ECCENTRIC CIRCLES

An Uncommon Tale of Five Women

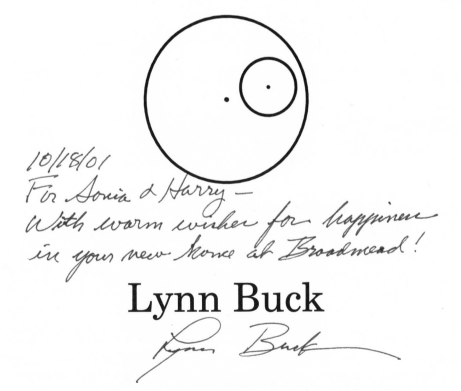

10/18/01
For Sonia & Harry —
With warm wishes for happiness
in your new home at Broadmead!

Lynn Buck

Lynn Buck

DORRANCE PUBLISHING CO., INC.
PITTSBURGH, PENNSYLVANIA 15222

ISBN # 0-8059-4014-6
Printed in the United States of America

First Printing

For information or to order additional books, please write:
Dorrance Publishing Co., Inc.
643 Smithfield Street
Pittsburgh, Pennsylvania 15222
U.S.A.

Acknowledgments

My first inkling of this book came upon reading a passage in Robin Morgan's *Anatomy of Freedom* offering her fanciful view of the ideal life in an "Old Feminists' Home." But my own view of women living communally might never have taken form without Erika Duncan's workshop in which she and members of the group, particularly Jean Hoffmann and Sue Wartur, encouraged me to persevere. During a later revision, Professor Robert Reeves deserves credit for teaching me the hard lesson that *less* is nearly always *more*. My gratitude also goes to the Serendipity Women Writers who watched the book evolve and lent encouragement, to feminist friends in chapters of the National Organization for Women in Long Island and Baltimore, and to Canio who gave me opportunities to read portions in progress in his Sag Harbor bookshop.

My thanks to Barbara Kouts who believed in the book from first read, also to my most serious critics, Ali MacDonald, Mary Randall, and Carolyn Dettmer, to Joyce Everett, my safety valve in a variety of ways, to Lisa Kombrink for helping me bring authenticity to the court scene, to Sandy Rapp for permission to use her song, and to Jill Bart who encouraged bold actions for my characters. I thank the many other people who read this novel in various stages and offered helpful comments: Thelma Becherer, Melissa Bishop-Morgan, Margaret Brehmer, Elizabeth Cory, Pat and Joe Cubells, Pat Eddington, Alice Goode-Elman, Eva Leah Milbouer, Sandy Rapp, Marion Sforza, Pam Thiele, Phyllis Tyler, Kim Walters, Hildegard Wilson, and Lorraine Zingone. Thanks to Sarah Cooper for not only reading the book but lending a listening ear. I am grateful to Sylvia Baruch for her book on houses of the South Fork—and to Marion Staley for her sketch of the house on my book jacket. And special appreciation goes to my husband, Hans, who lived only long enough to see completion of the first rough draft. It would not have been possible without his strong support. After I finished each chapter, he would read it, smile and say, "Now, what happens next?"

For my daughter, Susan Celia Hammond,
and in memory of my mother, Lora Crow Beck,
my cousin, Barbara Crow Pirtle,
my grandmothers, Elvira Jane Crow and Nancy Malinda Beck

After all, every circle has a point for a center. The size of the circle is determined by the energy with which it is expanded, not by the magnificence of what it may or may not take off from.

Elizabeth Janeway

* * *

Time and trouble will tame an advanced young woman, but an advanced old woman is uncontrollable by any earthly force.

Dorothy L. Sayers

1

D-Day for the rescue of Ada from Tranquil Acres sparkled with sunlight and clear skies, warmed by a breeze out of the southwest, unseasonably mild for early March. At breakfast Lee had said laughingly the Goddess was smiling on them. Not that she seriously believed there was a Goddess—but then she did not exactly believe in a God either, at least not the Presbyterian God of her early upbringing.

The four women, from late sixties to early eighties in age, clustered in the parking lot of the nursing home, going over their strategy—actually listening to Minerva, taller than the others, with the erect posture of a general, blue woven cape draped over her angular figure, white hair tucked beneath a cloche hat. "All right," she said briskly, "let's get on with it." She gestured toward the building. "Everyone knows what to do."

Lee, in tan corduroy pants and sneakers for a quick getaway, shivered and pulled her suede jacket more tightly about her. She bit her lip and ran her hand through short-cropped gray hair. Minerva, as if sensing her fear, gave her a hug. "Don't panic," she said.

"What about her roommate?" Elizabeth toyed nervously with the button of her camelhair coat and pushed back a strand of neatly coiffured gray hair.

"We'll just have to play it by ear." Minerva took her arm. "Come with me." She checked her watch and turned to the other two. "Let's meet here in half an hour."

"Isn't this exciting!" said Vivian. Her make-up was perhaps a bit too heavy, her frizzy curls a touch too blond, tucked beneath a green headband matching her high-heeled shoes and green mascara'd eyes. She linked arms with Lee, and they hurried along a tree-lined walk toward the terrace. Suddenly she pulled away and started to skip, her hair bobbing up and down, coat flying out behind. Watching her exuberant motion, Lee tried a hesitant skip-hop. She winced at the arthritic pain in her knee. "Damn!" she muttered. Again she tried and stopped, feeling strangely lead-footed and wobbly.

Vivian skipped back. "That felt good!" She linked arms again. "Lighten up, Lee. You don't want to go in with a long face and upset Ada."

They crossed the brick terrace. Lee pulled hard at the heavy door. It did not budge. She tugged again. This time the door swung open, nearly throwing her off balance. In the corridor the stale warm air was heavy with the scent of herbal deodorant, only slightly masking the faint stench of urine. They walked along the hall toward Ada's room. Elizabeth, approaching from the other direction, joined them.

"Say a prayer," Lee whispered to her.

"I thought you didn't believe in . . . ."

"Coming from you, it can't hurt."

Elizabeth, a devout Episcopalian, rarely missed a Sunday in church. They frequently clashed over Lee's view of the Bible as sexist.

From the doorway they could see Ada clad in pink-striped flannel nightgown and blue terrycloth robe, her long gray hair hanging in a thick braid over one shoulder, sitting in a wheelchair by the window eating her lunch. In the diffuse sunlight through lace curtains, she resembled a nineteenth century painting. She paused, soup spoon in hand, a puzzled expression on her face. "Who are . . . ?" Then a flash of recognition . . . "Well, why . . . what are you folks doing here?" Her voice once vibrant and clear was now strangely muffled, words slurred.

When Lee first met Ada in the 1950s she was struck by her resemblance to Eleanor Roosevelt. The same large teeth and generous smile, prominent nose, high forehead, same way of speaking, the vigor of her words—remarkably alike. Of course Eleanor was older by perhaps twenty years. But the resemblance was even stronger now that Ada had more or less caught up with her in age. The former Ada, of course, not this weak-voiced woman with the vacant gaze.

The room was small and sparsely furnished—two metal beds flanked by little tables, a bureau, two chairs, and against the far wall a square table and chair. The walls were an unsavory institutional green. If Ada were her normal self, she would surely do something to brighten the place—cover the walls with posters, perhaps even a mural, wheeling through the room in her blue smock, a cyclone of energy, flourishing her paintbrush. Lee smiled at the thought, but her face clouded when she looked again at Ada slurping her soup.

Claire, the roommate, sat at the square table eating her lunch. She was a frail little woman with sharp-boned birdlike face. Elizabeth crossed the room and pulled up a chair by her. She greeted the woman hesitantly and got no response. Then she took a small kaleidoscope from her bag. Looking through it, she exclaimed over the beautiful colors and shapes and handed it to Claire, showing her how to hold it to the light.

Lee walked quickly over to Ada and kissed her cheek. "How are you, Ada dear?"

Ada dropped her spoon, sloshing vegetable soup over her robe. "Oops! See what you made me do?"

Vivian sat down in a chair next to Ada who pushed the bowl of soup toward her on the tray. "Good soup," she said. "Want some?"

Vivian smiled and shook her head.

Lee bent down and whispered to Ada to hurry and finish her lunch so they could go on an outing.

"Speak up. Why are you whispering?" Ada's voice pierced the air. She had needed a hearing aid for quite some time but refused to acknowledge it. Apparently her hearing had deteriorated even more—another side effect of the medication perhaps. Lee's hands felt clammy. Things were getting complicated.

"Shhhhhhh!" Vivian cupped her hand and talked directly into Ada's ear. "It's a big secret."

"Secret about what?"

"If we told you, it wouldn't be a secret." Vivian started to take away the tray.

"Wait! I have to finish. They want you to clean your plate." Ada clutched the tray, pushing Vivian's arm away, and the tray fell to the floor with a loud clatter.

Claire put down the kaleidoscope and stared at them. "What are you doing to Ada?" She stood up unsteadily and raised her cane as if to defend her at all costs.

"What's Claire up to?" Ada demanded loudly.

Lee froze on the spot, envisioning a noisy melee . . . nurses and attendants rushing to the aid of the cane-wielding Claire and the shouting Ada. Whatever made them think this scheme would work?

Elizabeth firmly pushed Claire back into her chair. "Calm down, my dear, they only want Ada to hurry with her lunch so they can take her out on the terrace."

"I want to go along. See, I've finished my lunch." The shrill voice rose to a sharp crescendo. "Take me with you!"

There was an appealing quality to this little bird-woman. It seemed a shame to trick her. Maybe she was over-medicated as well. Too bad they couldn't take her along. And Ada? How would she feel about leaving her? The adjustment might be difficult. Lee gave a worried sigh, feeling suddenly overwhelmed by the chaos she was helping to create.

"What's wrong with Claire?" Ada's voice was increasing in volume.

"Don't worry. She's fine," Vivian said.

Elizabeth handed the kaleidoscope to Claire who peered into it. "My sister's in here, all gold and glittery," she said.

Ada tried to get out of the wheelchair but couldn't. Vivian started rolling it toward the door, her high heels clicking rhythmically against the polished linoleum.

"Wait! My tuna sandwich!" Ada was almost shouting. "And my ice cream!"

"Shhhhhhhhh! Remember our secret," Vivian said. "We'll take them along. Maybe you can eat them outside."

Lee quickly wrapped the sandwich in a napkin and put it in

4

her tote bag, along with the ice cream cup. Then she pulled Ada's cape from the closet, placed an envelope addressed to Dr. Prudence Runkles, Director, on Ada's bureau, and followed Vivian out. She could hear Ada muttering that people were trying to starve her to death.

Elizabeth remained behind with Claire and the kaleidoscope.

As they hurried down the hall, Lee wondered how Minerva was getting along on her interview with the director. She had a fleeting image of the unpleasant Dr. Runkles sitting behind her desk, tight-lipped, thin face pulled into a frown, regarding Minerva suspiciously as she handed her some brochures. The plan was to divert her attention, keep her safely out of the way by pretending she wanted information on being a volunteer. It could backfire. But Minerva was a good talker, and her proper Boston accent usually helped.

Suddenly a nurse came around the corner, walking briskly, almost colliding with the wheelchair. She stared at them quizzically through horn-rimmed glasses.

"We're just taking Ada on the terrace for a breath of air," Vivian said hastily.

Lee could feel a knot forming in her stomach.

"Well . . . ." The nurse hesitated. "We don't want our Ada to catch a cold now, do we?" She was using the tone frequently directed toward an older person as though addressing a child of less than average mentality.

Vivian squeezed Lee's hand, warning her to keep silent. With the pounding of her heart, she could not have spoken anyway.

"Not to worry," Vivian said brightly. "We brought her cape."

Lee held out her cape, hoping Ada would not say anything.

Then, to her horror, she heard Ada's slurred voice. "We have a secret."

"What is your secret, my dear?" The nurse sounded suspicious.

Ada shrugged dramatically and rolled her eyes. "They won't tell me."

"It's not really a secret," Vivian said quickly. "Dear Ada likes to make a game out of every little thing." She smiled sweetly. "We thought some fresh air would do her good."

The nurse was silent for a moment, lips pursed. Glancing at

5

her watch, she said she supposed it would be all right for a short while. Turning to Ada, she added, "When we come in, we must take our nap like a good girl."

Lee gritted her teeth, Ada nodded, and Vivian smiled. She pushed the wheelchair rapidly toward the terrace door. Lee had to lengthen her stride to keep up. Safely outside, she collapsed on a stone bench. "I thought I'd die! You were marvelous, Viv!"

Vivian laughed. "So far, so good!" She pulled the wheelchair alongside the bench and sat down. Lee studied her vivacious face, her trim figure. Vivian did not look sixty-eight, although in the glare of sunlight a network of wrinkles showed beneath the make-up, and the pale skin of her veined hands revealed a few tell-tale splotches.

"We'd better keep going," Lee said. "Our time is nearly up."

"What are you two mumbling about?" Ada asked. Then, suddenly remembering . . . . "Where's my strawberry ice cream?"

"Might as well sit here for a few minutes," Vivian said. "The old bat might be spying on us from the lounge."

Lee draped Ada's cape around her. In this outdoor setting she looked especially fragile, her robust figure of only six weeks ago slumped in the chair, her face strangely gaunt in the harsh noonday light. Removing the lid, she handed the cup to Ada who spooned the ice cream, now soft, into her mouth. Some of the pink liquid dribbled down her chin. "It's delicious," she said. "You sure you don't want any?"

Before Ada could finish the ice cream, Vivian stood up abruptly. "I can't stand this delay! Let's go." She pulled the wheelchair away from the bench.

"But my ice cream! You promised!"

"We've no time to lose." Vivian took off, pushing the wheelchair at top speed across the terrace and down the uneven surface of the walkway.

Lee hurried after them, feeling the nagging pain in her knee with every step. Glancing back, she noticed some movement on the terrace, unable to tell whether it was a person or a play of light and shadow from the trees. "Faster, Viv!" I think I see somebody!" Vivian quickened her pace, and Lee followed, limping.

Suddenly Vivian tripped on a crack in the cement, lost her

footing and lurched forward, sprawling on the sidewalk—the same sidewalk she had skipped along so joyfully before. Those ridiculous high heels! Lee stood motionless for an instant, then turned in time to see the wheelchair slowly rolling down the walk under its own momentum, accompanied by Ada's faint cries for help. With a burst of adrenaline, she rushed after it, grabbing the handles just in time to prevent the runaway wheelchair from crashing into a large oak tree.

"What's going on?" A dazed expression clouded Ada's face as she twisted around in the wheelchair toward Lee who was breathing heavily, her knobby hands grasping the handles. "Are you folks trying to kill me or something?"

"Oh, Ada dear, are you all right?"

"I guess so." Her voice sounded wavery.

"How about your hip? Any pain?"

Ada gazed at her, bewildered. "What happened to Vivian?"

"She fell," Lee said tersely. Setting the brakes on the wheelchair, she admonished Ada to stay there, as if she could do otherwise, and hurried back to Vivian.

She was picking herself up from the sidewalk, wincing with pain as she put her weight on her left foot. "I think I sprained my ankle. Go ahead with Ada. I'll get myself to the car." Vivian grimaced as she took a few halting steps.

"I can't believe this is happening!" Lee's heart was racing. A nightmare come true. Trying frantically to escape but unable to make any headway . . . pushing the wheelchair . . . a massive treadmill . . . her knee throbbing, breath coming in quick, short gasps . . . Vivian, stocking-footed, hobbling along some distance behind.

After what seemed hours in her panic, she reached the incline leading to the parking lot. Summoning all her energy, she shoved the wheelchair over the slope to the car, then turned back to help Vivian, now limping badly. Lee offered her arm for support, and the two of them struggled back to Ada who waited, confused and disheveled, strands of gray hair pulled loose from her braid and hanging about her face, her eyes darting wildly from one to the other. "What's going on?" she demanded again.

Out of breath and trembling, Lee did not answer. "We'll never make it!" she said to Vivian.

Just then, Minerva came running over. "Hurry!" Lee said. "We don't have a minute to spare." With difficulty, the three of them managed to pivot Ada from the chair into the car, far more cumbersome than they had imagined, Lee worrying with every movement about possible disastrous effects on Ada's hip.

Then came Elizabeth, flushed and breathless. "I thought I'd never get away! Claire finally dozed off. I slipped out the terrace door."

"They nearly ran me into a tree," Ada said, the words slurring into each other. "We have a secret." She smiled mysteriously. "Bet you didn't know that." Leaning back against the seat, she yawned and closed her eyes.

"Well, we did it!" Minerva said, giving them each a hug.

The wind had shifted, clouding the sky and bringing a wintry chill to the air. Lee carefully tucked Ada's cape around her and pushed back a wisp of hair from her lined face, relaxed now in sleep. How peaceful she looked, yet how vulnerable. "We'll make it work, Ada, I promise," she said softly.

The women got hastily into the station wagon, Vivian at the wheel, insisting she could manage, only needing her right foot to drive. As the car screeched out of the parking lot, Lee replayed in her mind the recurring image of Ada's fall in January at the rally, like slow-motion video though it had happened in a split second . . . Ada resembling an Amazon warrior, handsome in her black cape . . . tripping on a stone, crashing to the pavement still clutching her sign WOMAN'S VOICE/PRO-CHOICE, her cape flying outward like huge wings . . . Lee dropping her megaphone, kneeling beside her . . . Ada struggling to get up then collapsing, her face drained of its ruddy color, pain shooting from her eyes even as she insisted she was "perfectly all right." Lee tearfully repeating, "I'm so sorry, so very sorry!" The circle of grave faces surrounding Ada's crumpled form . . . the shrill siren of the ambulance, attendants lifting Ada onto a stretcher . . . the four women piling into the station wagon, careening after the ambulance . . . .

Lee closed her eyes, tried to erase the image. But she could not erase the guilt. If she had not organized the rally and insisted on the others attending, none of this would have happened. It was really her fault. If only she could turn back the clock, make everything the way it used to be when they first came together . . . but no turning back now.

2

A blustery wind rattled the French doors of the living room and rain beat upon the panes. The predicted change in weather had come with dramatic speed. But the fire crackling and sputtering in the fireplace dispelled the twilight gloom and warmed the four women clustered about it. Lee to one side in the walnut rocker, drinking a bourbon and soda, the calico cat on her lap, Elizabeth to the other side in the Salem rocker, sipping her glass of Chablis, Vivian, with bandaged ankle, curled into a corner of the couch, the glow of the fire reflecting in her face and her dry Manhattan. Minerva at the opposite end of the couch, her stockinged feet propped against the coffee table next to her glass of seltzer and cranberry juice, Ada's cat draped over her legs. Between Minerva and Vivian sat Daisy, Elizabeth's beagle. They were enjoying their customary Friday happy hour. This evening Ada's rescue dominated the conversation.

The Seth Thomas clock on the mantle struck six. Lee checked her watch. The old clock was nearly fifteen minutes fast. She must remember to set it back. But she liked to leave it a little ahead because of her tendency to cram too much into any given time.

Vivian raised her glass. "Here's to us. We pulled it off!" She had changed into a hot-pink warm-up suit, the color bringing to her face an almost youthful flush, her blond hair shimmering in the firelight. Amazing, the kindly effect of soft light in eradicating wrinkles and minor blemishes. Women of their age who wanted to preserve the illusion of youth should never show their faces in anything but lamplight and firelight.

"May our luck continue," Minerva said.

"We might need it," Elizabeth said, a worried frown wrinkling her brow. Lee studied the angularity of her face, the sharpness of bone, a suggestion of brittleness, softened somewhat by her gray hair stylishly permed, swept back from the high forehead, deep-set eyes serious behind gold-rimmed glasses. Was she having second thoughts?

"Well, the worst is over," Lee said quickly. For the next several minutes they replayed the rescue mission, toasting each one in turn.

That afternoon, after helping to get Ada settled, Elizabeth had gone to Southampton Hospital for her shift. She was still wearing the pink smock of the volunteers. Vivian, after wrapping an ace bandage around her ankle, had rushed back to her real estate office for an appointment. Ada was quite groggy when they arrived home, and Lee had simply told her she was spending the weekend with them as a special treat. After they got her into bed, she had asked, "Where's Claire?" and then dozed off without waiting for an answer.

Lee had persuaded her own physician to come by the house and examine Ada. When she told him about it over the phone, he was reluctant to get involved, but she had taken advantage of their long friendship, suggesting that it would hardly be fair to endanger Ada by refusing—in case she might have been on medications that needed to be tapered off gradually. Dr. Stone had phoned the doctor at Tranquil Acres, making it clear that he had absolutely nothing to do with their *crazy scheme* and was only involved on an interim basis until a proper disposition of the case could be arranged. He referred to their action as *irresponsible and impulsive,* stirring in Lee a sense of betrayal. Their rescue was clearly the only moral choice. She felt certain Dr. Stone must have realized it upon learning about Ada's medications—a potent sleeping pill, Dalmane, as well as Haldol to which she appeared to be extra sensitive. But physicians had this irksome professional bond preventing them from criticizing a colleague. Hypocritical, to Lee's way of thinking. He had taken

11

Ada off of both medications, leaving her only on a blood pressure pill and a reduced dosage of Motrin for pain.

Then the doctor had phoned the agency to arrange for a nurse until they could determine how much care Ada needed. And Minerva had called her friend, Margaret, a nurse, who offered to come over until the agency nurse started the next day.

"I imagine Ada is going to need a nurse or a health aide for quite a while," Elizabeth was saying, as if reading Lee's mind scanning the events of the afternoon.

Elizabeth's face was drawn into a frown—perhaps not so much out of concern for Ada as for the disruption of her cherished routine. Lee wondered if she would want to be personally involved in the care of Ada on a day-to-day basis. If it dragged out too long, she might lose patience. She and Ada had never been particularly compatible—Ada, the artist, a whirlwind of disorder, leaving a trail of her Bohemian attire throughout the house— Elizabeth the epitome of neatness exemplifying the old adage, a place for everything and everything in its place.

Last year when the five of them had decided to pool their resources and live together in this quiet Long Island village of Quintauket, it seemed so simple, so perfect. The plan evolved following the death of Elizabeth's husband, Parker Sherwood, when she had put her house on the market. Vivian, recently divorced and in search of an apartment, had come to list the property but instead convinced Elizabeth she should keep her house, sharing expenses with some other women. The ideal communal setup—harmony personified. In the course of the year, they had more than a few clashes, but today Lee had felt a strong sense of unity as they pulled together for Ada.

She glanced at Minerva who also appeared to be studying Elizabeth intently. They would have to be on guard, try to keep things smooth.

"Perhaps we should get an orthopedist to examine her," Vivian said. "She'll need some physical therapy."

"I wonder if her Medicare covers all this," Elizabeth said. "Of course, we wouldn't be held financially responsible. It's up to Arthur to pay what she can't." She seemed agitated, rocking vigorously.

12

Lee got up and poked the fire, then put on another log. She resented Elizabeth's penny-pinching focus on medical fees. Money, for Lee, had never been a top priority. Not that she ever had much, but she always figured it would turn up when she needed it, and generally it did. Even growing up during the Depression had not tempered her casual approach to matters of finance—an attitude probably inherited from her father who would blithely have given away his last dollar. Fortunately, in those lean years her mother had taken charge of their meager funds to put food on the table and pay the mortgage. Elizabeth, on the other hand, had grown up in an atmosphere of wealth, probably never had to skimp on anything in her life. She and Parker had lost some money in the market crash of '87, but she was reasonably well off and still managed to drive her Mercedes. Lee gave the logs an angry poke.

Minerva stretched and leaned back against the pillows. "What a beautiful fire!"

"How did you find time to fix it?" Elizabeth seemed more relaxed now. Her rocking had slowed down.

"Lee would lay a fire if the world were collapsing around her," Vivian quipped.

"I needed it this evening," Lee said.

The metallic ring of the telephone interrupted them. Minerva picked it up.

His voice crackled over the phone. "For Christ's sake, are you out of your mind? What have you crazies done with my mother? I couldn't believe my ears when the director called."

Minerva turned to the others. "It's Arthur." She held the phone away from her ear as the voice continued.

"Of all the stupid tricks!" He was shouting now. "How could anyone in their right mind . . . ."

"Now calm down, Arthur." Minerva's voice was carefully modulated. "We are not out of our minds. It's Ada's mind that was endangered. We had to rescue her from that den of false tranquillity."

"What are you talking about?" he sputtered. "I always knew you people were flaky. I warned Mother about you. I told her . . . ."

"You don't have to shout, Arthur. Why don't you hop in your

13

car and come out to the house. We can discuss this over a cup of tea like reasonable people." Minerva's solution to any problem, however weighty or trivial, was a cup of tea.

"Reasonable people!" he exploded. "You call this abduction of my mother reasonable?" His voice grew louder. "I could have you arrested and put behind bars!"

"Calm down, Arthur." Minerva held her hand over the mouthpiece. "He's threatening to send us to prison."

"Do you think he means it?" Lee asked.

Elizabeth, her face strained, was rocking furiously back and forth.

"He'd have to take us to court first," Vivian said. "He can't just cart us off to jail."

"Are you still there?" His voice was shrill. "Listen to me. I'm coming over all right. And I'm sending an ambulance for Mother — and a paddy wagon for the rest of you. I knew all along she should have come to live with Dolores and me instead of you maniacs. We have a perfectly good guest room. And she most certainly would not have been out marching around in protest rallies like some sort of sixties hippie!"

"What time should we expect you?"

His words were garbled now. Lee could not make them out.

"Don't be foolish, Arthur! It would be too great a strain on Ada to move her again. We'll talk when you get here."

Minerva hung up. "They will be out after dinner."

"Oh, dear me!" Elizabeth said.

* * *

Ada had roused enough to eat some chicken from a tray in bed, then aimlessly watched the television news before dozing off, hardly noticing her surroundings. Lee had given Ada her room, the only downstairs bedroom. Margaret, a robust, no-nonsense nurse, immediately took control. She had moved a file case, shoved aside the word processor, piled books and papers on the floor, rearranging the room for efficient nursing care.

The others had hurried through their dinner before the doorbell rang. A fine sleet was slashing at the windowpanes, and wind howled about the chimney. Lee shivered. She added a log to the fire and hastily poked it into a blaze. She could hear Vivian greeting the guests in the front hall.

Then the grand entrance. Arthur, tall and skinny, a few wisps of gray hair carefully combed over his balding head, grim-faced, exuding the pent-up energy of a Wall Street broker. He was still wearing his dark business suit, white shirt, and striped tie. Dolores, clinging to his arm, had on a navy silk print, its white collar accentuating the prim lines of her triangular face framed in a fringe of tight curls a trifle too red. Her pale blue eyes squinted through rimless glasses.

Lee moved away from the fire to greet them. A perfect pair for a comic poem, *American Gothic, 1989.*

Minerva had changed into beige pants and a soft green top she had woven. She was shaking hands with them, her very gesture imparting confidence. "Come sit here by the fire. It must be turning quite cold."

"Miserable night!" Arthur growled, rubbing his hands together.

Elizabeth, her face flushed, had greeted them and was busily fluffing the couch pillows.

The two sat on the couch, their angular bodies rigid, as if ready to pop up at any moment, reminding Lee of the wind-up toys she used to have. "May I get you a cup of coffee? Or tea?"

"No thanks, we just had our coffee with dinner." Dolores's voice was high-pitched, nasal.

Lee hated it when her guests refused any form of refreshment. In her Midwestern upbringing, food was a focal point of hospitality.

Daisy came bounding across the room and leaped on the couch, climbing over Dolores's lap, wedging herself between the two guests, her tail wagging vigorously. Elizabeth, her face now a deep red, grabbed the dog and dragged her out of the room, Daisy yelping in protest. Lee could hear her whining and scratching at the kitchen door.

"Where's Mother?" Arthur asked abruptly. "I want to talk to her."

"She's in the bedroom asleep," Minerva said. "Surely you don't want to wake her."

"Asleep! That's ridiculous! Why at this hour?"

"She was over-medicated, just as we suspected. But you wouldn't listen when we tried to discuss it with you last week on the phone."

"Nonsense!"

"Allow me to finish." There was a note of impatience in Minerva's voice. "Our doctor checked with their doctor this afternoon. Ada was on Haldol since the day you took her there."

"So?"

"For older people who are sensitive to the drug, it can be very dangerous," Lee said. "I just read an article . . . ."

"I'm sure Dr. Morris is a responsible physician."

"I read that a tremendous number of people in nursing homes are getting unnecessary sedatives," Lee said. "It keeps them under control. Ada is hardly the docile type, you know. We couldn't sit by and watch her deteriorate."

"A gross exaggeration! I want to talk to Mother. I drove all the way out from Manhasset." His voice was growing louder with each word.

"If you don't keep your voice down, you will wake her," Minerva said.

"Fine! That's my general intention." His face was flushed, the veins of his neck pulsing against his collar.

Elizabeth sat silently, head bowed over her knitting. Lee expected her to walk out of the room any minute. Elizabeth detested loud arguments. The same had been true of Lee's mother. Lee herself welcomed a lively debate. As a child she used to join in the disputes between her father and brother at the dinner table—whether the Socialist candidate, Norman Thomas, would make a good President, whether the Cardinals were the best ball team. Usually, at the peak, her mother would sigh heavily and leave the room. Today, of course, was hardly the time for an argument.

Just then Vivian limped into the room with a tray of glasses and bottles. "How about a liqueur?" She smiled her best smile at Arthur. "You need a little something after the drive out here."

Her voice had a lilting quality that usually appealed to men.

Arthur hesitated. "Well . . . do you have any Cognac?"

Vivian smiled brightly and poured some for him. Dolores and Elizabeth chose Amoretti. Minerva shook her head. She poured a B & B for Lee and herself. The tension was eased momentarily.

Arthur held the glass in both hands, sniffing his Cognac. "Nice bouquet." Taking a sip, he leaned back against the couch.

Minerva pulled over a chair facing Arthur and Dolores. "Now, Arthur," she said in her most Bostonian voice, "suppose we talk over this matter of Ada and try to come to some reasonable agreement."

"Reasonable! For God's sake! Kidnapping my mother and not letting me, her closest relative, talk to her!" His face was growing more flushed. "You call that *reasonable?*"

"We only want to help Ada," Lee said.

Arthur slammed his glass on the coffee table and stood up. "I've had enough! If you people won't let me see my own mother, I'll get a court order and have her moved out of here once and for all."

Minerva stood facing him. "Very well, Arthur, if you insist." She walked across to the door of the adjoining room, followed by Arthur and Lee. Dolores, Elizabeth, and Vivian remained seated, startled by the abrupt turn of events.

When they entered the bedroom, the television screen was on, with the sound turned off. Ada, sitting up in bed to watch, had dozed off, gray braid draped over her shoulder, mouth open, snoring lightly. Margaret stood up to greet them.

Arthur walked over to the bed and tapped Ada on the shoulder. "Mother, wake up. I must talk to you."

Ada gave a startled jerk, opened her eyes, staring blankly at him. "Who are you?" She rubbed her eyes and squinted.

"It's *me*, Arthur." He bent down and gave her a perfunctory kiss on the cheek.

"Oh, it's you. What are you doing here, Son?" Her voice was slurred, words garbled, like a poorly tuned radio signal.

"We must have a serious talk." Arthur pulled up a chair and sat down by the bed. Ada, meanwhile, had leaned back on the pillows and closed her eyes. "Mother, wake up!"

Ada opened her eyes, yawned, and glanced toward the

17

television, turning on the sound with her remote control. "First let's watch the show. I forget what it's called." She turned to Lee.

"It's 'Beauty and the Beast,'" Lee said.

"I want to see how it ends."

"Mother, for God's sake! This is serious." Arthur's voice was growing louder by the minute.

Ada sighed and flipped off the sound. "All right." She adjusted her pillow and gazed at Arthur. "Son, I believe you've lost some more hair since I saw you last. But it runs in the family. Your Uncle Oscar was totally bald at your age."

Arthur's face turned a shade redder. "Never mind my hair."

Ada propped herself up on her elbow. "Now, Son, what's bothering you?" Before he could answer, she looked at Minerva and Lee. "What are you folks doing here? I thought visiting hours were over."

"This isn't the nursing home," Lee said. "You're here with us."

"Oh." She fumbled for her glasses, dropped them, finally put them on and gazed at Arthur with a vacant smile. "Now, what's bothering you?"

"I want to talk to you—if you will just stop fidgeting around, for God's sake!" Lee relished his exasperation. "I want to know *why* you let these crazy ladies do this?"

"Son, why are you shouting? I'm not deaf, you know. You're getting yourself all worked up. It's not good for your blood pressure." Her face was puzzled. "Now, tell me, what is all this about?"

"That's precisely what I want to know, Mother. What is this all about?" He had lowered his voice and was studying Ada with a worried frown.

"Can't we talk about it tomorrow?" Ada yawned. "I'm . . . what was I saying?" Her eyes drooped closed, and her head relaxed against the pillow.

"Mother, please listen to me!" His sharp-edged voice softened.

Ada gave a soft snore and mumbled something unintelligible.

"But, Mother . . . ."

Lee took off Ada's glasses, tucking them into the case on her nightstand. "Shhhhhh!" she said to Arthur.

"Now, are you satisfied?" Minerva said as they left the room. "It's true, isn't it—what we told you?" Lee envisioned Arthur erupting into a Mount Vesuvius before their very eyes if Minerva pushed him too far. "Admit it, Arthur," she persisted. "Ada is not her normal self."

"Well . . . ." Visibly shaken, he appeared to be struggling between the actuality of her condition and his need to save face. "She did seem a bit muddled."

"A bit muddled! What you witnessed this evening did not even faintly resemble the real Ada."

When they entered the room Elizabeth stopped knitting, and Vivian set her glass on the mantle. Dolores remained on the couch sipping her Amoretti. "Well, dear," she chirped, her head cocked to one side, "did you talk things out with Mother Abernathy?"

"Talk?" Arthur snorted. "All she wanted to do was watch television or sleep!" He sat down beside her on the couch and folded his arms, staring straight ahead.

"A little more Cognac?" Vivian said.

"I still have some." Arthur reached for his glass on the coffee table and took a sip, frowning. Then he stood up and began pacing nervously back and forth. Walking over to the window, he pulled the drapes aside and looked out. "That damn sleet has changed to snow."

Lee said a vague prayer that they not get stranded here.

Arthur downed the final drops from his glass, then turned, facing them. "Well." He cleared his throat noisily. "Obviously we can't move Mother out of here in this storm. But Monday morning I want you to have her packed and ready to go back where she belongs. I'll work things out with Tranquil Acres."

Lee glared at him. "We'll do no such thing!"

"Over my dead body!" Vivian said. "Not after all we went through to get her out of that place."

Arthur was pacing the floor again. "After what *you* went through! Good Lord, think what *I* went through to get her there. The strings I had to pull, the deals." His voice had risen a few decibels. "They have a waiting list a mile long. It wasn't easy!" He scowled at them, his face nearly purple, the veins of his

19

temples pulsing. "And then you antique hippies come along with your smart tricks!"

"Do calm down, Arthur," Elizabeth said. "You're getting yourself needlessly worked up." She paused to count some stitches. "Why don't we just wait until Monday and let Ada decide where she wants to stay? Doesn't that sound reasonable?"

"*Reasonable!*" he bellowed. "There you go with that word again! Not one thing about this whole episode has been *reasonable.*" He lowered his voice. "Now get this straight, all of you. Come what may, first thing Monday morning I'm taking Mother out of here, and that's that."

"You can't do it against her will," Minerva said.

Arthur looked out the window again. "Damn snow!"

"They're right. Ada is the one to decide," Lee said. But would she be capable of deciding by Monday? Unless she improved markedly, she might choose to return to Claire and the strawberry ice cream.

"Well, I can't stand here arguing with you people all night. So here's what I propose we do." Elizabeth was watching him intently over her knitting. Vivian was twisting the stem of her glass and biting her lip. Minerva, about to put a log on the fire, dropped the log and turned to look at Arthur. Lee held her breath. "On Monday we'll see what Mother has to say. But if she is incapable of making a decision on her own, which I expect will be the case, she will definitely come with me so I can arrange for her proper care—away from your negative influence."

"You're rushing things, Arthur," Minerva said. "By Monday the Haldol might still be affecting her brain."

"It would be homicidal to send Ada back there," Vivian said.

"On Monday," Lee said firmly, "Ada stays with us."

"Now get this straight," Arthur said, the line of his jaw becoming more rigid, his flat gray eyes glaring at them. "She's my mother, and I shall be the one to decide. I am quite prepared to take legal action if necessary." He paused. The room was silent except for the ticking of the clock.

Finally Elizabeth said, "Let's not prejudge Ada's capabilities this evening." Her voice was beautifully precise and calm. "Monday will be time enough for that."

Arthur turned abruptly to Dolores. "We'd better start home before this damn weather gets any worse."

Minerva started collecting the glasses on a tray, humming softly to herself, the way she did when she was upset.

Lee shook hands with the two of them. Vivian and Elizabeth escorted them into the hall, helping them on with their coats and seeing them out the door, Elizabeth cautioning them to drive carefully in the snow.

When she heard the front door close, Minerva turned to Lee. "Thank God!"

Lee gave her a hug.

Vivian came limping triumphantly into the living room. "We did it again!"

Elizabeth sank into her chair with a heavy sigh. "I'm exhausted!" Her face looked haggard, strangely old. Would she have the patience, the stamina, to see it through? "I wonder if we weren't a little too hard on Arthur," she added. "After all, Ada *is* his mother."

Lee studied her more closely. Lips tightly pursed, hands clenched on the arms of the rocker. Why was she making excuses for Arthur? She was viewing it, of course, from a different perspective, being a mother herself with a son just about Arthur's age. Maybe motherhood gave her a better insight. Lee had come to terms with the reality that bearing children was not the only way for a woman to prove her worth. But she retained a degree of awe for any woman who had successfully raised a child to productive adulthood. Elizabeth certainly knew more than she about the mother-son relationship. But maybe she simply wanted out of a complex situation, wanted to turn the responsibility for Ada over to the dutiful son. Lee could feel her stomach tightening with anxiety.

Minerva yawned and stretched, then crossed the room toward the stairs, telling everyone good-night. Elizabeth got up slowly and followed her out of the room without a word. She seemed preoccupied.

"I'm sleeping in tomorrow," Vivian said. "If anyone calls, take their number if you don't mind." When she reached the door, she turned and said to Lee, "Why don't you call it a day?"

21

"I'm all keyed up. I'll just sit here and unwind." A vague sense of uneasiness crept over her. She had expected everyone to sit around talking about the evening, celebrating—and here she was. Alone, feeling somehow rejected. Were they perhaps having second thoughts? *No,* she told herself firmly, *only positive thinking!* She gave the fire a poke then curled up on the couch, staring at the embers and listening to their faint sizzle and sputter. In the quiet of the night, she became acutely aware of the ticking of the clock, a trifle off-balance on the mantle, causing an uneven rhythm, tock-tick, tock-tick. She got up and shoved the edge of the clock key under the base, and the rhythm became more even. Not perfect. But better. Nothing in this world was perfect anyway, particularly antiques—one of their charms. Perhaps that applied to aging women as well. *Face it. You are getting to be something of an antique, regardless of how youthful in spirit you claim to be. You must give yourself a little extra push to get up from a chair, and you hardly dare sit on the floor any more.*

Patches, the calico cat, jumped on her lap, purring loudly. As Lee stroked the silky fur, her tense muscles relaxed, breathing slowed. Ada's cat came over to the coffee table, stretched, rubbed his head on the corner of it, meowed, and leaped on the couch, lying beside Lee, his head on her knee. "Poor old Brother Gray." She scratched his chin. "You miss her too, don't you?"

She reached for the B & B. According to her friend Laura, B & B was a cure for anything from knocking out a cold or soothing a toothache to wiping out the blues. She needed that tonight, an all-purpose remedy. Lee filled her glass and held it to the light, admiring the sparkle of the amber liquid. These delicate glasses had been Matt's gift to her on their first wedding anniversary—a dozen of them. There were only six left. Arm in arm, they had toasted their happiness and a long life together, Matt saying, "May we drink from these glasses on our Golden Anniversary." And she, laughing, "If we live so long!" Just one more year now . . . . But you don't celebrate an anniversary alone. Never in those early years had she imagined outliving Matt. They had married with the comfortable notion of growing old together, surrounded by a throng of loving children and charming grandchildren. Now, here she was . . . Lee

22

Cranford, an old woman . . . well, approaching old age anyway, nearly seventy. Yet Matt would remain eternally youthful, at forty—handsome, smiling, strong. Time . . . what strange tricks it plays on its victims!

Sipping the tangy sweetness of the liqueur, Lee tried to retrieve some of the euphoria she had felt that afternoon after Ada's rescue. But now the dark shadow of doubt engulfed her. What if Arthur was right? What if they could not take proper care of Ada? Maybe this was indeed a foolish scheme. She had a tendency to act impulsively, involving others without completely thinking things through. Generally it worked out all right. But perhaps this time she had carried it too far. What if Ada fell? Or what if they did something to injure her hip? Or suppose Ada never got back to normal. What if Arthur came on Monday with a court order demanding Ada? And what if . . . .

Lee tucked a pillow behind her head, closed her eyes to screen out the disturbing possibilities chattering through her mind, took several deep breaths to put herself into the state of relaxation she had learned through long practice. She imagined herself in a circle of white light to ward off negative intrusions, and felt her body sinking into the depths of that other dimension. With deep longing she recalled the harmony of their early days together, her dream that they might be another Brook Farm or Blithedale. She could see Ada in a blue smock, hair braided with bright ribbons, in the garden at her easel, Elizabeth in broad-brimmed hat tending the roses, Minerva reading in the hammock, Vivian flitting about like a butterfly, herself—off to one side shaded by the maple tree, capturing the scene in a lyric poem vibrant with color and dappled sunlight.

Outside the snow continued to fall, blowing against the windowpanes, drifting across lawn and terrace, outlining porch railings in geometric design, swirling around hedges and fence posts, frosting the needles of pine and spruce, blanketing the area in the pristine silence of its whiteness.

23

3

Lee was careful to grip the shovel low and bend her knees with each scoop of snow. She had read this would reduce the risk of back injury and put less strain on the heart. Better leverage or something. But the wet snow was heavy.

Today she felt overburdened, not only by the snow but the nagging fear that Arthur would carry out his threat of legal action. At this point Ada might not pass a competency test. Her speech, though improved, was still hesitant, her thoughts slightly off focus, as if her brain were powered by a diminished current, an electrical brown-out.

She stood leaning on her shovel. Minerva came through the snow with vigorous strides, face glowing from exertion and the cold, a purple skating cap at a jaunty angle over her white hair. She wore a blue jacket over blue corduroys tucked into her high boots. How did Min always manage to look so striking, Lee wondered, while she looked so ordinary, no matter what she wore? Min could easily pass for sixty-something, rather than her actual seventy-five years. Of course, anyone who practiced yoga and walked a couple of miles a day deserved to look great. Lee thought back to the first time they met, some fifteen years ago at a consciousness-raising group . . . Minerva sitting barefoot on the couch, hair pulled back from her face with a bright scarf, laughing that light sparkling laugh, gray eyes smiling at her, and she knew she wanted this woman as a friend. Over the years, Minerva had become more than a friend. She was the sister Lee had always yearned for.

"I've cleaned off the cars, cleared a space for the birds and put out some seed." She took a deep breath. "Beautiful, isn't it?"

"As a child I would have agreed. But at the moment, I hate the stuff!" Lee resumed her shoveling.

"You look tired. Let me help."

"Well, thanks, I am a bit frazzled." She knocked some snow off her shovel. "At least the snow kept Arthur away Monday."

Minerva laughed. "I don't think he'll make it today either. Roads still aren't plowed."

"He's probably having conniptions."

"Couldn't even call us, poor fellow."

"By the time he gets here, perhaps Ada can stand up to him."

"She did pretty well when she was bonkers." Minerva walked toward the woodshed. "I'll start down there and meet you halfway."

Arthur had his mother's nervous energy but none of her creativity. In his confined world everything was based on facts, simple cause and effect, proceeding with resolute logic from point A to B to C. No detours or scenic by-roads. Lee shivered, uncertain whether from the cold or dread of their next encounter.

This was one of those wild storms when the bulk of it swerved out over the ocean, dumping its cargo on Eastern Long Island, leaving some fifteen inches, with three-foot drifts, labeled by the weather bureau a bizarre March blizzard. The weekend had been an adventure of sorts—the worries of Friday night put aside. They kept a fire blazing in the fireplace, munched popcorn, played cards, watched television together. Ada, slowly regaining her equilibrium, had joined them at the table for dinner. But she still slept a lot and seemed confused, occasionally asking for Claire.

Sunday night the agency nurse had canceled. Minerva took that shift to sleep on the folding bed in Ada's room, and Lee took the Monday shift. It had been a restless night. She was so afraid she might not hear Ada if she needed help she slept very little. Ada was so dependent on them now, like a child. This triggered in Lee a dormant fear of some looming disaster that might someday incapacitate her, force her to turn to others for her every need, give up her freedom. The thought tormented her.

25

Lee paused again and straightened her back. She clapped the wet snow off her gloves and stamped her feet to warm them. Her toes were beginning to have that familiar burning sensation, bringing to mind sleigh rides down snow-packed hills on her Flexible Flyer. How she had loved the exhilaration of the sharp wind against her face—so close to the ground, so close to danger, the chance of colliding with cars or other obstacles. In those reckless days she had not bothered to think about consequences. She, like others of her generation, took delight in living close to the edge. Today's young people seemed to have a similar attitude, just different modes of risk-taking. Worse, really—with the proliferation of drugs and hard sell of the media enticing them to by-pass childhood altogether and become mini adults, with designer clothing and world-weary attitudes.

The pain in her feet intensified. She tended to force her body to its furthest limit. Her father had been the same way, pushing himself beyond the breaking point, dying of a massive coronary at sixty-six. She had passed that hurdle, outliving him by over three years now. But she should not be too careless.

"When we finish," Lee called to Minerva, "let's have a bowl of Elizabeth's vegetable soup."

"Good idea," Minerva called back. "And a cup of hot chocolate."

"With a marshmallow on top."

The two shoveled in silence. By tomorrow the roads would be cleared, their drive plowed out, linking them to the outside world. And there would be Arthur to deal with. Arthur with his miserable fox face, flint eyes glaring at them, his piercing voice issuing ultimatums. And there would still be Ada's incessant needs, along with the worry of what she might say to Arthur. And they would have to face all the decisions, the endless details of living. But today they were still suspended between two worlds, free-floating, where everything beyond the immediate moment was a blur, the patterns hazy and indistinct.

* * *

Early Wednesday morning Arthur phoned, telling Elizabeth the Highway Department said the roads were passable, and he

26

would be out within the hour to take Ada back to the nursing home. Elizabeth reminded him that Ada was not to go with him unless she chose to do so. "We'll see about that," he snapped— and hung up, leaving her complaining that some people have no manners whatsoever.

Promptly at 9:30 Lee heard the clang of the front door knocker. *Remain calm*, she told herself sternly. Ada was sitting at the breakfast table, still in her nightgown and flannel robe, her gray braid neatly tied with small ribbons to match the robe and the clear blue of her eyes. Lee sat next to her drinking a second cup of coffee. Minerva, at the far end of the table, was glancing over the *New York Times*.

Morning sun slanted through the casement windows casting rainbow glints on the soapy water in the sink where Elizabeth stood nervously doing the dishes. Outside Lee could see the spruce trees, still heavy with snow, glistening in the sunlight. Such a beautiful morning to be spoiled by this intrusion.

Vivian entered the room, followed by Arthur, his manner brisk and businesslike. "Is she packed?" he asked. "I don't have much time." He set his briefcase on the floor and walked over to Ada. "Good morning, Mother." He bent down to place a kiss on her cheek, a near miss.

Ada gave him a vague smile. "What brings you here, Son? Sit down and have a muffin." She held out her plate.

Arthur remained standing. "Why aren't you ready to go?"

"Go where? Were we planning to go anywhere today?" Ada looked over at Lee, who shook her head. "You must be mistaken, Son. Leaping to conclusions, just like your father." She took another bite of muffin. "You should slow down."

"Good Lord, Mother! Didn't they tell you?" His eyes darted about the room.

"Tell me what?" Ada squinted her eyes. "I don't believe they told me anything in particular." She looked up at Arthur. "Sit down, Son. Elizabeth can fix you a muffin and some decaf."

"I'm not hungry." He drew up a chair beside her and lowered his voice, speaking slowly and distinctly, as if to a child. "Now listen, Mother, I've arranged for them to take you back at Tranquil Acres, but you must get dressed. I don't have all day."

27

Lee was seething but restrained herself. So far, Ada seemed to be holding her own.

"Tranquil what?"

"Tranquil Acres, for God's sake! The place where you were before these cr . . . ahh, these ladies carted you off."

"Oh. Well, why didn't you say so?"

"By the way," Vivian cut in, "we're having strawberry ice cream tonight."

"You stay out of this," Arthur snapped.

"It's a free country, so far anyway. I can say what I please."

Ada eyed Arthur suspiciously. "Are you trying to trick me into something?"

"Of course not, Mother. I'm merely looking after your best interests."

"Then what's your rush? Why can't we sit here and have a normal conversation?" Vivian, across the room, stifled a laugh.

"I just want to settle you in there as soon as possible so I can get to my office." Arthur leaned forward in his chair.

"Will Claire be there?" Ada's face brightened.

"Who's Claire?"

"I doubt that you could be with her any more," Lee said quickly. "They probably gave her another roommate by now." She felt cruel saying it, but this was all-out war.

"Oh. Well, I don't want to go back anyway." Ada glanced around at the others. "I wouldn't want to leave these folks." She shook her head emphatically. "No!"

"No?" Arthur shouted. "What do you mean, No?"

"No means no. I'm not going. I'm staying right here."

"You put her up to this, didn't you?" Arthur sputtered, his eyes shooting daggers at Lee. "You planted these ideas in her head! I knew all along I couldn't trust you."

"I did no such thing."

Elizabeth, who had been rattling the dishes in her agitation, put down her towel and came over to the table. "No need for accusations." Her voice rang firm. "Let's all have a nice cup of coffee and some coffeecake."

Arthur shoved back his chair and stood up. Rage filled his face and erupted from his voice. "You talk of coffeecake when my

28

own mother sits there defying my judgment?" He picked up his briefcase and strode toward the doorway. "I've had enough of you, all of you!" He emphasized his words with a sweeping gesture of his arm to include the whole kitchen. "But this isn't the end of it. I shall ask my attorney to set a court date."

"Court date for what, may I ask?" Minerva said.

"A hearing to have Mother placed under my custody as her legal guardian."

Lee stood up and faced him squarely. "You can't do that against her will."

"I can if she's proven mentally incompetent—and you crazies are shown to be unfit companions." At the door he turned. "See you in court."

Lee could hear his car taking off down the drive. "Whew!" she said.

"Well," said Ada, "he certainly left in a huff!"

"He'll get over it," Vivian said.

"I'm afraid not," Lee said.

"What did he say about court?" Ada looked confused, as if trying to piece together a tedious puzzle. "Is Arthur in some sort of trouble?"

"No, Ada, nothing of that sort. Nothing for you to worry about now," Minerva said.

"He said something about my hearing. I got that much." She looked bewildered. "I admit my hearing is not quite up to snuff, but what does that have to do with the court?" She shook her head. "It doesn't make sense."

"There's a lot about him that doesn't make sense," Lee said.

"Well, I'll take some of that coffeecake, Elizabeth, if you don't mind," Ada said. "Arthur can wear a person out!"

4

"Ada, do pay attention. Pretend I'm the judge asking you these questions," Minerva said. She was sitting cross-legged on the couch, with Lee beside her. Ada was across from them in the rocking chair.

"Shoot. I'm game."

"What's your name?"

"Mary Alice Screwdriver."

"Ada, be serious!" Lee said. "This is important."

"How can I be serious over such a stupid question?"

"All right, we'll assume you know your name, but when the judge asks you, don't give him any smart answers," Minerva said patiently.

"I thought that was the point. To prove to the judge that I am smart—smart enough to look after myself."

"She means smart-ass answers," Lee said.

"What's your mother's maiden name?"

"Elizabeth Barrett Browning."

"Ada!" Lee shouted in exasperation.

"All right. Mama's maiden name. Let me see." She twisted the end of her braid and stared out the window. "Well, the Elizabeth part was right. The rest has slipped my mind at the moment."

"We can look it up on your birth certificate," Minerva said.

"I have no idea where it is. Probably packed away in the attic somewhere." Ada paused. "Why not make up one. Who will know the difference?"

"Arthur, for one," said Lee.

"Well, then why don't we just ask him?"

"No, we don't want to show any sign of weakness," Minerva said.

"Never mind. I remember it now. Perkins. Elizabeth Ann Perkins."

"Well, don't forget it," Minerva said. "That's a question everyone should be able to answer. And where was she born?"

"How should I know? I wasn't there."

"Ada! Come on now!" Lee could not hide her impatience.

"Indianapolis, I think—or some outlying town." She smiled at Lee. "Don't get upset. Can't we have a little fun? The whole thing is utterly stupid as far as I'm concerned."

"Well, it might seem stupid," Minerva said, "but Arthur means business. He wants control of you and your future."

"All right, continue." Ada gave an exaggerated sigh and rocked back and forth, a bored expression on her face.

"How many children do you have, Mrs. Abernathy?" Lee asked.

"One, if I remember correctly. And at this particular time, I'd say that's one too many!"

"What's his or her name?" Lee asked, ignoring the aside. "And where does he or she live?"

"Trouble, with a capital T! I think he's from some other planet."

"I give up!" Lee exploded. "Don't you realize what's at stake?"

"Well, then, stop asking me such asinine questions. I'm not senile, you know."

"But that's exactly what we have to prove," Minerva said quietly.

"Is this the kind of questions they're going to ask me?"

"We don't know. We're just guessing. But whatever the questions, it's important that you give straight answers, none of your quirky humor. The judge might not be amused."

Lee could feel the fury building up inside of her, fury at Arthur for putting them through all this. During the past week, they mistook his silence for a willingness to let Ada make her own

31

decisions. But this morning Ada was served with papers requiring her to be in court the following Wednesday. Arthur was petitioning to be her conservator. The petition pointed out his concern for the financial and personal well-being of the proposed conservatee by reason of her advanced age, infirmity, mental weakness, and substantial impairment of her ability to care for her property and provide for herself. When Lee read it aloud, Ada had listened quietly with a baffled expression, then shaking her head in disbelief, exclaimed, "That Arthur! Why would he do such a cockamamie thing?"

Lee picked up the legal envelope from the coffee table. She felt a strong urge to rip it to shreds, but this petition was a reality they could not ignore. Fortunately the effects of the medication seemed to have worn off, except for an occasional lapse of memory. And they still had a week for further improvement.

"What's today's date?" Minerva asked.

"Wednesday."

"The date?"

"Oh. Now let me see." Ada began counting on her fingers. "March 15—the Ides of March,'" she said triumphantly.

"Good. And when we go to the hearing, it will be March 22nd. Keep that in mind."

"March 22nd." Ada nodded her head. "I can remember that."

"Here's one," said Lee. "Suppose you went to the supermarket and bought two pounds of apples at eighty-nine cents a pound and handed the checker a five dollar bill. How much change would you get?"

"With tax?"

"Skip the tax."

"Will they let you do that?"

"It's just a hypothetical question."

"Well, in the first place, I wouldn't pay eighty-nine cents a pound for apples. That's too much money. And in the second place, if I were to bother to go into a supermarket, I'd certainly come out with more than a bag of apples."

"Just answer the question. How much change?"

Ada sighed. "All right. Let's see . . . She mumbled to herself, Two times 90 is 180 minus 2 is 178 from 500 is . . . then

32

triumphantly, "$3.22."

"Good!"

Ada glanced at Lee with a worried frown. "I hope they don't give me many like that. It's not exactly my strong point."

"Well, you have to prove you're able to manage your own money."

"Now, one more question. What's the name of the President?" Minerva asked.

"President of what? General Motors?"

"You know what I mean."

"That's easy. Reagan."

"Think again. That was last term."

Oh, of course. George Bush. Can't stand the man! Guess that's why I keep forgetting. At least Ronnie could put on a good show, give us a little entertainment along the way. But George is an impossible bore!"

"The judge won't be interested in your political opinions," Lee said. "Just stick to the facts."

"And who is Vice President?" Minerva asked.

Ada thought a minute. "Partridge?" she said tentatively.

Lee rolled her eyes in dismay. "Are you serious?"

"I forget," Ada said in a low voice.

"Quayle," Lee said.

"Oh, of course. Well, I knew it was a bird of some sort. You'll have to admit, he doesn't stand out in a crowd."

Minerva got up from the couch. "I think we've practiced enough for today," she said briskly. "I'll put the kettle on for some tea."

* * *

After Ada had gone to bed that evening the four women gathered about the fireplace talking strategy for countering Arthur's challenge, the vague threat that had suddenly taken on a vicious life of its own.

"We must have a plan of action." Minerva laid aside the woven tunic she was edging with a crocheted border. "We can't just sit here complaining that it isn't fair."

33

"Honestly, that Arthur!" said Vivian with a defiant toss of her head. "I'd like to wring his scrawny neck!"

"There's no time to lose," Lee said.

"Oh, dear!" Elizabeth gave a deep sigh, not looking up from her knitting. "How can we manage? Ada will need an attorney."

"I know a lawyer in Riverhead," Vivian said. "He's been involved in a number of our closings. Very sharp fellow."

"But does he know anything about conservators?" Minerva asked.

"What is his fee?" Elizabeth said. Worrying about money again. But a legitimate question. Lee had heard any number of horror stories about outlandish legal fees."

"I'll talk to him about it. I think he's fair-minded," Vivian said.

"But wouldn't it be better to have a woman attorney?" Lee asked.

"There she goes again—a woman this, a woman that!" Vivian said. "Can't you ever give men credit for anything?"

"I could get a referral from the County Office for Women," Lee said. "This is decidedly a women's issue." She felt a surge of impatience. Everything jagged, sharp-edged.

"I don't think we have to label it," Elizabeth said. "A competent attorney is our chief concern." She counted some stitches on her knitting. "Parker's attorney was a splendid fellow. But he's semi-retired now, still in Florida for the winter I believe. He had a young associate who might do. Let's see, what was his name?" She resumed her knitting, rocking slowly back and forth.

"Wait a minute!" Lee stood up. "No one is even considering my suggestion of a woman attorney. I don't understand you people!"

"Well, I don't doubt that we could come up with a clever woman perfectly capable of handling the case," Minerva said quietly. "But I wonder if she would be aggressive enough to hold her own against Arthur's lawyer. From what I've heard he's quite a loud mouth. He might out-talk her."

"That's a sexist view if I ever heard one." Lee was pacing back and forth. She couldn't believe Minerva would take this approach.

"Well, we mustn't let our feminism stand in the way of Ada's security," Minerva replied. "You have to admit it is conceivable that a woman attorney might have a tough time dealing with a misogynist judge and a bully of a lawyer."

"And people tend to listen more to a man than a woman. Their voices carry more weight," Vivian said.

"Speak for yourself! I'd listen to a woman any day!" Lee sat down and started leafing through a magazine on the coffee table.

"But you do not represent the average man on the street," Elizabeth said.

"I should hope not!" Lee glared at the other three.

"I think they're right," Elizabeth said. "A man will make a stronger case for Ada. Why don't you check with your friend, Vivian. But remember to discuss his fee before you make a firm commitment."

"I don't think we have time to be choosy. We'll be lucky if he can do it on such short notice."

Lee got up and poked the fire, then threw on another log, sending up a shower of sparks. How she hated Arthur! Slithering his way into their lives. The room was quiet except for the sizzle and crackle of the fire, the slow ticking of the clock, and the click of Elizabeth's knitting needles.

Minerva picked up Arthur's petition from the table. "Arthur is a shrewd opponent. We have been regarding him as just an annoyance to be circumvented. But he's nobody's fool!" She read the petition, frowning. "Listen to this. He lists advanced age, infirmity, mental weakness. That's outrageous! Eighty-four is not all that old." She threw the paper on the table. "But we have to deal with the infirmity and mental weakness."

"With another week, her mind should be back to normal," Lee said.

"Whatever that is." Vivian shrugged. "Ada has her own standards for normalcy. They might not sit too well with a judge."

"Maybe we should have her examined by a psychologist," Elizabeth suggested.

"I've never trusted psychologists since the kooky professor I had in college," Lee said. "She gave short-answer quizzes that had nothing to do with the real world."

"Viv should check that out with the lawyer," Minerva said. "But what about this infirmity on the petition? We must step up her physical therapy, try to get her walking without the walker, just a cane perhaps."

"She's making good progress," Lee said. This past week she had begun driving Ada to Southampton for physical therapy— hot packs and ultra sound, massage, and a series of exercises to strengthen her legs. "I'll talk to the therapist, but I doubt that she can do much more."

"Let's ask the lawyer to seek an adjournment," Vivian said.

"A what?" Minerva said.

"A postponement. It's common practice."

"I'm worn out before we start!" Lee stared glumly into the red-orange flames twisting over the dark outline of the log. If only she could untangle them from this wretched web, free all of them to be the bright bold spirits they had been when they first joined forces last year for the good life.

5

Lee sat in the attic studio staring at her word processor, unable to concentrate. She did not adapt easily to new surroundings. When she insisted on giving up her room downstairs for Ada, she had not considered the ramifications—not so much the bother of climbing the stairs as the unfamiliar openness of this space compared to the cozy compactness of her room where, surrounded by her books, she could screen out the world. Up here she felt strangely vulnerable, even with the entire attic to herself at the moment.

Fluffs of clouds skittered across a windy sky on this day of the vernal equinox, mid-point between light and darkness. Patterns of sun and shadow from the skylight played across a stack of typewritten pages. Lee shuffled aimlessly through them. All morning, her first free one since Ada had come home, she had been trying to prepare a table of contents for her collection of poems. The manuscript, overdue at the printer, had been put aside for Ada's rescue and care, then for the legal complexities of Arthur's petition, yet to be resolved. But now they had a two-week reprieve. Rather than appearing in court tomorrow, Ada was free until April 4. A breather anyway.

The attorney search had unexpectedly resolved itself. Vivian's lawyer declined the case, saying it was not in his area of specialization. And the one Elizabeth had in mind did not have the time. Then Minerva remembered an attorney, Mary Graverton, who had recently moved out to Southampton from

Manhattan. They met at a Westhampton forum on AIDS a few months ago. Her credentials were excellent—extensive legal background and specialization in Elder Law. Minerva felt she was assertive enough to hold her own in the courtroom. Lee was delighted. Vivian and Elizabeth would have preferred a man. And Ada didn't seem to care one way or the other, apparently in a state of denial that Arthur would do such a thing. Their attorney had requested an adjournment to prepare for the hearing.

Today Elizabeth was keeping an eye on Ada, now capable of looking after many of her own needs. Lee savored this interval of freedom. But the poems seemed fragmented, refusing to form the organic whole she had envisioned. She stroked the cat curled up on the desk. "What's the matter with me, Patches? Am I losing it?" Patches yawned and rested her head on the papers, purring loudly.

Perhaps she was expecting an impossible degree of perfection. These had been strenuous days. Driving Ada three times a week to physical therapy, maneuvering her into the car, checking her routine with the therapist—nearly three hours from start to finish. And every morning supervising her exercises, listening to her excuses that she was too sore, too tired, or too something. Almost more than Lee could cope with, though she tried not to show her impatience. Ada was quickly becoming her old eccentric self. Always on the opinionated side, she seemed even more extreme now.

Lee hated to admit it, but Ada was beginning to grate on her nerves. Their friendship dated back to the St. Louis days when Ada was on the staff of the People's Art Center with Matt. His death had drawn them even closer. It was Ada who convinced Lee to go back to the university for her degree and Ada's recommendation that helped her get into college teaching. They had drifted apart when Lee moved to New York, but later Ada retired and settled in Greenwich Village where she had lived in the 1930s. Perhaps their lives formed some overall pattern—a giant jigsaw puzzle they could not discern because they were the pieces within.

Was she being hypocritical by pretending everything was fine? Or, even worse, was she playing the role of martyr? She had no love for hypocrites or martyrs. Small wonder she felt out of harmony. She had been imagining some sort of contract by which, if she did her part well, everyone would pitch in and do her share. How naive! The others could have taken on some of the therapy routine, adjusted their schedules too. But to bring that about would call for confrontation, and she hated that sort of thing among friends—so unfriendly.

Idly stroking the cat, Lee found her mind drifting back to the January rally, Inauguration Day, remembering how unified they had felt, the five of them, joined with that vibrant cross-section of people . . . Lee with the megaphone, "We must not allow President Bush to turn back the clock!" The crowd chanting, "Read our lips! We're Pro-Choice!" Sandy Rapp with guitar singing one of her songs, "Remember Rose," all joining in the chorus, "Get your laws off me; I'm not your property. Don't plan my family; I'll plan my own . . . ." The exhilaration . . . and announcing the March on Washington planned for April, amid wild cheers . . . If only they could feel that same unity today! But everything was changed now, changed by the whim of that ancient Trickster.

The cat rolled on her back with a luxurious stretch, knocking several pages of poetry on the floor. Lee did not bother to pick them up. She turned off her word processor and cuddled the cat against her shoulder. "Come on, Patches, let's see about lunch."

In the kitchen she found Ada and Elizabeth sitting at the table, laughing together. Ada's face, in contrast to the zombie expression of two weeks ago, was animated, full of life.

Lee put her cat on the floor beside Ada's. Brother Gray took a swat at Patches who retreated, hissing, beneath Ada's walker. Lee pulled up a chair at the opposite corner of the table. She felt strangely like an intruder.

"What have you been up to?" Ada asked. "All of a sudden you were gone. Hocus-pocus!" She snapped her fingers. "Vanished!"

"I told you I was going upstairs to work on the poetry book." Lee tried to keep the irritation out of her voice. She glanced at Ada sitting there in the sunlight, her lined face accentuated by her thick gray braid interwoven with red ribbons. She wore a simple blue denim vest over red print blouse and long denim

39

skirt that hid her lame leg. A sharply chiseled image against the white wall behind her.

"Well, I've begun rereading *Mrs. Dalloway*. And when I get lost in a book, I don't hear what's going on around me."

"How can you keep rereading Virginia Woolf? Can't you move on to something new? Why not try Alice Walker or Margaret Atwood or some other contemporary writer?" Lee felt the cutting edge of her words which she regretted but could not retract.

"Because she's the only writer with anything worth saying."

"Would you care for a sandwich?" Elizabeth asked.

"No thanks." Lee put a slice of bread in the toaster and took a container of yogurt from the refrigerator.

Ada made a face. "How can you eat that stuff?"

"What's wrong with it?"

"Nothing's *wrong* with it. I just don't see how anyone can like the taste of it."

"Well, *I* do. And, besides, it's good for you. Leads to a long life." Lee began eating the yogurt.

"Now don't give me that nonsense about those old fellows somewhere in Siberia who ate yogurt and chopped wood all their lives and lived to be a hundred and ten." Ada leaned her elbows on the table and propped her chin in her hands, looking across at Lee. "Who wants to live to a hundred and ten anyway?" She gave a mock shudder. "Especially if the price you pay is a lifetime of chopping wood and eating yogurt."

Lee got up to butter her toast without responding. She stood at the counter with her back to the table. Ada and her exasperating arguments! Yet Lee knew she should be grateful that she was now capable of arguing, after those terrible days of being unable to focus on anything. Why was she feeling so perversely negative? Sun sparkled against the row of spice jars above the stove, highlighted the copper teakettle. But she was not seeing it through the darkness of her mood.

"I, for one, most certainly don't!" Ada's voice broke through her thoughts.

"Don't what?"

"Want to live to one hundred and ten. I don't even know if I want to live past eighty-five."

40

"Why do you say that?" Elizabeth asked. "You really don't look your age."

"According to Arthur, I most certainly do, and then some! He thinks I'm infirm and off my rocker." Ada paused. "Or something to that effect. Who knows?" She looked intently at Elizabeth and Lee. "Maybe he's right."

"Don't be ridiculous, Ada!" Lee said quickly. "You'll soon have your strength back, and there's nothing wrong with your mind."

"Lee's right. You mustn't get yourself all worked up."

"But what if we can't prove it?" Ada's voice trembled.

"Of course we'll prove it," Elizabeth said.

"It's Arthur who's off his rocker," Lee added. "Getting back to what you just said, I want to know how you can even think such a thing"

"Why not? We just determined that I am of sound mind."

"Don't be impossible!" Lee's voice grew louder. "After *all* we went through to rescue you from that horrible place, and *all* we're doing now to keep you here, how can you say you don't want to live past eighty-five when that's almost what you are now?"

"I have a few more months to go," Ada chuckled. "Don't rush things."

"You make me sick!" Lee slammed her knife on the counter.

Elizabeth stood up with a heavy sigh and walked toward the door.

"Where are you going?" Ada called after her. Elizabeth left the room without responding.

"What's eating her?" Ada asked, staring at the closed door.

"She can't stand our arguing. And neither can I."

"Well, pardon me! You used to relish a good little battle of words." Ada's voice was puzzled. "But today you're like a firecracker about to explode."

Lee stared glumly at the blue-checked tablecloth. She couldn't say to Ada, *YOU are what's the matter with me.* No, she couldn't say that. "I'm just on edge—no particular reason. If I were thirty years younger, I'd say it was PMS."

"PMS? What in God's name is that?"

"Come on, Ada, surely you've heard of premenstrual syndrome?" Lee carried the dishes to the sink.

"Oh, *that.* Yes, I have read about it. But I can't remember all these crazy letters they use these days. Almost as bad as back in the '30s when we had WPA and NRA and CCC. Anyway, this PMS, I don't take much stock in it. Women today pamper themselves, make such a big thing about their hormone balance, their nutritional balance, their rhythms. And when they start menopause and get a few hot flashes, you never hear the end of it. In my day, we just toughed it out."

Lee knew that Ada was aware that she did not agree with her, but she refused to take the bait. Instead, she walked over and gave her a hug.

"What was that for?" Ada looked flustered.

"Nothing in particular. I just don't like for us to quibble over little things, and I don't like myself for the way I feel, and I don't like the way you insist on picking a fight, and . . . oh, I don't know . . . everything is off-balance."

"My dear Lee." Ada took her hand, giving it a squeeze. "I had no idea you were in such a state. Forgive me."

"It's not your fault. It's something inside of me, twisting at me. But what you said awhile ago troubles me."

"And what was that?"

"About not wanting to live past eighty-five. You didn't really mean that, did you?"

"Well, as I recall, I didn't say flat out that I didn't want to. I merely said I didn't know for sure whether I wanted to." Ada's voice was serious now, her eyes cobalt blue in their intensity. "But when you reach eighty-five, you begin to deteriorate, physically if not mentally. All sorts of maladies you have staved off through the years attack the body, sometimes the mind. I've seen it happen to a number of friends. And I'm not at all sure I wish to join their ranks. When I make my exit, I don't want to be carted off on a stretcher. I want to walk away from this planetary life under my own power, trumpets blaring and banners waving."

Lee sat quietly, her eyes blurred with tears. She could not bear to think about such an eventuality. *Not yet. No, not yet, please. Let us have a few more good years together.* Suddenly she stood up and moved Ada's walker closer to the table. "What do you say we practice your walking for a few minutes?"

"Fine with me. Only let's not be too strenuous." Bracing

42

herself, Ada stood up slowly, giving a wince of pain as she changed positions and grasped the handles of the walker. She looked so fragile standing there, so much more vulnerable than when she was sitting at the table. In the coming weeks she would need all the strength she could muster.

6

"I'm going on that march, come what may!" Ada brandished her fork for emphasis.

"Don't be ridiculous. You can't afford to take that risk." Lee poured some more coffee in her cup.

"Craziest thing I ever heard of!" Vivian said. "What if Arthur found out?"

"Arthur doesn't own me," Ada said quietly. "Not yet anyway."

Minerva was drumming nervously on the table. "But this will play right into his hands."

"Who says he has to find out? And besides, didn't that lawyer, Gravely or whoever, didn't she just tell us there's another adjournment until the end of April?"

"Her name is Graverton," Lee said, "Mary Graverton."

Ada always had trouble remembering the names of people she was not impressed with. Last week when they met with her, Ada had been stubbornly uncommunicative. When Lee asked afterwards what she thought of her, she said, "Too polite. Probably no match for Arthur's man."

"This new delay worries me. I wonder what Arthur's attorney is up to," Minerva said.

"He's not necessarily up to anything, Vivian said. "Maybe he just had a conflict of dates."

"It worries me too," Lee said. "I wonder if he's snooping around for evidence of some sort."

44

"You two watch too much 'L.A. Law,'" Vivian said. "Just enjoy our dividend of extra time."

"I don't see how we can relax until this is over and done with." Elizabeth got up to clear the table.

"Well, in any case, we deserve a weekend off, so let's get started on our Washington plans. We only have a few days," Ada said.

"Good Lord, Ada, be reasonable! What if you were to injure your hip again? What then?" Lee said. "And how do you think you could walk the two miles and back from the Monument to the Supreme Court Building?"

"I'll manage somehow."

"Why is this so important to you, Ada?" Minerva draped an arm about her shoulder.

"Well . . . ." Ada paused, biting her lip. "I have my reasons."

"Oh, she has her reasons. That explains everything." Lee slammed down her cup. "I give up!"

"I thought you wanted to go," Ada said. "It was all you could talk about when they first announced the march."

"That was before all this mess." Lee lowered her voice. "Of course I wanted to go. But now it's just too risky."

"Well, you don't have to be a martyr on my account because I am going, and that's that." Ada glanced around at the others. "You see, it's something I *have* to do because I still remember the pain of it, the desperation, the fear when I . . . ."

"You mean . . . " Vivian interrupted, "you're telling us that you had a back-alley abortion?"

"I've never talked about it before. It wasn't exactly back-alley."

"It couldn't have been legal," Vivian said with a laugh, "unless you were some sort of medical freak, getting pregnant at sixty-nine."

"I didn't say it was legal. But I took care of it myself."

"Not with a coathanger!"

"Not exactly. Something I rigged up with a knitting needle." Her voice quavered. "I had just started teaching. Fred and I weren't married yet. Babies were taboo for unmarried teachers." She buried her face in her hands.

"Oh, Ada!" Lee's voice was full of remorse. "I didn't know. All

45

these years, and you kept it to yourself." She pulled her chair over and gave her a hug.

"It's a wonder you didn't kill yourself!" Minerva gasped, the color drained from her face.

"Guess I was one of the lucky ones." Ada blew her nose. "Don't want our girls going through it again."

"Now it's clear—why you want to be there." Minerva ran her hands through her hair. "But I'm afraid Arthur would use this against us." She paused. "What's the name of that church he belongs to?"

"The Gospel something or other."

Vivian groaned. "You know how they feel! A woman's only choice is babies and more babies. He would really be upset!"

"If Arthur could get pregnant, he'd change his tune in a hurry," Ada muttered. "Actually it's Dolores' church. He probably goes just to keep her happy. Anyway, there's no need for him to find out."

"We can't be too careful until we get the court hearing out of our way," Elizabeth said, worry lines creasing her forehead.

"Well, what Arthur doesn't know won't hurt anyone." Ada's voice was defiant. "And even if he were to find out, which is unlikely, there's nothing mentally unstable about a harmless little excursion to Washington."

"His attorney might twist things around and make us seem to be unfit companions for you," Lee said.

"Plenty of time when we return to worry about Arthur and his smart-aleck attorney. Meanwhile let's take a break, get away and do something fun together—the five of us. It's a rare opportunity." Ada glanced around the table at the others. "I'm not too adept at expressing my feelings—except maybe through painting. But I want you to know how much it means . . . how living here with all of you . . . how alone I felt before, how you've changed . . . no, I mean . . . *enriched* my life." She paused, her face flushed, clearly embarrassed by the sentiment. She wiped her eyes on the sleeve of her blouse. "What would I ever do without you?"

The dining room had grown dark except for the light from candles in the two silver holders. Flames flickered and cast dancing shadows on the circle of women sitting around the table.

Vivian pushed back her chair and bounced up. "Stay where

you are, everybody." She hurried out of the room, returning with a bottle of sherry and five glasses. "This calls for a toast." She began pouring the sherry.

"What's the occasion?" asked Elizabeth.

"Only a sip for me," Minerva said.

"The occasion is that we are all together and we have every intention of staying together, and no earthly force will tear us apart, not even Arthur!"

The five clinked glasses and sipped their sherry.

"Let's all go to Washington! Here's to freedom! Freedom for *all* women—young and old, white and black, the poor, freedom of choice! And freedom for us, freedom from Arthur!" Smiling, eyes gleaming, hair glittering gold about her face, Vivian stood holding her glass like some twentieth century Goddess of Liberty—candle flames reflecting in the glass a myriad of amber sparks showering on the table. She fixed them in her gaze. "Well, what do you say, girls?"

7

Four overnight bags were stacked by the door in the front hallway, along with a thermos of coffee and a cooler of soda and sandwiches. Piled beside them were a stack of placards, the NOW banner, a large American flag, and a folding wheelchair.

"Liz, get your bag down here. Perry is expecting us at her place by eight-thirty. We've barely time to make it. And we have to pick up Linda and Quincy by nine o'clock." Lee gripped the stair railing impatiently. Her face was flushed with excitement, masking the wrinkles. Today she felt far younger than her years.

Elizabeth appeared at the head of the stairs, still in her bathrobe.

"Why aren't you dressed?"

"I have something to explain." Elizabeth came slowly down the steps. "But I don't quite know how."

"Get to the point, Liz. What's up?" Vivian entered the hall, car keys in hand.

"Well," Elizabeth cleared her throat, "to make a long story short, I can't go with you."

"You *what?*" Lee said. "What do you mean—can't go?"

"Well, when the phone rang a little while ago, it was John calling to tell me a friend had given him two tickets to a concert at Carnegie Hall tonight, and he asked me to go with him. First I told him *no*, on account of Washington. But he sounded so disappointed, I . . . I just couldn't turn him down." She fiddled nervously with the tie on her robe. "I'm truly sorry, but you know how I love Carnegie Hall."

48

"Oh, Johnnie, oh, Johnnie, how you can love!" Vivian began singing in a shrill treble. She, of course, didn't have much room to talk—being out on the town just about every weekend herself, with an assortment of men, all ages and types. It was remarkable that she had actually canceled a date to go on the march. Decidedly out of character.

Elizabeth had met John Berkley, a retired banker, in her volunteer work at the hospital. He now served as a volunteer cashier in the coffee shop. They had been going out occasionally for the past month or so. When Vivian started teasing her the other day, she blushed and said, "It's nothing serious—not so soon after Parker's death."

Lee looked at Elizabeth with dismay. "How could you back out at the last minute this way? Some feminist!"

"I never claimed to be a feminist," Elizabeth snapped, the lines of her face growing taut, her back stiffening.

While in their teens Lee and her friends lived by the unspoken code that it was quite acceptable, even expected, that you break a date with the girls to go out with a boy, any boy at all. Even among adults it used to be standard behavior. But times had changed. Or had they? Maybe it was just wishful thinking—the notion that living together, caring for one another, would create a genuine spirit of sisterhood among the five of them. Now here was Elizabeth standing there with her wrinkles and gray hair, over eighty, canceling her arrangement as if unaware of any obligation.

Elizabeth broke the uncomfortable silence. "I said I was sorry. But I've made up my mind."

A troubled frown clouded Lee's face. Perhaps this little romance was blossoming into something more serious. What if Elizabeth were to team up with John permanently, move in with him? What then? She tried to push the bothersome thought out of her mind. But it triggered a vague sense of uneasiness.

Before she could sort it all out, Ada came into the hallway twirling her cane, followed by Minerva who was wearing a white jacket with her message on the back in large purple letters: MY CONSCIENCE IS THE HIGHEST COURT.

"Do be careful, Ada. We'll be in a real pickle if you take another fall," Lee said.

Minerva turned to Elizabeth standing rigidly at the foot of the steps. "Liz, you're not dressed!"

"She's not going!" Vivian rolled her eyes and extended her hands skyward. "At the last minute she tells us."

"Not going?" Minerva looked at Elizabeth with concern. "Is something wrong?"

Elizabeth shook her head, eyes downcast, her face a deeper pink than her robe.

"She has a date with you-know-who." Vivian puckered her lipsticked mouth into an exaggerated kiss.

"A concert at Carnegie Hall is not just an ordinary date. I couldn't say *no* to that." Elizabeth glanced about at the four of them. "I do hope you understand."

"But you'll miss this historic occasion. They're expecting the largest turn-out ever," Minerva said. "Are you sure, Liz?"

Elizabeth nodded.

"Well, maybe it's a good idea for you to be around here at least part of the weekend in case Arthur calls," Minerva said.

"Why should he call?" Lee's voice was edgy. Since his petition for the conservatorship, communication had taken place through their attorneys. Lee had not told Mary Graverton about their Washington trip, fearing she might advise against it. Ada would not have listened anyway.

Lee turned to Elizabeth. "If Arthur should call, make up a reason Ada can't come to the phone. Or maybe you should just leave the machine on and monitor it."

"Right," Vivian said. "You might somehow give it away. Just don't answer the phone, Liz—unless it's one of us."

The very mention of Arthur had set Lee's pulse racing. She could feel a tightness in her jaw and a tension in the muscles of her shoulder and neck. One more thing to worry about—what scheme he might be up to, what trap he might be laying. Worrying had become one of her specialties lately. Even before they were on their way, she had begun worrying about maneuvering the wheelchair on and off the subway, hunting elevators instead of stairs, and who knows what other complications? At first, Ada had objected strenuously to taking the wheelchair but finally admitted she could not walk the distance. "Listen," Lee said abruptly, "we've got to get out of here. We'll be late as it is."

"Yes, folks, let's be on our way." Ada lifted her cane like a drum major and started out the door which Vivian held for her.

Elizabeth had slipped on her coat to see them off. She put the last bag in the wheelchair and pushed it down the drive to the car.

Lee gave her a hug. "Take care now, and don't get carried away." There was something very touching about Elizabeth standing there . . . . Lee searched for words for the feeling that had come over her—a sense of the ephemeral nature of their lives, so fragile . . . . Gripped by the strong desire to preserve every image, like pressed flowers in a scrapbook, she made a silent wish for their safe return.

"Be prepared to bail us out in case we get arrested," Vivian said, climbing into the driver's seat.

"Oh, dear, don't do that!"

"Just kidding, Liz."

Lee looked back as the car pulled out of the drive and saw the lone figure, still waving good-bye.

8

Holding firmly to the handles of Ada's wheelchair, Lee felt a certain disbelief that they were actually here in Washington, part of this tremendous surge of humanity. The morning was sunny, unseasonably cool for April, with a sky of brilliant blue marbled by white swirling clouds. Three weeks beyond the intersection of the sun's path with the celestial equator, each day an acceleration of light, producing in Lee a parallel quickening of spirit. In this green season alive with unfurling leaves and tender shoots of grass, she always experienced a joyful anticipation, seduced by its lavish promises.

Giddy with lingering fragrance of cherry blossoms and the massive chanting crowd, Lee tried to capture and preserve the moment, create an internalized videotape, knowing she would not be able to find words to describe it in her journal. Throngs of people covered the hill at the base of the Washington Monument and flowed out onto Constitution Avenue, a cross-section of generations. Colorful signs and banners rose above them. Chants and songs filled the air, an atmosphere charged with camaraderie.

Lee could feel the dynamic energy pulsing through her, the exhilaration of this page in history she was helping to create. She was clad in the white of the suffragist—white pants, sweatshirt, jacket, beret, and a diagonal gold sash decorated with CHOICE buttons.

Ada sat in her wheelchair with regal bearing. She wore a long white skirt and high-necked blouse with puffed sleeves, a multicolored wool shawl draped around her shoulders. Her beribboned braid hung gracefully over one shoulder, and she carried a white ruffled parasol encircled with the slogan NEVER GO BACK. She drew many admiring glances and played her role with gusto. Arthur would have a fit if he knew. A worrisome thought. But, of course, he had no way of finding out.

Minerva stood beside them carrying the large fringed banner of their chapter of the National Organization for Women—panels of lavender, white, and gold, replica of those carried by their foremothers. It was flapping vigorously in the wind, and she struggled to hold the pole steady. Lee noted with concern that her face looked pale and tense. She seemed to lack her usual vitality. Lee recalled the two of them at past rallies—against the Shoreham nuclear plant, for human rights, for peace in Nicaragua—Minerva striding ahead and Lee struggling to keep up. She studied her face more closely, noting with a stab of fear that she did seem strained, older somehow. Inevitable, of course, the aging process. Perhaps she only appeared older today in contrast to the three younger women she was standing beside, Lee's former students—Quincy, Linda, and Perry.

Turning to Linda, Lee suggested she give Minerva a hand with the banner. She was a slender woman in her twenties with a bush of red hair pulled away from her face by a white headband. She wore a sign, MOTHER BY CHOICE. Linda quickly circled over to Minerva, who seemed glad to relinquish the banner.

Lee moved closer to Minerva. "Are you all right, Min?"

"I'm fine. Just a little worn out from the long ride yesterday and not much sleep last night."

The seven of them had congregated in one room, clad in gowns, pajamas, and robes, drinking wine, soda, and juice, munching on potato chips, talking far into the night—starting seriously with the familiar question: If abortions were declared illegal, what would become of women who have them anyway—and people who perform them? Would there be enough jails to hold them? And Minerva lashing out at the church patriarchs who couldn't stand for women to have sex without paying the penalty . . . then a chronicling of early sexual experiences. Blurred by the wine, a bit more than her usual limit, Lee's memory was hazy

53

today . . . something about Ada's first kiss . . . Vivian's first time to go all the way . . . Perry in a miniskirt of the '60s when her sanitary napkin came unfastened . . . Quincy's first encounter with a diaphragm . . . silliness spiraling about the room until they were laughing uncontrollably . . . Lee doing a parody of Nancy Reagan advising the women of the world to *Just say No!* Meanwhile Minerva and Ada had drifted off to sleep, Ada snoring loudly by the time the three younger women went back to their room.

It was well after two o'clock when Lee got to bed. But she had awakened full of vitality, keyed up for the big day. She loved those night sessions with the women—the talk, the laughter, the room fairly crackling with energy. Back in her teaching days, she and a colleague in Women's Studies would gather up a vanload of students for their annual pilgrimage to Seneca Falls in July—tracing their heritage, the first Women's Rights Convention. She recalled the thrill of visiting Elizabeth Cady Stanton's home, sensing the power of that magnanimous spirit, sitting where she might have sat to write her historic Declaration of Sentiments, paralleling the founding fathers' Declaration of Independence. Above the din of the crowd, her revolutionary words bombarded Lee's memory—a long list of inequities, ending with a pledge to fight the *misconception, misrepresentation, and ridicule* that lay ahead. Thanks to Stanton and that audacious little group of women, things had changed since 1848, but not enough. Such a long time to wait! If she were alive today, she would surely be with them in Washington leading the march.

Lee glanced over at Linda holding the banner high, confident and strong. What a contrast to the timid young woman who had hesitantly entered her office, standing with downcast eyes, clutching her frayed coat—attending college in defiance of an abusive husband who bullied her and threatened their young son. Now she was divorced and working part-time, about to graduate and go on to the State University. Next to Linda stood Perry, a robust woman of forty, short-cropped brown hair framing her ruddy face. She wore a sign, CHOICE—THE AMERICAN WAY, and carried the American flag, faded and stained from years of marches and rallies. Strong and resolute now, but a few years ago devastated by the agony of her decision to have an abortion, intensified by a rigid Catholic upbringing. "Isn't this great!" she exclaimed.

Ada pivoted around in her wheelchair. "Reminds me of the rallies back in the 1930's when folks from the Village would come together protesting one thing or another. Same spirit, just different slogans."

"That long ago!" said Quincy, her tawny brown face serious beneath a mass of cornrow braids tied in tiny white ribbons. Her sweatshirt bore the words *A WOMB OF ONE'S OWN*. "What sort of things were you protesting back then?"

"Well, it was called the Red Decade, and we, my artist and writer friends and I, all of us, were passionately anti-Fascist. We would attend these street rallies, handing out pamphlets supporting the Loyalists in the Spanish Civil War. I was working crazy hours in a restaurant and trying to find time on the side for painting—so I tried not to get too political. But I was swept up in it along with the others."

"Did you ever get arrested?" Perry asked.

Ada shook her head and adjusted her parasol. "No, but some folks did. We so fervently wanted the Loyalists to win, we would get carried away. I remember some of those huge gatherings—how unified we felt, supporting our soldiers in the Abraham Lincoln Brigade. We must have seemed pretty fanatical." Ada smiled, reliving that little fragment of time. "We wanted to do anything possible to help them in their crusade for freedom, not just for the people of Spain but for people everywhere. We foolishly thought we could change the world!"

"I hate to show my ignorance," said Linda, "but we never studied much about that in school. Did the Loyalists win?"

Ada shook her head. "But it was a brave effort. Hemingway wrote about it, you know, in *For Whom the Bell Tolls*. Folks back then should have paid attention—just as they should now." She sighed. "But who's listening?"

She was interrupted by chanting: *Two, four, six, eight. You can't make us procreate!* Everyone joined in, repeating it several times until Lee began to feel hoarse.

Ada had talked of life in the Village, but this was the first

Lee had heard about her involvement in that radical decade. A decade she herself had managed to drift through, sheltered in her Midwestern suburb, largely out of touch with the outside world. Of course she was almost fifteen years younger than Ada. But it was more than just age. She had grown up in the same conservatism Ada had rebelled against by leaving her home in St. Louis and striking out on her own. In the 1930s Lee had been more interested in practicing the cello and daydreaming about boys than righting the wrongs of the world. She vaguely remembered how Tim, a high school boyfriend, had talked earnestly about Fascists, Brown Shirts, and Silver Shirts, but she had paid scant attention, not grasping the significance until the day she heard on the radio chants of *Heil Hitler!* by thousands of voices, sending shivers of fear down her spine. But even then she had remained on the fringe.

Perry's voice jolted her back to the present. "Did you and those others ever march on Washington?" she was saying to Ada.

"Yes, but not about the Spanish War. Against Japan." Ada chuckled. "We were boycotting Japanese imports, silk hose and such. And we marched on Washington wearing those horrible cotton stockings. Nobody had thought up nylons yet. We didn't have a group this size. But we made our point. That's what you have to do—speak out!" Ada's voice rose loud against the throng, her face flushed from the memories.

Suddenly a cheer went up as the crowd began to move forward. Lee felt a quickening of pulse as she grabbed hold of Ada's chair and pushed it along. But they had only progressed a short distance when the movement ceased as quickly as it had begun..

Lee searched her memory for the pivot point when her life started moving in this other direction. Probably the year she renounced her Republican heritage and voted for Kennedy. The beginning. And then Matt's death, forcing her to fend for herself . . . moving to New York, protesting the Vietnam War, a chunky middle-aged widow carrying placards, along with the hippies, the flower children. A late start—and so much still to be done, so little time.

"My God!" Linda shrieked. "Look at those people over there on the side. Oh, I can't stand it! That sign. GOD HATES

ABORTIONISTS! And those pictures of a dead fetus. Makes me want to puke!" Her hands that carried the banner were shaking, her face splotchy red.

"Calm down, Linda," Lee said. "We just have to ignore them."

"But it infuriates me! All their talk about saving the lives of the unborn. What about the lives of the women forced to give birth if *Roe v. Wade* is set aside? And what about those who die from butchered abortions? Don't they count?" Anger was choking her words.

Minerva put her arm around Linda's waist. "You don't have to convince us. That's why we're here."

Lee turned to Vivian standing to one side, neatly dressed in white slacks and sweater, her curls tied back with a lavender band. She had been unusually silent. "Why so quiet, Viv?"

Ada twisted around in her wheelchair. "We've hardly heard a peep out of you."

"I'm remembering something I don't like to think about. But today it's haunting me." Her voice could barely be heard about the rumble of the crowd. "One reason I'm here."

"What happened?" Minerva draped her arm over Vivian's shoulder.

She remained silent, her face pale and strained, hands clasped tightly together.

"Something about an abortion?" Perry squinted against the sun.

Vivian hesitated. "I've never talked about it before . . . a long time ago, 1968, a few years before they were legal."

"Would it help to tell us?" Lee studied her grim face. "If you'd rather not . . . ."

"I don't really know." She paused. "Gives me a queasy feeling, just thinking about it. I was forty-six. Sounds young to me now. But, God, I felt pretty old at the time!" She gave a nervous laugh. "Thought I was safe, you know, into menopause, irregular periods . . . got a bit careless. Ben and I had decided from the start that we didn't want to be tied down with kids. And at that time our marriage was getting shaky—on again off again. The next year, actually, we went ahead with our divorce."

The others had gathered around, listening intently. Lee,

57

screening out the noise of the crowd, had to strain to hear.

"When the doctor told me I was pregnant, I burst into tears, and he said he was sorry but there was nothing he could do. He told me to get dressed and wait for him in his office. Then he said, *Don't look at any phone numbers on my desk.* Of course, when I went into his office the first thing I did was check his desk, and there was a piece of paper right on top with a phone number which I quickly copied.

"God, this sounds like a real underground deal!" Linda set the banner pole on the ground and moved closer.

"It was! My doctor took a chance even doing that much."

"Whose phone number?" Perry asked.

"A Unitarian minister on Long Island. When I called, he gave me a number in the city, and that turned out to be another minister who gave me the number of a doctor—here in Washington."

"Such intrigue!" said Perry. "Sounds like a TV mystery."

"When I phoned for an appointment I was told to send $500 cash, and then the doctor would set a date to see me."

"Gross!" said Quincy.

"But I had no alternative. I was lucky to find someone." The memory clouded her face. "By then I was two and a half months pregnant . . . no time to lose." Vivian's voice had an angry edge to it now.

"Anyway, about ten days later it was arranged. I took off work and flew to Washington. It was done in his office . . . without anaesthesia."

"No anaesthesia? Why, that's absurd!" Minerva exclaimed.

"Unbelievable in this modern day!" Linda chimed in.

"You forget. It wasn't today or yesterday. It was over twenty years ago," Vivian said tersely. "The doctor was taking quite a risk. He could have lost his license, gone to jail. Said they were worried about a possible police raid. They gave me a sedative, but I was so scared, it didn't do much good. I was shaking all over, couldn't stop. They told me to relax, that I was making it harder for myself—but I couldn't help it." Her face had turned even more pale, her voice barely audible. "The nurse stuffed a Kotex in my mouth to keep me from screaming."

58

"Poor Viv!" Minerva squeezed her shoulder. "How dreadful!"

"I watched him throw the fetus in his disposal can . . . ." Her voice quavered. "And I felt a sense of relief, almost disbelief, the lifting of a crushing burden . . . but then a strange sadness, even though I felt I had made the right choice." She heaved a sigh. "Emotions get all jumbled sometimes."

During Vivian's account, the crowd had moved only a few feet. Lee, shuffling along with them, focused only on Vivian's words, ignoring the background noise. And Vivian now seemed oblivious to her surroundings, intent on spewing it out, a cleansing perhaps. Strange that she could reveal something so deeply felt, here among all these people.

"They had me wait in an adjoining room for a time before starting home. The doctor gave me a shot of penicillin and told me to see my doctor for antibiotics. He couldn't risk giving me a prescription. When I left his office, I was bleeding, not a lot, but enough to scare me." She paused to wipe her eyes and blow her nose. "I didn't mean to talk about all this."

Lee could feel a surge of voiceless rage rising up, choking her. How many thousands of women had this happened to? Or even worse? And to think that Vivian had kept it to herself for so long, just like Ada. A reluctance, no doubt, to dredge up bitter memories. But if more women were to speak out, tell of their own agony, perhaps there could be more understanding.

"How did you manage?" Ada's face was almost as pale as Vivian's, her hands gripping the arms of her wheelchair.

"Well, I stocked up on tampons and Kotex and took a plane back to Long Island that afternoon. Went to bed as soon as I got home and just about cried my eyes out. It was so hard not talking to anybody. Phoned my gynecologist, of course, and told him I had a miscarriage. Then he took over."

"It's an outrage!" Perry was sputtering with anger.

Lee found herself thinking about Maxine, her friend who had an abortion shortly after they became legal. She still mourned that little life she had not given birth to. Perhaps it had not been the right choice for her—although with four children and her marriage on the thin edge, a child was the last thing she wanted. Right perhaps in a pragmatic sense, but not emotionally. She

59

still bore the scars, so deep she could not bring herself to go on the march with them. Choice—a complex word. But what it boiled down to was simple enough. Each woman should have the freedom to determine *who* she is and what *she* needs. A choice Lee had never needed to face personally. For years she and Matt had tried, without success, for a baby. When her friends started getting pregnant, she could hardly conceal her envy, plagued with recurring dreams that she had given birth and was bringing the baby home. A deep yearning. Even now she could feel the pain.

If faced with an unwanted pregnancy in her child-bearing years, Lee wondered whether she could have gone through an abortion. She felt a peculiar empathy for the emotional zeal of the anti-abortion people—their emotions but certainly not for the desire to impose their beliefs upon others. What a shame the two sides could not come together, talk it out instead of pitting woman against woman!

"I wish we would get started. It's chilly just standing here." Linda was jumping up and down, clapping her hands together.

"Might as well relax. They never start on time," Lee said. "How about grouping yourselves around the chair here? It would make a good picture."

Her request was met with groans. "Oh, not another photo! You took us by the van, standing in front of the hotel, and in front of the White House. How many do we need?"

"But we don't have one in front of the Washington Monument."

"Come on, folks, cluster around Ada," Perry said.

"Why don't I get out and cluster—and let someone else sit in this chair? I'm sick of it!" Ada said. "*Everyone* should spend an entire day in a wheelchair. It would be an eye opener!"

"Don't be silly!" Lee snapped. Of course, she did have a point. Lee could not quite imagine spending any length of time in a wheelchair. It must be hard on Ada.

"Bear with it awhile longer, Ada. You'll be grateful for it before the day is over," Minerva said.

"Might as well give in," said Perry. "The General has spoken. Cluster around, folks." She propped the flag against the wheel of the chair and draped herself over the arm. "Smile! And say *CHOICE*."

9

Standing beneath the Washington Monument, they could see people on a platform at the base of the hill—a woman playing a guitar, another holding a microphone—but could not hear anything because of a malfunctioning speaker. Nearly two hours had passed, and they had moved only a few hundred feet, surging first one way, then another without any apparent sense of direction. Lee's leg was beginning to ache, her discomfort aggravated by a chill wind.

To one side a cluster of five women caught her attention. Pillows stuffed under their clothing made them appear pregnant. Around their arms and necks were chains linking them to a huge papier-mache effigy of a balding black-robed Chief Justice Rehnquist held aloft on a long pole, his face looming grotesquely above his prisoners.

"I'll be right back." Lee handed her tote bag to Quincy, asking Minerva to hold onto Ada's wheelchair. "I want their picture."

She pushed her way over to the chained women where other photographers had converged. It took a few minutes to focus her camera and get a clear shot without people in the way. This was one of the times she wished she could add several inches to her height. Being short seldom bothered her—except in places like supermarkets where items were shelved too high. But lately her shortness seemed more pronounced. Maybe she was shrinking— the dreaded osteoporosis. After taking the bizarre group from various angles, she maneuvered over to snap a large purple and white banner, CATHOLICS FOR CHOICE. Then she saw a sign resembling a huge perpendicular frankfurter topped by a wire halo. A gigantic penis! The sign underneath said: IF MEN COULD GIVE BIRTH, ABORTION WOULD BE A SACRAMENT! She must get a picture of that. Elizabeth would be shocked.

Lee looked around for the others. They had disappeared from view, but no cause for alarm. She could catch up with them after a few more photos. She felt a delightful sense of freedom—being able to snap one shot after another without comments from the sidelines. Nearby stood a young woman with a coat-hanger suspended above her head, as if coming out of her ears. Unlimited photo opportunities! When she was nine years old, Lee had started taking pictures with her mother's old fold-up Kodak, and from then on, she was hooked, saving money for weeks to buy film. Her brother let her use his darkroom. She loved the acrid smell of the developer and fixer, the magic of watching images take form.

The crowd was surging upward toward the monument now, and Lee was being pushed along with them—massed together like a giant amoeba. There had been no orders, at least none she could hear. The flow seemed self-generated. After perhaps a hundred feet, they stopped as suddenly as they had started. She felt dizzy, the ground tilting beneath her. She must find the others. But no need to panic. Just find their banner. Elbowing her way toward one that looked like it, she discovered it was New Hampshire. From a distance they all appeared the same. And the women all resembled one another in their white clothing. She was engulfed by a wave of anxiety. Her feet felt weighted to the ground, as if she wore sneakers of steel. Her heart was pounding rapid drumbeats, her breath coming in short gasps.

Suddenly she was swept back through time to a St. Louis Department Store where, at the age of four, she was lost in a maze of legs, none of them her mother's, and she sat down by a rack of dresses crying softly until a salesperson found her. But now she could not just sit and cry, waiting to be found. How stupid of her! Lost without her wallet or glasses or even a tissue to blow her nose.

Lee shouldered her way through the mass of people, asking

first one, then another, "Is this the New York contingent?" A gust of wind whipped her scarf across her face and twisted the CHOICE sign hanging around her neck. She shivered and drew her jacket more tightly around her, arms crossed over the sign to hold it in place. The sun had disappeared behind a cloud, shadowing the crowd. She could not stop shivering. With misgivings she remembered all her strict warnings to the others to stick together and not get lost from the group. And she had violated her own rules. A lost leader!

They were now within range of the speaker system on the platform near 14th Street. Perhaps she could make an announcement over the microphone. She tried to push her way through the crowd, but it was against the flow. Even if she got there, what would she say? *May I have your attention? I am Lee Cranford, lost leader in search of her group."*

Her nose was beginning to run. She sniffled, wishing for a tissue or handkerchief. A proper lady, her mother used to say, was never without a handkerchief, neatly ironed, scented with lavender sachet. Lee wiped her nose on her sleeve and kept walking. The marchers abruptly came to a standstill. Unable to move in any direction, she felt as if a steel vice were squeezing the air out of her lungs. She shifted her weight from one foot to the other. This invasion of her space upset her equilibrium. Words of the artist, Betsy Damon, came to mind. *We need to find space for ourselves, space to feel, think, be strong, be completely female.* The time Damon had visited the college, she captivated them with her performance workshop when they painted each other's faces, frolicking with the abandon of children. She explained how they needed to *collectivize* their energy, bring people together in a new space to change their consciousness. Today was also a space ritual of sorts, generating its own collective energy, but without the joy and security of that earlier one.

A voice rattled over the microphone asking them to be patient, saying it was human gridlock clear to the Capitol Building. Lee looked at her watch. One-thirty. She had been lost well over an hour.

Of course she could simply find her way to the hotel after the march, meet the others there. But she would have to take the

Metro to Arlington. She had an inexplicable fear of the subway, that underground realm with the darkness of a tomb. In Manhattan, she would walk blocks to avoid it—or take a bus or cab. Here, with the group she had managed fine. But going back alone would be different—finding the right station, right color code, getting off at the right stop. And anyway her return ticket was in her tote bag with everything else.

She didn't even have a map, though she had given a copy to everyone to keep handy, just in case . . . . She had been in Washington on other marches but couldn't remember much about the streets. Years ago she had been here with Matt but never worried about finding her way when he was along. She recalled the hours they had spent in the Smithsonian. Now one of his silver chalices was there, with slides of his silversmithing techniques. Such a pity he didn't live to see that. Dear Matt . . . . What would he think of this march? Women's liberation had not been an issue at the time of his death. Most women were busy cooking, cleaning, raising children. But he had encouraged her to go back to college. Today, no doubt, he would be marching beside her.

Near the intersection Lee noticed several motorcycle cops and patrol cars. The city was saturated with police. So many thousands of women assembled in one place—a threatening situation! It crossed her mind to ask the police for help, but she rejected the idea before it took shape. Hardly the approach for a mature woman. Her outward appearance suggested she had it all together. Who could know the timid child hiding beneath the surface! Face it, she told herself. You might be an intellectual warrior, but you are a physical coward. She could fearlessly match wits with the wiliest of bureaucrats and usually come out well ahead, but she was afraid to follow a mountain trail or find her way in a strange place. She was plagued by a recurring nightmare—trying to meet someone in a large building but unable to find the right room. The more she searched, the more confusing it would become—rooms changing location, locked doors, endless hallways, and she would awaken in a cold sweat.

They were jammed together now in a bottleneck at the corner. Lee glanced around. Maybe she could borrow a dollar for the subway. She had never asked a stranger for money. She was fighting back the tears. Perhaps she should try the Goddess—some sort of prayer to Her. But she had never prayed seriously to any but her Biblical God. The Goddess was merely a mythical tool for speculation—not one to turn to in real trouble. But it might be worth trying. How should one begin—*Our Mother who art in Heaven* or *Our Sister of the Elements . . . Earth, Air, Fire, and Water . . . ?*

"Is something the matter?" Startled, Lee turned to see a tall woman next to her, a woman who looked strangely like Minerva—same erect posture, angular face, same short-cropped hair, except hers was dark with just a tinge of gray. Probably in her early fifties.

"Oh, I'm all right," Lee said quickly. But her voice sounded strained. The fear—did it show in her face? She must look a mess.

"You appeared so worried. I just wondered."

"Well, to tell the truth, I am a bit upset. I've lost the others in my group." She gave a nervous laugh. "It was foolish of me. I wandered off to take some pictures. Then they disappeared."

"Oh, my! That *is* a problem."

"No telling *where* they are by now." She wiped her eyes on her sleeve.

The woman reached in her pocket and handed her a small packet of tissues. "Here, this might help."

Lee took it gratefully. She wiped her eyes and blew her nose. "That's better." It was a relief to talk to someone, especially such a kindly person, someone like Minerva. If only she were Minerva. She would throw her arms around Lee, and they would laugh together. "I feel so stupid. I gave Quincy—she's one of our group—I gave her my tote bag to hold, and now I don't have anything but my camera."

"That *is* a predicament. But I wouldn't call it stupid. You just got caught up in the moment."

"Amazing!" Lee said. "You not only look like Minerva, you talk like her. Are you, by any chance from Boston?"

"Well, originally not far from there—a town on the outskirts called Hingham, but I'm living in Connecticut now."

"I knew it!" Lee was smiling broadly. "Minerva is from Boston too. What a coincidence!"

"But tell me, who is this Minerva I so resemble?"

"Well, she's a very fine weaver—or fiber artist, that's what she prefers to be called, and a retired English professor. She's considerably older than you, but there's a strong resemblance, the way she carries herself, as well as her manner of speaking."

The woman laughed. "What fun to have a double! I should like to meet this Minerva sometime."

"I'll see that you do—if we ever find her, that is." Finding the group seemed less urgent now. She was beginning to feel quite comfortable in the company of this woman. "I guess it's time I introduced myself." She extended her hand. "I'm Lee Cranford."

The women shook hands. She had a nice firm handshake. "My name is Bernice Dianachild. Just call me Bernie."

Lee smiled. "Diana was your mother, I suppose. I have a friend who changed her name that way a few years ago. Such a stir it caused!"

"Yes, it shook up a few of my family members. But they've accepted it now—most of them." Her face clouded. "Families must learn, and friends too, that we must make our own choices, in names, and other matters. There's a great power in naming—a primal power, deeper than the name itself." Her voice was serious.

Their eyes met. "I like the concept, but I don't know if I would want to take all the static it generates."

Bernie smiled. "It's not so bad nowadays. People are getting used to the idea of women claiming their own identity. And those that don't approve are at least learning to tone down their criticism."

Lee nodded in agreement. She felt a very real rapport with this new friend. "Minerva says . . . ." She paused. "Forgive me for referring to her so much, but we're together a great deal. She's sort of a role model." She could see for a moment Minerva's face, pale and strained beneath the banner, then the image faded.

"Are you living together?" Bernie shaded her eyes against the sun and looked at Lee.

"Yes, we are." Lee paused. "But don't get me wrong," she stammered. Bernie was studying her intently. "It's not what you are probably thinking. I mean . . . we are together, but . . . ."

"And what do you think I'm thinking?" Her voice was sharp-edged.

"That we're . . . ." Lee hesitated. She still had difficulty using the word *lesbian*, though she was not homophobic. Or was she? A troubling thought. She looked away from Bernie.

"That you're lovers? Is that what you thought I thought?" Her manner seemed to have changed abruptly.

"Well," Lee cleared her throat . . . *lovers,* another word she was uncomfortable with. "I guess I don't know for sure what you were thinking, but some people might jump to the conclusion that, because we share the same house, Minerva and I have ahh . . . a relationship." She quickly corrected herself. "A sexual relationship, that is." She could feel the blood rushing to her face. "And that is certainly not the case." She was growing more embarrassed by the minute. Why was this woman making her feel so defensive? "We're simply good friends who happen to live together. Along with three other women. That's all." Bernie still seemed to be eyeing her suspiciously, and every word Lee said was making it worse.

"Forgive me," Bernie said softly. " I thought for a moment you might be one of us."

Lee remained silent. What could she say? So wrapped up in her own immediate worries, she had not even considered that possibility . . . Bernie a lesbian. And now she had offended her. Hadn't all her years in the women's movement taught her anything? "So thoughtless of me!" she said finally. She could feel a flush coloring her face.

"Let's just call it a misunderstanding." Bernie smiled at her, a broad smile that crinkled the corners of her eyes and mouth.

"Yes, let's. We're all in this together, after all. I hate labels and categories."

"But we can't deny what we are. In fact, we must not." Her tone was emphatic.

Lee met her gaze, deep, penetrating. Her eyes, dark topaz, had a luminous quality to them. "Are you here with a group?" She glanced around at the women in their vicinity, wondering if her friends would be as open to her as Bernie. She generally felt awkward, out of place, when she as a heterosexual was in the minority. It happened occasionally at women's studies conferences or other gatherings. She would sense that she was being scrutinized, every word, every move.

"No, I'm alone," Bernie said. "Several friends drove down yesterday. I was planning to meet them here but haven't found any of them. I took an early flight this morning. Saturday is my best day at the shop. I couldn't afford to close up."

"What sort of shop do you have?"

"Primarily a book shop. But I also handle a line of feminist cards, note paper, decorative T-shirts, and sweatshirts. I happen to be wearing one now." She unzipped her jacket to reveal a white sweatshirt with a lavish sunburst of gold sequins and lavender embroidery.

"How beautiful!" Lee was beginning to like this woman more and more. "What do you call your shop?"

"Womanspace."

"Perfect! Strange, I was just recalling a while ago something Betsy Damon once said about women and space—how we need to find space to discover our strength."

"Damon . . . yes, I saw her environmental sculpture, *A Shrine for Everywoman*, I think she called it—in Copenhagen during the 1980 Mid-Decade Conference. Impressive."

"You were there? I wanted to go—but convinced myself I couldn't afford it." Lee paused, thinking of things in life she had missed because of physical cowardice. She had never taken an overseas trip alone. "Damon's sculpture was at the finale of the Decade in Nairobi as well. I wanted to go there too but wasn't adventuresome enough."

"Well, you're here. And that's an adventure in itself. Speaking of women and space, have you read John Berger's *Ways of Seeing?*"

Lee said she had seen references to it but had not read the book.

"You would enjoy it. Quite astonishing in his perception of the differences between a man's presence and a woman's presence."

"What's his basic premise?"

"He focuses on space and the human form in art, but what he

says can apply to the world in general. He says, *A man's presence suggests what he is capable of doing to you or for you.* In other words, he has power which he directs toward others."

"He has the power all right."

"A woman's presence, according to Berger, *defines what can and cannot be done to her.*"

"Amazing!"

"He writes that woman is split into two, always watching herself. Anything she does, she simultaneously envisions herself doing it."

The crowd interrupted with a lilting chant, *All we are saying is give us a choice.* Lee and Bernie joined in, repeating it until it faded into the rumble of background noise.

"There's a lot of truth to what he says about being split," Lee said when the chanting stopped. "I often find myself trying to step aside and see myself, analyze what I'm doing. But I never thought of it as typical of all women. Just considered it peculiar to me as a poet."

"A poet? I'd have never guessed."

"You mean I don't look the part?" Lee tried not to sound annoyed.

"Well, somehow you seem more professorial than the poetic type. But there I go, stereotyping!"

"If it makes you feel like a more proficient judge of character, I *am* a retired professor. I only discovered I was a poet within the past few years. Maybe I haven't been at it long enough to look like one." Lee laughed. "But I envy you—having your own book shop. That used to be a dream of mine."

"We do a pretty good business."

"Where is this wonderful shop? I'd love to browse around in it."

"New Haven."

"I can't believe it! We're practically neighbors. I live on Eastern Long Island, in a proper little village called Quintauket where most of the inhabitants have grown up or summered since childhood. They can trace their ancestors back to the pre-Revolutionary Period."

"Sounds rather stuffy."

"It must have been a shock to them when the four of us moved

69

in with Elizabeth. She's one of them, you see, perfect credentials."

"Have any of them confronted you?"

"No. I just feel their presence." Lee paused. "We're about a forty-five minute drive to Port Jefferson. I could take the ferry from there to New Haven."

"Do. We'll have lunch."

Once again the crowd started moving, this time with greater speed. Lee linked her arm through Bernie's "I don't want to get lost twice in one day." They laughed and walked in step to the chant: *Not the Church, not the State. Only we decide our fate.* They were headed down Constitution Avenue now, amid a sea-swell of people, signs, and banners.

Lee felt a quickening of pulse as she kept pace with the crowd. In between chants and songs, she told Bernie about her housemates and the students who had come to Washington. Bernie told how she had been a professor of history in a small Midwestern college, how the year she was up for tenure, word got to the administration that she was a lesbian, and that was that. A traumatic upheaval in her life. Rather than risk a recurrence of the situation, she had come back east and taken her savings to open a book shop, choosing New Haven where she had relatives and some good business contacts. At present she was living alone, having broken with her lover last year.

"How unfair! Just because of some turkey of an administrator!" Lee said. "Couldn't you fight it?"

"That wouldn't have done any good."

"Didn't you have a faculty union, a grievance procedure?"

"Yes, but even if I had won, which I doubt, they would have made life miserable for me. It wasn't worth it."

"I understand. Our whole society is homophobic."

The line of Bernie's jaw hardened, face muscles tightened. They walked on in silence. Finally she said quietly, "I doubt that it's possible for you to *understand*, in the true sense of the word."

"What do you mean?" Everything had been going so smoothly between them, and suddenly Lee was feeling on the defensive again. True, she was not a lesbian, but did that mean she was not allowed to identify with their feelings? Hadn't she spent years speaking out for equality, defending the rights of all women?

70

"Why do you think I don't understand?"

Bernie sighed. "I know you're really trying, but it's not that simple." A barrier had slid between them, a glass door blocking the flow of their conversation.

Why was this woman making her feel so ill-at-ease, over . . . over what? She couldn't even define it. "Doesn't the fact that I am clearly woman-identified qualify me to have some understanding of oppression?" Lee glanced at Bernie who was staring straight ahead. The stubborn set of the jaw and erect, unyielding posture reminded her once again of Minerva.

"I just get tired of dealing with it—tired of trying to explain something that can't be explained, something that has to be personally experienced." Bernie glanced over at Lee. "A brand of discrimination you won't ever truly know, regardless of how well-intentioned and woman-identified."

They continued to walk, the pace quickening. "How can you be so sure?"

"Let's put it this way. If you were to announce to the world that you are a lesbian, live your life that way for a few days, give up all claim to all the heterosexual privileges you take for granted, perhaps you might gain some glimmer of understanding." Bernie pushed back a lock of hair from her face. "But even then, it would not be a true experience because you would know that at the end of the little experiment you could return to your previous status." Her voice was taut, like a guitar string too tightly tuned.

Lee remained silent. What could she say? She felt confused, betrayed by the very feminism she so strongly advocated, as if someone had slipped in a new set of rules. Among her lesbian friends, they had spoken, of course, about oppression, among other things. But, come to think of it, they had never really talked one to one about this, about how it feels on a personal level. Maybe she had unconsciously chosen to avoid it.

Bernie turned toward Lee. "Perhaps I was a little hard on you." The lines of her face had relaxed, her voice softened. They walked along in step. "It's just something I have strong feelings about."

"It's strange," Lee said. "Earlier today Ada told us we should all spend some time in a wheelchair so we could understand how

71

she felt, and you tell me I can only understand how a lesbian feels by pretending to be one . . . and, I don't know . . . sometimes it just gets to me, this business of trying to be sensitive to all our diverse needs, weighing everything I say and do, for fear of offending someone."

Linking arms a little tighter as their pace accelerated, Bernie said, "It's not exactly easy these days for any of us. But would you want to turn back the clock, undo your awareness?"

Before Lee could respond, another chant swept through the crowd: *What do we want? Freedom of Choice! When do we want it? NOW! What do we want?* . . . Lee gave Bernie's arm a squeeze. "I guess that's the answer," she said.

"The answer?"

"We each make our choices, whatever the price."

They had traveled at a brisk pace, about three-quarters of the way. Rising above the banners and flags was the dome of the Capitol Building. *Read our lips. We're Pro-Choice!* they chanted defiantly as they were heckled by a handful of sidewalk demonstrators.

Lee was beginning to tire, finding it difficult to keep step. Her feet throbbed, and a dull pain extended through her leg and knee. Leaning heavily on Bernie's arm for support, she felt too short of breath to continue the chanting. One foot after the other, just keep walking.

"It's getting rather warm, don't you think?" Bernie said after a few minutes. "Let's move over to the side and take off our jackets, rest awhile. Maybe we can find a place to sit."

"It *is* warm. I don't dare sit down though. I'd never get up! But I suppose I could lean against a telephone pole for a minute or so." They stepped out of line. Lee took off her jacket and looped it around her waist. Propping herself against the nearest pole, she sighed heavily. "That feels better!"

"Are you sure you don't want to sit down somewhere?"

Lee wondered if she looked as bad as all that. Her hair must be a tousled mess, her face sweaty and wind-burned. But she was definitely not going to play the role of fragile elderly citizen. "No, I'll be fine. Just need a few minutes to catch my breath." She closed her eyes and let the pole support her weight. It smelled of creosote. She hoped it wouldn't rub off on her clothes. Anyway, she was too tired to care.

Suddenly she heard Perry's voice. "Lee! Oh, God, Lee! Where have you been?" Lee opened her eyes and looked down the street to see Perry at the edge of the marchers, bounding toward her, red-faced, the flag flapping wildly overhead. When she reached Lee's side, she gave her a fierce hug. "We've been looking all over for you! What happened?" Her voice was a blend of exasperation and relief—the way a mother might greet her wayward child.

"Well, it's a long story . . . not so long really, just long in the making." Lee told about the pictures and how she lost sight of the group, keeping her voice light. No need to reveal how she had panicked. Bernie was standing to one side watching them quizzically, a faint smile on her face. Lee introduced the two of them.

They smiled and shook hands. "So you're Perry," Bernie said. "Lee told me about you."

"What did she tell? Only the good stuff, I hope."

"Well, let me see . . . I don't think it was *all* bad."

Perry's face turned a shade redder.

"Aren't you the one working for the MSW degree?

Perry nodded.

"Lee said something about you following in her footsteps."

Perry, grinning broadly, gave Lee another hug. "We have to get back to the others," she said. "They're waiting for us on the edge of the Capitol grounds. It's just a couple more blocks. Such a mob, you can't get any closer. Can't see much from there, but it's within range of the speaker system. We can go on the sidewalk and by-pass the marchers. Follow me."

They got back with the group just as the voice of Molly Yard, President of NOW, boomed over the speaker announcing an estimated record-breaking crowd of 600,000. "And they're still coming!" she added amid a roar of applause. As far as Lee could see in any direction there were people, texturing the Capitol grounds, like a myriad of pebbles on a beach, and still flowing in, pushed by a tide of tremendous force. She could not see Molly or Jesse Jackson or Bella Abzug or any of the other speakers on the Capitol steps. They were indistinguishable from the blur of faces beneath the panorama of flags and banners.

Lee's return was greeted with jubilation and a round of hugs. She surveyed them fondly . . . Ada looking less regal now, her parasol tattered by the wind, hair tousled, some gray strands pulled from the braid and flying about her face, Quincy's white pants stained with grass and mud, Linda's red hair flying wild, pale skin splotched by the sun, Vivian, minus her make-up, looking her age, Perry's face smudged, shiny with perspiration, even the usually neat Minerva a bit worn and frayed. Yes, a bedraggled assortment of women—but how beautiful!

They were interrupted by the voice of Gloria Steinem over the speaker. At least it sounded something like her. The P.A. system distorted everything. "Women who come to Washington either get to the top by marrying in or they march in. Barbara Bush used to be Pro-choice, but now she's not allowed an opinion." The crowd cheered. "We must free Barbara Bush!" Steinem said. And the crowd began to chant: *Free Barbara Bush!* Lee felt her voice growing hoarse but continued chanting.

Then someone on the platform began to sing, *We are gentle, loving people. And we are singing, singing for our lives.* The crowd joins in, their voices filling the air, vibrating in all directions. Lee raised her voice with the others, draping one arm over Bernie's shoulder and the other over Quincy's who draped her arm over Perry's shoulder. Perry propped the flag against the wheelchair and placed her hand on Ada's shoulder. Minerva, on the far side of the wheelchair, reached down for Ada's hand, extending her other arm to Linda who linked arms with Vivian. *We are old and young together* . . . . This sad, lilting song always brought tears to Lee's eyes, no matter how hard she would fight them back. She could feel them welling up now . . . *gay and straight together. And we are singing* . . . . Tears began trickling down her cheeks, but she could not wipe them away without letting go of the others . . . *angry, loving people* . . . . Tears were streaming down her cheeks now as she continued to sing, in harmony, swaying to the rhythm of the music, embraced by shimmering layers of sound, vibrant waves of voices lifting her high above the crowd into the blue of the sky, yet intertwining her with the others like the lavender and gold ribbons of Ada's braid.

10

Vivian sat at the breakfast table, chin in hand, eyes closed. "Oh," she groaned, "every bone in my body aches!" She took a sip of coffee. "I think I'll call in sick today." Minus the usual make-up, her pale skin showed every wrinkle and groove, accentuated by the sunlight streaming through the casement windows. The aging process—sneaking up on all of them. The cruel reminder jabbed at Lee . . . their time so limited. Something she preferred not to think about.

"I waited up for you until after midnight," Elizabeth said.

"At midnight we were still on the Jersey Turnpike." Minerva poured herself a cup of tea. "Traffic was bumper-to-bumper from Washington to Baltimore and didn't thin out much till we got to the Verrazano Bridge."

"It must have been about three-thirty," Lee said, yawning. She limped across the room to get some milk for her cereal. "Oh, my feet! They'll never be the same!"

"Well, how was it?" Elizabeth asked.

"How was it?" Ada stood in the doorway leaning on her cane, still in her robe, her braid hanging limp down her back, several gray wisps dangling about her face. "Let me tell you, it was spectacular!"

"And you should have seen Ada decked out in her costume . . . all sorts of people coming over to snap her picture," Vivian said.

"Did you catch any of it on TV?" Lee asked.

"Only about two minutes on the evening news."

"They do their best to ignore us," Minerva said.

"Maybe it's just as well. With our luck, the TV camera would just happen to focus on us in the crowd, and Arthur would just happen to tune in, and then fireworks would erupt," Lee said.

Vivian buttered a piece of toast. "You're such a worrier, Lee."

"I can't help it." Lee laughed. "It's in my genes I guess. But I do worry about Arthur's attorney. He could claim that we endangered her health by taking Ada there in her fragile condition."

"Wait a minute!" Ada plunked down her cup. "I'm perfectly sound."

"But some lawyers are adept at twisting the truth," Minerva said.

"Well, you weren't on TV, and Arthur didn't call—so there appears to be no cause for concern," Elizabeth said.

"Wouldn't that be a panic! Arthur watching us on TV." Vivian laughed. "I can just see his face!"

"Let's drop the subject of Arthur for the time-being." Lee resented the way his very name could disrupt their peace and quiet.

"Let's see what *The New York Times* has to say about the march." Minerva got up from the table and went out the door to the front lawn.

Lee turned to Elizabeth. "How was the concert?"

"Beautiful! Really an inspiration."

"And how did you and John make out?" said Ada.

Elizabeth blushed. "Oh, fine. We had a delicious dinner at a little Swiss restaurant before the concert. He's so well-mannered. Thinks of every little thing."

"Did you stay in his apartment?" asked Vivian.

"Oh, no, we drove home," Elizabeth said hastily, her face a deep pink.

"Ohhh?" Vivian smiled and arched her eyebrows. "Didn't he invite you to stay over?"

"We've only known each other a short time." She cleared her throat nervously. "Spending the night wouldn't have looked right."

Vivian shrugged her shoulders. "Who's looking, for God's sake!"

Lee was relieved to see Minerva coming in with the paper.

76

This conversation about Elizabeth and John and their growing relationship bothered her—something else she did not want to think about.

Minerva held up the paper. "Our march made a big splash on the front page!"

"And a huge picture!" Lee said. "The women leading the procession with that banner. You can even read the words, it's so big: KEEP ABORTION AND BIRTH CONTROL SAFE AND LEGAL." She was smiling broadly. "I can't believe they gave us such a spread!"

"The headline says, RIGHT TO ABORTION DRAWS THOUSANDS TO CAPITOL RALLY." Minerva frowned. "Why doesn't it say *hundreds of thousands?* We were certainly more than just thousands."

"Let's see." Vivian leaned over her shoulder. "Calm down, Min. The opening words of the article are: *Hundreds of thousands of people marched . . . .*" She took the paper from Minerva. "And listen to this next paragraph: *It was a crowd of mothers and daughters, self-described aging hippies . . . .*"

"That's us all right." Ada laughed. "*Aging hippies!* What else does it say?"

"I can't read it if you keep interrupting. Let's see . . . *aging hippies and politically emerging college students, Hollywood stars and young professionals, all gathered on the broad grassy Mall of the Capitol . . . .*" Vivian continued reading while the others listened, tossing in a comment here and there. She leafed through the pages to the continuation. "Another big picture!" She held up the paper. "There's Molly Yard and Bella Abzug and Whoopee Goldberg and . . . ."

"Wait a minute," Minerva said. "Let me see those pictures at the bottom of the page." Vivian handed her the paper. Minerva's face paled as she stared at the page. "It can't be true!" she gasped.

"What is it, Min?" Lee asked.

Tight-lipped and silent, Minerva handed her the paper, pointing to one of a group of small pictures in the lower corner. There was Ada in her wheelchair, clearly recognizable with her long braid, white ruffled gown, straw hat, and parasol, surrounded by several other marchers of assorted ages, framed by Perry's flag and Linda's NOW banner.

Lee sat stunned. "No! I don't believe it! Ada, how could you?"

"How could I what?" Ada asked, bewildered.

"What's the matter with everybody?" Vivian grabbed the paper. "Oh, my God!" she shrieked. "It's Ada, big as life—right here in *The New York Times*! Even worse than TV. What are we going to do?"

"Let's see." Ada reached across the table for the paper. "Yes siree, that's me all right. Not a bad picture really—except my hat's on crooked, and I'm kind of squinting into the sun." She chuckled. "Never in my life thought I'd make the *Times*!" She looked at the picture again. "Too bad they didn't get you folks in it too."

"Ada, are you out of your mind?" Lee shouted. "If Arthur sees this, it's a disaster!"

"Take it easy," Ada said. "You're making a mountain out of a molehill. Arthur is not likely to see it. He generally only reads the *Times* on Sundays. Weekdays he takes that stuffy *Wall Street Journal*. So relax." She handed the paper to Elizabeth. "See the aging hippie—that's me."

"Oh, dear!" Elizabeth sat twisting her napkin. "Maybe you shouldn't have gone after all."

"That's water over the dam." Minerva took a sip of tea. "We *went*, and did what we felt we had to do."

"Could someone pour me a cup of coffee?" Ada said.

"I just don't understand how you can sit there so calmly, Ada, drinking coffee and acting as if nothing is the matter!" Lee's voice bristled with annoyance. "Why did you let that reporter take your picture?"

"How was I to know he intended to publish it? Folks were shooting pictures everywhere. What was I supposed to do—post a sign, *No Photos Allowed?*"

"Arthur might not even see it," Minerva said quietly. "Perhaps we are making too much of it."

"Her name isn't listed—one thing in our favor. And it's not a very big picture." Vivian stretched and yawned. "So let's simmer down and enjoy our breakfast."

Lee tried to eat her cereal, but it tasted like soggy sawdust.

She stared out the window at the pattern of sunlight through the fresh green leaves. Maybe Elizabeth was right. Maybe they should not have gone. With this as further ammunition, the court might rule in Arthur's favor. She sat motionless, steeped in misery.

Ada, meanwhile, had put on her glasses and was scrutinizing the picture. "Well, at least a couple of your students got in. "See, there's Perry and the one with the bushy hair, I forget her name." She held out the paper for Lee.

"I've seen all I care to see." Lee pushed it aside.

Ada continued to examine the picture. "And over at the edge is Minerva's back—I can tell by her jacket . . . . Oh, and here's that colored girl with the funny name."

"She's African-American, not colored," Lee said sharply, "and she's a woman, not a girl!"

"You and your words," Ada muttered. "Some folks are so picky!"

"We're all a bit on edge this morning," Minerva said. "What would you like for dinner tonight? It's my turn to cook."

Before anyone could respond, the phone rang. Vivian picked it up. "Just a minute, I'll see if she's up." Holding her hand over the mouthpiece, she made a face and formed the words, "It's Arthur."

Lee could feel her heart pounding. The worst had happened.

Ada shook her head vigorously. "I'm still in bed. Can't talk now."

Vivian kept him waiting a minute or two, then said, "I'm sorry, Arthur, she's still sleeping."

She held the phone out from her ear as his raspy voice crackled through the line. "Well, she'd better get herself to the phone or I'm coming out there in person!"

"I don't think that's necessary. Can't she call you later?"

"I want to talk to her *now,* not later!"

Vivian, phone in hand, looked over at the others. "What should we do?" she whispered.

Lee's throat was so dry, she could not utter a word.

Minerva leaned across the table to Ada. "You might as well see what he has to say. We don't want him coming out here."

Ada shook her head. "I don't want to talk to him."

"Give him the benefit of the doubt," said Elizabeth. "Maybe it has nothing to do with that picture."

"Oh, all right." Ada got up and walked slowly to the phone. "Hello, Son." She faked a yawn. "What's so important that you had to get me out of bed? . . . Picture? . . . What picture? . . . Where?" She turned and grimaced in their direction, then hunched herself over the phone. "Listen, Son, you'll have to speak up. I can hardly hear you . . . . What's that? Must be a poor connection. Why don't you hang up and I'll call you back." She hung up the phone and turned to them. "He saw it!"

"So much for *The Wall Street Journal!*" said Vivian.

"Now, what do we do?" Lee said, twisting her hands tightly together, barely able to form the words.

"We might as well face up to it," Minerva said. "After all, we didn't violate any law. Nobody told us Ada couldn't go."

"Well, I think . . . ." Elizabeth was interrupted by the ringing of the telephone.

Ada let it ring four times. "What should I say?"

"Pick it up!" Vivian said. "Just wing it!"

Ada sighed and picked up the phone on the sixth ring. "Hello?" Her voice sounded weak, unsure. "No, I was just in the bathroom . . . . Yes, this is a much better connection. Now what were you saying before? Something about a picture?"

Ada was holding the phone tight to her ear. The four women sat silently listening intently to her words.

"No, I haven't seen the paper. You woke me up from a sound sleep. I haven't even brushed my teeth yet." She turned toward them, holding up her crossed fingers.

Vivian suppressed a laugh. "That Ada!"

"Shhhhh!" Lee said.

"A picture of *me* in *The New York Times*? Now, Son, don't be ridiculous! I've never even had my picture in *The Hampton Chronicle.*"

There was a pause as she listened, a faint smile on her face. Ada had missed her true calling, Lee thought. She belonged on stage.

"Well, just because it looks like me doesn't mean it has to be me. We all have our double somewhere, they say." Another pause.

"Does it have my name under it?" She turned to them, smiling. "That's what I thought. Then what makes you think it's me?"

Ada was clearly in her element. But she couldn't keep up this pretense indefinitely. Arthur would persist, Lee was certain of that.

"The braid? Well, I don't have a monopoly on braids." She frowned. "Grandma's parasol? Oh, I gave that away when I moved out here." She turned toward them and held up the phone in exasperation. "Listen, Son, you know you're always jumping to conclusions. Now, if you don't mind, I want to have my coffee . . . . Yes, I'll look at the paper. I'm curious to see this imposter . . . . Your lawyer? Well, that's fine with me, Son. You just tell him to contact our lawyer right away. The sooner we can get this over, the better!"

Ada hung up and walked slowly back to the table. "Well, he didn't buy the *double* idea. He knows it was me. Sounded just a tad angry." She shrugged and gave a nervous laugh. "But I had a perfect right to go." Her face was flushed, and there was a slight tremor in her hands.

"Now what?" Minerva said.

"I'll talk to our attorney," Lee said. Hindsight told her they should have cleared the trip with her, and with Kevin Maloney, the court-appointed guardian. She sat immersed in worry and guilt. Arthur was a very clever adversary. A nagging voice clattered away in her brain reminding her that none of this would have happened if she hadn't held that January rally. They would be their old carefree selves now, free of the devilish Arthur and his poison seeds of disharmony, free of his threats, his invasion of their space.

11

Fragrance of azaleas, andromeda, late-blooming forsythia, and daffodils filled the air. It was one of those balmy evenings in early May, soft as eiderdown. Lee hummed along with a Mozart piano concerto coming through the livingroom speakers as she put fresh candles on the coffee table, yellow to match the bouquet of daffodils on the bookcase. She pulled the chairs and couch into a circular arrangement. The poets were about to arrive for their monthly meeting. A close-knit group, they had been coming together for nearly five years now, sharing and critiquing their work.

She had been eagerly looking forward to tonight as an escape from worries about Ada and the court case. Following Arthur's flare-up, Lee had called Mary Graverton. The attorney, after lecturing her sternly about the need for extreme caution and warning her to refrain from taking any further risks, had requested another adjournment from the court, to allow time for Arthur to simmer down. The case was now scheduled for the end of June. The court guardian had also given them a severe reprimand, but at least they got to him before Arthur did.

This past month had been the first opportunity for Lee to resume serious writing. With Ada's gradual recovery, she had started catching up on her own clutter of bills and correspondence but still felt fragmented. It was only after their return from Washington that she felt able to concentrate on new writing. The words had begun to flow, slowly at first, then pouring forth, demanding to be set down on paper. Elated by the joy of finding her own voice again, she would sometimes sit up until one or two o'clock writing.

For Ada as well, the Washington trip seemed to have been a turning point. Having proved herself, she behaved now as if nothing could deter her—not even Arthur. She had resumed her painting with renewed vigor. And she was planning to move from Lee's room back to her attic studio as soon as she could maneuver the stairs. If only the court case were not hanging over them, everything would be perfect.

Elizabeth usually managed to be away on this particular Friday of the month. She did not relish the idea of these extraneous women invading her well-ordered life and living room. Tonight she had gone to a movie with John. Lee rather liked him, despite her fears about his growing interest. A bit on the quiet side, tall, silvery hair accentuating his tan, a Florida tan from frequent trips to Fort Lauderdale to visit his daughter and grandchildren. Elizabeth clearly enjoyed his company but when teased by the others would blushingly deny any serious intent.

Vivian was having dinner with Nathan, her newest admirer, a large, balding man in his seventies with a loud voice and overbearing manner—not exactly Vivian's type. She generally preferred more docile younger men. But, in her words, "Nat's got more money than he can count, and nobody to spend it on, so I might as well help him unload some of it."

Minerva and Ada were doing the dinner dishes. Though not poets, they often joined the group. Minerva's field at Columbia had been seventeenth century metaphysical poets, but she also admired Blake and a wide range of contemporary poets. Her keen ear made her a valued critic. Ada was a colorful addition, though her comments were unpredictable, focusing on her off-beat aesthetic views and her philosophy of the world as a place dominated by the Jungian trickster archetype.

Lee leafed through the poems she would read tonight—a couple of lyrics and a long narrative about the rally. Anxious for feedback, she had been counting the days. She glanced at her watch. Nearly eight o'clock. She placed copies of her poems on the coffee table, shoving aside some books and magazines to make

83

room. A scrap of blue paper fell to the floor. Picking it up to throw in the wastebasket, she noticed Minerva's handwriting. Might be something she needed. The name of Minerva's gynecologist caught her eye. The page had been torn from the pad by the telephone. Strange. She hadn't said anything about an appointment. Minerva was in the habit of jotting down a list of questions or points she wanted to clarify before making a phone call, then checking them off and noting what was said. Carrying the paper over to the lamp, Lee put on her glasses. It was not easy to decipher. Maybe she should just put it aside for Minerva. She hesitated for a moment, started across the room toward the telephone table, then turned. If something was the matter, she ought to know. She held the note close to the light. Today's date. Something was crossed off. Beneath that, *Spotting for ten days.* Another illegible word, then, *Bleeding heavier today.* Then some doodles, arrows and jagged lines, followed by what the doctor must have said. Again, Lee could not read all of it, but she caught the word, *abnormality.* On the next line, *D & C Monday morning, 8th — outpatient.*

Bleeding! Such an ominous word. Trembling, Lee sat down on the couch, wishing she had not seen the note. Of course that wouldn't make it go away. Why had Min kept this to herself all these days? By nature she was reluctant to discuss personal matters. But after all, Lee was her closest friend. She looked at the paper again. Maybe she was making too much of it. A bit of bleeding was not the end of the world. It did not necessarily mean . . . Lee did not even like to think the word . . . *cancer.* There could be any number of causes, a simple polyp or something. The knot of fear tensing the muscles of her stomach disputed those hopeful thoughts. Bleeding was not to be taken lightly.

The mantle clock had begun to strike. The poets would be arriving any minute. Lee held the note in her hand wondering what to do with it. The image of Minerva's face at the Washington rally, pale and strained, flashed through her mind. But after a few days of rest, she had apparently snapped back to her usual vigorous self, and Lee had put it out of her mind. Despair obliterated the glow of anticipation she had felt earlier in the day. Maybe she should tell the others she wasn't feeling well, send them home. No . . . Minerva would be upset. She would just have to get through the evening, then talk to Minerva. A car pulled into the driveway, then another. Hastily she folded the paper and tucked it in the pocket of her corduroys.

When the doorbell rang, Daisy went bounding to the door with joyful barks. Laura entered carrying a bottle of wine. She wore yellow tights with a yellow and white striped sweater. Her dark hair, streaked with gray, was pulled back from her face in a ponytail tied with a small yellow ribbon. Lee greeted her with a hug. "You're the very personification of spring." Her voice quavered.

Laura studied her intently. "Is something the matter?"

"Nothing really." Lee hesitated. "Well, yes, but . . . ." She paused, biting her lip and turning away. Laura had a warmth about her, a brightness of spirit, that was very comforting. During the stressful days of caring for Ada, Lee had confided in her. And when the situation would become intolerable, with Lee almost at the breaking point, she would escape to Laura's house for tea and sympathy, returning home revitalized. But Minerva would surely resent it if she told anyone. "I can't talk about it." She turned toward Laura. "Does it show that much?"

"You look fine." Laura gave her a reassuring smile. "You just seemed a bit on edge. Maybe we can talk later."

They were interrupted by Rachel and Katherine with noisy confusion of warm greetings and hugs, comments on the gorgeous weather, blended with Daisy's jubilant barking.

Katherine handed Lee a bakery cake. "For Nicole's birthday."

Birthdays . . . something Lee usually enjoyed—the little girl in her who refused to grow up—but not tonight. "Glad you remembered. I'll take it to the kitchen." She turned to Laura. "Just put the wine on the coffee table, and I'll bring out some glasses.

"Let me help." Laura followed her to the kitchen.

Ada had finished the dishes and was headed for her room. Minerva had gone upstairs, saying not to wait for her.

After Ada left, Laura put her arm around Lee's shoulder. "Wouldn't it help to talk about it?"

Lee hesitated. "I really shouldn't." She took a deep breath.

Minerva . . . the strong one, suddenly vulnerable . . . . "But I'm so afraid. Maybe I'm just over-reacting." She reached in the cupboard for the wine glasses. One slipped from her hand, shattering across the floor. "Damn!" She stooped down to pick up some pieces of glass. "I'm a total wreck!"

Laura took Lee's arm, leading her to a chair by the pine table. "Just relax while I clean this up." She began sweeping up the glass splinters. "Sometimes we need to see things from another angle."

"Well, I found a piece of paper with Min's handwriting from a phone call . . . . Lee cleared her throat. "Maybe it's nothing at all, but at her age it could be serious, and now . . . ."

"What did the note say?"

"I couldn't read all of it, but the gist is that she has been bleeding for several days, and her gynecologist has scheduled a D & C for Monday." Lee glanced at Laura whose face reflected her concern. "And she hasn't even told me about it, not a single word—*me,* supposedly her close friend, and I know she must be worried, yet she won't talk about it, and she'll be terribly upset when she finds out I've read the note, and I don't know what to do . . . ." The words came tumbling out. She felt on the verge of tears.

Laura put her arms around her, saying, "There, there," the way one might talk to a child. She smelled of soap and fragrant lotion. "It's all going to work out. Try to put it aside and enjoy the evening. That's what Minerva would want. And we'll figure out a way to talk to her later."

Lee wished she could just stay in those arms, protected and secure. "If Min hasn't shared this by now, she doesn't intend to." Her voice broke. Swallowing hard, she tried to clear away the hurt, but it remained. She pulled away and busied herself with setting some seltzer, ice, and yellow cocktail napkins on a tray. How pleased she had been this afternoon to find napkins to match the bouquet of daffodils and the candles—a special touch of spring. It seemed so long ago—this afternoon, when a color was important, when the sun came slanting through the casement windows flooding the room with splashes of light and melodic sparkles. Now she could focus on nothing but the icy fear flowing through her. What if the bleeding changed to hemorrhaging? She felt strangely dizzy.

"You look a little pale. Are you all right?"

"I think so." But how could she be all right—with Minerva sick?

Laura picked up the tray, and they walked to the living room. Nicole had just arrived, greeted by hugs and birthday wishes. Her auburn hair hung in soft waves about her face, flushed with excitement. "Sorry I'm late. Had to wait for my sitter."

Lee gave her an affectionate hug. "Happy birthday!" She tried to force some happiness into her voice.

The poets had begun taking their places around the room. Lee sat down in the walnut rocker. Laura went to call Ada. "Where's Minerva?" Katherine asked.

"She said she might be a little late." Lee tried to keep her voice casual.

Laura returned, curling up at one end of the couch near Lee's rocker. She glanced around the room. "Who wants to begin?"

Rachel volunteered, handing out copies of two poems. She was about to start when Ada made her dramatic entry, wearing a long lavender skirt, a blouse of soft blue silk, silver and turquoise beads, and lavender ribbons in her braid. Crossing over to the Salem rocker, she hung her cane on the mantle. "According to Santayana," she announced with a flourish, *"Beauty is a pledge of the possible conformity between the soul and nature, and consequently a ground of faith in the supremacy of the good."* Ada always dug up a quotation, and Lee liked the challenge of analyzing the layered meanings. But tonight she could not focus on the words.

"I'll drink to that!" Laura raised her glass. Turning to Lee, she said, "You don't have any wine. Let me give you some."

Lee shook her head. "Not right now."

"It might help," she said softly, pouring some wine in a glass and handing it to Lee.

Rachel proceeded with her poem. Lee, sipping her wine, had the uncanny sense that she was merely going through the motions of being here, saying her lines. When Rachel finished reading, Lee was not certain what the poems were about. One had to do with an apple orchard in Israel. The other was in a cafe in Paris or somewhere. Usually she particularly enjoyed Rachel's poems, strong and lean with vivid imagery; but now, leaning back in the rocker, eyes closed, barely listening, she was unable to participate. The others appeared not to notice. Words rose and fell but did not register. She wondered uneasily about Minerva. She should have come down by now. Her thoughts drifted back to the Minerva of those blissful yesterdays . . . bounding out of bed at daybreak for her morning walk, striding briskly along, arms swinging, face shining. One time Lee had gone with her but could not keep the pace, returning home breathless and exhausted.

Laura had begun to read one of her poems. Lee fidgeted in her chair. Just when she felt she could not sit there another minute, Minerva walked in. Lee watched her intently. Laura paused.

"Please go ahead," Minerva said. "Sorry I'm late." She poured a glass of seltzer and pulled up a straight chair on the edge of the circle. She seemed calm, but there was something rigid about the way she was sitting. Why hadn't she chosen the couch where she usually sat? Plenty of space between Laura and Rachel. Deliberately isolating herself. She wore a pair of loose-fitting harem pants with a plain woven top of silk and linen fabric. The wheat tones, unrelieved by any touch of color, made her skin look sallow tonight, unhealthy. Beneath the lamp, she appeared old and fragile. Lee was suddenly overwhelmed by the depth and intensity of the love she felt for this friend who could disappear from her life altogether. A flood of memories swept over her . . . the two of them admiring the paintings in a gallery, window-shopping on Job's Lane, sitting quietly by the fire, swimming in the bay, laughing at nothing or everything . . . . All of it might be taken away.

Laura was reading a poem now describing an old photo of herself as a child with knobby knees and pigtails, holding her grandmother's hand. Afterwards she said, "I didn't know it would be the last time we were together."

Lee thought of her own grandmother, some lines she had written in her memoirs shortly before she died . . . about *traveling*

88

up and down the hills of her life, wading in the little creek, drinking from the old gourd at the green rock spring, walking among the pines . . . . The serenity of one in harmony with herself and the universe . . . . But Lee felt no harmony, only fear and anger at the threat of death that had entered their lives.

Then she became aware of Minerva's voice quoting from a Blake poem: *Memory, hither come, / And tune your merry notes* . . . . Lee watched her face, as if to memorize it, so beautifully animated, reciting in her rhythmic New England voice. It ended with the lines: *Walking along the darkened valley / With silent Melancholy.*

Minerva appeared more relaxed now. But why had she chosen a poem ending on darkness and melancholy? Was it an indirect message? Suppose the tests indicated she was inoperable. Lee couldn't bear to think about it. But negative thoughts kept spinning through her mind . . . . Why hadn't Min told her? The question gnawed at her. She felt a nagging sense of betrayal.

Katherine's poem was next—opening with praise for winter over spring. Lee's brain refused to assimilate the words, fogged by conflicting signals. She gazed at the daffodils across the room, a burst of sunshine captured in a blue Chinese vase, but such short-lived beauty. By tomorrow some of the delicate blossoms would be wilted. Without Minerva would she be able to face spring with its green surge, its galaxy of intoxicating colors and fragrances?

The group had broken off into little conversations around the room. Ada was engaged in a lively discussion with Katherine . . . something about her poem denying the beauty of nature, and Katherine saying she failed to see beauty in a nature that leads us to our death.

Lee studied Katherine's flushed face, serious in the defense of her poem. Glowing with vitality in the summer of her life, it was easy for her to contemplate winter. But when winter approaches and the body begins to deteriorate, that is a different matter. One yearns for spring. Lee recalled her grandmother's delight in the first spring flowers, her almost childlike anticipation each year—until the year she died, when spring had lost its meaning.

Fragments of words floated about, but Lee could not grasp them. Something about a cyclical view of time, voices merging and fading . . . cycles of nature, of seasons, of day and night . . . life and death . . . But there was a finality about death, defying anything cyclical. When the curtain comes down, there are no encores. The ultimate paradox, Lee mused . . . that we must spend our lives burdened with the knowledge that living is dying, a little each day.

She rocked slowly back and forth, attempting to channel her mind in another direction, but she gave up trying to concentrate. The words had become a blur of sound. After what seemed an interminable time, the mantle clock began to strike eleven, deep tones resonating through the room. She saw Laura get up from the couch to bring in the cake. Katherine followed to take care of the tea and coffee.

Lee sank back in the rocker and closed her eyes, suddenly feeling tired and exceedingly old. The voices were just a murmur in the background, rising and falling. She found herself thinking about a hike she and Minerva had taken in the Adirondacks last fall along a quiet wooded trail, the crisp cool air, the crunch of leaves underfoot, the sense of harmony they had felt, the two of them. Minerva, with her eye for beauty, stopping to admire a cluster of crimson leaves or an arrangement of moss and stones . . . Minerva, sitting on a log by a mountain stream, picturesque in woven knickers and heavy knit sweater, white hair tied back with a red scarf, Minerva encircled by a haze of sunlight filtering through the leaves, laughing at something Lee has said, pointing upward, to a bird perhaps or some cloud formation . . . dear Minerva, so perfectly in tune with nature . . . Lee allowed the fresh pungent aroma of balsam to envelop her, the autumn breeze to caress her, the trickling of water over the rocks to soothe her troubled psyche.

12

Laura and Katherine carried in the cake sparkling with thirty candles, and everyone began singing *Happy Birthday*. Lee tried to join in but still had trouble focusing her attention. Rachel was reminding Nicole to make a wish . . . Katherine ridiculing the idea of wishes . . . Rachel defending the magic power of candles and stars, saying it was wise to play it safe.

Lee, too, played it safe. As a talisman on important occasions she always wore a silver and gold ring Matt had made, and she often went through the ritual of knocking on wood. Even at her happiest, she was haunted by a shadow hovering over her, waiting to mete out a penalty for being too happy, too confident or too self-sufficient. By acknowledging its presence through these little gestures, she could keep the dark force at bay.

Nicole, eyes shining in the tiny flickers of light, took a deep breath and blew out the candles, followed by applause and Laura asking what she wished and Rachel cautioning her not to tell. Lee closed her eyes again, but the voices persisted . . . Nicole saying she wished she could stay thirty for the rest of her life . . . Katherine saying the only way to stay thirty would involve dying, hardly a viable alternative.

Lee studied Nicole's expressive face, envying her youthful beauty. How had she felt at that age? Too long ago to remember. So much potential, so much vitality. How could one appreciate it until it was gone, drained away by time and trouble? "You make me feel positively ancient," Lee said to her.

"Don't start talking *ancient*," Nicole said quickly. "You're ageless, Lee."

Lee sat quietly. *Ageless indeed!* What did she know?

"Oh, to be thirty again!" Katherine sighed.

"Oh, to be thirty and know what I know at forty-eight!" Laura's ripply laugh flooded the room.

"I wouldn't want to relive my thirties!" Rachel said. "But, I don't look forward to anything beyond my fifties."

This mindless prattle by these women, all in their prime, was grating on Lee's nerves. Rather inconsiderate of them, in view of those in the room approaching the stage that might be termed *truly old,* as if they had no feelings whatsoever. Lines from a Hodgson poem kept flitting through her mind . . . *Time, you old gypsy man / Will you not stay, / Put up your caravan / Just for one day?* Bargaining with Time . . . a hopeless task, even for a poet.

Ada's voice rose above the chatter. "You young folks! All this moaning about being thirty or forty. That's prime time! Just wait till you're almost eight-five. Now there's a different story."

"Ada, you're the youngest almost eighty-five I ever saw," Nicole said. "What's your secret for growing old gracefully?"

"Gracefully?" Ada snorted. "Let me tell you. There's nothing, absolutely *nothing,* graceful about growing old—when your eyesight fails, your hearing diminishes, your balance gets off-kilter, your teeth and hair start falling out. Everything coming apart! No, don't ever think you can grow old gracefully. It's impossible!" Ada was leaning forward in her chair, waving her hands for emphasis.

She was right, of course. Those who tried to deny the dismal process of aging with face-lifts, implants, bleach, and heavy make-up generally looked ridiculous, like circus clowns, in their frantic quest for eternal youth. Yet those who let nature take its course suffered the indignities of sagging contours or a hardness of features, the wrinkles, the graying—becoming caricatures of their former selves. A cruel paradox. And hanging over all of them, the threat of Alzheimers or paralysis or other illnesses to deprive them of their dignity and independence. The whole thing was grotesque.

Lee looked uneasily at Minerva who had moved over to the couch where she had kicked off her shoes and was sitting cross-legged between Laura and Rachel. How was she reacting to all this dreadful talk?

Someone handed Lee a cup of coffee and a piece of lemon cake, her favorite. But tonight she could eat only a few bites. Voices rose and fell as the women chattered away. She was not listening—intent on planning what she would say to Minerva after they left . . . when she became aware of Minerva's voice. "I must take issue with Ada's negative view of aging. There is some truth in what she said about physical deterioration, but there *are* things you can do to keep your body in shape with exercise and good nutrition."

Minerva did indeed keep herself in excellent shape, with her yoga, jogging, swimming. But, ironically, she now faced the possibility of a malignancy that could destroy her beautiful physical fitness. "There's another side to consider," she added, "the freedom of spirit we acquire as we grow older. Unlimited freedom. We can soar like seagulls if we've a mind to. And we are aware of the value of time, knowing it could soon come to an end."

Come to an end . . . The words echoed through Lee's mind. Was this another hidden message?

"The true secret of growing old gracefully," Minerva continued, "is to stay flexible. Open your mind to new ideas, new people . . . . "

Ada interrupted. "But no matter how flexible you are or how high you fly, it won't help if your body is stricken with a deadly disease."

"Well, that's when a person needs a strong support system— friends or relatives to see her through the crisis."

Support system! Min hadn't even mentioned the bleeding to anyone for support.

Rachel started gathering up the cups and plates. "Now it's Lee's turn to read."

Lee shook her head. "It's getting late. Let's save mine for next time." By then maybe this nightmare would be over—maybe just a false alarm. She remembered with a pang her joyful anticipation, only that afternoon. Now she simply wanted everyone out of the way.

"Lee's right." Laura yawned. "It wouldn't be fair to the poems at this hour." She stood up and stretched. The others gathered up their belongings, and after hugs and farewells they were gone—Ada as well, saying it was past her bedtime.

The room was suddenly quiet, except for the slow ticking of the clock. They usually sat and talked for a while after such a gathering, but tonight she felt ill-at-ease. "I think I'll heat some water for tea," Lee said to Minerva. "Care to join me?"

"Why don't you just sit down," Minerva said, motioning toward the rocker, "and I'll take care of it. You look all in."

She returned shortly with their tea and pulled up a chair near Lee. They sat quietly, sipping their tea for a few minutes. While Lee was trying to decide how to bring up the subject, Minerva broke the silence. "Lee, whatever was the matter with you tonight?"

"Nothing. Well, not with *me* anyway. Why?"

"You seemed distracted, not yourself at all."

Reaching into her pocket, Lee pulled out the crumpled piece of blue paper and flung it into Minerva's lap. "This! I found it when I was clearing off the coffee table, just before the meeting. Maybe I shouldn't have read it, but I couldn't help seeing the part about the bleeding and Dr. Johnson.

Minerva's face flushed as she held the paper, not looking at Lee. "Oh, I'm so sorry you had to come across it that way. It must have slipped out of my book. I was going to talk to you about it later, truly I was, but I didn't want to spoil your meeting."

Lee was silent for a minute. Minerva's explanation did make sense, but it was not easy to put aside the hurt. "When I found the note . . . well, you know how I tend to exaggerate things." She gave a nervous laugh. "Before the evening was over, I worried myself into quite a state. And it was so frustrating—not being able to talk to you."

Minerva reached over and took her hand. "I suppose it would have been easier for you if I had mentioned it sooner."

Lee nodded. "What did Dr. Johnson say about the bleeding?"

"She said I should be examined as soon as possible. She will do a D & C Monday."

"It could be just a polyp or something minor of that sort—nothing serious perhaps, not necessarily . . . ." Lee could not bring herself to say the dreaded word.

"Dr. Johnson won't know if it's a malignancy until she gets the pathology report. Cancer is a possibility, of course."

Lee squeezed her hand. She swallowed hard, trying to keep her voice cheerful. "I'll drive you to the hospital. You'll be an outpatient, I suppose?"

Minerva nodded. "If it does turn out to be serious, Lee, promise me you won't go all to pieces." Minerva's clear gray eyes examined Lee's face intently. "I'll need your strength."

Lee felt the tears welling up. It was impossible to envision life without Min. She added a richness of texture that no one else could duplicate. "I can't bear to think about it."

"Well, let's not anticipate." Minerva smiled at Lee and took a sip of her tea. She cleared her throat and shifted her position, as if uncomfortable with their solemn mood. "I found a fascinating book at the library, by the way. Maybe you'd like to take it with you Monday."

Minerva's idea of fascinating books did not always coincide with Lee's. "What's it about?" she asked dubiously.

"Reincarnation."

"I had no idea you believed in *that*."

"I didn't say I believed in it. I merely said I was reading a book on the subject." Her tone was defensive. Minerva took another sip of tea. "It's by a psychiatrist whose patients, in hypnotic regression, supposedly described scenes from past lives.

Lee's face clouded. "It seems against your grain somehow." She was aware of a tensing of the muscles of her neck and shoulders—a signal she could not ignore. A way of *knowing* that her mother used to call *sixth sense*. Did Minerva have a premonition of death?

"The idea interests me—that's all."

Lee remained silent, studying Minerva's face, her gray eyes gleaming in the firelight, reflecting its glow like moonstones.

"And while they were in the hypnotic trance, in between lives, they would channel messages back from some sort of spirit realm."

Lee frowned. "Messages? What kind?"

"Oh, various things—what it's like after death . . . I don't remember all of it." Minerva sounded vague. "You know, resembling what those patients of Kubler-Ross describe.

"I have trouble believing those accounts."

"Me too. But if one could believe in the concept, it might be comforting." Minerva finished her tea and set her cup on the tray.

Lee sipped her tea without comment. Perhaps Min had turned to reincarnation in denial of impending death . . . an image of the four women floated through her mind . . . black-gowned, clustered about Minerva's coffin. Lee shuddered. Her imagination was clearly out of control.

Minerva meanwhile was explaining something about a progression of astral planes, but the words flowed over Lee uncomprehended. She felt numb. Minerva squeezed her hand. "I don't believe you are even listening to me. Are you sure you're all right?"

Lee gazed at Minerva's face, pale in the shadowy firelight. The pent-up tears began to flow, streaming down her cheeks. Minerva gave her a hug, murmuring, "Don't cry."

She wiped her eyes and blew her nose. "Forgive me, Min. I know I'm over-reacting. But you're supposed to be the healthy one. I just can't deal with this."

"I haven't been diagnosed yet. It might be nothing at all," Minerva said lightly.

"Do you really believe this weird book?"

"Not exactly. But I have always felt there *might* be an afterlife. When we die, I think our spirit remains—out there somewhere." She made a circular gesture. "Maybe something within us, so intangible we can't even describe it, remains—hovering around somewhere."

"Well, I used to think so too, but now I don't know."

"We tend to rely so heavily on the rational, perhaps we fail to nurture our spiritual selves."

Pondering Minerva's words, Lee thought about Agnes, her much-loved Missouri colleague who died some twenty years ago. At times Lee could still feel her presence, especially when faced with a tough decision. She would ask herself what Agnes would do, and frequently the solution would become quite clear. "Do you think we can communicate after we die?"

"I'm ambivalent. What do you think?" Minerva said.

"I feel there is an energy source we can connect with if we know how, helping us accomplish far more than we otherwise could. And I would like to think this same energy might activate our spirits after death, but I have my doubts. Living on in some other dimension is intriguing . . . but I don't know . . . might just be wishful thinking. And reincarnation—well, that's too far out!"

"Would you choose to come back if you could?" Minerva was watching her intently.

"It wears me out to think about it!" Lee sighed. "I'll settle for the life I'm living now. The next one might not be as good. I wouldn't want to risk it." She closed her eyes trying to imagine starting over again. "What about you, Min?"

"If given the choice, I might."

Lee smiled. "You always were adventuresome. One of the things I love about you."

Minerva's eyes smiled back at her. They were quiet for a few minutes, each lost in her own thoughts. Then Minerva went to the kitchen for more tea. Upon returning, she sat staring into her cup, as if trying to read the future. Abruptly she said, "Lee, do you think when your time comes you'll be afraid?"

The question startled her. "Surely, Min, you don't think your *time* is approaching!" Lee laughed, trying to turn it into a joke.

"Seriously. What do you think?"

Lee could not avoid her gaze. "Well, I'm not the bravest person when it comes to anything physical—and I have to admit, I 'm a little afraid to imagine my own death. I hope I go quickly—a heart attack or something so I won't even know it's happening. I certainly don't want to linger and feel myself deteriorating." Lee shivered. "I don't want a long illness."

Minerva nodded in agreement.

"But maybe I shouldn't be so afraid—considering the extraordinary experience I had some forty years ago. I haven't ever told anybody."

Minerva was leaning forward, teacup poised in midair. "Please tell me. I'll keep it to myself."

"Even though it happened long ago, I still recall it vividly." Lee settled back in her chair, folded her hands in her lap, wondering where to begin. "I was in a St. Louis hospital after a miscarriage, very ill with some strange infection they could not diagnose. And I was allergic to several of the medications, making matters worse. I'd been there for a couple of weeks with a high fever and severe chills. Each day I grew weaker, more fearful and tense. I slept very little, afraid to let go, afraid of dying perhaps. And when I did sleep, I'd wake up soppy wet from night sweats. I truly felt the end was near. My fears seemed to be confirmed when Matt was called home from a conference out of state, and I heard my brother was on the way from Boston. You know, preparing for the final deathbed scene." Lee closed her eyes, reliving the experience. "So that night I felt I was at the end of the line. I said my usual night-time prayer, the Lord's Prayer . . . being in my super-Christian phase then." She gave an embarrassed laugh. "But when I got to *Thy Will be done,* I stopped and said, *All right, God, Thy Will be done. If it's time, go ahead and take me. I'm just too tired to fight any longer.* Then I closed my eyes, perfectly relaxed, and felt as if I were floating— just drifting away. I could hear music in the distance. I remember thinking, to my great surprise, *If this is dying, it's not at all bad!* Then I fell into a deep sleep. When I woke up the next morning, I was free of fever and all my symptoms, delighted to discover I was still alive! I knew it was a miracle." She smiled broadly. "The doctors and nurses were astounded. You should have seen their faces when they found me sitting on the edge of the bed asking how soon I could go home. I didn't *dare* tell them what happened. They would have thought me a bit wacky."

Minerva was smiling at her. "Amazing! After such an experience, I don't see how you could be at all fearful of death."

"It wears off after awhile."

"That energy source you mentioned—I'm quite certain it's out there. The trick is knowing how to draw on it when needed. It would be comforting," Minerva added, "to believe in some form of immortality."

Lee nodded.

"If we could believe that life never really ends—that our spirits remain out there, communicating with each other and those we leave behind, the threat of death that clouds our days might disappear."

"That's an awfully big *if*. I doubt that I could believe it. But I suppose I could at least keep an open mind." Lee smiled at Minerva.

They sat together in silence for a few minutes. Then, before going to bed, Minerva gave Lee a good-night hug and kiss. Lee sat in the old walnut rocker listening to the arrhythmic ticking of the mantle clock. Picking up the poems she had intended to read, she glanced through them and pulled out one, revised from last winter. Tonight it seemed to represent her outlook more closely than Minerva's suggestion of some sort of afterlife. She read it softly aloud as she rocked slowly back and forth:

Without a Trace

My footprints
in the snow
criss-cross
from house to woodshed
to bird feeder
intersecting
the straight path
of a solitary cat,
each paw tracking
the one before.

Overhead
frosted jet trails
form a massive X
against a cobalt sky;
sharp outlines
blur, fade
feather away.

In time
mine too
will vanish.

Returning her poem to the stack on the coffee table, Lee blew
out the candles, turned off the lamp, and walked slowly through
the darkened room toward the stairs.

13

Bright sunlight splashed through the maple branches, warming the four women sitting on the porch along the side of the house— Minerva on the wooden swing crocheting an edge to a piece of handwoven fabric, Lee beside her writing in her journal with Patches curled up between them, Ada at her easel by the railing, Vivian in the Adirondack chair polishing her nails. Elizabeth was in the living room playing a Chopin nocturne, its bittersweet melody floating through the French doors.

The air was charged with an uneasy undercurrent as they awaited the phone call from the doctor with the results of yesterday's D & C. The portable phone was on the swing by Minerva. Both Vivian and Elizabeth had rearranged their schedules—to stand by. Lee glanced at Minerva, intent on her work. Today her color seemed healthier than in recent days, perhaps because of the dusty-rose woven top she was wearing. She had come through the D & C very well, the doctor commenting on her excellent physical condition for a woman of seventy-five. Except for some wooziness yesterday and slight weakness today, she seemed none the worse for it. But now the interminable waiting. *Let it not be cancer,* Lee prayed silently.

"What time did she say she would call?" Vivian painted a swish of red across her thumbnail and waved her hand in the air to dry the polish.

"This afternoon after she received the pathology report." Minerva did not look up from her work.

"This waiting can drive a person berserk," Vivian said. "How do you stand it, Min?"

"Do I have any choice?"

"Well, knowing how these bureaucracies function, she might not even receive that report today," Ada remarked. "I know how those . . . . " She was interrupted by the ringing of the telephone.

Minerva picked up the phone. The piano music ceased. Ada stopped painting, her brush in mid-air. Lee put down her pen. Vivian leaned forward in her chair. "No," Minerva said after a moment. "To reach the fence company, you have to dial area code 718." She hung up. "That wrong number we get every so often."

After several minutes of silence, Ada asked the time. Vivian told her it was 3:45. Lee was having trouble concentrating on her journal. How could Minerva sit there crocheting as if nothing were the matter? "If you haven't heard by four o'clock, Min, perhaps you should give Dr. Johnson a call," Lee said.

"We'll see." Minerva continued with her work.

A few minutes after four, the phone rang. Minerva picked it up amid hushed silence. "Oh, hi," she said. "No, we're still waiting to hear. That's all right. Yes, we'll give you a call." She hung up. "That was Bernie. She just wanted to know the news. Apologized for calling. Thought we would have heard by now."

"Why don't you try the office?" Vivian said. "It can't do any harm. Maybe she got busy and forgot."

"I'll give her till 4:30," Minerva said quietly.

Ada, announcing that she was chilly, went inside for her shawl. Vivian stood up and stretched, saying she would put on the kettle for tea. The sun was obscured now by the corner of the house and a cluster of spruce. Lee felt shivery but did not dare leave to get her sweater. She put down her journal, holding Patches on her lap for warmth. Minerva had stopped crocheting and was staring across the lawn.

"It's nerve-wracking, isn't it?" Lee said softly. The cold fear had lodged in her stomach.

"I'd just like to know, one way or the other."

For the next few minutes there were no sounds except the chatter of finches at the feeder and the creaking of swing chains against the ceiling hooks. The phone rang again. For a split

102

second, Lee imagined how it would be if the news were good, how they would hug and laugh, joking about their premature worries . . . .

"Yes," Minerva was saying. "Yes . . . I see. Thursday at eleven? All right, I'll be there. Thanks for your call." She hung up, her face drained of its color. Lee sat motionless, waiting to hear what she already knew. Minerva's voice was calm and steady. "Dr. Johnson says there's a cell change indicating an early malignancy. She recommends surgery. Wants me to come in Thursday and talk it over."

Lee put her arms about her and held her tight, unable to speak. She had promised she wouldn't go to pieces. Finally she said, "It's going to be all right, Min, I know it will. The doctor said you were in fine shape, remember? Try not to worry . . . . "

Minerva, tight-lipped, expressionless, pulled away and started rolling up the piece of weaving. "Thanks, Lee." She gathered up her crochet materials.

Vivian, Ada, and Elizabeth were standing at the French door. They knew. "I'm so sorry, Minerva dear," Elizabeth said.

Minerva nodded but said nothing, tucking the fabric and thread into her work basket.

Vivian suggested they come inside and have some tea.

Minerva shook her head. "I think I'll go up to my room." She walked across the porch, her gait unsteady compared to her usual confident stride, and disappeared into the house. Lee could hear her slowly climbing the stairs.

* * *

In the red Volkswagen Minerva sat beside Lee at the wheel. The drive to Stony Brook had not been pleasant. Grim-faced and silent, Minerva stared out the window, apparently oblivious to the roadside shrubs bursting with riotous color, the trees with their fresh leaves unfurling, a tapestry in delicate shades of green. The burgeoning new life seemed out of place today. Lee had tried to make small talk, but Minerva's responses were monosyllabic.

They had at last exited from the Long Island Expressway onto Niccolls Road and were approaching the Stony Brook

103

University Medical Center—two gigantic structures dominating the skyline of this wooded residential area. The one consisted of twin hexagonal towers of a black shiny substance some twenty stories high, each hexagon supported by enormous pillars and topped by a round flat cylinder. The dark towers were joined at an angle by a narrow sheath of concrete extending from top to bottom. The other building, white cement, was formed by eight massive cubes, four in a square on the bottom layer and four stacked on top, the layers separated by a space, perhaps one story in height. Topping the upper section was a large round tower. This grotesque pair, the dark and the light, were connected by a crosswalk near the top. From a distance, they resembled two monstrous robots shaking hands. The sight of them filled Lee with foreboding.

As they drove down the road from Niccolls toward the medical center, the buildings became somewhat less malevolent, their overall shape not apparent at close range. But the feeling persisted that some ominous force might be lurking within. Lee entered the ramp to the multilayered garage, took a ticket from the automated gate, and squeezed into a narrow space on the ground level. She gave a sigh of relief. She hated winding around in garages to the upper tiers. Reminded her of a rollercoaster, rekindling childhood fears.

Entering the building of the black towers, Lee found herself shivering, probably more from anxiety than from the air-conditioning. She had a stubborn distrust of most doctors and all medical facilities. The U.S. Surgeon General, she thought, should require hospitals to hang over the entrance a sign: WARNING! ENTERING THESE PREMISES MIGHT BE DANGEROUS TO YOUR HEALTH.

The circular lobby was immense, high-ceilinged, with assorted information and registration desks and wedges of purple and beige upholstered chairs arranged to conform to the circular structure. Despite its size, Lee felt closed-in. The air was oppressive, perhaps too many times breathed and recycled. The lobby at ground level was actually the fifth floor. Laboratories and offices were on the lower windowless levels. The two women found their way through a maze of circular corridors down the

104

elevator to Dr. Johnson's subterranean office. The lack of windows contributed to Lee's feeling of suffocation and the irrational fear that they could be trapped in there forever unless a supernatural power, such as Ariadne's ball of twine, came to their rescue.

While Minerva conferred with her doctor, Lee sat in the cramped waiting room filled with patients, most of them young women in various stages of pregnancy, some with small children who climbed over their laps or sprawled on the floor playing with blocks and toy cars. One lone man sat balancing a toddler on his knee. He looked as out of place as Lee felt. She stared at the large watercolor dominating the beige wall. A weatherbeaten rowboat partially submerged at the edge of a marshy shore, intended perhaps to have a soothing effect. But Lee found it depressing. Everything in gray tones—water, reeds, sky, boat. They needed something cheerful—maybe a still life of sun-filled zinnias and marigolds.

She rummaged through the magazines—*Family Circle, Good Housekeeping.* At the bottom of the pile she found an old *New Yorker* but couldn't concentrate, even on the cartoons. She sat glumly staring into space. Why did this have to happen? It wasn't fair. The old refrain—not fair, not fair! As if there were some open-minded Monitor out there making sure everyone got an even break. She tried to remember what Mark Twain had said . . . something about life being a combination crying machine and laughing machine, and if you managed to laugh as much as you cried you could consider yourself lucky. Today it was hard to imagine ever laughing again. Minerva, her rock and her strength, now in need of her support. She felt woefully inadequate, with no more backbone than a jellyfish.

Finally Minerva emerged from the doctor's office. There was a vague air of uncertainty about her as she walked slowly across the room, her steps less sure, her posture less erect. Lee linked arms with her. "What did she have to say?"

"Well, we had a good long talk." Her voice had that guarded cheerful tone she used when she wanted to evade the issue.

Lee was not certain she really wanted to hear the doctor's verdict but knew she must face it. "Did she tell you anything more specific?" They were walking down the hall now toward the elevator, and she noticed that Minerva was leaning rather heavily on her arm.

"I'll tell you about it when we got out of this place. It gives me the jitters."

When they reached the ground floor, Lee looked about with dismay, trying to remember which direction to take, this circular structure providing no familiar landmarks. Then she spotted the familiar wedge of purple chairs and beyond them a door leading to freedom. She took a deep breath as they stepped out into the fresh air. "Now tell me, word for word, what Dr. Johnson said."

"Let's get to the car first. I'm a bit tired." Rarely had Min acknowledged any feelings of fatigue or weakness.

"I tell you what. Let's go somewhere we can talk. I'll treat us to lunch."

Minerva hesitated. Most restaurants, she frequently observed, charged too much for very mediocre food.

Before she could give a negative response, Lee cut in. "A reward of sorts. We've earned it." She loved eating out but seldom did without a special reason. Today there was good reason. "I know the perfect spot—only a short drive from here."

In the car their conversation was haphazard, each pointedly avoiding the major topic. At the Three Village Inn the hostess, costumed in a ruffled Eighteenth Century gown, seated them by a large sunny window overlooking Stony Brook Harbor. Their talk focused on inconsequentials—the luxury of lobster salad and hot rolls, the antique furnishings, the weather. Finally Lee could stand it no longer. "All right," she said abruptly, propping her chin on her hands, looking across the table at her, "tell me everything, Min."

"Well, there appears to be a malignancy, but they won't know for sure, or how extensive, until they get in there and look around." Her voice was calm and precise, but as she talked she was running her hands through her hair, avoiding Lee's eyes.

"And what else?"

"She recommended a hysterectomy." Minerva took a sip of water. "Said I didn't have to make up my mind instantly but shouldn't delay too long." She toyed with her glass. "Those cells could spread, you know."

106

Lee nodded, fighting back the tears.

"I told her I wanted a second opinion."

"Good idea."

"She referred me to an oncologist at Sloan Kettering." She handed Lee a slip of paper with the doctor's name and phone number.

The very name of the place filled Lee with dread. Thinking back some twenty years, she saw the face of Leah, her political friend and ally of the sixties—protesting the Vietnam War together, running the campaign headquarters for an anti-war Congressman, mourning the assassinations of Kennedy and King, the Chicago Convention, celebrating victories and defeats together. Leah had died in that hospital. Breast cancer with rampant metastases. Nothing could save that frail, pain-wracked body, not even her spunk, her valiant laughter to the very end. "That's certainly one of the best medical centers in the country." Lee glanced away from Minerva as she said it.

"I've been reading up on this in *Our Bodies, Ourselves,* and it says hysterectomies are among the highest percentage of unnecessary operations." Minerva twisted her napkin around her fingers.

Dear Min—grasping at straws. "But I doubt that their statistics apply in cases . . . where there is a suspicious cell change . . . a possible malignancy." Lee sputtered out the hateful word.

"At any rate, I do want a second opinion," Minerva said firmly. She took several sips of water and stared out the window. "They will give me the slides to take to the other pathologist."

"If they advise surgery, would you have it done there?"

"I think not. Too inconvenient." Her voice quavered. She drained her water glass and forced a smile. "Besides, I have confidence in Dr. Johnson."

Lee nodded and reached for Minerva's hand. It seemed unreal, here in this cheerful atmosphere, to be discussing such remote things as hospitals, pathologists, and surgery. "Let's splurge and have some dessert," she said.

Minerva shook her head. "I think I've had enough."

"Oh, come on, Min. Otherwise I'll feel like a glutton if I have to eat mine alone." Lee took an almost childish pleasure in desserts but, in the never-ending battle to control her weight, made it a rule not to eat any except on weekends or special occasions.

"Well, if you insist." Minerva's gray eyes smiled across the table at her.

Lee ordered the Black Forest cake, and Minerva, after scanning the menu critically for a few minutes, chose a lime sherbet. Savoring every bite of the rich chocolate cherry sweetness, Lee contemplated the soothing effect of chocolate, like an opiate, making anything seem possible, temporarily anyway. "This is sinfully delicious! You want a taste?" She held out a bite on her fork.

Minerva made a face. "Much too rich for me. How can you eat it?"

Lee took another bite of chocolate whipped cream topping. It seemed inappropriate for her to be eating with such gusto.

"A penny for your thoughts."

Lee flushed, trying to explain her feelings of guilt over her enjoyment of the chocolate cake at this time of crisis.

Minerva laughed as she scooped up her last bite of sherbet. "There you go again! Must you always justify every ounce of pleasure?"

"I guess I'm just a hopeless case."

"Promise me one thing, Lee." Minerva's voice was serious now.

"I don't like to make promises I might not be able to keep."

"Well, this one you can keep. Promise me if anything goes wrong," Minerva paused, looking at Lee intently, "you won't wallow in guilt, convinced that it is somehow your fault."

"Don't be ridiculous, Min. What makes you think something will go wrong?" Lee felt her throat tighten at the very thought of the *something* neither of them wanted to name.

"I don't anticipate any mishap, but one never knows." Minerva gazed steadily at her. "Promise me, Lee, no guilt!" Sunlight from the window reflected in her eyes, tiny glints of silver.

"All right, Min, I promise."

14

It was one of those rare Saturday afternoons when the five women were all at home together—an unspoken need to support Minerva on this last weekend before the operation the following Thursday. Lee was helping Elizabeth plant a border of coleus alongside the house. Ada and Vivian were playing chess on the terrace. Minerva had stretched out on a lawn chair reading. Some ten days had passed since her visit to Dr. Johnson. In the meantime she had gone to Sloan Kettering in Manhattan for consultation. After the diagnosis was confirmed, she had asked for the hysterectomy to be scheduled at Stony Brook.

A brisk breeze from the bay ruffled Lee's hair. The smell of salt air, blended with fresh-mown grass and moist earth, produced in her a sense of well-being. Removing her garden gloves, she allowed the cool, sandy soil to trickle through her fingers, her mind momentarily free from worries about what lay ahead. She lifted a scraggly red coleus from its plastic cubicle and placed it in the ground, mixing in a trowel of compost and firming the soil around it. "There," she said in a low voice, "doesn't that feel better? Now you must grow!" Ever since reading a study about plants thriving on music and conversation, she talked to anything she planted and to the houseplants as she watered them. But she tried not to let anyone hear her. She had enough quirks without that.

"Did you say something?" Elizabeth asked. She had started planting at one end, Lee at the other.

Lee looked up, startled. "I must have been talking to myself."

With blue chambray sundress and matching espadrilles, broad-brimmed sun hat, and unsoiled green-thumb gloves, Elizabeth could have stepped right out of the pages of *House and Garden*. Lee surveyed her own torn jeans, faded shirt, smudged sneakers, and grimy hands with mild dismay. There were times when she had a secret longing to look the part of an Elizabeth.

"We'll just sprinkle on some peat moss, and it will be finished," Elizabeth said, smiling. "Thanks for your help."

"My pleasure—as long as someone shows me what to do. I'm not much of a gardener on my own."

"You could learn."

"I suppose so. Mother had a beautiful garden. Grandmother too." Lee trailed her fingers through the soil, remembering her mother's array of iris, coral bells, snapdragons, and poppies—and her grandmother's hollyhocks, roses, and hydrangeas. Both women dead for many decades, yet those gardens remained sunlit and fragrant in memory. "I feel very close to them when I'm digging in the garden . . . as if we're communicating somehow."

Elizabeth nodded. "My sister was quite a gardener too. I often think of her as I work in mine—especially in springtime. She was so impatient to start planting, even before the last frost."

"It takes time to keep up a garden properly. I guess I'm not willing to pay the price." A matter of priorities. Writing was supposedly her top priority. So why was she always getting sidetracked?

From the terrace came the voices of Vivian and Ada in a heated argument—Ada saying Vivian was obliged to move the chess piece, once she touched it, and Vivian denying she had touched it.

Lee got up with difficulty, stiff from kneeling so long. Brushing the dirt from her jeans, she walked over to the terrace and pulled up a chair to observe the game. Her brother had taught her to play when she was twelve—that, along with poker and blackjack which she much preferred. Chess seemed so ruthless—the idea that to win you must corner or trap your opponent. "Mind if I watch?"

"It's all right by me," Ada said.

Vivian, intent on the game, did not reply.

"It's your move," Ada said.

"Don't rush me."

"Maybe we should get one of those chess clocks."

Vivian studied the board with a frown. "You didn't leave me much choice." She moved her bishop to take Ada's knight.

Ada took Vivian's bishop. "Check!" she said with a grin.

"Damn! How stupid!"

After a few more moves, Ada won the game. "Nice play," Lee said.

Vivian gathered up the pieces and put them in the box. "It drives me up the wall to play with Ada! She's so damned unpredictable."

"That's what makes life interesting," Ada said. "If you knew in advance what I was going to do, why bother to play?"

"But she . . . ."

Elizabeth, who had pulled up a chair across the table, hastily suggested they all have some lemonade.

"Make mine a gin and tonic," Vivian said.

"Mine too," Lee said.

"Not a bad idea," Ada said. "Triple that gin and tonic."

"Isn't it a little early in the afternoon to start drinking?" Elizabeth's voice registered her disapproval.

"Not for a Saturday." Vivian looked at her watch. "It's nearly three-thirty, the traditional time to start a happy hour on Saturdays."

"I never heard of that," Elizabeth said. A pink flush colored her neck and face. Turning abruptly she walked across the lawn.

"Where did you hear that Saturday rule?" Lee asked.

"I made it up." Vivian laughed. "I'd better go help."

Minerva, carrying her book, came over. "What's the matter with Elizabeth? She seemed perturbed."

"I think she's worried that we might turn into alcoholics." Ada gave a hearty laugh. "Always wanting folks to measure up to her highbrow standards."

"Let's not be too hard on her." Minerva—ever the balanced, kind-hearted one. Lee wished she could be more like her.

"What are you reading, Min?"

Minerva handed her the book. *"Womanspirit* — Hallie Iglehart. Remember that woman who did a workshop on feminist spirituality a few years ago?"

"How could I forget? Rutgers, wasn't it?" The energy circle . . . women sitting cross-legged on the floor, linking hands, their energy circulating to create a dynamic force . . . Lee smiled at the memory.

"And how we formed a human chain, chanting as we walked down to the lake?"

"I can't recall what we were chanting, but I remember throwing leaves and flower petals into the water."

"Weren't they supposed to represent our negative thoughts?" Minerva said. "That seemed awfully foolish at the time."

"Because you rarely have any negative thoughts to get rid of. With me it's different." Lee recalled how light and free she felt, watching her trouble-laden petals float away.

"And when we passed a clump of huge old cypress trees you hugged them all, telling them how beautiful they were."

Lee laughed. "I took a picture of you beneath one."

"The whole thing sounds weird to me!" Ada said, frowning. "Especially that part about the leaves and flower petals. I didn't know you folks were into that sort of nonsense."

"I suppose it does seem strange unless you experience it yourself." Lee remembered the tears streaming down her face when they were in the circle, each woman sharing fears, worries, and guilt — followed by her giddy happiness at the conclusion of the ritual. Would she ever again feel so free and light-hearted?

"I was wondering . . . I know this might sound silly, but I was wondering if we could do an energy circle the night before I go to the hospital. I'm having a few negative thoughts I'd like to dispose of."

"What a great idea!" Lee tried to mask her surprise and concern. Minerva must be genuinely worried.

"I remember watching you — how tense and edgy you were at the start . . . the end of the semester — all those exams you had graded . . . and how relaxed you seemed when we finished the ritual." Minerva smiled. "I know it sounds contradictory, but I believe I'm in a more receptive frame of mind now for a ritual or something that might strengthen me to embark on this surgical

112

adventure. I don't feel particularly brave." She softened her words with a laugh, covering up her uncertainty.

It was not like Minerva to admit weakness. "Well then, let's do it!" Lee turned to Ada. "I hope you'll join us?"

"Better count me out!" Ada's braid flipped across her face as she shook her head vigorously. "The whole thing sounds like bullshit to me! I'd feel like a fool!" Her voice was emphatic.

"Oh, come on, Ada. We'll need *all* of us to make it a success," Lee said.

"Welllll . . . ."

""I'd truly appreciate it," Minerva said quietly.

Ada's face softened. "Well, all right," she said, taking Minerva's hand, "for you, I'll do it. But that doesn't mean I will believe any of it. No, not one iota will I believe!"

"Nobody is asking you to take an oath on it," Lee said. "Now, let's see—who else can we get?"

"I doubt that Elizabeth will do it," Ada said, "or Vivian either."

"I think they can be talked into it." Lee closed her eyes, envisioning all of them sitting cross-legged in a circle in the moonlight . . . no, not sitting cross-legged . . . easy enough for Minerva, but impossible for Ada, and difficult for herself as well. Perhaps they could sit on the lawn chairs . . . yes, in a circle, barefoot, hands entwined, raising them to the stars and moon, invoking a healing energy to flow through each of them to Minerva.

"I'll bet my bottom dollar they won't do it," said Ada.

"Well, I don't want to deprive you of your bottom dollar," Lee said, "but I bet they will."

"I can't, in the wildest stretch of my imagination, see Elizabeth in one of those crazy circles!" Ada gave a loud laugh. "Vivian, maybe. But not Elizabeth, not in a million years."

Just then Elizabeth came out with the lemonade, followed by Vivian with the gin and tonics. They distributed the drinks and joined the others around the table.

"Well, speaking of the devil . . . ." said Ada with a broad smile, "Elizabeth, you arrived at precisely the right moment for Lee to pose an important question."

Elizabeth's eyebrows narrowed into a frown. "A question?"

113

Lee glared at Ada. She had intended to lead into it casually, offhand. "I think Min can explain it better than I." Lee gave Ada's foot a light kick under the table.

"Ouch!" Ada winced as if in pain.

"Are you all right?" Elizabeth asked.

"Fine, fine . . . ." Ada glanced at Lee. "Just a twinge in my bum leg."

"What are you and Lee up to?" Elizabeth turned to Minerva.

In somewhat garbled fashion, she tried to explain the concept of an energy circle and how she thought it might be a good send-off for her hospital trip.

"Tell about the leaves and petals,'" Ada said with a grin.

"Leaves and petals?" said Vivian. "What on earth are you girls talking about?"

Lee flinched at her use of *girls*. But she had about given up trying to reform Vivian's language. "We won't do anything of that sort," she said quickly. "We'll keep it simple." She tried to catch Ada's eye, but she was poking at her ice cubes. Lee turned to Elizabeth and Vivian. "I do hope the two of you will help us out."

"Well, I don't know . . . " Elizabeth said. "The last time I went along with one of your schemes, I found myself at Tranquil Acres making conversation with a woman who saw her sister in the kaleidoscope. I vowed I'd never let you talk me into anything like that again."

"But look what we accomplished. We rescued Ada. And now Minerva needs us. When we all pull together, we can do miracles," Lee said.

"Sounds harmless enough to me," said Vivian. "I'm game."

"Thanks, Viv," Minerva said.

Elizabeth cleared her throat, a warning signal. "Don't you remember, Lee, what our attorney told you about not doing anything else out of the ordinary before the court hearing? This sounds considerably beyond the ordinary. We mustn't risk offending Arthur any more than we already have." Her frown had deepened.

"I'm sick of hearing about Arthur all the time and what he will think!" Lee exploded.

"What we do for Minerva in our own backyard is none of Arthur's business," Ada said.

"And besides," Vivian said, "how would he ever find out?"

"Well, I think you could accomplish more by coming to church with me and saying a prayer." Elizabeth gazed earnestly at Minerva.

"I don't have any faith in that patriarchal institution." Minerva took a sip of her lemonade. "I'm afraid you will have to pray for both of us."

"This ritual, it sounds so . . . so pagan." Elizabeth was creasing her napkin into accordion pleats, folding and unfolding it.

"Liz, if you would prefer not to participate, I'll understand," Minerva said.

Ada, twirling the ribbons in her braid, gave Lee one of those I-told-you-so looks. *Damn Elizabeth anyway! So rigid and self-righteous. And damn Ada for her smugness!*

Elizabeth sat quietly sipping her lemonade, staring toward the bay. She put down her glass, still frowning. The others waited in silence. Finally she said, "Well, Minerva, if it were anyone else, I would definitely refuse. But if you think it will help, I'll do it."

Vivian clapped her hands. "Marvelous! Now tell us how it works, Min."

"Thanks, Liz." Minerva was beaming. She turned to Vivian: "It's not magic. I just think the ritual process might strengthen me. I'm hoping Lee will work out the details." She glanced over at Lee.

Lee nodded. She felt she owed Elizabeth an apology—but one did not usually apologize for one's thoughts. "Fine," she said to Minerva, picturing them in the circle holding hands, chanting. She looked at Elizabeth sitting stiffly in her chair, tight-lipped, hands twisting nervously in her lap. An image came to mind of Elizabeth sitting in church, discreetly clad in tailored suit, every waved hair in place beneath a proper hat, with matching gloves. But Lee had difficulty seeing her barefoot in an energy circle.

"Now, who else might come?" Minerva said.

"Oh, I thought it would be just the five of us," Elizabeth said.

"To make an effective circle, we need at least eight or ten,"

Lee said. "Only special friends, of course. We don't want any negative vibes."

"I noticed some ritual suggestions in this book, in case you want to look it over," Minerva said.

"And Starhawk has some in her books," Lee said. "But I want to create something unique, especially for you."

"How about giving Bernie a call? She might have something new on healing rituals in her bookshop," Minerva said.

"Let's check the ferry schedules. Maybe she can come over Wednesday evening," Lee said. Since their chance meeting at the Washington march, Lee and Bernie had advanced their friendship by letter and telephone. And Minerva had joined them for lunch one afternoon in New Haven. The three of them had established an instant rapport.

"I thought you stipulated *special friends*." Elizabeth's frown reappeared. "I don't recall ever meeting someone named Bernie."

"The one who befriended me in Washington—I told you about her," Lee said.

"Oh, yes." Elizabeth nodded. "But is she a close enough friend?"

"Isn't she the lesbian?" Ada asked.

It sounded innocent enough, but was it? Ada loved the leading question, loved to insert an element of friction and then watch the sparks. "What difference does that make?" Lee snapped.

"Well, I've got nothing against the lessies. What they do in private is their own business." Vivian rolled her eyes and shrugged her shoulders. "But do we want to include her in this intimate gathering of really close friends. I mean, wouldn't she feel like an outsider?" *Same old excuses . . . same old tired phrases.*

"I think Vivian has a good point," Elizabeth said. Was she worried about holding hands with Bernie—squeamish at the idea of that lesbian energy pulsing through her fingers, fearful that it might be somehow contagious? Lee glanced at Elizabeth's tense face. Perhaps she should not be too hard on her, considering her own awkward behavior upon meeting Bernie. We're programmed from earliest childhood, she mused, instilled with irrational prejudice and fear. No wonder we have trouble breaking free.

Minerva leaned across the table. Her voice was firm. "Bernie

116

is no outsider. I'd like to have her for the ritual." She looked around at the others. No one spoke. Lee smiled at Minerva. Their eyes met, signaling victory.

Elizabeth, obviously aggravated, announced she was going inside to start dinner. Ada challenged Vivian to one more game of chess.

Minerva and Lee walked down to the shore and sat on an upturned dinghy. Seagulls soared high above. Sailboats skimmed across the bay.

"What a peaceful scene!" Lee had taken off her shoes. She wiggled her toes in the moist sand.

"I'll miss this view and this salt air in the hospital."

"But it won't be for long, only a few days."

"If all goes well."

"What do you mean, *if*?" But even as she said it, Lee recalled the friend who had died from a blood clot after routine gallbladder surgery.

"Things do sometimes go wrong. I've prepared a Living Will, and I'd like to designate you as my power of attorney."

"A Living Will?" Lee had never seen such a document, although she knew it allowed one to die naturally when there was no expectation of survival. Fear gripped her, choking her words. "I don't care to consider that horrible possibility, Min."

"Neither do I. But if something happens, I don't want to be kept alive by machines." Her eyes reflected glints of steel.

"I wouldn't either. But what's this about power of attorney?"

"That's in case a medical decision has to be made that I am not capable of making."

Lee shivered, despite the warm sun slanting across her back. "That's an awful responsibility. How do we know I would make the right decision?"

"Just remember what I've told you, and you will know. I trust you to do what's necessary."

For an instant she saw Minerva in the hospital bed, pale, skeletal thin, a fleeting image but vivid in its stark intensity— entrapped in a network of tubes, machines, flashing lights. The tears Lee had been struggling to hold back came streaming down her face.

Minerva reached in her pocket for a tissue and handed it to her. "Cheer up, Lee. You'll have me dead and buried before I even go to the hospital." She was laughing her light ripply laugh.

Lee blew her nose and wiped away the tears. "I'm sorry I broke down. It just suddenly hit me. It's all so cruel. Why, Min? Why?"

"I don't know." Minerva tossed a stone into the water. It landed with a splash, ripples circling outward until they reached the shore. They sat together in silence. Lee was not sure how long . . . until the incoming tide washed across their feet. Picking up their shoes, they started back along the shore.

"All right, Min, I'll do it," Lee said finally. She swallowed hard. "But I hope I never have to use it."

Minerva stopped, shading her eyes against the sun shimmering across the water. "Just one last look." She stood motionless for a time, her slender form statuesque against a backdrop of reeds, sea, and sky, the fringe of her dress blowing against her legs, her arms and face tinted golden by the late afternoon sunlight.

Lee wished she could hold the moment, tuck it away in a locket and keep it forever.

"I'm ready now," Minerva said at last. Smiling, she linked her arm through Lee's. "Thanks, Lee dear."

"For what?"

"For being you. My rock, my strength."

Unable to respond, Lee gave Minerva a quick hug. Turning away from the water, the two women walked arm in arm through the marsh grass toward the house.

15

The nine women sat barefoot in a circle of lawn chairs beneath a rose-tinted sky, sheltered by a cluster of spruces and one large maple, overlooking the bay. It was that quiet time at day's end, suspended between light and darkness when the raw edges are softened, when the tempo slows and bird songs subside, when only the peepers accelerate their strident chorus. An evening breeze rustled the leaves and lifted the corners of the purple woven cloth on the round table in the center of the circle.

Lee had envisioned their ritual by moonlight under the stars, but Minerva preferred to do it immediately after dinner so she could get to bed early. And twilight, she said, was her favorite time—when the worries of the day fell away and all things seemed possible. For Lee this was not the case. To her it was a depressing time, this hour of indeterminate light, the stillness, the day sliding into darkness. A time for facing the solemn thoughts of one's own mortality—thoughts that could be pushed aside during the activities of the day.

It stemmed from childhood, this feeling about twilight, her first awareness of it coming when she was seven or eight. It must have been about this time of day one spring when she and her family were driving in their old Chevy to her grandmother's cottage in the Ozarks. She had been alternately singing *Old MacDonald* and counting all the horses and cows, every so often asking how many more miles. Leaving the open fields, they drove down a steep hill into a valley where the road ran through a dense woods, sunless and dark. Looking into that tangle of trees, she felt a chill run through her—suddenly struck with the realization that one day all of these people so dear to her would be dead. Her grandmother, to her young eyes already quite ancient, her mother, her father, even her older brother. And she would be left alone—until she, too, would have to die. She sat huddled in the corner of the back seat, crying silently at this dreadful revelation. Then, as the car emerged from the wooded area to more farmland with the last rays of evening sunlight slanting across the fields tinting everything golden, the cloud of dejection lifted as abruptly as it had descended upon her, and she put the whole thing out of her mind—or so she thought. But, time and again, in the early evening hours that dark feeling was to return with vivid clarity.

Impatiently Lee pushed aside the memory to focus on the ritual about to begin. On the table in the center of the circle burned a large citronella candle, its pungent aroma floating around them. Beside the candle were a blue bowl of salt water and an angular quartz rock, four or five inches in diameter. Clustered at random around these items were gifts for Minerva, placed there by each woman to remain throughout the ceremony and absorb any positive energy that might flow into them.

From Ada there was a curvaceous wooden candlestick on which she had painted a woman's face and body in a blue and red peasant costume, with a bayberry candle emerging from her head. Vivian brought a small porcelain cup decorated with pink roses and elaborate gold lettering, *From a Friend,* saying she had found it in an antique shop years ago and had been waiting for just the right friend to use it. Elizabeth gave her a brass goat bell from Norway, suggesting she could ring it if the nurses did not give her proper attention. Laura brought a small crystal vase containing a single red rosebud.

Perry contributed a bronze labris on a purple cord, telling how the Amazons had used one side of the double axe to chop down trees and till the soil and the other side to kill their attackers. "Every good feminist needs one," she said. Margaret who, despite her scientific background as a registered nurse, practiced therapeutic touch and believed in harnessing the energy of outside forces, brought a highly polished rose quartz, advising

Minerva to hold it in her hand before going to the operating room—to strengthen her heart and give her courage.

Bernie constructed a mobile of shells and beach stones which she hung on a branch of the maple tree over the table, where it would jingle whenever it caught the breeze. She had arrived just in time for dinner. Elizabeth, rallying to the occasion as a proper hostess, greeted her warmly. Ada and Vivian had also been on their best behavior. Lee's gift was a silver locket with a photo of herself in one half and a pressed four-leaf clover in the other. "For good luck!" she had said, giving Minerva a quick hug.

Minerva, not one to show her emotions, was clearly touched by this array of gifts. She had excused herself and run into the house, saying she would be right back. When she returned, it looked as if she might have been crying. She was carrying a small narrow fringed tapestry, finely meshed, of delicate linen thread with a few slender seedpods interwoven. She hung it on the branch beside Bernie's mobile, saying she planned to take this along to hang in the window at the hospital and wanted it to absorb all the positive energy she could feel right now. Her voice sounded a bit husky.

So far, everyone had been remarkably cooperative, though some had objected to removing their shoes and stockings. Elizabeth worried about stepping on a snail or a slug, and Vivian complained that the grass prickled her feet. Lee herself was a bit squeamish about walking barefoot on ground she could not see clearly, but she dared not admit it. When she announced that it was time to begin, the women who had been chatting among themselves gradually became quiet and attentive. She heard a giggle from Vivian's direction and waited a few seconds for complete silence. Then she asked them to sit erect, feet flat on the ground, and take several deep breaths, trying to feel the earth's energy. "Now, link hands," she said, "and continue to breathe deeply, sending your energy clockwise around the circle." Lee was seated between Perry and Minerva. She concentrated on directing the flow to Minerva on her left, and on around. Her fingers felt tingly and warm.

Perry was squeezing her hand so tight she winced. Perry eased up, whispering, "Sorry. I got carried away." Beyond Minerva was

121

Bernie, then Margaret, Laura, Elizabeth, Vivian, Ada, and back around to Perry. Lee glanced about the circle. Everyone was serious now, absorbed in the energy flow, bodies and faces at ease.

"Continue breathing together. Inhale slowly . . . and exhale . . . inhale . . . exhale . . . and feel yourself relax. With each breath, feel the strength of the circle flow through you." Her voice droned on. "Feel yourself becoming one with the circle . . . Inhale . . . exhale . . . ." Disengaging her hands from Minerva's and Perry's, she stood up, linking their hands across her empty chair, and moved to the center. Over her white slacks she wore a loose-fitting blue velvet coat, lined with white satin. A golden sunburst was appliqued on the back and two silver crescent moons on the front. Bernie had brought it along as a loan from a friend who was into feminist rituals. Lee had been hesitant about wearing it, but the minute she put it on, she felt inches taller, and stronger too.

Arms outstretched, she said she was going to invoke the powers of the four elements. Facing the East, she began:

> *Draw forth the light,*
> *that first violet tint*
> *of Aurora we invite*
> *to cast her ethereal glint*
> *on bright wings in flight*
> *and disperse any hint*
> *of gray-clouded night*
> *with her aerial imprint.*
> *Draw forth the light.*

Lee had put considerable time into memorizing what she had written for the invocation. Though not at all sure she really believed in this, she wanted to make it as authentic as possible. She had spent a restless night worrying about making a fool of herself—either forgetting her lines or not convincing the women to take it seriously. But now she was feeling more confident. Perhaps it was the blue velvet coat or the energy from the circle— or perhaps a little of each.

She picked up Ada's bayberry candle and lit it. Facing the South, she continued:

> *Draw forth the flame*
> *From Arinna's crimson spark*
> *helping us proclaim*
> *power of the matriarch.*
> *Let fresh breezes frame*
> *our circle as we embark*
> *on this journey without name,*
> *magic making its mark.*
> *Draw forth the flame.*

She set the candle in its holder and picked up the bowl of salt water, holding it as she turned toward the West:

> *Draw forth the wave*
> *of Tiamat's salty abode*
> *to free our minds and save*
> *us from the weighty lode-*
> *stones that will enslave.*
> *We drink to strength bestowed*
> *in twilight upon the brave*
> *traversing the windswept road.*
> *Draw forth the wave.*

Returning the bowl to the table, she scooped up a handful of sandy soil and faced the North to conclude her invocation:

> *Draw forth the song*
> *of graceful Gaia who made*
> *this earth to which we belong,*
> *green mountain and glade,*
> *Mother of weak and strong,*
> *through night's deep shade*
> *guide us firmly along,*
> *women united, unafraid.*
> *Draw forth the song.*

When she finished the last line, Lee felt a strong sense of relief. The women had listened in polite silence, but were they laughing inwardly? Goddess invocations were not her usual poetic style. She rejoined the circle, linking hands with Perry and Minerva. Perry squeezed her hand, and Minerva gave her a warm smile. She glanced around the circle. The faces were expectant, awaiting her next signal.

"Now," she said, "it's time to release hands and invite our mothers and grandmothers to join us, to enter the circle. I'll begin." She took a deep breath. "I'm Lee, daughter of Ethel, granddaughter of Mary Leandra and Almira Jane." Saying their names, she had a fleeting image of each one . . . her mother beneath an arbor of roses, gray hair framing her face, dark eyes gazing at her with a haunting sadness . . . Grandmother Leandra—a wiry old woman in a long dress, hair slicked back from her angular face, smiling grimly as she clutches a plump, curly-headed crying baby—Lee, her namesake . . . and Grandmother Almira in her garden in gingham dress and sunbonnet, her face crinkling into a smile . . . Lee continuing, "I invite them to join our circle."

The voices started around the circle: "I am Minerva, daughter of Mildred, granddaughter of Prudence and Emma" . . . Lee wondering what sort of woman her mother had been . . . the voices continuing . . . to Bernie . . . then to Margaret, only knowing the name of one grandmother but inviting the other in spirit anyway . . . to Laura, remarking how she and her mother could never communicate on the same wave length but she could talk to her grandmothers . . . Elizabeth, looking ill-at-ease in her bare feet, yellow linen dress, white sweater and pearls, saying she doubted that her ancestors would feel comfortable here but supposed it would do no harm to include them . . . then on to Vivian . . . then Ada.

"I am Ada, daughter of Amanda," her voice loud enough to be heard down at the bay, "but I definitely am *not* inviting her!." She was shaking her head vigorously, red ribbons on her braid flipping back and forth as she spoke. "Mama gave me nothing but trouble when I was growing up—inhibitions and prohibitions, and I don't intend to re-establish any foolhardy connections with her or her ghost or whatever." A murmur flowed around the circle. Lee flinched. She might have known Ada would pull something like this. Then, to her relief, Ada lowered her voice, calming down as she named her grandmothers, terming them a couple of meek little old ladies who she reckoned could do no harm.

Then Perry, the last one . . . inviting her grandmothers but echoing Ada's views on her mother. "My mom would disrupt this entire ceremony—trying to convert everyone to Catholicism. No way will I invite her!"

Lee had planned this part of the ritual as a means of adding an extra dimension, strengthening the circle. She was startled by some of the responses, the vehemence of their rejection, the very mention of their mothers causing them to bristle. She felt her muscles tensing at the thought of the friction she might have unwittingly injected into this circle, her mythic circle intended to symbolize perfect harmony. But she must carry through.

"Now close your eyes," she said, " and try to feel the presence of these mothers and grandmothers among us. Perhaps you can see a mental picture of them. What would you say to them? What might they say to you?" Lee attempted to envision this array of spirits they had invoked, but it was too overwhelming. Women of all ages and types. Young mothers with red lipstick, rolled back hair and broad-brimmed hats of the forties, long-waisted beaded flappers of the roaring twenties, serious matrons of the fifties, sporty tanned grandmothers of the eighties. A collage of women intermingling with the nine in the circle . . . . But she must focus on her own threesome.

Drawing several deep breaths, imagining the air flowing through her body and releasing the tensions, she gradually reached a state of deep relaxation and concentrated on finding an image of her mother, but there was nothing—only darkness. Now the darkness was brightening to purple, a rich purple, the velvety color of iris—the iris her mother used to plant. Lee attempted to envision her mother the way she remembered her from childhood, beautifully young, her dark hair tied back in a red bandanna, digging in her garden surrounded by masses of iris. But she could not see beyond the purple haze. She felt cheated—on the verge of something she could not quite reach.

The circle was perfectly quiet. But Lee was acutely aware of the presence of these women, their breathing, the waves of energy they generated. The breeze had picked up, bringing an evening chill to the air. She pulled the velvet robe around her for warmth. From the nearby trees came the call of a whippoorwill, a mournful sound but a pleasant one for Lee, reminding her of evenings in the Ozarks with Grandmother Almira. Concentrating on her breathing again, she tried now to see her. Nothing appeared at first—only the hazy purple. Then she noticed the purple gradually changing into a bright blue, then to the gray-blue of twilight, and a memory invaded her mind . . . her grandmother sitting in the wicker rocking chair on her porch in the Ozarks . . . the family out there together to cool off from the heat of the day, the air breezy, a delicate aroma of honeysuckle floating about them. Lee sees herself as a child of perhaps eight or younger, sitting on the porch steps listening to the sounds of the grown-ups' voices blending the rise and fall of cicadas signaling the approaching darkness. Mother and Aunt Martha are sitting on the swing, its rusty chains grating against the ceiling hooks with a loud creeeek-craaaak. Father is tilted back against the wall in the old ladderback chair, and Mother is warning him he will either break the chair or his back, or maybe both, but he does it anyway . . . . They used to say Lee shared her father's stubborn streak.

She can hear Grandmother's rocker scraping softly against the floor as she rocks slowly back and forth. Lee remembers thinking she must be awfully old, she has so many wrinkles—beautiful wrinkles, and smiley blue eyes that crinkle up at the corners making still more wrinkles when she laughs . . . that wonderful laugh starting with a low soft chuckle deep in her throat, then growing louder and heartier until her whole body seems to be laughing.

The dusky air begins to grow chilly, and her mother is saying, "Don't you need a sweater, Mary Lee?" . . . *Mary Lee* . . . the name everyone called her back then. A few years later she was to drop the *Mary*, declaring double names too childlike. Strange how one can't wait to grow up, then yearns to find the child again . . . .

The scene began to fade as Lee allowed her mind to wander. She quickly concentrated on relaxing into the past to restore the memory. Slowly the shadowy images come back in focus . . . gray silhouettes in the dim twilight, the first katydid of the evening beginning its relentless call, accompanied by the voices of the whippoorwills, the twilight deepening, and in the distance the eerie call of a screech owl.

Shivering, the child climbs on her grandmother's comfortable, well-cushioned lap . . . . She used to feel sorry for anyone who had skinny grandmothers with bony laps . . . . Now Grandmother is hugging her close against her large soft bosom, sheltering her from the night sounds, rubbing her arms, saying, "My sakes, you've got goose bumps!" and hoisting her up a little higher on her lap, exclaiming, "Gracious, child, you'll soon be too big for my lap! See there—your feet nearly touch the floor."

And Mary Lee whispers, "I'm *never* going to be too big for your lap, Grandmother, and you're *never* going to die." She snuggles closer.

And Grandmother kisses her on the back of her neck, saying, with a hint of sadness in her voice, "Children have to grow up, and everybody has to die eventually," the wooden rockers of her chair pressing against the worn floorboards, squeaking faintly . . . .

Lee, her mind now gyrating crazily in time and space, recalling her childish denial of death, realized keenly that death was still a fact she was reluctant to accept. At this moment she longed for some magic power to grant her the serenity of that Ozarkian grandmother, roughly the same age then as she was now, but stronger by far—strong as Missouri granite.

"Not me!" the child says emphatically. "I don't want to die— *ever*." The shadows are darkening. She is shivering again, and Grandmother tightens her embrace. Enveloped by the wispy fragrance of her lavender perfume, she can hear the rhythmic thump of her heart and feel the vibrations of her voice as she resumes her conversation with the others. Mary Lee relaxes to the gentle motion of the rocking chair. A soothing sense of oneness with that calm quiet little universe flows through her—the rise and fall of Grandmother's breasts, the strong heartbeat, the voices blurred in the background, the creaking of the swing, the katydids, the whippoorwills, her own breathing in unison with her grandmother's. Catching sight of the faint glimmer of a star, she begins chanting, *Starlight, starbright, first star I see tonight* . . . . And Grandmother is telling her to make a wish. And then Mother says it is her bedtime, but Mary Lee wheedles permission to stay up just a little longer. Savoring those precious moments of borrowed time, the child closes her eyes and makes her wish: *Let us stay this way forever,* she says to the star, yearning to remain safe and secure on this generous lap, protected from the night and the shadowy darkness—but knowing the wish can't come true—even if she doesn't look at the star again . . . .

Lee sat quietly in the circle, stunned by the graphic intensity of that scene dating back over sixty years. All of them dead now, except her. A wave of sadness washed over her. She had been right, of course, about the wish. So why did she persist in making wishes? Slowly she opened her eyes and glanced about the circle, concerned that the women might be growing restless. The light was too dim now to see her watch. The others were all sitting in relaxed positions, apparently engrossed in their visualizations or memories or thoughts . . . whatever. Hers had not been what she expected—some new vision, a communication across the barrier of time. Nothing like that—only a disconcerting memory, leaving her shaken and bewildered.

The light had dwindled to the point that she could not see any faces clearly except those on either side of her. A hint of a smile softened the lines of Minerva's face. Perry appeared troubled, her forehead puckered into a frown. The women across the circle were shadow forms, like those in her twilight memory. Some day they, too, would be gone, all of them.

Lee felt strangely weak and wobbly—but she must continue the ritual. Walking slowly to the center, she stood by the table, leaning against it for balance. Lilacs scented the air, blending with the salt breeze. *When lilacs last in the door-yard bloomed . . .* " Whitman mourning the death of Lincoln . . . *Please, no more thoughts of death tonight . . .* She rubbed her fingers along the sleeves of the blue ceremonial coat, taking comfort from its velvet softness, the feeling of the satin lining against her arms.

Picking up the bell and ringing it, Lee asked the women to concentrate on letting the energy flow upward from the earth through their bodies in preparation for the next step. She was acutely conscious of the grass, small stones, and sandy soil beneath her bare feet. Except for a vague discomfort and a dull ache in her arthritic knee, she had not been able to sense anything out of the ordinary. But now she thought she could discern a tremor originating in her feet and traveling upward . . . perhaps her hyperactive imagination . . . but she was sure she sensed *something*. Maybe this paraphernalia—the bell and the magic coat—was getting to her. But wasn't it a sacrilege of sorts to lead a ritual she was not certain she believed in? The old familiar weight of guilt pressed in on her. But she was *trying* to believe—for Minerva's sake. That was the best she could do. She became aware of a faint rustling as the women shifted positions, a murmur of voices. Then a hush fell over the group.

Lee rang the bell again, its brass tones encompassing the group. She picked up the large quartz rock, asking that they pass it around, concentrating on some specific worries or problems and symbolically depositing them into the rock. She gave the rock to Minerva who cradled it in both hands, staring at it intently. Lee took her place in the circle. While the rock made its way around, she tried to free herself from the twilight Ozark memory which still held her in its grip, a memory both comforting and disturbing.

When the rock came back around to her, it seemed to feel heavier . . . all those burdens . . . or was she imagining again? The hard angular surface pressed into her hands. *It's death . . . That's what worries me . . . I don't know what I'll do if . . . .* She continued to hold the rock. *Help me find whatever strength . . . . .* For an instant she could see the shadowy form of her grandmother in the wicker rocking chair.

She walked back to the table, hoping her legs would not collapse, wishing she could end the ritual but determined to complete it. Immersing the rock in the bowl of salt water to cleanse it, wash away their worries, she started it around the circle again for the women to draw strength from it. Lee surveyed the group. Though she could see only their dim silhouettes, she sensed they were taking the ritual seriously. No silliness so far, no negative comments. Everyone apparently suspending any

129

skepticism they might have and entering into the spirit of it, including Elizabeth—though one never could tell for sure what Elizabeth was thinking beneath that polite facade.

Daylight had faded into dusk, making the flames of the bayberry and citronella candles more visible, flickering in the breeze, casting faint wavery shadows across the table of treasures. The sound of the whippoorwills had crescendoed—one nearby and another replying in the distant trees—intermingled with the persistent chorus of peepers. The whippoorwills called her back to that little town in the Missouri hills, its strong ties tugging at her. But she must move forward. She should have brought more candles to ward off the darkness which had so suddenly descended.

When the rock came back around to her, she had the uncanny perception that it was lighter. Probably her overwrought imagination. But, whatever the cause, a sense of elation came over her as she held the rock, warm now from much touching. She had a strong desire to laugh and leap about but repressed it. The others would surely think she was out of her mind—which might indeed be the case.

She carried the rock to the table, suggesting that everyone stand up and stretch but remain in place before drawing the ritual to a close. The women broke their silence, conversation flowing freely around the circle, though in hushed tones, as if still partially under the spell of the ritual. It sounded harmonious, Lee noticed with a sense of relief. Returning to her place in the circle, she realized, with a pang of remorse, that she had forgotten to try envisioning Grandmother Leandra during that part of the ceremony. Well . . . too late now.

Perry gave her a hug. "Lee, you really pulled it off!" she said with a grin.

Minerva was beaming. "It was splendid!"

"Maybe the Goddess was with us," Lee said.

"Which one?" asked Perry. "You invoked four, didn't you?"

"Collectively," Lee said. "All of them in one—*the* Goddess."

"When do we get to the petals and leaves?" Ada asked.

"I told you we weren't going to do that tonight." Lee tried not to show her annoyance.

130

"I feel beautifully relaxed," Margaret said.

Lee flushed with pleasure. "Let's join hands," she said to the group, "and pay tribute to Minerva." She reminded them to concentrate on their breathing. "Now," she added, "allow your breath to become a hum." A low *hmmmmmm* started around the circle. Someone raised her voice to a higher pitch, someone else lower, in harmony. Lee felt a shiver of delight. "Now let the humming change into words—words that might bring strength and healing to Minerva."

Woman, Woman, Woman chanted someone in a low monotone, and they all joined in, then *Wise Woman,* repeated several times, their voices growing louder, changing to *Power,* then to *Womanpower, Womanpower, Womanpower,* their voices crescendoing in the darkness, reaching their peak with *MINERVA! MINERVA! MINERVA!* their clasped hands rising into the air simultaneously.

Breathless and exhilarated from the chanting, Lee wished she could conclude the ceremony right now, but she felt an obligation to bring it to a proper end, in keeping with the tradition. Asking the women to join hands, she moved to the center. Facing each of the four directions, she offered a simple thanks to each of the four elements before the final action—a formal *opening* of the closed circle. Reluctant to break the magic, she stood for a moment with arms outstretched, then chanted the lines she had prepared:

> *Open circle, open*
> *but remain unbroken.*
> *Let each one depart*
> *with joyful heart,*
> *the flame of this night*
> *burning ever bright*
> *until, our circle complete,*
> *again we shall meet.*
> *Open circle, open*
> *but remain unbroken.*

With the last words of the chant, Lee blew a kiss to the shadowy forms encircling her and rushed across to Minerva to give her a hug. Then everyone was hugging Minerva and Lee and each other.

Suddenly Lee heard the sound of a car door in the driveway. She could see someone emerging from the car with a flashlight . . . . No, it was two people. Who in the world? The police? Had the neighbors complained? No, not the police—no flashing lights or sirens. The two forms, one tall and one short, were dimly silhouetted against the porch light which Elizabeth, with typical forethought, had turned on. As they came closer, Lee grabbed Minerva's hand. "Look over there, Min, quick," she whispered. The figure in front walked like Arthur. Impossible! No reason for him to be here. "Do you see what I see?"

"It couldn't be Arthur!" Minerva said.

"I'm afraid it could," Lee groaned. "And Dolores too! What should we do?"

"What can we do—other than welcome them—and pray they decide to go home immediately."

"I don't believe it," Lee said. "Tonight of all nights!"

"Just leave the talking to me." Minerva's voice was calm. She gave Lee's hand a squeeze.

As the two figures drew nearer and the tall one spoke, Lee had no doubts about their identity. She would know that rasping voice anywhere. "Hello? Hello? Anybody home?" It was Arthur all right, asking his usual stupid questions. Obviously they were home.

"Over here, Arthur," Minerva called.

"What in God's name are you ladies doing out here?" He had come within full view now, his lean face ghostlike above the flashlight, his voice loud and querulous. "I hope you're not up to your old tricks. Where's Mother?"

Dolores was beside him, stumbling awkwardly in her heeled sandals, clutching his arm with one hand and her pocketbook with the other.

"I might ask the same of you, Arthur. What are *you* doing here?" Minerva said crisply, pulling herself up to her full height, looking regal despite her bare feet.

"We stopped by to see Mother. Where *is* she?" Arthur repeated, suspicion edging his voice.

The other women stood in their places, immobile, as if playing

Magic Statues. Then Ada came forward. Lee watched with admiration as she approached, resembling a barefoot gypsy queen, with her embroidered blouse, silver beads and bracelets, her gray beribboned braid over one shoulder, her full red skirt swirling as she walked. "Arthur?" she said, her voice dazed, "Is that you?"

"Hello, Mother." Arthur gave her a peck on the cheek. His dark business suit made him look especially funereal. Dolores was standing to one side, as if waiting for her cue to speak. The tight curls framing her pinched face were a bright orange above the flashlight. More like a puppet than a person.

"What a surprise!" Ada was staring at Arthur, but somehow looking beyond him, as though still under the spell of the ritual. "What brings you here, Son?"

"We were in the neighborhood—met some friends for dinner at The Post House in Southampton. We just thought we would stop by and check up on things."

"It's too bad . . . " Ada said, her eyes still focused on some distant plane.

"What's too bad, Mother?" Arthur was clearly puzzled.

"Too bad you didn't come a bit sooner. You could have met your Great-Grandmother O'Malley. Such a dear old soul . . . . " Her voice trailed off into the darkness.

"Meet who?" Arthur's ghost face was looking startled now.

"Your Great-Grandmother O'Malley . . . my mother's mother." Ada smiled vaguely. "I didn't invite Mama. She would have disrupted the ritual. Your Great Aunt Viola came in her place. I hadn't invited her either, but suddenly there she was, big as life. Remember her, Son? Always used to give you pennies for candy?" Ada was smiling broadly now. "She sent you her love."

Arthur was shaking his head in disbelief. "*What* ritual, for Christ's sake?"

"For Minerva."

Arthur, completely baffled, stood gaping at his mother. "What's all this nonsense?" he sputtered. "Rituals . . . meeting some great grandmother and great aunt who have been dead for a half century or more?" He paused, apparently at a loss for words, and shined his flashlight directly on Ada. Staring at her feet, he frowned. "Mother, what on earth are you doing out here *barefoot* at this time of night?" He glanced around at the other women, noting their bare feet.

Ada blinked, shading her eyes with her hand. "I'll thank you, Son, to quit shining that bright light at me as if this were some sort of police line-up! And could you keep your voice down a bit? I'm not stone deaf, you know."

Arthur lowered his light and his voice somewhat. "Just tell me, Mother, what are you and your loony friends up to now?"

Ada stood tall, in her gypsy queen posture, staring defiantly at her son. "I'll have you know, my friends are quite sane. And you have no right barging in here and breaking the spell." Lee felt like applauding.

"Break the spell? Good grief, Mother, what are you talking about? Have you gone completely out of your mind?"

Lee supposed the scene might seem rather off-beat to an outsider, particularly Arthur. He had not been around since that day back in March when he filed the petition. Too bad this had to be their first contact. Had he, perhaps, come by to patch things up? If so, she had spoiled all chances with this ritual. She felt a surge of the old familiar guilt and remorse.

"Well . . . " Ada was groping for words . . . "you see, we were doing this energy circle, this . . . ." Lee wondered if she should help her out. But anything she said would only aggravate matters. "This ritual to help Minerva before . . . you know, she's going into the hospital . . . and our healing energy . . . from the earth, that is . . . I mean . . . ." Her explanation was becoming more and more garbled.

"Wait a minute, Mother. I don't understand half of what you're saying. But surely you can't believe in all this hocus-pocus?" Abruptly he turned his flashlight on Lee, his eyes glaring at her. "What have you done to my mother? Is that what the shouting was about? What we heard when we drove in?"

"Not shouting, Arthur, *chanting*," Lee said.

"This was your idea, wasn't it? Involving my mother in your lunatic schemes!" He continued to glare at Lee, standing there barefoot in her blue velvet robe with its sunburst and crescent moons.

134

Before she could reply, Minerva spoke up, her voice crisp and firm. "This was *my* idea, Arthur—not that it matters."

"It matters to me what my mother gets herself drawn into, considering what happened when you-know-who staged that hippie rally in Riverhead." He cleared his throat. "I came here hoping we might work out some sort of compromise, but it is clear to me now that you people are *impossible!*" Arthur walked over to the round table where the candles were still burning and eyed Minerva's treasures. "What's this?" He started to pick up the rock.

"Don't you touch that!" Ada swished over and grabbed his wrist, edging herself between him and the other objects on the table.

"Why? What's so special about it?"

"Because it's our worry rock."

"Your *what?*"

"Never mind. You wouldn't understand." Ada was looking secretive. "But if you contaminate it, Lee would have to wash it with salt water again. And you mustn't touch the other things because you might de-energize them."

"Wait!" Arthur's tone was growing more suspicious. "Is this some sort of a cult?" He stared at the table and its strange contents. "That's it!" He spit out the words. "You were practicing witchcraft!" He turned his light on Ada again. "Mother, how could you!"

"Witchcraft?" Ada gave a loud laugh. "What on earth gave you that idea?"

"Don't try to deny it. You've got all the trappings right here." He gestured toward the table.

"Don't be silly, Arthur," Minerva said.

He wheeled around and faced them. "Who's being silly?" he demanded. "You witches have cast a spell on my mother. You've got her talking this crazy gibberish that no one in his right mind can understand." He glowered at them, his face demonic in the shadowy beam of his flashlight. "Just wait till I tell this to Mr. Maloney."

Lee could feel the blood pulsing in her temples. Kevin Maloney, the court guardian, would clearly not be in sympathy with this. She could think of no response.

135

"We come by for a friendly call and find my mother babbling incoherent nonsense, and we are treated with hostility by the rest of you!" His voice was trembling with rage. He grabbed Dolores by the elbow and started across the lawn. "We don't have to put up with this!" Then he turned, calling back to them. "But you haven't heard the last of it!"

As their forms faded into the darkness, Lee laughed. But her laughter was forced, covering up her fears. "Good riddance!" she said, wishing momentarily that she actually was the type of witch Arthur had in mind so she could put a hex on him. Substituting an age-old childhood gesture for the hex, she placed her thumbs in her ears and flapped her fingers defiantly at the departing shadows. Arthur was not to be trifled with. He might indeed find a way to use this against them.

The women clustered together in silence, watching the car lights pull out of the driveway.

16

"Exactly what did Arthur say when he referred to us as witches last night?" Elizabeth asked Lee. "I couldn't hear much from where I was standing, but he sounded quite upset."

Lee was curled up on the couch in the living room trying, without success, to bring her journal up-to-date. Things had been happening too fast lately. And tonight her mind was a gray haze, nothing in focus. The only image that would come through clearly was Minerva lying in her hospital bed waiting for tomorrow's operation. When Lee left there this afternoon, Minerva looked totally out of place, as if she ought to leap out of bed and start jogging down the corridors. All that vital energy restricted . . . just not right.

"What's that, Elizabeth? I'm sorry. My mind was wandering."

Elizabeth paused in her knitting and glanced at Lee with a worried frown. "Are you all right? Can I get you a cup of tea or something?"

"No, I'm fine, thanks. I just didn't hear what you said."

"I asked what Arthur meant about *witches*. I told Florence about our ritual when she called this afternoon, and she said it sounded as if we were some sort of a *coven*, of all things! Of course, I assured her it was nothing of the sort—just an energy circle for Minerva. But Florence said there are a number of women on Long Island who actually call themselves *witches*—who think they can perform acts of healing and all sorts of strange things." Elizabeth's daughter, Florence, was almost as annoying as

Arthur, in her own puritanical way, or maybe worse because she was inherently more clever. "Of course, you hear about some of these so-called witches now and then, but I've never taken it seriously." She paused to count her stitches. "Florence mentioned, as a case in point, the daughter of a friend of hers, a college girl about our Melanie's age, who has renounced her religion and joined a coven! That made me think about Arthur again and how irate he was last night. I *know* it had something to do with witches."

Lee could feel Elizabeth watching her. "Oh, Arthur—he was just jumping to one of his hasty conclusions." She slid the top off and on her pen as she talked, wondering if she should try to explain anything to Elizabeth or just let it ride. "You know how he is."

A steady rain beat upon the paned windows, driven by a wind out of the northwest, bringing a damp chill to the air. Unseasonably cold, according to the tri-state forecast, with temperatures dropping into the forties tonight. Lee pulled her sweater tight around her, shivering. "We're lucky this change in the weather didn't happen last night." She started to add something about the Goddess helping them out, but refrained. Elizabeth was too uptight for any references to divinity beyond the Father, the Son, or the Holy Ghost.

"Well, after Arthur stormed out last night, everybody was busy saying good-night, and I hated to upset Minerva by discussing it then." Elizabeth paused to roll up her yarn. "But I kept thinking about it after I went to bed. You know, how a question keeps buzzing around in your head and won't leave you alone?"

Lee did not feel like dealing with the issue, especially now, with her mind so muddled. But she could sense Elizabeth's determination not to let the question go unanswered. Standing up and stretching to get the stiffness out of her back, Lee walked over to the casement windows. All she could see were rivulets of rain trickling down the glass. She stared into the darkness, then pulled the curtains closed to shut out the gloom. She returned to the couch where she sat, chin in hands, thinking about a way to explain the concepts behind their ritual. Elizabeth had resumed her knitting but was still waiting for a reply, Lee knew by her posture, a certain tautness of shoulders and spine.

"I think Arthur was angry because he leaped to the irrational conclusion that we had indeed somehow been transformed into witches and were engaging in some form of black magic. You know, witches in the old stereotyped notion of pointed hats and broomsticks, in cahoots with the Devil."

"Oh dear me! Surely there was nothing evil in what we were doing."

"I said it was an *irrational* conclusion. But he was already suspicious from Ada's garbled account of the ritual, and then when he saw that strange assortment of gifts to Minerva . . . and when Ada wouldn't allow him to touch them . . . " Lee smiled at the memory of Ada in action . . . . "Then our *worry rock* . . . ." She was laughing now as she recalled the scene. "Too much for his logical Wall Street mentality!"

Elizabeth was not laughing. She sat rocking silently back and forth. There was no sound but the click of her knitting needles and the slow ticking of the clock. "Surely people, except for that radical fringe of women Florence mentioned . . . *respectable* people, I mean, don't believe in witches in this day and age."

"It depends on how you define the term. Certainly not in the old traditional sense—except maybe on Halloween." Lee shifted her position on the couch. This was not going to be easy. "But there are people who believe in a divine spirit in *everything*—rocks, plants, water, the earth, the sky—people who honor the forces of nature through various rituals."

"You mean Pantheists. I know all that. I don't need one of your lengthy lectures." There was an edge of impatience in her voice. "But precisely what does it have to do with witches?"

The rain was coming down harder now, driving against the windows and French doors, the wind howling with demonic fury. "Listen to that rain!" Lee said. "I'd better draw some water in case the pump goes out." She hurried to the kitchen, glad to escape the inquisition. She functioned on the theory that by not preparing for a catastrophe you are inviting it to happen.

When she returned, Elizabeth was holding up her knitting to check her progress. A loose-knit bed-jacket, in soft rose yarn. "It's looking good," Lee said. "Minerva will love it. Her favorite color."

139

"I'd like to finish it this evening. Then you could take it with you in the morning."

Lee thought about Minerva coming back from the operating room , weak and pale, half-conscious. "Min probably won't need it for a day or two." She could feel the onset of a headache, the tension in her shoulders and neck working its way upward.

"Arthur also said something about Mr. Maloney. Do you suppose he will report this?" Elizabeth sounded apprehensive.

"I wouldn't be surprised." Lee tried not to show her concern— but it was a worry. Young Kevin Maloney, though congenial enough, was not likely to be in sympathy with any deviation from standard behavior, especially a goddess ritual. When he had come to the house, as the court guardian, to talk to Ada, she was on her best behavior, and Lee had the feeling he was on their side. But Arthur's version of last night might change his attitude. Perhaps she should speak to him. Lee's head was throbbing. Why did everything have to happen at once? Minerva's operation was all she could deal with right now. Maloney would have to wait.

"And about the witches . . . ?"

Lee sighed. If Ada or Vivian were here, perhaps they could divert Elizabeth's attention. But Ada had gone to her room to read in bed, and Vivian was at a meeting for realtors. She wished they could just drop the subject. But Elizabeth, like a bull terrier tugging at a bone, was determined to pursue it. "Okay, the witches," Lee said after a lengthy silence. "Some of these Pantheists we just mentioned might consider themselves modern-day witches practicing their religion, known as *Wicca* or *the craft*—to bring back the wisdom of the ancients."

"Witchcraft, in other words," Elizabeth said sharply. "So there was some validity in what Florence was telling me." She stopped in the middle of a stitch, staring at Lee. "No wonder Arthur was upset!"

The wind had increased in velocity, rattling the shutters, scraping low-hanging branches against the house. Lee wished she had built a fire in the fireplace. But who could imagine they might need one the last week of May? Besides, Elizabeth had cleaned out the ashes, polished the glass doors and brass fittings,

140

closing it for the season. Lee tried to imagine the cheerful crackle of flames, feel the warmth, to bolster her sagging spirits. There was something so elemental, so comforting about an open fire — just as in the power of rituals relating to fire and the other elements to the inner self. If only she could get that across to Elizabeth, persuade her to put aside her distrust and grasp the essence of their ritual—understand the depths of its meaning for Minerva, and for Lee as well.

Elizabeth's rocking had accelerated. In another era, sitting there frowning in the black Salem rocker, she could be one of those self-righteous seventeenth century Massachusetts citizens, passing judgment on those poor innocent women on trial for witchcraft, calling them wicked *She-Devils* . . . . But even as the thought crossed Lee's mind, she quickly erased it, feeling immeasurably guilty for even thinking it. After all, Elizabeth *had* expressed doubts about the ritual, participating solely to please Minerva.

Except for the noise of the storm, the only sound in the room was the slow ticking of the old clock and the creaking of the rocker against the floorboards. The gray cat sitting on the piano by the window staring into the darkness, stood up, stretched and arched his back in one graceful movement, and came across the room, leaping onto Lee's lap. She stroked his fur, thinking about the unfortunate cats of times past, cats tortured and burned as surrogate witches. "You're a lucky fellow, Brother Gray," she murmured. She was beginning to feel a stubborn determination now to convince Elizabeth, somehow win her over. "Do you know why peasant women of the Middle Ages were labeled witches?"

"I haven't the slightest idea." Her voice sounded remote.

Lee gritted her teeth. She doesn't know, doesn't care, but she *should* care. "Because they were *healing* people, healing with herbs rather than the traditional prayers and religious incantations. So they were considered evil because such healing couldn't possibly be the work of God." She glanced at Elizabeth who said nothing, intent upon her knitting. "So, in the narrow-minded logic of those old patriarchs, the women were assumed to be in league with the Devil!" Lee was becoming more and more agitated. "And those poor peasant women were burned as witches, thousands and thousands of them, simply for the art of healing, doing their harmless rituals . . . women coming together—dancing, singing, celebrating life . . . scary stuff!" Her voice quavered with anger. She knew it was a mistake to get so worked up, but she couldn't stop. Elizabeth always clammed up when anyone became emotional.

Lee could almost feel the heat of those ancient flames—searing her own flesh. She stared at Elizabeth, willing her to speak, react to the horror. But she sat quietly rocking and knitting, not even looking up. Finally, in exasperation, Lee said, "I get the feeling you're not listening."

"Yes, I heard you . . . . It's a shame, of course."

"A shame! Is that *all* you can say?"

"Well, I don't know what else to say. Those church people must have somehow felt they were justified."

"God, Elizabeth, I can't believe you would calmly sit there defending those cruel killers!" Lee's voice rose into a shrill crescendo.

"I wasn't defending them. I was just trying to see it from their point of view. Customs were different back then." Elizabeth's voice had also become several decibels higher.

At that point, Ada entered the room. "What in the world is going on down here?" She rubbed her eyes and pulled her flannel robe about her. "Why are you two shouting at each other?"

"Nobody's shouting," Lee said. "I was merely trying to set Elizabeth straight about modern witchcraft."

"Witchcraft?" Ada began to laugh. "Witchcraft! If you aren't a sight, the two of you, glaring at each other arguing about . . . . Wait a minute . . . does this have something to do with Arthur calling us witches?"

"Why don't you just keep out of this!" Lee snapped. Ada was more than she could contend with now.

"That's it, *witches*!" Ada said, ignoring Lee's suggestion. "Well, how about that! Our little ritual was some kind of witchcraft? Is that what you are trying to explain?" Her laughter increased. "Then Arthur was not so far off base. I do declare!"

Lee scowled at her. "I fail to see what's so funny."

142

Elizabeth, rocking at a furious pace, did not look up from her knitting.

"Well, I can tell when I'm not wanted." Ada started across the room, still chuckling, shaking her head and murmuring "Witches!" At the door she turned. "Do me the favor of keeping your voices down so a person can get some sleep . . . or better still, why don't you call a truce?" Lee wished they could but didn't know how.

Elizabeth sighed heavily. "I wish you had told me ahead of time."

"Told you *what* ahead of time?

"That this so-called energy circle was actually a form of witchcraft." Elizabeth's face was flushed and her eyes flashed behind the gold rims of her glasses.

"I *told* you," Lee said, trying to keep from shouting, "it had nothing to do with the old false notion of witches." Ada was right . . . they must look ridiculous—the two of them yelling at each other this way. But the words kept spouting out. She could feel the blood throbbing in her temples. "Some of it was *like* feminist witchcraft—not exactly, but similar. Anyway, it was a meaningful ritual for Minerva—so what difference does it make what we call it?"

Elizabeth sighed again. "Well, the Bible says witches are an *abomination* . . . somewhere it says that . . . in *Exodus* or *Deuteronomy*." The lines of her face were tightly drawn. "And somewhere else God says, *Thou shalt not suffer a witch to live.*"

"Well, I don't happen to be a witch, if that's what you're implying!" Lee could not conceal her irritation.

"I said no such thing!" Elizabeth had stopped knitting altogether. "But how is one to know?" she added testily.

Lee knew their argument had reached a fairly ludicrous stage, but it was beyond her control. "What it says in the Bible is just a lot of sexist patriarchal crap, written by men, for men, against women!" She stood up, knocking a startled Brother Gray off her lap, and stormed out of the room. She did not look back, but she could picture Elizabeth sitting there piously like Whistler's Mother, face composed in a mask concealing her anger, calmly rocking and counting her stitches.

143

No sooner had Lee started up the stairs than she began to have misgivings, wishing desperately she could retract those last words, blot them out. Halfway up she paused, leaning against the railing. She could retrace her steps and apologize. It would only take a minute to clear the air. She could say, *I'm sorry. I didn't really mean those things I said about the Bible.* And Elizabeth would smile and say, *I understand. You were upset . . . so much stress.* And they would hug and everything would be fine. She hesitated, her foot balanced on the step. There was only one problem with that happy scene. She would be a hypocrite. Did she owe anyone an apology for stating what she felt was true? She continued up the steps. Of course, she might have chosen a less offensive word than *crap*—maybe *propaganda* or some such. But Elizabeth had not been very kind to quote those Biblical pronouncements against witches right after Lee had pointed out their tragic history of persecution. The nagging question, one that plagued her intermittently, jabbed at her now . . . . How could she have been so stupid—blindly teaming up with a woman so diametrically opposed to her view of life? Why couldn't it have been somebody else's house where they had come together?

In her room the wind sounded even louder—howling through the trees, humming along the utility wires. She drew the curtains and opened the window just a crack. The rain was still coming down in torrents. After getting into bed, she told herself to quit thinking about the argument and get some sleep. She would need to be rested for tomorrow, for Minerva. But her tense muscles would not relax. She felt rigid, as if stretched taut upon some medieval torture rack. If only she could replay the evening. How much better if, through calm moderate words, she had convinced Elizabeth of the validity of their ritual rather than getting so passionate about it. But, oh no, she had to say those cruel words . . . . If only . . . .

Finally she fell into a fitful sleep, dreaming she was on trial by the townspeople for witchcraft, accused of turning into a cat and putting a hex on Arthur . . . . Elizabeth helping them build the bonfire and Minerva trying to stamp out the flames pleading, *Wait! This is a horrendous mistake!* Elizabeth suddenly changing into Arthur saying, *I told you so! . . .* joined by Kevin Maloney, his sandy hair and beard now spiked in fiendish red, throwing chunks of wood on the fire . . . and Minerva saying they could erase everything by joining hands . . . and Lee shouting, *I'm sorry! I'm sorry!*" She awoke in a sweat, her heart pounding, and lay awake till daybreak.

17

The storm had blown out to sea during the night, bringing air that was breezy and clear. From Minerva's room on the thirteenth floor of the hospital, Lee could see an expanse of trees beyond the university complex and, in the distance, the Long Island Sound, a slash of slate blue against the horizon. She and Vivian had arrived at eight-thirty, an hour before the operation was scheduled. Minerva had insisted on a minimum of sedation and was quite coherent and calm as they waited together. The nurse came in around ten o'clock saying there would be a delay because of a bottleneck of some sort in the operating room. Lee immediately began to worry about possible adverse effects of this. She was growing fidgety. It was like telling someone good-bye at an airport, waiting endlessly for the flight to be announced, passing the time with mindless talk. Vivian was chattering away, and Minerva appeared to be listening, occasionally responding. But Lee had tuned her out, concentrating on some cloud formations outside the window.

It was nearly eleven when the attendants finally came for Minerva. As they wheeled her out of the room, she waved, smiling, and blew them a kiss. She looked so vulnerable, stretched out there on the cart, Lee could not keep back the tears. She dabbed at her eyes, hoping no one had noticed. Minerva was holding the rose quartz and wearing Lee's locket until the last minute when she handed them to Lee saying, "Take care of these until I return." Lee nodded, putting the locket around her neck and holding the quartz in her hand, absorbing its warmth.

An emptiness pervaded the room after she was gone—as if devoid of its center, though many visible traces remained. Her melon-striped terrycloth robe draped over the foot of the bed and her slippers by the chair . . . at the window her little woven tapestry with the seedpods silhouetted against the light, along with Bernie's mobile of stones and shells . . . on the bedside table, a rosebud, and Elizabeth's bell. On the corkboard above her bed she had tacked a snapshot of the five of them framed by lilac blossoms. Lee had suggested maybe that area was intended for hospital records, but Minerva said she might as well make use of it. Her arrival the morning before had created quite a stir in the gynecological wing. Remembering it now, Lee couldn't help laughing.

"What strikes you so funny, Lee? Are you all right?" Vivian asked.

"Oh, I'm fine." Strange how we keep on saying we're *fine*—even if we're at death's door with walking pneumonia or in the depths of despair. "I was just remembering Minerva's grand entrance yesterday, carrying that bottle of spring water and all her other trappings—how she refused to get undressed until she had arranged the room to her liking."

Vivian laughed. "That's Min all right. I can just see her driving the nurses nuts!"

"Actually the head nurse was impressed. She said she knew she had an intelligent patient when she saw that bottle of spring water."

"Why did she bring that?"

"She read in *Our Bodies, Ourselves* that bedside hospital water is sometimes contaminated by bacteria. It advised bringing water, along with your vitamins, which she also brought, of course."

Vivian smiled. "She's certainly not your ordinary patient."

"Then the nurse came back, apologetically, saying there must be a mistake in their records because her birthdate was entered as 1914. She supposed it was a typo. Should it have been 1924? Well, Min went into peals of laughter. And the nurse just stood there looking bewildered—until Min told her it was no mistake, that she was indeed seventy-five."

147

"She'll be the star of the thirteenth floor before the week is over."

They sat in silence . . . Vivian flipping through the pages of a *People* magazine and Lee staring out the window. She could hear the usual confusion of hospital sounds—a doctor being paged, a patient's call-bell, orderlies conversing as they pushed their carts down the hall. She was still cradling the rose quartz in her hands. *Let her come through safely.* She was not certain whether she was addressing the stone or the Goddess or just some vague source of healing power.

Vivian gave a loud yawn and tossed the magazine onto the bed. "Excuse me. I didn't get my beauty sleep this morning."

"I didn't get enough sleep either. It was a restless night." But she could not tell Vivian about the nightmare.

"What was eating Liz this morning, by the way? She hardly said a word at breakfast."

Elizabeth had been coolly polite, saying almost nothing except when she handed Lee the brightly wrapped package and asked her to take it to Minerva. And Lee, not knowing exactly what to say, had taken the package with only a nod.

"Definitely not herself," Vivian added. "What do you suppose was on her mind?"

"I think she was miffed about certain things I said last evening." Lee could feel a flush creeping up her neck into her face.

"What sort of things?" Vivian, chin in hand, was studying her closely, her green eyes glimmering with curiosity.

Lee stared into the depths of the rose quartz, rubbing its smooth surface with her fingers. "I really don't care to discuss it."

"Suit yourself." Vivian shrugged her shoulders. "But, speaking of Liz, what do you think of her budding romance with gallant John?"

"Well," Lee said, relieved at the change of focus, "I rather like him, don't you?"

"He's definitely not my cup of tea, but I suppose he's a good match for her. Proper almost to the point of perfection. He would drive me up the wall!"

Vivian was right. John would be a real mismatch for her. But he and Elizabeth seemed quite compatible. Lee admired his soft-spoken manner, despite her growing concern over the way he monopolized Elizabeth's time and occasionally intruded on their privacy. When he stopped by for her, he would join in their conversation as if he belonged there. Recently when Elizabeth had invited him for dinner, he was quite charming, toasting them individually and saying something special about each. Not many men would bother.

"He's a very congenial fellow," Lee said. "But he's not my cup of tea either." She had not been serious about any man since Matt's death, not even in those days when she was an attractive young widow of thirty-something. Not that she hadn't gone out with men occasionally and enjoyed it. But they all fell far short of Matt with his warmth and wit and tenderness, his way of making her feel loved.

"Who would be your cup of tea if you were making a choice?"

"I haven't given it any thought, really."

"Well, you'll never find a man at that rate."

"Who said I was looking for one?"

"Oh, come on now, Lee, *every* woman would like to team up with *Mr. Right* if she could." Vivian took out her mirror, applied a swath of red lipstick to her full lips, and rearranged the fringe of curls about her face, smiling at the result.

"Not necessarily. Maybe once was enough. Maybe it's better to stop while you're ahead." She wished Vivian would drop the subject. Strange that she should feel this way, considering that she had suffered through two unhappy marriages and stormy divorces. But whenever a few weeks passed without a man on the scene, she was miserable. Her current attraction was a mortgage specialist—a macho character, into stock-car racing.

"But what *is* your type, Lee, if you ever happened to be shopping around? You never go out with anybody on a one-to-one basis. You're only with men if they're part of a group you happen to be in. One would almost think you were anti-male." She gazed at Lee beneath heavily mascara'd lashes.

"Not at all. But I am pro-woman." In those lonely days after Matt's death, she might have considered remarriage if the right

149

someone had happened along. But now, with Minerva and the others, she felt no desire to seek male companionship. Why couldn't Vivian understand? They were clearly poles apart, and today she was in no frame of mind for a lengthy argument.

Lee stood up and walked over to the window. Touching the mobile, she watched the beach stones and shells twirl and sway back and forth, listening to the sound of the sea as they brushed against one another. She must concentrate on Minerva, keep transmitting positive energy to her.

A nurse walked in, her manner as brusque as the angles of her starched cap. Not at all like the pleasant ones on duty yesterday. She checked the blood pressure machine, intravenous pole, and the array of equipment behind the bed, then asked them to find another place to wait while she changed the bed and prepared the room for the patient's return.

"But we want to be here when she comes back," Lee said.

The nurse glanced at her watch. "It's not quite twelve. The operation is probably just getting underway."

"But she's been down there an hour. It ought to be nearly over by now," Vivian said.

The nurse, as if addressing young children, explained that patients were not whisked from their rooms directly into the operating room. There were routine procedures to follow. Generally one might expect a wait of twenty or thirty minutes. But with the pile-up today, it was certain to be much longer. Therefore they might as well relax. They would have ample time to go to the cafeteria for lunch. Lee wondered why such a patronizing tone was so frequently used toward older people, as if they had reached an advance stage of senility.

Having no choice, she and Vivian headed for the door. Lee turned to take a last look at the little seedpod tapestry glimmering in the sunlight. Then they started down the circular corridor in search of an elevator. The serpentine nature of these hallways had the same suffocating effect on Lee as on her first visit to the place with Minerva. At the elevator, she took note of the purple doors, a marker for their return trip. Though aware of the irrational nature of her fear, she could not free herself from the constriction of throat and chest that attacked her every time she ventured forth in this monstrous building.

"Why isn't there a 13 button?" Vivian asked as she pushed the elevator button for the lobby. "Isn't that Minerva's floor?

"It's that MR button," Lee replied. "Stands for *Medical Records,* but it's really the Thirteenth Floor—where they stored records until Gynecology took it over, but they still refer to the floor as MR. Weird isn't it?

Vivian laughed. "There must be some superstitious people around here."

Lee nodded. She did not like the connotation of thirteen, but calling the floor by another name did not change the truth of it. Her brother had always claimed thirteen as his lucky number, that being his birthdate, the date he started his first job, and his wedding date. He died on a different date, which also fit the pattern. One should not die on one's lucky date.

After a number of false turns, they found the cafeteria where they sat at a table overlooking a sunny courtyard. Lee only wanted coffee but, at Vivian's urging, had taken an English muffin that she was attempting to eat.

Vivian kept up a steady stream of small-talk. Lee was barely listening. She focused on Vivian's hand holding her teacup—lovely hands if you overlooked the few tell-tale liverspots, none of the unsightly arthritic joints Lee had developed. Too bad she wore her nails so long and painted them such a ghastly blood red. But she was grateful for Vivian's company despite the nails and empty chit-chat. She had gone out of her way to arrange time off from the office. Ada could not come because of the amount of walking, and Elizabeth was not able to switch her day at the hospital.

Lee had not expected to feel so jittery. "I'm glad you could come along," she said abruptly.

Vivian smiled and took Lee's hand in hers. "She's going to be all right, I'm sure."

Lee glanced at her watch. A quarter to one. Dr. Johnson had been vague about the length of time, saying something about an hour and a half or possibly more. "They must be well along by now," she said.

"She'll probably be back in her room by two." Vivian's voice was upbeat. Lee wished she could feel more confident. She had a fleeting image of Minerva on the operating table under fierce glaring lights, a mask over her face, enshrouded by snakelike tubes, blood gushing from the incision. She felt her own blood draining from her face.

"Are you all right? You look a little pale," Vivian said.

"Just a bit dizzy. I'll be fine in a minute. Probably the lack of sleep."

"You just sit there while I get you a Coca Cola." In Vivian's world, a coke was the sure cure for anything. While she was at the coke machine, Lee reached into her bag and pulled out the rose quartz, cupping it in her hands, hoping it might somehow transmit the healing energy to Minerva lying there so helpless in that room of cruel lights and tubes surrounded by masked people wielding sharp instruments.

* * *

Lee glanced nervously at her watch. "If Minerva is not back by three o'clock, I'm talking to the nurse again." They had been sitting in Minerva's room for nearly two hours.

"Better wait till a few minutes after three. Maybe old stoneface will be off duty by then."

"I wonder what's taking so long." She walked to the window and looked out at the expanse of sky, cloudier now, the white cotton fluffs of the morning transformed into layers of heavy gray felt, obliterating all but a few patches of blue.

"Even if she didn't go into the operating room till noon, it's been almost three hours." Something must have gone wrong. Her stomach contracted with fear. But surely they would have notified her if . . . Minerva . . . if . . . . Again she was haunted by the image of Minerva and the blood and the maze of tubes.

Vivian had kicked off her shoes and was sitting on Minerva's bed sorting the contents of her tote bag—an array of lipsticks, comb, mirror, pens, matches, scraps of paper. "How about a game of double solitaire? I just found these cards in my bag."

152

"No," Lee said abruptly, "I couldn't possibly!" How could Viv be so relaxed? "I doubt that they want anyone to sit on the bed, by the way." Her voice had a sharp edge to it.

"Why? Who's hurting anything?" She had very little regard for rules and regulations..

The nurse appeared in the doorway. "Miss Wingate is in the recovery room now," she said briskly. "They will bring her to the room after she comes out of the anesthesia."

"How long will that be?" Lee asked. "How is she?"

"Anywhere from thirty minutes to an hour or more, depending on the type of anesthesia and how she reacts to it." The nurse spoke in a clipped monotone. "As to her condition, I have no specific information. You will have to check with the doctor." Turning to Vivian, she said firmly, "Perhaps you are not aware that visitors are requested to sit in the chairs provided, not on the beds."

"I wasn't aware of that rule." Unruffled, Vivian smiled, gathered up her things, and hopped off the bed.

As the nurse left the room, Vivian made a face at her back. "She's probably afraid to smile," she said with a light laugh, "afraid her mask might crack."

Lee sat down in a chair facing the door. She tried once again to read her book, *An American Childhood,* but kept rereading the same paragraph, unable to concentrate. She chewed nervously at a hangnail that started to bleed.

After another thirty minutes, Lee had just said she was going to check again at the nurses' station, when a young doctor in green surgical gown came to the door. He was slight of build with stubby black hair and deep-set dark eyes. "Which one is the sister?" he asked, glancing from one to the other.

"I am," Lee said quickly, standing up and extending her hand. "Lee Cranford." As they shook hands, she felt his eyes studying her. Was he sizing her up as an unlikely prospect for Minerva's sister? They had agreed ahead of time that she would be listed that way to avoid bureaucratic hassles. But Lee could feel her face flushing with this simple violation of the truth. Breaking rules did not come as easily for her as for Vivian. Abiding by the law had been rigorously instilled in her—even the simplest of warnings, such as *Keep Off the Grass*.

"I'm Dr. Gomez, surgical assistant to Dr. Johnson. She asked me to stop by now, and she will talk to you later."

Vivian walked over and extended her hand. "And I'm Vivian Gould, Minerva's first cousin."

"Is she all right—my sister?" Lee asked. Her voice, faint and quavery, seemed to be coming from someone else.

"Yes, she's doing fine." He smiled at her, but there was something guarded in his manner.

"The operation . . . " Lee hesitated . . . "How did it go? I mean, did you get it all . . . the cancer?"

"Well, I think Dr. Johnson wants to explain the procedure to you, along with her recommendations."

Lee felt another spasm of the fear that had gripped her throughout the day. What was he trying to tell her—or trying to hide? "I have to know." Her voice was her own again. "Please tell me."

"She's out of the anesthesia, though still groggy. Her general condition is quite satisfactory."

"That's a relief!" Vivian said. She was standing by Lee now, her arm around her waist.

"But about the operation . . . " Lee said. "Is everything all right?"

He paused, as if deciding how much to tell. "Well, we found the area of malignancy to be more extensive than expected, and the biopsy indicated the cell changes were somewhat further advanced." He adjusted the tie of his gown as he spoke. "But the hysterectomy itself went well." Another pause. "There was some hemorrhaging shortly after we began, but it was controlled. Your sister is in remarkably good physical shape for a woman of her age."

Lee flinched. Hemorrhaging . . . . Her ghastly image might have been close to the truth.

"We gave her a transfusion, to be on the safe side."

The *safe* side? What about the chance of hepatitis or, worse still, the AIDS virus? They had discussed the possibility of a transfusion, and Minerva wanted to give some of her own blood to be set aside for that purpose, but there was not a long enough

154

interval. And Lee, who had the same blood type, offered to donate some to be stored for Minerva. But the blood bank did not store specific blood for specific people. How she hated these institutions!

"How soon will Minerva be back in the room?" Vivian asked.

"She should be along in a few minutes. They're probably just waiting for an attendant." He started toward the door, then turned. "Dr. Johnson will be up shortly." And, as if sensing Lee's fears, he added, "Don't worry now. She's going to do fine." Shaking hands with both women, he made his exit.

18

"What did Dr. Johnson tell you about the operation?" Minerva said. She was propped up in bed after a short walk down the hall. Her face had good color today, enhanced by the soft rose of Elizabeth's bed-jacket. A remarkable contrast to the day before, when they finally brought her back from the recovery room, her face ghost-pale with a greenish tinge. Lee, in a frenzy of worry, had been on the verge of collapse. But Vivian had efficiently taken over the bedside care, giving Minerva small sips of water, then persuading the nurse to bring her a cup of tea which she held for her to drink. She had insisted that Lee stay in the easy chair and relax. Later Dr. Johnson had come by and talked to Lee in the lounge.

"Well, she didn't go into much detail." Lee was sitting in a straight chair near the bed, her eyes focused on the little seed-pod tapestry, wondering how much she should tell. "Have you talked to her?"

"She was in to see me this morning."

"And?" Lee studied Minerva's face. How much did she know?

"She told me the surgery went well, though it took longer than expected. Said she would discuss her follow-up recommendations with me in a day or two." Minerva paused. "But I had the distinct impression she wasn't telling me the whole story."

Lee walked over to the window, rearranging the potted plants on the sill to avoid looking directly at Minerva. "Well, I don't know that I should be talking about things she plans to explain later." She pulled a withered blossom off the tuberous begonia.

"Let's not play games, Lee." Minerva's face was serious. "We've always been honest with each other. Precisely what did she tell you?"

"Well, as I said, she was not too communicative. She explained that the operation took longer because of the location of the cancer."

"Is that all?"

"Just about." Lee pressed her finger into the soil of the pink azalea plant. "This needs water. They dry out so fast in the hospital air." She turned abruptly and went into the adjoining bathroom for a cup of water which she poured into the pot. "I'd better get some more for this flower arrangement too."

"Lee, please sit down and stop puttering with those plants."

She returned to her chair. She could feel Minerva's eyes searching her face.

"What is it you're not telling me?"

"Well, she said something about it being farther advanced than the initial biopsy indicated."

"Anything else?" Minerva's voice was calm, low-pitched.

"Listen, Min, I really think she should be telling you all this, not me. She's the doctor, you know, and she can use all the proper terminology.

"No, don't give me that excuse." Their eyes met. Then Lee looked away. "I know you used to be a medical secretary. You're familiar with all those terms. Tell me the truth, Lee." Her voice was louder now, with the sharpness of steel.

"Well it's not a disaster," Lee said softly. "Nothing that can't be taken care of quite adequately with a little radiation."

"Oh, so that's it." Minerva leaned back against the pillow, her face grave.

"I didn't want to have to tell you this." Lee reached over and took her hand, holding it in both of hers. "I wanted the operation to clean it all out—nothing more to worry about." She paused, noticing the way the sun glinted against the red begonia blossoms and slanted across the side of Minerva's face. "Everything perfect, that's what I wanted for you, Min."

157

"Things don't always go the way we want," Minerva said quietly.

"Dr. Johnson said the radiation was really just a safety measure. So I don't think it's anything to fret too much about." Lee was trying to keep her voice light.

"Did she mention how long the treatments would take? I mean, how many treatments over what time span?"

"This is really something she will want to discuss with you, Min, I'm sure."

"Do stop being so evasive, Lee. The less you tell me, the more I'll worry. The darkness of the unknown—that's the hardest to face. As a child, I used to lie in bed at night watching the shadows of tree branches against the wall, cast by the streetlight, imagining all sorts of spooky things about them. I would be afraid to hang my hands or feet over the side of the bed for fear some unknown creature would grab them." She smiled at the memory.

"I shouldn't have said anything at all."

"If you hadn't, I wouldn't have forgiven you." Minerva reached out and gave Lee's hand a squeeze..

"Well, I'm hazy on the details. But I believe she said something about five days a week for maybe five or six weeks—something to that effect."

Minerva's smooth forehead crinkled into a worried frown. "That seems like a tremendous amount of radiation!"

"Perhaps you could ask her about doing less." Lee shared Minerva's aversion for excess medication, let alone radiation. Both of them always refused to have as much as a dental x-ray without being convinced it was essential. "Surely they wouldn't prescribe more than necessary." But she wondered if the doctors were indeed as precise as they might be. It was just not fair— such an ordeal for Minerva who had always taken such good care of herself, having to subject her body to those deadly rays. There were so many horror tales about side effects. Life seemed little more than a grotesque gamble—a toss of the dice by that Indifferent Mastermind of the Cosmos. What was the use of prayer or rituals or anything else?

Lee pulled a pen and small pad of paper from her bag and handed them to Minerva. "Maybe you'd like to make a list of questions for Dr. Johnson."

Minerva laid the pad and pen on the bedside table, then leaned back and closed her eyes, as if shutting out the suggestion.

"I don't want to tire you, Min. Would you like to take a little nap?" Today was clearly not the time to face such a formidable procedure.

"No, I want to talk this out." She opened her eyes, opalescent in the sunlight, and looked over at Lee. Her mouth was drawn into a tight line, intensifying the angles of her face.

Such a strong, beautiful face. Why was this happening to her? A pointless question. If there was indeed a God capable of answering, Lee had to acknowledge the capricious nature of his role as dispassionate Puzzlemaker who did not care which piece might come up next in this absurd scheme of things.

"I'm not at all sure I want to go through with the radiation," Minerva said abruptly. She was gazing out the window. "Maybe I'll just take my chances with the surgery."

Lee remained silent, wondering how to respond. It was typical of Minerva to say this. Maybe she was right. But despite her recent interest in alternative medicine, Lee retained a certain respect for traditional doctors and the conventional scientific approach—far from flawless but perhaps less risky than the rash of strange practitioners cropping up everywhere. "It's a tough decision," she said at last.

"What would you do if you were me?"

Lee sat staring at the intravenous fluid dripping through the tube into Minerva's arm. She felt the weight of her response. "I don't think you should be too hasty in rejecting the radiation. I imagine they've improved their techniques, probably their equipment too." Maybe so . . . but how could she know? Was she willing to put blind faith in technology? But refusing radiation could lead to death. Lee reached over and straightened Minerva's pillow, pushing back a lock of tousled white hair and stroking her forehead. "Of course, the ultimate decision is up to you. Before deciding, why don't you have a serious talk with the doctor?"

"I have a feeling she'll try to talk me into it. I must decide ahead of time. And I need your help, Lee."

"Then my advice is to go ahead and get it behind you." No

159

sooner had she said the words than she regretted it. What if Min suffered terrible complications from the radiation—a bowel disorder or incontinence or blood deficiency? She would never forgive herself. Lee glanced at Minerva whose eyes penetrated hers.

"Do you really mean that?"

"Well, I *think* so. You asked me what *I* would do. But what I would do is not necessarily what you ought to do. Don't put this burden on me, Min." Lee looked away. "It has to be your choice." Her voice sounded wavery, unsure. Her head felt as if some giant were pounding on it with a mallet.

The late afternoon sun had shifted away from the red begonia, away from Minerva's face now in the shadows, taking on a faint lavender tinge. But her contours seemed softer, more relaxed. "You're right, Lee," she said after a long interval of silence. "It has to be my own decision. And my inclination is to refuse anything that will do further violence to my body." Her fingers were toying with the edging on her bedjacket, but her eyes were focused on Lee. Her voice was resolute. "I think I'll try the holistic approach. There's supposed to be a good practitioner up island. And I can do some imaging on my own. Perhaps we could do another healing ritual."

"Oh no, I couldn't do that, Min!" Lee said quickly. "Not with so much hinging on it. I wouldn't know how." It was not as if she were a bona fide *green witch,* accomplished in the healing arts of *wicca.* That was totally out of her realm.

"Well, we don't need to deal with all that now." Her voice had grown stronger—the old Minerva taking charge of her life. "I'll talk over my decision with Dr. Johnson, but I doubt that she can persuade me to change my mind."

The pounding in Lee's head had accelerated. Her throat felt like sandpaper. She wanted to cry out, *Don't be so hasty!* But she had insisted it was Minerva's decision to make. Now she must accept it. She got up hastily and went into the bathroom for a paper cup and some water.

Minerva turned sideways, propping herself up on her elbow. "Now, let's talk about more pleasant matters—your book of poems, for instance. How is it going, Lee? I've been so wrapped up in all this, I've lost track."

"It's not exactly going anywhere at the moment."

"What is that supposed to mean?"

"Well, the book just doesn't seem all that important right now." Lee drained the last drops from the paper cup and folded it nervously into sections, not meeting Minerva's gaze.

"Not important? Don't be ridiculous, Lee! You know how hard you've been working on it all these months. Of course it's important. What's your timetable?"

"I don't really know. Everything is off schedule."

"You must have some sort of deadline. You'll need the book for your reading at Canio's. Isn't that coming up soon?"

"About a month from now. But I think I'll cancel it." She spoke in a monotone, still not looking at Minerva. "I can't cope with poetry these days."

"Why, Lee Cranford, how can you say that? You've been talking about that reading since last fall." Her voice reflected her disbelief.

"Well, it's such a hassle, trying to get the book finished in time for the reading—all those pesky details for the printer and everything. I just haven't felt like dealing with them."

"I thought you sent the proofs off last month."

"I did. But there were some last-minute additions on the publication credits and a change in the wording for a couple of poems, and I was waiting on a blurb which just arrived a few days ago from one of the poets, and the cover design needed some modifications, and the printer couldn't find the right ink color, and my photo for the back cover didn't have enough contrast for printing, and . . . well, the final decisions are endless. It just doesn't seem particularly relevant now anyway."

"You can't mean that!" Minerva said sternly.

Lee sat watching the slow drip-drip-drip of fluid through the intravenous tube, wishing Min would not press her on this. The book, of course, had been very special to her from the moment she started compiling it nearly a year ago—her best poems assembled and reassembled with painstaking care. And it was still special, her firstborn, in a sense. But lately all thoughts of poetry were dwarfed by the magnitude of Minerva's illness. But how could she explain it without appearing to blame her?

"How long will it take to print the books, once you supply the printer with everything?"

Lee shrugged her shoulders and stared out the window. "Forget it, Min. After we get through with all this medical stuff, I'll try to pick up where I left off."

"I'll do no such thing!" Minerva's voice was firm. "Surely that printer must have given you some idea of the necessary time."

"I believe he said to allow a couple of weeks."

"Well, then, you can still make it!" Minerva said emphatically.

"It would take a miracle."

"Knowing you, I imagine a good night's work would clear up everything. You could very likely send it out in a day or so. Why don't you stay home from the hospital tomorrow? Bernie's coming over. She can do the honors while you take care of all those knotty details."

"Well, even if the book were to be completed in time, which I doubt, I'm not sure I'm up to doing a reading right now."

"What has come over you, Lee?"

"I'll be all right. Probably haven't quite got over the strain of yesterday." Her head still ached, and a dull pain radiated from her knee down her leg. She wished she could curl up in a corner somewhere out of everyone's sight and sleep away all thoughts of cancer, metastasis, and death, eradicate all of it, dream of being in a canoe on an Adirondack lake, floating along without any decisions to make except when to go ashore or when to take a swim . . . the way life had been years ago, the freedom she yearned for now.

"Lee, you must not allow yourself to become trapped in the martyr role. I know how much your writing means to you." Minerva was gazing at her with great tenderness. "I appreciate all you have done to help me through this, but the worst is probably over now."

"I hope so!" She leaned over and took Minerva's hand. Tears were welling up in her eyes. She couldn't hide them.

"My recovery will take some time. You shouldn't let it interfere with your writing."

Lee reached for a tissue on the bedstand and wiped her eyes.

She watched the jagged pattern of light and shadow against the far wall, resembling a ziggurat. "I mustn't tire you, Min." She stood up and stretched. "Let me lower your bed so you can rest. Perhaps I'll go downstairs and pick up a sandwich."

"Not that I want to get rid of you, Lee, but why don't you go on home now and concentrate on the finishing touches of the book."

Lee smiled. "You won't give up, will you?"

"I can be just as stubborn as you." Minerva laughed her ripply laugh. Then her voice grew serious again. "Promise me you won't give up on the book and the reading?"

After adjusting the spread and the pillows, Lee stood silently by the bed wondering if she dared make a promise she might not be able to keep.

Minerva caught her by the wrist, saying, "I'll not let you go until you promise."

"I'll try."

"That's not exactly a promise, but I suppose it will have to do." Minerva released her wrist.

Lee bent down and kissed her quickly on the cheek then walked across the room, blowing another kiss as she went out the door.

"And don't come back until you have mailed the final corrections!" Minerva called after her.

19

Five kites of rainbow hues swooped and swirled, shimmering in the sunlight, soaring with each gust of wind higher into a sapphirine sky. The blue one, resembling an eagle, appeared to be in pursuit of the red one, bat-shaped, with long twirling tail. Just below fluttered a yellow dragonfly and a giant butterfly with purple wings. A paper pyramid with panels of red, orange, and green hovered above the others, making a humming sound. Some mystical power seemed to propel them on their upward spiral, the freedom of these gaudy ornaments of the sky limited only by five slender strings, barely visible.

On the beach below, the five women holding the strings rivaled the kites with their antic behavior and colorful clothing. Ada, her full blue skirt flapping against her legs and her long braid lifted by the wind, stood barefoot in the sand. When her kite lurched ahead, she would follow it with uneven gait, having tossed aside her cane. Smiling broadly, she pointed toward the multicolored pyramid. "You see which one is leading the procession, don't you?"

"Some of us don't happen to be artists with a flair for this sort of thing," Vivian said, leaping over the sand to catch up with her. "So why spend time trying to make them when you can buy them just about anywhere?" The sun had tinted her fair skin a bright pink, almost matching her coral two-piece bathing suit and the striped scarf tying back her curls.

"Mine was cheaper," Ada said.

"But think of all the time you wasted on it."

"Wasted! How about the time you spend watching those stupid game shows?"

"I didn't intend to start an argument," Vivian said lightly. "It's too beautiful a day for that." She glanced over her shoulder at Elizabeth, walking briskly to catch up. "Better hurry, Liz. Mine is outflying yours."

"Well, it's not a competition." Elizabeth was breathing heavily from the exertion, her face flushed beneath her beige straw hat, an extraordinary hat that only someone like Elizabeth could wear, its broad brim decorated with a large cluster of artificial cherries. The paisley skirt of her sundress fluttered gracefully with each step. She looked up at the kite tugging at her string, an eagle she had fashioned from wire and bright blue plastic bags from the *New York Times*. Vivian's red bat dipped and twirled several kite-lengths ahead of it.

"You look tired, Liz. Perhaps we should rest a few minutes," Vivian said. "The kites will fly without any help from us, if the wind keeps blowing and we hang on to the strings."

"No, I'm fine. Just a bit out of breath." The three women continued down the beach at a slower pace.

Lee had stayed back a short distance with Minerva who was seated in a canvas chair, partially shaded by a striped beach umbrella. They showed no concern over the fact that their two kites, the dragonfly and butterfly, were lagging behind the others. Occasionally as they talked, they would glance up at them. In the three weeks since her surgery Minerva had made steady progress. Despite tiring easily, she was clearly enjoying this afternoon at the beach. She was comfortably dressed in a loose-woven outfit of teal blue, knee-length pants with sleeveless low-necked top. Stretching out in the chair, she dug her toes into the damp sand. "How delightful it feels!" she said. "I had no idea something as simple as flying a kite could wipe out the troubles of the world, not to mention my own."

Lee nodded, gazing up at their two kites diving and twisting almost as if choreographed. Unfolding the other chair, she sat down next to Minerva. Though she was wearing a bathing suit beneath her shorts and T-shirt, Lee had decided not to go in the water. She and Matt used to dive into the surf and jump with the waves, braving the roughest of waters. With him at her side, it had seemed easy. But after his death she had lost her courage. She would only go in when the sea was relatively calm—today it was quite turbulent. The sound of the waves breaking and pounding against the shore took her back to Myrtle beach where she and Matt had spent a glorious three days in the summer of '44 when he got a pass from the air base. One entire night they slept beneath the stars, wrapped together in a blanket on the sand. Why did these memories keep crowding her today—at such a different point in her life? "I love this salt air!" she said, taking a deep breath.

"It makes me sleepy," Minerva said with a yawn.

"Do you want me to hang on to your kite while you take a nap?"

"No, I hate to waste time sleeping. It's such a precious commodity, time . . . ." Her voice trailed off into the wind.

Lee nodded again. Was Minerva thinking about the unspoken—how limited her own might be? Strange how everything always seemed to gravitate to time and its relentless passage, even here surrounded by this wild beauty. She closed her eyes and leaned back in the chair, listening to the roar of the surf, feeling the salt spray on her face.

Minerva nudged her arm, pointing to their two kites which had drifted far behind the others. "See how they glide along so smoothly, almost as if self-propelled?"

"The other three are getting smaller and smaller," Lee said. "Little rainbow splotches darting around up there." Shading her eyes against the sun, she suddenly noticed a cluster of black particles like tiny gnats. She tried to brush them away, but they did not disappear. Quickly she closed her eyes for a moment, then opened them. The black specks were still there when she looked out toward the sky or the bright sand—floating wildly about like a blizzard in one of those small glass globes you shake to make a snow scene, only this was a miniature storm of cinders inside her eye. She tried closing first one eye, then the other, determining that it was her left eye these ominous black dots had invaded. She could feel her heart pounding. *Don't panic,* she told herself. Perhaps by focusing on the kites she could make the dots disappear. But when she tried to look beyond the dark spots, they partially obstructed her view of the swirling kites. Her left eye—the same eye in which she had noticed strange glints of light for the past two nights. Quick jagged flashes at the far edge of her vision—so fleeting she first thought she was imagining them. Her inclination had been to ignore the whole thing, but the following night, going to her car after dark, she noticed them quite clearly whenever she turned her head to the side—those minute streaks of lightning. Because she did not see them at all during the day, it had been easy to forget about them. But now these weird specks . . . . Might they somehow be related to the bright flashes? She shut her eyes again, but as soon as she opened them, there they were, that swarm of dark speckles dancing against the glare of sand and sea, in vivid contrast to the multicolored kites dotting the sky.

"What are you day-dreaming about, Lee? You seemed miles away."

"Nothing in particular."

Minerva dug her feet deeper in the sand. "I'd like to throw away my shoes and go barefoot the rest of the summer. It's good for the feet—massages important pressure points."

Lee sat gazing up at their kites darting about in the sunlight, intermingled now with a multitude of the dark flecks.

"Do you happen to have a pencil and some paper?" Minerva asked.

Lee rummaged around in her tote bag and pulled out a note pad and pen, handing them to Minerva who sat holding the pen and paper, staring toward the ocean.

"Now it's my turn to ask what you are day-dreaming about," Lee said.

"I'm trying to think of an appropriate message to send up."

"A message?"

"Didn't you ever do that as a child?" Minerva tore off a sheet of paper and folded it into a small square. "You just take the paper like this, put it on your string, and it will deliver a message to your kite.

"Sounds like magic."

"I suppose it's the wind or vibrations or something that carries it up. Shall we try it?"

"Why not?"

"Here, you can write a message too." Minerva handed her the pad and pen. "I'm still thinking."

Lee doodled scrolled designs around the edge of the paper, frowning in concentration. Finally she sketched a stick figure of herself looking up at the butterfly kite, her hand to her mouth shouting, *WHY?* Then she folded the paper.

"Aren't you going to show me your message?"

Lee shook her head. "Messages to kites are supposed to be kept secret, just like wishing on a star."

"I thought you said you never did a kite message before."

"I did. I mean, I did say I didn't. But my intuition tells me it should not be revealed to anybody or anything but the kite."

Minerva looked at her with a quizzical smile for a moment, then took the paper and pen, quickly writing a few words and folding the paper. "Mine is a secret too," she said.

"Now, how do we get them on the strings?"

"Do you have any scotch tape? We could tear a little slit and then patch it together."

"I have a Band-aid."

"That would do. Is there anything you *don't* have in that bag?"

Lee laughed. "I guess it's my early Girl Scout training. Can't seem to shake it."

Together they attached their messages to the strings and watched them climb slowly upward.

The other women were headed back now, pulling in their kites as they walked. Lee could hear their voices, but their words were swallowed up in the sound of the surf. Vivian led the way, close to the water's edge, splashing her feet as she walked. Ada followed, limping slightly, and then came Elizabeth, stumbling through the sand, her sandals tucked under one arm. The kites twisted and gyrated as if rebelling against their return to the earth.

"It seems a pity to make them come down, take away their freedom," Lee said.

"I know," Minerva replied. "But they're not really free. It's

168

only an illusion. We have control over them."

"Sort of like the Presbyterian doctrine of Predestination and Free Will." It had always perturbed and sometimes angered Lee, this contradictory concept inculcated in her impressionable young mind by the church, that you were free to make your own choices, but a true Christian would, of course, choose to do the Will of an omniscient God who had already determined how your life would turn out before you even started living it. This had never made sense to her, and eventually she had rejected the idea. Freedom, by its very definition, indicated that you could make decisions without external control, not accountable to any higher Power.

She smiled, remembering how this realization had pulled her out of the abyss of despair, guilt, and self-pity she had plunged into after Matt's death. A university drama course she was taking at the time had led her to Sartre's *The Flies,* contemporary version of the *Oresteia.* A passage near the end of the play drastically changed her entire outlook. Zeus is explaining to King Aegistheus the dangers of letting his subjects find out the *dark secret*—the knowledge that they are free. *Once freedom lights its beacon in a man's heart,* he says, *the gods are powerless against him.* It was for Lee a kind of epiphany. She could still remember her profound sense of joy upon reading those lines, how she sat at her desk reading and rereading that page. *Yes,* she had told herself, *enough of this mourning and moping around, brooding over what Fate might have in store. It's time for me to take control.* Miraculously she felt, Sartre's bold existential doctrine of freedom had offered her a means of survival, encouraging her to choose her way rather than waiting for life to determine it for her. Not that she invariably chose wisely, but at least she chose, unhampered by that self-defeating shadow of Predestination and the amorphous Will of God.

They watched their two kites darting first one direction then the other as the wind shifted, tugging at the strings to climb higher. Such fragile beauty, tethered only by two slender strings.

"Let's stop playing God and free them all the way," Lee said. She fished around in her bag and found a small pocketknife which she held out to Minerva. "What do you say, Min?"

"Not a bad idea." Taking the knife, she cut the string, then

169

handed it back to Lee who quickly severed hers.

Minerva draped her arm around Lee's shoulder as they silently watched the yellow dragonfly and the purple-winged butterfly careening madly for a moment, then plunging earthward, freed from the tension of their strings and the hands which had allowed them to fly.

20

Oblivious to the outer darkness, the oppressive heat, and the steady hum of the attic fan, Lee sat at her writing table trying to decipher one of her poems through a flurry of black specks. In the glare of the lamp against the white page they seemed even darker and more numerous than before. She had not particularly noticed them last night after they came home from the beach, too tired to read or do anything requiring close vision. But tonight, with less than forty-eight hours before the book party at Canio's, she was under pressure to make her selection of poems to read.

Shoving aside the disorderly pile of papers, she picked up her book of poems and held it an arm's length to admire the cover, multicolored beach stones against a beige background with the title, *Earth Stones,* superimposed in strong black letters, and beneath that, *Poems by Lee Cranford.* Rubbing her fingers over its rough texture, she tried to recreate the giddy joy she had felt when she first opened the carton of books . . . but that was before the invasion of the black particles.

She leaned her head on her arms, dozing off momentarily. Awaking with a start, she sat up and propped her chin on her hand, trying to fight off the drowsiness. Since most of the poems for the reading would come from her book, she should choose them first. Opening the book at random, she began reading a poem. But the sinister black flecks intruded. She was gripped by panic. Tomorrow perhaps she should call the eye doctor. But he might tell her not to use her eyes—or put her in the hospital for tests. No, she couldn't risk that. After the reading she could check with the doctor. Maybe in the meantime the specks would disappear.

For the next hour she sorted poems, selecting and rejecting, changing her mind . . . and battling the demonic spots, trying to ignore them. Her head was throbbing. Perhaps she would do better in the morning by daylight. She could get up early and have the place to herself before Ada started painting. Sharing the studio with Minerva had worked fairly well these past months. And now that Ada could manage the stairs, Lee had planned to return to her downstairs room. But, with Minerva's operation, it had seemed better for her to move into Lee's room until she got her strength back. Lee had not anticipated the difficulty of sharing this attic space with the loquacious Ada who seemed unaware of how difficult it was to concentrate while someone was talking. Tonight she yearned for the snug security and comfort of her own room.

Abruptly she closed the book of poems, stacked her papers in three neat piles marked: USE, DON'T USE, and UNDECIDED, then walked to the door and flipped off the light.

* * *

The two women sat at the breakfast table enjoying the early morning coolness, the quiet broken only by the chittering of finches and wrens and occasional melodic trills from a mockingbird perched on top of the spruce outside the kitchen window. Minerva sipped her tea, elbows propped on the table, the sleeves of her lavender kimono draped over the edge. Lee was staring vacantly across the room, a spoonful of cereal halfway to her mouth, in suspended animation.

"Lee, is something the matter?"

The spoon clattered into the bowl. "Why do you ask?" Lee could feel a flush coloring her face.

"You seem so . . . so far away. You've hardly said a word since we sat down."

"You know I don't like to talk until I've had my coffee."

172

"But you seem so ... *out of kilter*, as Ada would say. Something is bothering you."

Lee looked away and took a sip of coffee. "Well," she said, staring at the cup, "I'm having a terrible time deciding which poems to read Saturday."

"Are you sure that's all?"

Lee did not answer. She could feel Minerva's sharp gray eyes trying to pierce her protective barrier.

"You have plenty of splendid poems to fill the hour."

"I seem to have lost my confidence. Maybe just an advance case of stage fright." Her laugh sounded forced.

"Nonsense! After some thirty years matching wits with college students and giving lectures before whole auditoriums of people, you would get stage fright over a reading among friends and writers at a local bookstore? I don't believe it!" Minerva set down her cup. "Be honest with me."

"Something seems wrong with my judgment." Lee poured another cup of coffee. "I keep shuffling poems around and can't come to a decision on which ones to use." This was no lie, of course—but if her eyes were functioning, she would be able to concentrate on choices. Maybe it was enough of the truth to satisfy Minerva.

"Well, perhaps I can help." She sounded relieved. "Let's run through some of them. I'll pretend I'm a listener at Canio's—and select those I think would come across best."

"I'll get them." Lee stood up, tying the belt of her blue terrycloth robe, faded with many seasons of wear, but comfortable—like an old favorite book. She brought the poems down from the attic, and the two sat on the porch swing. "Let's hear 'Twilight.'" Minerva handed Lee the poem. "I've always liked it."

"Why don't you read it?" Lee said.

"No, you read it so I can listen—and get the proper effect."

Lee turned to catch the light on her paper. But it was a splotchy mixture of sunlight and shadow. Squinting, she started to read. After a few lines, she stumbled over a word, corrected herself and continued haltingly. The black spots were darting about crazily. Finally she reached the end and tossed the paper aside without looking at Minerva. "I'm tired of that one. I don't think I'll use it."

"Lee, what's the matter? The way you read it—as if it were a foreign language or something." Minerva took her by the shoulders and turned her around so they were facing one another. "What has happened, Lee dear?" Her grip was firm. "This is more serious than merely deciding what poems to read." Her eyes scanned Lee's face.

Lee shut her eyes to avoid the intensity of her gaze.

"Whatever is wrong, you shouldn't keep it all bottled up." Minerva released her grip and leaned back in the swing, one arm around Lee's tense shoulders. She pushed the swing gently with her feet and sat humming her little nameless tune. Lee relaxed into the curve of her arm. She could feel slow tears seeping from her eyes, trickling down her cheeks. Hastily she wiped them away with the back of her hand.

"It has something to do with your eyes, doesn't it?" Minerva said after a few minutes.

Lee nodded. Pulling a tissue from the pocket of her robe, she wiped away fresh tears and blew her nose. "All right, I give up! You're determined to find out, aren't you?"

"What can you expect from a Scorpio?"

"Well . . . . " Lee hesitated, still reluctant to discuss the dark spots, as though naming them would somehow confirm their reality. She took a deep breath . . . "It's these damned little black specks floating around in my left eye. I first noticed them yesterday at the beach." After blurting it out, she felt a strong sense of relief.

"Why didn't you tell me?"

She studied Minerva's face, noting with a start how much thinner it had become, pale in the sunlight, strained. The operation had taken its toll. And if she continued to refuse radiation . . . so fragile . . . . "I didn't want to worry you, Min. You have enough to think about, just getting yourself well."

"You'd better check with the eye doctor right away."

"I figured you would say that." Lee gave the swing a push, listening to the slow squeak of the chains against the hooks. "But I'm not going to the doctor until *after* the reading."

"Lee Cranford, are you out of your mind!" Minerva stopped the swing with her feet and looked directly at her.

174

Lee sat silently untying and retying her robe. Maybe she *was* out of her mind, but she knew she wouldn't risk a visit to the doctor on the day before the reading.

"It might have something to do with your retina, and that could be serious." She continued to look into Lee's eyes, as if probing to see inside and find the problem. "What do they look like, these specks?"

Lee tried to describe the effect of a black snowstorm and the little jagged flashes of light that came with darkness.

"It sounds like more than ordinary floaters. There's probably still time to make an appointment for today if we call right away."

Lee shook her head.

"Why are you being so unreasonable?"

"It's no use, Min, I'm *not* going." Her tone was emphatic. "And I'm *not* being unreasonable. I've invited all these people—I don't even remember everybody I asked, and I don't have an accurate list—and it's been announced in the paper, and Elizabeth has bought all the food for the buffet afterwards. Postponing it at this point would be pure chaos."

"People would understand a medical emergency." Minerva's face was pulled into a worried frown. "Recently I read in the *Times* something about retina problems—such as a little hole or a tear. The symptoms sounded similar to yours."

Pulling away from Minerva, Lee picked up the poems, shuffling through them.

"And if neglected, it could lead to a detached retina."

Lee remained stubbornly silent, gazing up at the blue porch ceiling, thinking about flying the kites, how carefree they had felt at the beach, wishing now she could be one of those kites swooping around in the sky, free from all this worry.

"On the other hand," Minerva's voice intruded, in a lighter, coaxing tone, "maybe it's nothing serious at all. We could go to the doctor today, and he might tell you not to worry. Think how relieved you'd feel."

"If it turns out to be nothing, it would be a waste of valuable time. Anyway, he would dilate my eyes so I couldn't read a word for hours, and he would do all sorts of tests . . . . No, I can't put up with that, not today. My book is too important to me."

175

"Do you want to risk being a blind poet, just for the sake of that book?" Minerva was clearly exasperated now. She shoved her feet on the floor, causing the swing to jerk noisily back and forth on its chains.

A blind poet? Lee shuddered at the thought. Blindness was a state she had never been able to fathom, that all-encompassing darkness, the black density, absence of shades and tones of color . . . the unseen dangers . . . groping around to find the way, needing help for some of the simplest routines, never again seeing the natural beauty she took for granted—the stars, whitecaps on the bay, cloud formations, pine trees, marigolds—and, above all, people, those she loved. No, she did not want to be a blind poet. She looked intently at Minerva as if to memorize every detail, noticing the way her white hair swooped back in waves from her face, softening its angularity, the fine wrinkles texturing her skin, the quizzical mouth, the sun glints in her gray eyes. What would it be like not to see her except through memory and imagination?

Lee recalled how she and the neighborhood children used to ask one another, *Which would you rather be—blind or deaf?* A foolish question in retrospect. Who in her right mind would choose either? With her love for music, she had always resisted any thought of deafness, but blindness she dreaded still more. She remembered how she used to close her eyes to test whether she could find her way around the house, counting steps and establishing familiar pieces of furniture as markers. She even sent away for the braille alphabet which she and her best friend memorized so they could punch out notes to each other in raised dots—their secret code. An unconscious blend of fear and fascination must have stimulated this preoccupation with blindness.

"No, of course I don't want to be a blind poet," she said, turning to Minerva. "But aren't you exaggerating a bit? A slight delay in seeing the doctor doesn't automatically mean blindness." She fingered the heavy chain of the swing. Why couldn't Minerva understand this choice—just as Lee had accepted Minerva's choice about radiation?

The two sat for a few minutes saying nothing, letting the

motion of the swing carry itself, Minerva humming her little tune, the bird songs intensifying, the drone of an occasional small plane or helicopter carrying the city people eastward for the first weekend of summer. Finally Minerva said, "How are you going to read, with those little black things obstructing your vision?"

"I'll manage somehow. A few poems I know by heart. Perhaps I can memorize a few more—just refer to the text when I need to. The longer ones I'll practice today till I'm comfortable with them."

Minerva sighed. "I think you're making a mistake, but I admire your spunk." She picked up some poems. "Let's finish sorting these."

"Thanks, Min." Lee gave her a quick hug.

"Here's your title poem, 'Earth Stones.' Do you want to open the program with that?"

"I'm not sure whether to open or close with it."

"Let me read it aloud. That might help you decide." Leaning back in the swing, Lee closed her eyes, listening to the flow of words in Minerva's crisp New England voice:

Clustered in the small black
enameled tray on my table,
they talk to me,
these multifarious stones
shaped by fire
polished by water, wind
and the weight of time.

One by one I pick them up,
rub my thumb over
their hard smooth surfaces,
hold their glossy coolness
against my cheek, cradle
them in my hand
until they absorb my warmth,
try to translate
their fragmentary messages.

Cloud white and earth brown

beach pebbles
and a free-form red, deep
from ancestral fires, lean against
a pyramidal Amazon stone,
grass green. On the edge —
an oblong, without sheen,
diagonally divided
black and white. Jung wrote
of such a stone symbolizing
the twofold nature of our souls.
Years ago it seemed to be roughly
half and half. Now the dark
creeps into the light
nearly three-quarters, my soul
stone. Alongside, balancing it,
a rose quartz,
translucent, heart-shaped.

"What counts?" I ask
stone by stone.

Lee was smiling now, relaxed. "It will be my final poem. I'll end on that question."

The rest of the morning passed quickly, the two of them looking through the poems, Minerva reading them aloud. A feeling of harmony enveloped her as the program took shape. The tensions and doubts gradually slid away, leaving her confident about tomorrow. She envisioned the colorful bookshop abuzz with the energy generated before a reading, all the chairs filled with an expectant audience, Canio introducing her in his quiet way, with just the right touch of praise and wit, holding up her book for all to see, the applause . . . .

* * *

That night Lee dreamed she was standing at the lectern at Canio's attempting to read her poetry. Some of the words were obliterated, and the ones she could see were all jumbled. Her mind was equally jumbled. The words coming out of her mouth were not those on the page. To her bewilderment, she was reciting little sing-song nursery rhymes: *Mary, Mary, quite contrary, How does your garden grow?* in a voice barely audible. *Louder!* shouted someone at the back of the room. The audience was sparse, only a scattering of people fidgeting in their seats, coughing. Some had left their places . . . looking at books, chatting as if she were not even there, drinking wine. She felt strangely hollow, as if speaking in a vacuum. She could see Elizabeth and John whispering in a corner, Vivian flipping through a newspaper, Minerva crocheting, Ada studying the paintings on the wall . . . someone hurling a book, hitting her in the eye . . . someone else shouting, *This isn't poetry. You must be blind!* Then a barrage of notebooks, pens, pencils, erasers flying through the air, forcing her to duck behind the lectern.

She awoke thrashing about in bed, tangled in the sheets, gasping for breath, calling out, "I'm not a blind poet! Please listen! I'm not! I'm not blind!"

21

Everything was blurred. Lee's eyes refused to focus on her book, *The Accidental Tourist,* brought along to serve as protection against any negative energy from other patients and to calm her own well-concealed fears that always smoldered within her, even upon the most routine visit to a doctor's office. Well-concealed, that is, unless they took her blood pressure, which had a way of shooting up at an alarming rate. This afternoon the minute she walked into this small annex of the hospital laser room, the nurse had put drops in her eye to dilate it, repeating the procedure every few minutes. Lee tried shutting the dilated eye and reading with the other one, but it was too great a strain. She closed her book with a sigh and stared at a painting on the opposite wall. Was it a French Impressionist or her hazy vision? She tried squinting at cartoons in an old *New Yorker* . . . but no use. Why didn't they stock this place with large-print books?

Today her fears were intensified by the way the eye doctor had put her on an emergency status, ahead of other scheduled patients, as soon as she mentioned her symptoms over the phone. That was this morning. He had told her to come to his office immediately, warning her not to bend over or lift anything in the meantime.

Though only a few hours had elapsed, the particulars of the morning office visit were a bit fuzzy. Terrified by the reality of possible blindness, she had not been able to take in all of the doctor's scientific explanations. His examination revealed a small hole in the left retina, that much she knew . . . and then something about the black specks being drops of blood which would gradually disappear . . . and the jagged flashes having to do with a sort of gelatinous stuff moving around or shrinking or some such. That was where he lost her completely. Normally a smiling jovial person, today he looked strangely demonic—sitting there opposite her on his stool, the light strapped to his head, backed by an array of menacing equipment, scowling as he lectured her about the gravity of her condition, the danger of a detached retina, and her foolishness for not calling sooner . . . . After endless talk, he had asked her to meet him at the hospital early in the afternoon for the laser treatment.

Elizabeth, who had rearranged her hospital duties to accompany her, had treated Lee to lunch while they waited for the appointment. John was taking Elizabeth's place today as volunteer cashier. Lee could not help but notice how his lean, serious face lit up when he saw Elizabeth walk in, how she smiled at him and blushed when he complimented her on her outfit, a subdued rose print with scoop neck and full skirt that flattered her figure. Despite her white hair and wrinkles, there was a youthful air about her, especially when with John, that belied her eighty-one years.

During lunch Lee had only been able to pick at her food and take a few sips of coffee. But she was grateful to Elizabeth for driving her there and standing by. Too bad they did not see eye-to-eye on more things. At least the rift following their bitter dispute over witchcraft and the Bible had mended, more or less anyway. But she still resented Elizabeth's attitude about their ritual and regretted her own angry response. She wished she had the power to wipe out the words.

Elizabeth was sitting beside her on the couch in the laser waiting room now, knitting booties for a new great-grandchild in California. Ever so often she would pause to ask Lee how she felt, could she get her a glass of water or would she like her to read something aloud. And Lee would say she was fine, not to worry. She was never able to talk to Elizabeth the way she could to Minerva. And right now she just wanted to be left alone. She concentrated on projecting her mind into the place she had created

for herself as a retreat whenever events became too overwhelming
. . . a small sunny room in a cabin overlooking a mountain lake
bordered by cedars and spruce, the room containing no furniture,
only piles of colorful pillows, and she would sink into their
softness, allowing her tensions to drain away . . . . But today
worrisome thoughts of Elizabeth and John kept invading her
hideaway . . . . They had been going out together a couple of
times a week lately . . . . The old foreboding swept over her.
What if John . . . Lee tried to brush the thought aside, but the
hazy forms of Elizabeth and John persisted—his arm draped
around her shoulder, her face upturned toward his, the two lovers
reclining on her pillows—fading away, then returning. No use
trying to obliterate the image.

That left only the laser, an unknown quantity, to think about.
She shivered, despite the warm stuffiness of the room. If only
Minerva were here . . . she had offered to come, but Lee insisted
that she keep her post-operative appointment for today . . . too
important to postpone. And she still held out the hope that Dr.
Johnson might talk some sense into Minerva. Dear Min . . . not
facing the risk she took through her stubborn refusal of the
radiation . . . . But today Lee must try not to dwell on that. Think
positive thoughts . . . the Book Party last evening . . . its success
and her amazing survival . . . yes, wonder of wonders! Having
come through that unscathed, perhaps she would also survive
the laser.

Leaning back in the couch, Lee closed her eyes to savor the
memory. Canio's Book Shop crowded with people. A smiling Canio
clad in jeans and a black Amnesty International T-shirt, his gray
hair pulled back into a small ponytail, hustling about putting up
more chairs among the maze of bookshelves for the overflow
crowd, the atmosphere electric with anticipation . . . Lee suddenly
panicking, saying to Minerva she doesn't think she can manage,
but Minerva saying firmly, *Of course you can!* Lee focusing her
attention on a painting among those on display—a beach scene
with people in summery pastels against a cheerful blue sea . . .
relaxing with the memory of the salt air and their kites in the
wind, the waves breaking over the sand . . . listening to Canio's
introduction but not hearing a word of it, her heart pounding as

she steps up on the little platform and stands at the lectern, looking out at the faces of her friends, so many of them—Laura and Katherine and several of the other poets, Perry and a cluster of her former students, Bernie, and, of course, Minerva, Ada, Elizabeth, and Vivian, plus a number of summer visitors and Sag Harbor regulars, all waiting expectantly, applauding in response to what Canio has said . . . and now a hushed silence, Lee grasping the lectern to steady herself as she opens with a few words of thanks to Canio and greetings to the audience, words she has carefully rehearsed, her voice hesitant at first, then gaining in strength and volume.

She begins with a few short poems she has memorized, postponing the uncertain moment when she must cope with the black specks and the printed page for the longer poems, feeling now at one with her audience, attentive, listening with an intensity that draws them closer . . . finding, to her amazement, that she is able to read through the specks almost as if they were not there . . . as if she were under some sort of magic spell . . . perhaps related to the silk coat she wears, a gift from Minerva, ordered through Bernie as a surprise—bright purple with vertical sea-green panels and a stylized gold butterfly on the back. Luxuriating in the softness of the silk against her arms, Lee feels suddenly taller than her stocky five foot two—tall and invincible, remembering how Minerva had said the coat would give her power, enhance her words, thinking maybe it was true . . . .

Lee was jolted out of the memory by the nurse's voice calling her name, telling her the doctor was ready for her. She followed haltingly, somewhat off-balance from her blurred vision. Elizabeth put down her knitting to accompany her but was advised not to enter the laser room.

Shaky and fearful, Lee enters the room . . . . It seems to be spinning around, then, to her relief, rights itself, and the nurse is assisting her to a chair surrounded by a cluster of lights and imposing paraphernalia . . . Lee's mind reeling, unable to focus on any one thing . . . sitting here facing a sinister contraption resembling a combination telescope and machine gun . . . nervously clasping and unclasping her hands, sweaty and clammy cold, wondering what happens if the doctor aims wrong . . .

whether the laser beam might blind her with one zap or blow a hole in her brain . . . or who knows what, trying to erase that lingering thought . . . and then the doctor taking a seat at the opposite end of the machine, explaining in meticulous detail what he will do . . . something about fastening the edges of the hole in the retina like stitching around a hole in a piece of fabric—only his stitches will be minute laser burn scars . . . and Lee trying to envision this weird form of needlework in her eye, unable to concentrate on his words, feeling dizzy and wondering what would happen if she fainted dead away . . . no longer listening, only wishing desperately to get it over and done . . . the doctor placing Lee's forehead against a bar for support and her eye against the barrel of the laser gun, cautioning her not to move . . . adjusting the other end of the gun to his eye . . . Lee praying that he have clear vision and a steady hand . . . and then ZAP and a blinding flash of light inside her eye and another and another in rapid succession, ZAP/FLASH, ZAP/FLASH, a myriad of fireworks exploding in her head as the machine shoots its rays on their circuitous journey . . . Lee feeling strangely numb, wondering if it will ever cease . . . wondering how much more she can take . . . and suddenly it is over . . . dazed and motionless, relieved that her eye and brain are still intact . . . the doctor talking about percentages and how lucky she is and warning her not to bump her head or fall or lift anything heavy until the scar tissue forms, and something about taking it easy for a few days, this being a form of surgery . . . and to come back in a week just to play safe . . . and Lee nodding, wondering what he means by playing safe but unable to say anything coherent . . . .

Elizabeth appeared at the door to help her to the car. Lee, completely limp, her legs weak and rubbery, leaned heavily on her, marveling at the steadiness and strength of Elizabeth's arm encircling her waist, still unable to put into words anything of the bizarre experience.

22

Lee had dozed off while reading, propped against the pillows in her bed. Moist with perspiration, she awoke vaguely disoriented wondering momentarily where she was, what day it was. She was not even sure of the time. It felt like morning, but she could tell by the length of the shadows cast by the sun slanting through the open windows that it was late afternoon. Closing her eyes, she tried to focus her mind, but everything was foggy, the way it had been ever since the laser treatment on Monday. Physically, she supposed she was all right. In the dark she could still see the jagged flashes. The doctor had said it would take time. And the black specks were gone except for one small spot—something to do with the hole. It did not particularly bother her. But she felt strangely clumsy and unsure, afraid to move around, afraid of falling or hitting her head and jarring loose the fragile retina. She was not willing to discuss it with anyone, just wanted to be left alone.

It was more than that. No doubt some of it related to her typical pattern of falling into a depression after the completion of any important project, regardless of its degree of success. The letdown, the lack of an immediate goal, would throw her into an indeterminate state of misery for anywhere from a day to a week or more. But she had never felt quite like this. Of course, she had been under great pressure preparing for Canio's along with the strain of Minerva's operation, the question of radiation . . . . Her nerves were frazzled from the start.

Now, plagued with the recurring image of those blinding laser flashes, the sense that she was a hair's breadth from extinction, she was forced to acknowledge her own vulnerability, her mortality. All week she had not been able to shake the feeling. She examined the squiggly pattern of the varicose veins on her legs beneath her short pajamas—the legs of an old woman, yet until now she had never really felt *old*. She was in the habit of saying, "You're only as old as you feel," harboring the comfortable notion that she was *never* going to feel anything but young. How stupidly optimistic she had been!

During the past few days she had secluded herself in her room. Even something as simple as taking a shower seemed hazardous so she had substituted sponge baths or sometimes, like today, not even bothering with that, not bothering to get up at all . . . . But what day was it? Friday? Yes, it must be Friday because yesterday was Thursday, the day she had canceled the NOW board meeting over the objections of Minerva who had suggested it would do her good to get out of the house. Friday— the last day of June. Incredible how one day melted into the other an indistinguishable blur.

Lee glanced about her cluttered room, noting the boxes of books and stacks of papers waiting to be sorted and put in their proper place, her word processor waiting to be connected, her desk piled with mail waiting to be opened—everything in a state of upheaval. After the laser surgery Minerva had insisted that Lee take back her own room to avoid the strain of climbing the stairs, assuring her she no longer needed it and was eager to return to her own space. Lee had limply accepted, allowing the others to move her belongings back. But she could not bring herself to concentrate on rearranging things. Too overwhelming. She felt she was sliding down into a deep funnel from which there was no escape. With each attempt she would slide down a bit farther. She sighed and closed her eyes again, thinking she might rest a bit more before dinnertime.

In the background she could hear the murmur of voices from the living room. Then Vivian's rising above the others, high-pitched and penetrating. "Well, if you ask me, it's not normal, slopping around in her pajamas and robe all day and shutting herself in her room. She needs to see a therapist."

Then Minerva's voice, but it was so low she could not make out the words.

"A day or two maybe—but not the entire week. It's ridiculous." Vivian again.

How could they talk about her this way? They must assume she is asleep. But what right had they to pass judgment? Lee felt the blood rushing to her face.

Now Ada's voice. "I'm getting tired of this moping around, I can tell you!" Then some words Lee was unable to hear—something about "no good reason." Lee could hear the clink of ice rattling in glasses . . . their happy hour, and they had not even called her to join them. Ada still talking. "Her eyesight is perfectly fine . . . ." How could she say these things? Particularly in view of *her* erratic behavior Lee had to contend with when they brought her back from the nursing home.

"Well, I think she brought it on herself." That was Elizabeth. "Too much stress. Always biting off more than she can chew—manipulating everybody in sight to take care of every worthy cause that catches her fancy."

Lee sat hunched on the bed, hugging her knees to her chest, fighting back the tears, straining to hear, yet wanting to screen out the hateful words.

"With Lee," Vivian said with a laugh, "*everything* she encounters is a worthy cause." The others were laughing too.

"How true!" Ada's voice. "Many's the time I've wished she would leave well enough alone, quit dragging us to meetings on everything under the sun—Central America, groundwater pollution, wetlands, justice in the courts, *whatever*." More laughter. "She turns into a fanatic when she gets going."

So that's how they regarded her efforts. She could feel the angry tears welling up in her eyes. She swallowed hard and closed her eyes, wishing she could sink into oblivion. It would serve them right if she did . . . but she was unable to obliterate their words.

"She does tend to splatter herself out a bit." Minerva's voice, clipped and precise. "I do wish, for her sake, she would learn to be more selective. We all have to make choices." Even Minerva,

187

her nearest and dearest, rejecting her.

"And for our sakes too," Elizabeth said. "She can be dreadfully hard to please when she works herself into a state. Nothing suits her. I try my best to be amiable. I declare I do."

Lee listened in disbelief, wiping away the tears with a corner of her pajama top.

"The trouble is, she always thinks her way is *the* way, the *only* way." Ada's voice, sounding annoyed. "And she'll twist your arm until you go along with it."

"Exactly!" said Vivian. "Once she's made up her mind, that's it. She won't listen to anybody else. Or even if she does listen, you know good and well she has already decided."

"Maybe that's the problem," Elizabeth said. "Now she is compelled to acknowledge she can't control everything, that *she* is as much at risk as the rest of us." She paused. "It's too bad she doesn't have some religious faith . . . if she could turn to prayer . . . ."

"I doubt that she would pray." Vivian again. "Except to one of her goddesses maybe. But she doesn't seem interested in pulling herself out of this."

"I'm worried," Minerva said. "It's not at all like Lee to sink into such a funk." She paused. "I'll look in on her, maybe wake her to have a drink with us. It would do her good."

Lee could hear her footsteps approaching. Turning toward the wall, she feigned sleep, not responding when Minerva called her name, breathing slowly and rhythmically until she heard her tiptoeing out the door. Then she propped herself against the pillows again, staring out the casement windows overlooking a spruce tree and an expanse of the bay. Its water sparkled in the late afternoon sun, reflecting a wavery image of sailboats anchored in this sheltered cove. A light breeze ruffled the curtains, bringing a whiff of salt air. The voices droned on, but quieter now, and in her anger, Lee had tuned them out.

Minerva's cat, Ebony, who had been curled up with Patches at the foot of the bed, climbed up on Lee, with a plaintive meow. Lee cradled the cat in her arms. As she stroked the silky fur, Ebony nestled closer, rhythmic purrs vibrating against Lee's chest. "Lucky thing! You never worry about what people think, do you?" The amber eyes blinked at her, then closed as the cat snuggled into the curve of her shoulder.

Lee had no idea how long she had been sitting there, staring vaguely into the distance. Everything had become a blur, rather like her mind, out of focus. She felt totally alone, alienated from the others, from the world. Unwanted, unappreciated, unloved . . . well, perhaps *loved* by Minerva, but probably in much the same way as one would love a troublesome child. "How can I ever face them again?" she murmured. The cat purred a bit louder and snuggled closer. She heard the clock strike five, invading the silence. Suddenly she noticed what appeared to be the form of a woman standing near the window. Or was it simply the movement of curtains in the breeze and a certain play of light and shadow? Now it was moving closer to her. Though it appeared to be just an outline at first, it took on more substance as it approached. A slender woman with erect carriage, wearing a long dark dress trimmed with a tiny white pleated ruffle at the neck. Was it something in her emotional state that brought forth this apparition? Ghosts, she had always thought, would be wispy translucent forms clothed in white trailing gowns. Nothing as concrete and three-dimensional as this. Shutting her eyes tight, she lay quite still, hoping when she opened them the woman would be gone. But she could sense her presence—an indescribable heaviness in the atmosphere. Slowly opening her eyes, she was not surprised to see the woman still standing there, gazing at her through small-rimmed glasses, gray hair parted in the middle, pulled back from the angular face. Where had she seen her before? Lee frowned, trying to remember . . . of course—Grandmother Leandra—the photograph she had seen in the Family Bible. But what was she doing here?

"You ask why I am here?" the voice says. It has the same Midwestern intonation of the rural Missouri relatives Lee remembered from her childhood. But it seems to be just floating around in the air, that voice, not coming from the lips of the woman.

Lee feels the blood pounding in her ears. "Grandmother Leandra?" She hesitates. "Is it really you?" Her throat is so constricted she can barely speak above a whisper.

"Well, that all depends on what you mean by *really.*" The woman is smiling at her. "Please don't be frightened. And let's not be so formal Just call me Leandra. Or . . . you could call me Lee if you prefer. That's how I was known to my close kin and intimate acquaintances."

Lee is silent, startled by the idea of referring to her grandmother by her first name, her own name at that—rather a jolt to her psyche. Her frown deepens . . . but in a sense, through a quirk of time, she has nearly caught up with her in age, putting them more or less in the same generation now. This is the grandmother everyone used to say she resembled in temperament, a certain stubbornness and an irrepressible tendency to collect things, keep diaries and scrapbooks—or, in Lee's case, file folders overflowing with clippings, letters, and other papers. She recalls the hours she has spent through the years reading her grandmother's old diaries with their precise Spencerian script on crumbling yellowed pages, hours eagerly absorbing the thoughts and dreams of that idealistic country school teacher, poring over Leandra's clippings and pictures neatly pasted into bound volumes . . . . Yes, they have more in common than their names. But she feels unprepared to confront that startling image of her at this moment. Ill-at-ease under the steady gaze of the intruder, she tears at a hangnail until it begins to bleed.

Ebony has moved back to the foot of the bed next to Patches. If the cats are aware of this weird presence, they show no fear— merely a certain attitude of alertness, ears tilted slightly forward, eyes turned in the direction of the grandmother.

"But why are you here, in person this way?"

"*In person* might not be quite the right term, but let's not quibble over words."

"What I mean is—you're not a memory like the one of Grandmother Almira holding me on her lap—the memory I experienced during our healing ritual."

"I used to hold you on my lap when you were a baby—such a sweet little tyke," the voice responds, "but you always cried, every time I picked you up." Lee wonders vaguely if Leandra might be jealous of her other grandmother. She feels a twinge of guilt over forgetting to include this grandmother in the ritual.

"You died before I was old enough to remember. I always regretted that."

"I, too, my dear." There was an awkward pause. Then the voice again. "By the way, don't worry about leaving me out of the ritual."

A flush of embarrassment colors Lee's face a dull red. "I'm sorry."

"That's quite all right. Had I been invited, I probably would not have appeared. Things of that nature are not to my liking." Despite the Midwestern twang, her voice has a quiet dignity to it, commanding attention.

"You still haven't told me why you are here now."

"I sensed that you needed me." Lee feels a tingling in her shoulder, as if someone has reached out and touched her gently, although she has not discerned any movement on the part of the woman.

"They said such dreadful things!" Lee replies in a quavery whisper.

"Don't let it get you down, Lee dear," the voice says.

"How will I ever be able to face them again?" She reaches for a tissue on the bedside table and wipes her eyes.

"I know. I know. It did sound a bit cruel to me as well."

"How do you know what they said?"

The voice pauses but does not answer her question. "Perhaps one should consider it in context."

"I don't understand." Lee hugs her knees against her chest and stares hard at the grandmother.

"In the context of your recent behavior which, if I may say so, has been a trifle peculiar these past few days."

"Please, Grand . . . ah . . . Leandra, don't you start in on me too."

"My only intention is to help you break free from this negative state of mind." Her form has moved over to the rocking chair now and sits there rocking ever so slightly.

It's no use." Lee closes her eyes, wishing this woman would quit prodding her.

"You wish I would disappear, don't you?"

191

Lee nods her head, eyes still closed.

"But I don't intend to depart until we set things straight." The voice is firm. "All you have to do is go out there, head high, chin up, and talk things out."

"I can't do that." Lee sniffles and blows her nose.

"Of course you can, Lee dear." The voice is more gentle now. "We Bartons don't give up that easily."

Lee sits hunched against the pillows staring at the woman in the rocking chair. "I can't believe we're having this conversation," she says finally.

"You still have much to learn." The figure seems to be blending into the rocking chair. "Mercy sakes, I'm afraid I'm running out of time." The voice is growing dimmer.

"But wait, Leandra, I still need help. I don't know what to say to them."

The voice is barely audible now. "You will know when the time comes."

Lee looks at the chair, still gently rocking though its occupant has vanished. A strong sense of her presence remains. Uncanny how she knew exactly what everyone said. Had she been there, invisible, all along?

Lee had always felt cheated by never knowing this grandmother, cheated either because she died too soon or Lee was born too late. Now their lives appeared to be more intertwined than she realized. Years ago when Lee had decided to drop the *Mary* from her name, she had no idea her grandmother had also shortened her name to *Lee*. But she remembered the way folks used to say she had Leandra's eyes — hazel, deepset and serious, the same brooding mouth with a slight downward turn, a mouth that occasionally could break into a generous smile brightening the otherwise solemn face . . . Leandra had been smiling this afternoon. She was much more appealing in reality than in those rigid old photos. Wait a minute . . . *reality?* What was she saying? The person she had just seen, or thought she had seen, could not, in the wildest stretch of imagination, be described as *real.* Or could she?

Lee felt a sense of peace from within, linking her in some inexplicable way to that vague outer realm for which she could find no adequate word . . . . She relaxed against the pillow for a few minutes trying to define the feeling. Giving a long, luxurious stretch, she realized, to her amazement, she was smiling. If she hurried she could take a shower, get dressed, and join the others for dinner. But what would she say to them? Never mind. "We'll just play it by ear," she said aloud, glancing over at the rocking chair, now motionless.

23

"Tell me something, Min," Lee paused from her apple slicing to push a lock of hair away from her eyes with the back of her hand.

"Tell you what?" Minerva was sitting at the dropleaf table in the center of the kitchen flipping through the latest *New Yorker*, reading aloud an occasional editorial comment.

"Do you believe in ghosts?" Lee turned away from the counter, her eyes fixed intently on Minerva's face.

"I've never seen one, if that's what you mean." She put aside the magazine and leaned forward, elbows propped on the table.

"Not whether you've *seen* one. Whether you *believe* in them. You don't necessarily have to see something to believe in a particular concept do you?" Lee turned back to the apples and continued slicing them into a pie pan.

"Well, that all depends. In your case, being from Missouri the Show-me State, I suspect you wouldn't believe in anything you couldn't actually see with your own eyes." Warm July sunlight slanted through casement windows on the worn surface of a massive chopping block extending the length of the counter and reflected in the row of pewter trays and mugs on the shelf above. Frowning, Lee considered just how much of Friday's encounter with Grandmother Leandra she should tell Minerva. She felt an urge to talk it over, find a logical explanation. But trying to explain a visit from someone, dead for nearly seventy years . . . no, it would sound too ridiculous. She wouldn't even know what to call it. A ghost? *Listen, Min,* she could say, *the other day I had this strange conversation with this ghost who strongly resembled my grandmother.* Maybe she should call it an *imaginary conversation.* That would be more in keeping with Min's philosophy. Whatever she labeled it, she had, in truth, felt the presence of this entity. And by following Leandra's advice, using the direct approach, she had achieved a harmonious re-entry into the group.

Lee remained silent as she peeled and sliced the final apple. Suddenly she felt a jagged pain in her left index finger and saw blood oozing from the cut. "Damn!" she said. She turned on the faucet and held her hand under the cold water, sending a stab of pain through her fingers, once slender and tapered, now knobby with arthritis. Uncanny how closely her hands resembled her mother's. She had never expected those youthful hands to undergo such a metamorphosis. The aging process—slow, insidious, relentless in its destruction. She watched the blood spurt out of her finger and trickle down into the stainless steel sink.

Minerva quickly crossed the room, grabbed a paper towel, dampened it, and wrapped it around the bloody finger. "Hold your hand above your head," She said and walked with long strides into the bathroom, returning with a Band-aid which she applied to the wound. "Now keep your hand up till the bleeding subsides."

"What would I do without you?" Lee arranged the apple slices on the pie dough in the pan with one hand, arching the other high over her head. "I feel like a ballerina or something," she said lightly. But her frown deepened. "Honestly, Min, what is your opinion about ghosts or visitations of some sort?" A sharp image of Grandmother Leandra floated through her mind—erect posture, sharp inquisitive eyes behind tiny silver-rimmed spectacles . . . but how could she explain it to Min? She added another sprinkle of sugar and cinnamon to the apples. The aroma took her back for an instant some sixty years to a Missouri kitchen . . . . She is standing on a stool beside her mother rolling out dough for their pie . . . everything so beautifully safe and secure, Mother always knowing the right answers . . . .

Minerva looked at Lee quizzically. "Are you trying to tell me you think you've seen a ghost?" She reached for an apple slice.

"You do have a vivid imagination, you know. The writer in you, I suppose. Are you sure it was not just a case of the right brain getting carried away?" A smile flickered across her face.

"I don't quite know *what* I'm trying to say. But it wasn't my imagination. I know I saw *something*. I suppose you could call it a ghost—not that I've ever seriously believed such things existed." She turned, facing Minerva. "You haven't answered my question."

"Try putting your hand down and see if the bleeding has stopped." Minerva was sitting at the table now, chin cupped in her hand. "Do I believe in ghosts? Well, I've always enjoyed reading accounts of haunted houses and strange happenings, the supernatural, you know, unexplained psychic phenomena. The idea of some other realm superimposed on our own earthly experience—that sort of thing intrigues me." She glanced at Lee. "But I can't honestly say I believe in ghosts, as such. Tell me what you saw—or think you saw."

"Whatever it was, I did see it. No doubt about that."

"How's your finger, by the way?"

"Seems to be all right." Lee glanced at the band-aid. "But you keep changing the subject. Let me try to explain what happened." She quickly summarized the unexpected appearance of her grandmother and their conversation.

With a perplexed frown, Minerva sat staring at her clasped hands on the table. She rubbed one thumb against the other, as if it might be Aladdin's Lamp.

"I suppose you think I'm out of my mind. You don't believe it could really have happened, do you? I had trouble believing it myself, but I swear it's true." Maybe she should have kept the whole thing to herself. It did sound preposterous, especially when told here in the sunny kitchen while making an apple pie.

"Do you suppose you might have dozed off and dreamed it?"

"This was no dream. I know what I saw and heard." Lee was emphatic. "In fact, it was more than seeing and hearing. I could *sense* her presence—a kind of heaviness in the air. And I think the cats felt it too—not scared, just alert, curious. I tell you, Min, it was spooky." She crossed the room and pulled up a chair beside Minerva. "But very *real*."

How could she convince Min when she could not even identify

196

her own feelings? She pondered the incongruity of the whole thing—including the way she had felt like a child when she was talking to her grandmother, despite her awareness that they were now just over a decade apart, so to speak. Time . . . such a trickster . . . slowly but ever so surely destroying the body while leaving untouched the eternal child hidden inside, occasionally surfacing to shame us or delight or amaze us, according to its whim. Even if she were to surpass her grandmother and live to be ninety-something, she would probably still feel like a child at times. Could it have been the child's voice that had summoned Grandmother Leandra?

"I had such a peaceful feeling after she left . . . or faded out, that is. I realized, to my surprise, that I was feeling *in harmony* again, as you would say, after those horrible days of discord. And I was able to come out of my room to face the group, in spite of all those unpleasant things everyone said about me."

"None of us meant to hurt you." Minerva reached over and gave her a hug.

"I know *you* didn't, Min, but I'm not so sure about the others." Lee had felt a huge sense of relief when the women greeted her warmly as she entered the dining room, showered and dressed for dinner, all of them exclaiming over how nice it was to have her back in circulation. But this did not erase their words. The bitter taste remained.

"Well, getting back to your grandmother," Minerva said, her arm still draped around Lee's shoulder, "the important thing is not so much the reality or unreality of what you experienced but the fact that it enabled you to pull out of your doldrums and brought you back to us." She gave her shoulder a squeeze, then pulled her arm away, as if embarrassed at the show of affection. "I'm glad you've become your old self again."

"Thanks, Min, but I wonder . . . ." They were interrupted by the telephone. Minerva crossed the room and answered it. "For you, Lee." She held her hand over the phone. "Some radio station wanting your reaction to the Supreme Court Webster decision."

So it had happened, the long-awaited decision. Lee hesitated. "What should I say?"

"First you need to find out specifically what the decision was,

197

and take it from there." Minerva handed her the phone. "And if he's too vague, tell him you'll call him back."

It was the news chief of a Riverhead station. As he filled her in on the basic points, Lee felt all the frustration and anger of the battle rekindling in the pit of her stomach. He told her that the decision, though not overturning *Roe v. Wade*, did uphold crucial portions of the Missouri law banning the use of public facilities and public employees for performing abortions. He seemed hazy on the details.

"Well, I'm sadly disappointed." She paused. As a spokesperson for women of the area, she must say more. She struggled for words. "It's not a total defeat, but it's clearly a setback, a restriction of our reproductive freedom, well, not mine, you understand, I'm past that age," she stammered, "I mean women in general." She was botching it. "You're not taping this are you?"

"No, but I was about to." His voice came over the phone crisp, impatient.

"Let me call you back when I come up with something coherent."

"There's no time. We're on the air in five minutes."

Lee took a deep breath. She should have been prepared for this ahead of time. "All right, let's start again."

"We're taping," he said. "We go now to Lee Cranford, president of the local chapter of the National Organization for Women, for her reaction to the Supreme Court decision."

She tried to keep her voice firm. "I'm dismayed and angered by this erosion of women's right to choose. Although *Roe v. Wade* was not overturned, this decision weakens it. And it affects far more than the women of Missouri. It will encourage other states to place restrictions on abortions." Her own state, the root of this. She felt a rush of shame and anger. "It's blatantly unfair! A woman's access to abortion should not be determined by where she happens to live."

"Can you tell us what actions, if any, you intend to take?" His voice seemed to be taunting her, goading her on."

"Well, short of a revolution, I'm not sure at the moment." A revolution? Was that what it might take? "But I'll keep you posted." She hung up the phone and slumped into a nearby chair.

Her face felt flushed, the blood pounding in her ears.

"Oh, God, what a mess! It will be on the air in a couple of minutes."

"You did a fine job, Lee, just fine, considering that you had no advance notice." Minerva gave her an encouraging smile.

"I hate talking to these news people! I felt so awkward, groping for the right words, afraid of saying something altogether wrong. I should have said, *We'll fight this to the bitter end, state by state, if necessary! Uppity Women unite!* That's what I should have said."

"Let's turn on the radio and see how it sounds."

"I'd rather not." Lee stood up abruptly and walked over to the counter. Taking a rolling pin from the wall rack, she commenced vigorously rolling the dough for the top crust. "It's all so depressing . . . forced to fight the battle over and over again."

"But do we have a choice?" Minerva said with a sigh. She sounded tired.

"How are you feeling these days, Min?" Lee felt a stab of guilt. She had been so wrapped up in her own negative state, she had not given much thought to anyone else in the past week.

"Oh, pretty good," Minerva said quickly—almost too quickly. "I don't seem to have my old stamina, but I suppose it will take time."

"Speaking of choices . . . ." Lee hesitated. Was this the right time to ask the unspoken question, left dangling ever since the operation? Then she heard herself blurting it out. "Have you given any more thought to the radiation?"

"Considerable." Minerva was sitting at the table again, flipping the pages of her magazine without looking at them.

"And have you come to any conclusion?"

Minerva closed the magazine, rubbing her hand along the cover. "I think so," she said finally. "I think I'll probably go ahead with it."

Still holding her rolling pin, Lee crossed over to Minerva and gave her a hug. "I think it's a sensible decision." She paused, studying her closely. "But you don't look too happy about it. Are you sure that's what you want?"

Minerva, eyes closed, was resting her forehead on her hand. "No, not at all. It's the opposite of everything I have long believed, or thought I believed in—holistic medicine, nutrition, exercise, natural cures . . . . But I have already violated that with the surgery." She was silent, as if still weighing her decision. "The radiation is another violation, so debilitating. It's a gamble for survival."

"Have you discussed this with Dr. Johnson recently?" Lee felt herself absorbing some of Minerva's irresolution. Maybe for her it was not the right decision after all.

"We had a long talk last week, and she strongly recommends it. I asked her about the risks—you know, destruction of healthy tissue, blood disorders, other side effects." Minerva's voice wavered. "She assured me that the potential benefits far outweigh the possible risks." Minerva was sitting erect now, squinting her eyes the way she did when she was working out a problem. "This morning I phoned the oncologist for an appointment to discuss the details. But there's a feeling of unreality to this whole thing. I can't believe I'm doing it!" She glanced at Lee. "Does that make sense to you?"

Lee nodded. She felt too choked up to say anything. Turning away to avoid Minerva's direct gaze, she noticed the calico cat on the counter sniffing her pie dough. "Damn it, Patches!" Scooping up the startled cat, she threw her to the floor. "You know you don't belong there while I'm cooking!"

"Aren't you being a little hard on her? She often sits there by the window, you know."

"But she doesn't generally stick her nose into my food. These cats are getting spoiled. We should declare the kitchen off limits."

"That will be the day!" Minerva was laughing, a rippling laugh that reached out to Lee compelling her to join in, the tension broken.

"When is your Stony Brook appointment?

"This coming Friday at eleven."

"I'll drive you. Then afterwards . . . " Lee was interrupted by the phone. "Don't answer it," she said to Minerva. "He might be calling back."

But Minerva, who was crossing the room to the phone, picked

it up. "Melanie, hi! Yes, we heard just a few minutes ago. It's dreadful, yes." There was a long pause. "Hold on just a minute, Mel dear." Turning to Lee she said, "Melanie is calling from the college. Says she's *like devastated*! Sounds a bit tearful. Should I invite her over?" Lee nodded. "Come to the house, Mel, as soon as your classes are finished and have dinner with us. We'll talk then."

Lee still marveled over how Elizabeth's genes could have contributed to someone as vivacious and uninhibited as Melanie— so free from the religious and social restraints of her mother and grandmother. Lee delighted in her rebellious spirit. Like a fresh ocean breeze. Every so often she would drop by—just to talk or, as she put it, "to see what the *uppity oldsters* were up to." She had captivated them all. If Lee could have chosen a granddaughter, she would be exactly like Melanie.

The phone rang again. "If it's that newsman," Lee said, "tell him I've gone for the day, completely vanished, and you have no idea where to find me or when I'll be back.

Minerva picked up the phone, then turned to Lee. "It's a reporter from *The Southampton Press*."

"Oh, God! Tell him . . . ."

"I'm not going to tell him anything. You talk to him." She handed the phone to Lee.

Lee responded to the reporter's questions, making essentially the same statement she had given on the radio. When asked what actions might be taken, she dodged the question, saying she was awaiting word from the national office, that whatever President Molly Yard recommended, their chapter would probably take part in it "But I can assure you," she told the reporter as she ended the conversation, "we'll make our voices heard. We'll not give up until we can guarantee for every woman in this country complete control over her body." Her tone was firm. "In the words of Susan B. Anthony, *Never another season of silence!*"

Lee put down the phone and turned to Minerva. "How was that?"

"Splendid, absolutely splendid!" Minerva's gray eyes smiled at her. "Susan B. would be proud of you. And, no doubt, so would your Grandmother Leandra."

24

Vivian's station wagon pulled into the drive with a screech of the brakes. "Lee, where are you?" she called as she came in the door.

"In the kitchen." She was arranging cold cuts on a platter. "Is anything wrong?" Vivian had a tendency for minor accidents which always, according to her, were someone else's stupid fault. Lee sighed, expecting the worst.

"I just heard the news on the way home." She stormed into the kitchen, kicked off her pumps and plopped into a chair, stretching her legs and wriggling her painted toes. "It makes my blood boil! Those pompous men on the Court taking away our rights! Damned male chauvinists!" Her face was flushed a deep pink.

"One of them is a woman." Lee placed a cluster of parsley in the center of the platter. "Much to my dismay."

Vivian reached for a cherry tomato. "Do you mind?" she asked, putting it in her mouth.

"Go easy. I want them in the salad."

"Sorry." She went to the refrigerator, taking out a Coke. "What are you going to do about it, Lee?"

"Do about it? You're the third person who's asked me that today."

"Who were the other two?"

"A Riverhead radio newscaster and a Southampton reporter."

"Hey, not bad! I'll bet you gave them an earful!"

"Not exactly. I avoided saying anything too specific."

Vivian looked disappointed. "Why not? We can't let them get away with this!"

"I'm trying to think things through." After those cutting remarks only last Friday about her worthy causes, what right did Vivian have to expect her to come up with the answers? Although on the surface they had reached a friendly settlement, her resentment still smoldered. She handed Vivian a tray. "How about making yourself useful and carrying some dishes out to the porch? Supper's just about ready."

"Soon as I finish my Coke." She sat fanning herself with her skirt.

Lee was shredding the carrots and chopping the celery for the salad with more vigor than necessary. Ever since the phone calls, she had been brooding over the court decision and its implications. What were they supposed to do now? Start all over again?

Ada entered the kitchen from the back stairway, wiping the moisture from her face with her handkerchief. "It's a scorcher today." She was breathing heavily.

"It's not a good idea for you to come down those steep narrow stairs. You could fall, you know." Lee's annoyance with the Court and Vivian was spilling over on Ada.

Ada, in denim skirt and checkered blouse, flourished her cane like a baton. "Don't worry about me. I'm agile as a mountain goat."

"Well, don't say I didn't warn you," Lee muttered. She sounded like her mother who had constantly warned her about one thing or another.

"What do you think about it, Ada?" Vivian asked.

"Think about what?" Ada was leaning on her cane now.

"The news." Vivian stared at her. "Where have you been? Playing Rip Van Winkle?"

"Where was I? Well, I was on the porch sketching. Then I went upstairs and took a nap. What did I miss?"

"Merely the Supreme Court decision—the one we've been waiting for, the reason we marched in Washington. Get Lee to explain it to you. I don't understand all the shitty details." Vivian walked out of the room balancing the tray of dishes in one hand

and her Coke in the other.

Yes, count on Lee to figure it out . . . . Her head was throbbing. Women were trapped in a giant treadmill, like a bunch of rats, in some cosmic experiment to test human endurance, at the mercy of those patriarchs in their black robes. She didn't want to explain anything to anybody right now.

"Oh, the Supreme Court. How could I forget?" Ada looked over at Lee. "Do you suppose it's senility—like poor dear Mama? She couldn't remember the simplest thing. In one ear and out the other. I can't let that happen to me." She sounded worried.

"Of course, you're not senile. You were simply screening out the world to concentrate on your art. I envy the way you can do that." Lee sighed, remembering calmer times when she could close herself in her room and write for hours without interruption—the exhilaration she felt, watching a pattern of words take shape. Lately her life was too fragmented for that kind of creativity. Would she ever feel whole again? "Come sit down, and I'll tell you all about it." Lee explained the Court decision, based on what she had been able to piece together. "We'll have an early supper on the porch, then catch the evening news. I'm sure Molly Yard will make a statement for National NOW."

Ada snorted. "Molly Yard! She'll have something to say all right. That woman reminds me of a country preacher, booming out those words. But it doesn't make one particle of difference. Remember when we were in Washington, a good half million of us—Molly and everybody making speeches. Did those old geezers on the Court listen? The answer is *NO*. Nobody listens. We might as well keep our mouths shut and go about our business!"

Molly's speeches did tend to be overblown. But Lee respected her zeal for battle, her energy that could put many younger women to shame. And she admired her appearance, white hair pulled back from her strong lined face, the resolute jaw, flashing eyes, her bearing, clearly a woman to be reckoned with. Lee herself never felt that she looked the part of a leader—her short dumpy figure, her aversion for wearing the dresses and heels considered proper attire for women in the public eye. She had put all that aside long ago, focusing now on comfort.

"You're beginning to sound like Sonia Johnson," Lee said to Ada.

"In what way?"

"Your idea that we quit protesting. She says we should stay out of politics, break free from the senseless restrictions of the male establishment. Each of us should live our lives the way we feel is best for us, free ourselves from within. That would be a true revolution."

"Sounds pretty far-fetched to me."

"Perhaps—until you get to know her. She can make anything sound plausible." Lee had first met Sonia at a NOW convention in the early 1980s, shortly after she made headlines because of her excommunication from the Mormon Church, the publication of her book, *From Housewife to Heretic*, and a lengthy fast for the ERA. Despite her voice, a bit too high-pitched, the cadence too fast, she could mesmerize her audience by the intensity of her message. With her whimsical humor, impish face, slender figure casually clad, poised as if for flight, she seemed rather like a feminist Peter Pan.

"Didn't she run for President of the United States at one time? That's political."

"Yes—for the Citizens' Party several years ago—but that was before she formulated this new philosophy."

"Well, maybe Sonia has a point. Protesting gets us nowhere," Ada said.

"Sonia compares women who keep reacting against the patriarchy to puppets, dancing whenever the puppeteers pull their strings. I think it's in her book *Going Out of Our Minds*. If we break loose from the strings, she says the puppeteers could pull and pull, but we would not dance. We would be totally free."

"So, why don't we just free ourselves from the Supreme Court and all their nonsense?" Ada was smiling broadly.

"Cut the strings?" Lee said dubiously. She remembered that sunny, windswept day at the beach when she and Min cut their kite strings—how the kites catapulted to earth. Was it in their power to free themselves?

Lee tried to imagine being that free. No more letters to the editor about groundwater pollution, no forums on landfills, no

205

panels on battered women and hungry children, no rallies for lesbian and gay rights or reproductive choice, no picketing against nuclear disasters, no envelope-stuffing, committee meetings, no yard sales or cocktail benefits. no strategies for candidates, no more networking, however worthy . . . . With a snip of the scissors, she could free herself from all that, say, *I've done my share. It's someone else's turn,* and walk away, carefree, a feather floating in the breeze.

That would go against the grain of everything she believed, back to earliest childhood, perhaps beyond memory—the sense that we have an obligation to try to make the planet a better place, not only for ourselves but those around us and those who come after. Trying to shape it into words, she realized it might sound old-fashioned in today's world—egocentric to imagine that one person could make any real difference. But it was instilled in her—a deep and abiding moral obligation. When an injustice occurred, someone must try to right the wrong—and if she happened to be the someone on the scene, did she have any other choice? Perhaps she had been a slave all these years to an unduly rigid set of beliefs, burdened with excessive guilt if she did not follow through. Had she missed the true joy of freedom?

"Well," Ada repeated, "what do you think about it, Lee? Your mind seems a million miles away."

"I'd like to believe what Sonia says. Though it sounds great in theory, I doubt if it would work." Her voice trailed off in a wispy thread of uncertainty. Her dilemma—Molly Yard exhorting her to rally the troops, Sonia beckoning her toward flyaway freedom, the joy of solitude and time, so little of it remaining in her life span, the sand flowing relentlessly through the glass, ten years perhaps or, with luck, fifteen—time to create her own visions, shape her own words. Closing her eyes, she shielded her face with her hands.

What would Grandmother Leandra advise? Lee focused her energy to transmit a plea for help. Nothing happened. Taking several deep breaths, she tried again, concentrating harder . . . . Suddenly the face . . . gray hair pulled back from the center, deepset eyes behind the rimmed spectacles, the firm mouth . . . *What should I do, Leandra?* The face maintained its steady gaze but gave no reply. Lee was not certain whether it was Leandra this time or just a memory. She did not have the same strong sense of her presence, and the image kept going out of focus, like a TV screen with overlapping channels. *I wish you had given me some clue about communicating before you disappeared last week.* The face came clearly into view momentarily, then vanished. *Please come back.* The face did not reappear, but the word PERSEVERE floated through Lee's mind. A word Leandra might use. But, *persevere* in what direction?

* * *

Just as they were sitting down to supper, they heard Melanie's car, a bright orange Volkswagen Bug of ancient vintage dubbed the Rattletrap. She came bounding onto the porch, her face flushed, sandy hair flying. "Sorry I'm late. At the dorm I got into this humongous argument with Debbie. She can be, like, so pigheaded! She said I shouldn't get so freaked out over the Supreme Court decision because it wouldn't affect us in this state, and I said what about the women in Missouri and don't be too sure about New York because they could change the law here too." She paused to take a breath. "Some people are, like, impossible!" She glanced at the four women sitting around the table. "Where's Grams?"

"She's having dinner with John at the Yacht Club," Minerva said. "We've set a place for you over here by me. Come sit down. We'll watch the news when we finish eating."

"Out with John again? Do you think this is getting serious?" Melanie's face clouded.

"We wouldn't be surprised," Vivian said, arching her eyebrows.

"Why? Don't you like him?" Ada asked Melanie.

"Oh, he's all right. But he seems to be, like, well . . . stuffy. Gramps always, like, kidded around and laughed a lot. A really fun person. But John, like, takes himself so seriously."

Lee had once questioned Melanie about this mutilation of the language, the tendency of young folks to sprinkle their conversations with *like*. Her laughing response had been, "I never thought about *why*. Maybe because it, like, makes more sense—like, softens the reality." Lee was not sure she got the point but saw the futility of pursuing it further. She studied Melanie's expressive face, so intensely earnest. More vulnerable, in a way, than her own generation had been. Then she realized Melanie was speaking to her. "What do you think, Lee?" Her wide-set eyes, iridescent sea-green or blue changing with the light, met Lee's across the table.

"Well, your grandmother still loves your grandfather, I'm sure. She has always said no one could ever take his place." What Lee did not add was that Parker's name seldom came into the conversation in recent weeks. "I think she just finds John an enjoyable companion." Was she saying this to reassure Melanie or delude herself?

"I wouldn't be too sure about that," Vivian countered.

The increasing togetherness of Elizabeth and John continued to nag at Lee like a dull toothache, ever present. Although the five of them had been living here only a year and a half, it was unthinkable that they could be torn apart by some outside force. Their arrangement was far from the harmonious whole she had imagined—but certainly better than living alone.

Minerva changed the subject to Melanie's art classes. During the meal she entertained them with lively accounts of her life-drawing and difficulties with the model, her love of ceramics and the capricious nature of the kiln which either enhanced or destroyed her pots, according to its whim. It could, in her words, "like, drive you up the wall."

After supper they clustered about the television in the living room. The Supreme Court decision got top billing. They sat quietly listening to Justice Blackmun's dissenting opinion in which he said, "I fear for the liberty and equality of the millions of women who have lived and come of age in the sixteen years since *Roe* was decided." Lee thought of Elizabeth who had called that afternoon expressing dismay over the Court . . . Elizabeth and Melanie and the other granddaughter in California, and the two lively great-granddaughters, the problems these and future restrictions might generate for them, and thousands like them.

They heard Molly Yard label the decision "a disaster" and

pledge to carry on the battle for reproductive freedom. This reminded Lee of the night back in '82 when she and Minerva sat before the television listening to Ellie Smeal, then President of National NOW, announce that despite the failure of the Equal Rights Amendment to be ratified, they would continue the fight. She remembered their disappointment—how a few months prior to that they had enlisted as *ERA missionaries* during semester break to fly down to Fort Lauderdale, going door to door with petitions, walking until their feet ached, drenched in sudden downpours or sweating in the sultry sun, frequently rebuffed, attacked by dogs, cats, parrots, even a monkey—trying to behave *like Republicans* as instructed, neatly dressed in their green and white outfits. Ultimately they had failed. Would this new battle be worth the untold hours, the tremendous energy?

Now Faye Wattleton, President of Planned Parenthood was speaking. "This is a sad day for freedom. Now a woman's access to abortion will become hostage to geography." They watched her jostle with a representative of the National Right-to-Life Committee to keep her place at the microphone as he tried to push her aside while she was talking to reporters.

"Atta girl!" Ada exclaimed as Faye held her ground, saying to the intruder, "Please at least be courteous."

Vivian applauded. "You said it! The nerve of him!"

The news then shifted to other matters. "Talk, talk, talk!" said Ada. "And it doesn't do one iota of good."

Minerva turned off the set. "Well, now that we know the whole story, what is our battle plan?"

"I'd like to wring their scrawny necks, including Sandra Day O'Connor. What a traitor!" Vivian said.

"We suspected all along she wouldn't support us," Lee said.

"Well, we need a strategy," Minerva said. "I suppose the first step will be that Pro-Choice Rally at Melville. It's next week isn't it?" She looked at Lee.

Lee nodded. "But I told you I wasn't going. Remember? It conflicts with that special poetry workshop I've signed up for."

"But that was before the Court decision. You wouldn't want to miss the rally after today, would you?" Minerva eyed her with steady gaze.

"Of course she can't miss it now!" Vivian said emphatically. "How would it look if she didn't show up?"

"Folks are counting on her," said Ada. "She can't let them down. Right, Lee?"

"It wouldn't seem right—a rally without Lee!" Melanie chimed in.

Lee did not respond. Why were they referring to her in the third person, as if she were some sort of pawn in a chess game? This was her decision, not theirs. She had always maintained that a good leader should never be indispensable. The workshop . . . she had been looking forward to it for weeks, an opportunity to study with William Heyen whose poetry she greatly admired . . . . Of course, the rally *would* be exciting. Perfect timing—the women coming together, venting their anger and frustration. And there would be good press coverage. She could feel herself wavering. Perhaps they were right—people expecting her to lead their group at the rally, now of all times. She felt torn in both directions . . . but she had participated in enough protests in her lifetime. A parade of the signs, banners, and flags she had carried, the chants, the songs, the rallies, floated through her mind. Yes, she had done enough.

"Adele is in charge of reservations for the bus, and she's doing a fine job. We've checked all the arrangements. You don't need me."

"But you *are* coming along, aren't you, Lee? You wouldn't want to miss it would you?" Minerva's tone was incredulous.

Lee remained silent, sipping her coffee. Closing her eyes, she concentrated on retrieving the image of Leandra. *What should I do?* Nothing happened. But again the word drifted into her mind—**PERSEVERE**—in bold letters, as if painted on a billboard. What did it mean? She sat frowning into her cup. Then suddenly it came to her—the answer. Turning to Minerva, she said firmly, "I do hate to miss the rally, but I'll have to." She glanced around at the others who were observing her in stunned silence. "I doubt that you'll understand. But this poetry workshop is extremely important to me—an opportunity I can't, in fairness to myself, give up."

PERSEVERE . . . . Strange she had not seen it before. If she wanted to take her writing seriously, she must allow herself some

210

prime time, unfragmented by other demands. But did it mean escaping the world altogether? Maybe not. Maybe she could try to empower other women with words rather than actions . . . create an exuberant world—of sisterhood and striving and love . . . .

The others quietly cleared away the cups while Lee sat dreamily staring into that new direction, her body relaxed, a faint smile lighting her face.

25

Sprawled comfortably in a lounge chair beneath the Norway maple, Lee gazed out over the bay observing the swoop and swirl of gulls above water rippled by a southerly breeze. The same breeze ruffled the papers on her clipboard and stirred the sultry air, diminishing only slightly the heat of this August afternoon. She was working on a poem about the Moon Goddesses, Artemis and Hecate, in tribute to the impending eclipse of the moon. The clipboard fell off her lap as she stretched lazily and wiggled her bare toes against the fur of the calico cat curled at her feet. In her childhood going barefoot had been a delight, the freedom of grass underfoot, the challenge of gravel drives, cement sidewalks, hot tar of streets to toughen her feet for summer's endless cloverchain of days. That part of her had not changed. She would still kick off her shoes at every opportunity. Sunlight through the canopy of leaves patterned her legs and denim shorts in bright splotches. Not bad legs, she noted, for a woman her age, now that a summer tan masked the varicose veins.

She was totally alone for the first time in weeks. She relished the solitary feeling. It was Elizabeth's turn to take Minerva to Stony Brook for radiation. Ada had gone shopping, and Vivian was at work. The stillness was disturbed only by cries of the gulls and an occasional bark from Daisy frisking about on the lawn. Brother Gray and Ebony were investigating a mole hole by the hedge. A Tiger Swallowtail and a Great Spangled Fritillary fluttered about the butterfly bush. Lee smiled—her world in balance—too delicate to last. But nothing wrong with savoring the moment.

It had been a good summer so far. The court case was twice adjourned—once on account of the illness of Arthur's attorney, followed by the vacation of the judge during August—scheduled now for mid-September. The possibility of Arthur's petition being granted seemed far less likely than in March when he first took action. Though highly unpredictable, Ada was clearly of sound mind at this time. Lee had mixed feelings—relishing the postponements, yet wanting to get it over. Minerva's treatments were going well. In a few more days she would be finished. They had taken turns driving her to the medical center, with Bernie helping out on her day off. Minerva showed no drastic side effects beyond an occasional queasiness. After her initial agonizing over the decision, she had faced the radiation with resolute cheerfulness, determined not to let it interfere with her life.

The Long Island rally in July denouncing the Supreme Court decision had been a great success. *Newsday*, estimating the crowd at twelve hundred, quoted Betty Friedan saying, *We will prevail!* and the President of NOW New York State saying, *We're going to take to the streets and the ballot boxes. The time for civility is over!* Lee had some pangs of regret over not taking part but held firm in her resolve to focus on writing.

The workshop had been a tremendous boost for her, forcing her to set priorities and allow time not only for writing poetry but reading it as well. She felt rejuvenated. And the past week she had immersed herself in mythology of early goddesses, starting with Merlin Stone's *When God Was a Woman* and working her way through several other books that viewed archaeology and myth from a new perspective, studying goddess figurines, fertility symbols, and other early artifacts.

She picked up her clipboard and read over fragments of a poem taking shape. Images of fleet-footed Artemis, Goddess of many breasts, and her counterpart, Hecate, Goddess of the Dark Moon, Queen of Witches and Magic, guardian of the crossroads where three roads come together in the dark of the night. Lee was intrigued by the three roads. Perhaps that was where she stood now . . . good starting point for a poem. She was very susceptible to the power of moonlight. Nights of the full moon she was frequently unable to sleep, getting up to peer out the window where the moon patterned the lawn with lacy shadows, dark against its pale light. When she was a child, her mother had pointed out the exquisite cameo profile of the Woman in the Moon, more appealing to Lee than the traditional Man in the Moon. She recalled the world's excitement over the first moon landing, her own exhilaration mixed with sadness at the human pollution of something so celestially enchanting.

Her thoughts meandered back to the eclipse. She had seen an eclipse of the sun but never a total eclipse of the moon. How could she do justice to that in a poem? Perhaps a moon ritual would be better . . . yes, an eclipse ritual! But could she convince the others?

* * *

The night of the eclipse the weather had cooperated—no clouds or haze to obscure their view of the moon. The women were sitting in a circle, some on beach chairs, others on cushions and towels on the sandy shore of the cove opening into the bay, just below the road that ended at the shoreline adjoining Elizabeth's property. This was the only place they could get an open view to check the progress of the moon and its darkening shadow as it moved across the sky.

There were nine of them tonight—eight who had taken part in the healing ritual, plus Melanie who had dropped by and insisted on joining them. Elizabeth was not present. Though the disagreement over the validity of goddesses and witches had faded into the background, she had not forgotten. At the very mention of another ritual, Lee had seen by her frown and tautness of lip that she did not approve. She would have no part of it, declaring such things totally pagan, an affront to her Christian faith. Lee had not argued the point further. Despite Elizabeth's negative reaction, they had gone ahead with the plans. Lee felt some

214

misgivings, but it was not as though Elizabeth had laid down an ultimatum. She had simply withdrawn. To avoid any personal connection with the ritual, she had made a date with John to go to the city for a concert and dinner and to spend the night at his apartment. Lee wondered if she had unwittingly pushed them toward a closer relationship—their first overnight together.

When they discovered that the eclipse coincided with the last day of Minerva's radiation, they had decided to combine their moon ritual with a celebration of that milestone. Lee glanced fondly at Minerva, sitting next to Bernie, the two of them in animated conversation, interspersed with laughter. She thought about the previous ritual—how worried they had been, Minerva so fragile, facing the unknown. And now, a brief two months later, she had not only survived, she was thriving, despite the weakening effects of the radiation. And she had lost none of her sparkle in the process. Worth celebrating.

It was eleven-thirty now. The women had been sitting together in the circle for over an hour watching the copper-colored moon move slowly upward from the eastern horizon and become gradually darkened by the shadowed curve of the earth. The stars sparkled more brilliantly than usual tonight, undimmed by moonlight. How rare it was to take time for marveling over their beauty. As a child, Lee had felt a close kinship to them. She recalled distant St. Louis summer nights, hot and humid, when she and her mother, father, and brother would lie on quilts in the backyard to cool off, star-gazing, trying to see who could identify the most constellations. There was something reassuring about those old formations circling the skies, changing with the seasons, disappearing but always returning—returning long after those loved ones were gone. Beneath their vastness, Lee felt immeasurably small and ephemeral, unable to fathom such magnitude. From where she sat now, she could see Sagittarius the Archer aiming his bow and arrow at Scorpius, said to have bitten Orion, causing his death, obliterating him from the summer sky. It had always bothered her that so many of the constellations named by those old Greeks and Romans had such violence associated with them. She preferred the earlier matriarchal myths focusing

215

on fertility and natural life cycles.

Lee glanced about the circle of faces, made visible only by the lighted candle each woman was holding. She felt a rush of affection for all of them, wishing she could summon the Egyptian Isis to hover above them and extend her feathered wings to protect them always. So far, everything had gone well. She had opened the ceremony by invoking the Powers of the Four Directions. She was wearing her purple and green silk coat embellished with the gold butterfly—a little heavy for the warm evening, but it gave her confidence. And she felt it added to the sense of drama. Minerva had suggested a more simple format than before, but Lee wanted to retain at least a touch of formality.

Now the women were taking turns around the circle sharing a poem or story or an object relating to the moon . . . Margaret's moonstone ring that brought her good luck, its milky surface reflecting the light with a bluish sheen, Laura's abstract wood sculpture resembling the Goddess Diana, Vivian's Moonflower vine she would plant in the morning. Perry reading Marge Piercy's poem *The Moon Is Always Female*. Nearing the end, these lines: *Out of necessity's hard stones we suck / what water we can and so we have survived, / women born of women* . . . . Perry, eyes aglow in candle flame, saying "I just love this part!" And Lee thinking *she* would be one of those survivors, one to carry on the struggle. Yes, Perry and others like her would be the affirmation long after Lee had faded into oblivion . . . .

Now Minerva was displaying a long stick on which she had glued feathers, seed pods, and small shells, calling it her magic wand . . . Lee wishing she could use it to put this moment on hold, stop the tape unwinding at such a pace . . . and now Ada reading from a May Swenson poem, *After the Flight of Ranger VII*, her description of the moon as an *old fossil / to be scrubbed / and studied / like a turtle's stomach*, saying with a laugh that she felt a strong personal resemblance to that moon.

Lee had not written the poem she had intended, focusing on the dark power of Hecate, the lines stubbornly refusing to take shape. She read from an earlier poem about Artemis dancing wildly through the forest in luminous robes, ending with:

Her cosmic lantern beckons,
so bright it snuffs out the stars,
her magnetic current surging
through my veins
luring me to wander
along that celestial path.

And, as if to illustrate Lee's poem, Melanie stepped into the center of the group, leaping and twirling around with her candle, doing what she called a "Moon Dance."

Bernie completed the circle with a ghost story about a young woman in a blood-red gown who wandered about an ancient house on the night of the full moon. Noticing Bernie's arm draped over Minerva's shoulder, Lee felt a twinge of jealousy which she tried to suppress. After all, they were kindred spirits. She had known that from the beginning. But it made her feel a bit isolated . . . . The night air had grown chilly. Shivering, Lee pulled the silk coat close about her, hugging her knees against her chest and digging her toes into the sand.

It was midnight, and the eclipse was nearly complete. They could barely see the darkened moon, outlined with a faint sliver of light. An awed silence spread over the group as they sat with faces upturned, straining to see the pale remnant. There was something ominous about this eerie darkness . . . easy to see how it must have terrified their primitive ancestors to watch the moon slowly disappear, wondering if it would ever return.

Perry leaned over to Lee. "Is it time now?" Lee nodded, and Perry moved to the center where she picked up a bongo drum which she began beating, slowly, rhythmically. Lee asked everybody to stand and join hands for a chant to complete the ritual.

Bring back your light
O Sister Moon!
Cast aside the dark shadow.
Bring back your light
O Sister Moon
Join the celebration.
Bring back your light
O Sister Moon!

The nine women repeated the chant three times with exuberance, their voices and drumbeat growing progressively louder until the last time around, they were shouting, *O Sister Moon!* followed by a boisterous cheer.

The moon, continuing its journey, had moved ever so slightly out of the shadow, the faint sliver of light now on its westerly rim. Minerva, giving each one a hug, announced she was going to complete the ceremony by taking a swim in the nude to cleanse all traces of the hateful radiation. Slipping off her dress and panties, folding them neatly on her towel, she walked majestically into the water.

Lee watched her slim figure merge with water and darkness in astonishment. Why hadn't Min told her beforehand? While considering whether it was spontaneous or planned, she heard Perry say, "Come on, Lee, let's go in!" stripping off her shorts and top as she spoke.

Although she tried not to be a prude, Lee had always shied away from public nudity, even among women. The nude body of either sex embarrassed her. And she had no intention of taking off her clothes in front of everyone, even in the moonless dark. Soon it would become brighter, and she would be out there naked, her bulges plainly visible for all to see. No, she would not do it. In fact, she did not even want to watch the others do it. Everything was suddenly out of control.

She looked up to see Bernie running past, her naked body a lithe shadowy form as she leaped, laughing, into the water and started splashing Minerva.

"Come on, Lee." Perry was tugging at her arm. Large-bodied and sturdy, she seemed totally unconcerned about her nudity.

"You go ahead. I'm not sure I want to."

"Well, that's up to you." Perry waded in, shouting, "Come on, everybody!"

"Look how it sparkles." Minerva was sloshing the water over her head. "Millions of diamonds!"

"It's phosphorescent," Lee could hear Bernie saying . . . then something about microscopic plankton. A phenomenon Lee had seen before, but usually earlier in the season. Bernie

218

threw some water into the air. "Our own water sparklers—fireworks for Minerva!"

Now Margaret had removed her clothes and splashed into the water, with Melanie close behind her, squealing with delight. Laura was kicking off her sandals and pulling off her sundress. "What a grand finale!" She tossed her clothes on the sand and jumped in. Easy enough for her, Lee thought, noting the firm line of her breasts and thighs.

Ada, leaning heavily on her cane, walked over to Lee. "They've all turned into lunatics!" Then Vivian, despite worries about jellyfish and horseshoe crabs, stripped off her clothes and tiptoed gingerly into the water. Lee envied her slender body, the grace of her movements in the emerging moonlight. Ada, shaking her head emphatically, declared there had to be at least one sane person in the group. She sat on an upturned dinghy, saying she would just stay and watch. Lee longed to sit there beside her, but that might reveal how squeamish she was. Ada had her hip as an excuse, though she never needed an excuse or explanation for what she did or didn't do—an attitude Lee admired but had not yet achieved.

Why did she feel compelled to justify her actions? And the human body—such a miracle of creation, why were so many women, particularly American women, dissatisfied with their physique? Starving themselves with fad diets or changing their contours with plastic surgery. Most European women seemed far more accepting of their bodies. She thought of the nude bathers she had seen on the beaches of Denmark, how natural it seemed for them.

As far back as memory could reach, Lee had been self-conscious about exposing her body to the public eye. When she was quite young, in first grade, she had a vivid dream that she was walking to school in just her bloomers, humiliated, trying to hide . . . and the agony of high school gym classes, having to walk from shower to dressing room with nothing but a skimpy towel between her and the eyes of the other girls, embarrassed by her skinny frame and small breasts in an era when Mae West ruled supreme.

Even in marriage, nudity had not come easily for her. Though she loved the feel of Matt's body against hers, the electricity of his touch, she did not like to see their nakedness, preferring darkness to daylight for lovemaking. And when Matt would caress her, covering her with kisses, telling her how beautiful her body was, she had assumed his words were inspired only by the passion of the moment.

Lee looked out over the water sparkling with phosphorescent spray. One would expect those rowdy people splashing about out there to be teenagers, not a group of mature women. Through her mind flashed the image of her mother clad in a black skirted bathing suit in the style of the early 1930s. How she loved to swim! Many a day she would whisk through her housework saying, "Well, that's better than it was." Then she would round up the neighborhood kids and Mrs. Harrison next-door, pile them all in the Chevy, and take them for a swim at Forest Park Highlands. Lee had been proud that her mother was the only woman on the block who knew how to drive. But she had looked with young critical eyes at her plump figure, sagging-breasted and large-bellied, encased in the drab unflattering suit, her veined legs nearly as white as the tiles of the swimming pool, thinking if she ever were to get that old she wouldn't want to be seen in public looking that way. Calculating the years now, Lee was amazed to realize that her mother could not have been older than forty-five at the time. After swimming a few lengths, the two women would drape their arms and shoulders over the edge of the pool, floating on their backs, legs outstretched, talking and laughing over the antics of their young charges. Lee had not appreciated what a free spirit her mother was. What would she do if she were here tonight? Very likely she would be one of the first to go in.

Perry was calling to her. "You don't know what you're missing! Come on, Lee."

No use postponing it any longer. If she didn't join them, she would never live it down. Lee removed the silk coat, feeling strangely vulnerable without its comforting softness. Carefully folding the coat and laying it with her clothes on a beach cushion, she walked to the water's edge wrapped in a large towel which she put on a nearby log just before plunging in.

Within a few steps, the water was up to her waist, and she

began to swim sidestroke. Hesitant at first but quickly gaining confidence, she stretched out full length, sliding her arms through the water, one reaching out, the other pulling back, her legs beginning the slow rhythmic scissors kick propelling her forward. She was astonished at the sensation of the cool salt water on her skin, how much different it felt in the nude than in a bathing suit. With each stroke, she sensed the negative thoughts about her physical self slipping away. Phosphorescent bubbles swished and trailed after her as she glided through the water caressing her body with every movement of her arms and legs. She felt unbelievably free and buoyant in the gleaming spray that encircled her, as though in some other dimension unbound by constraints of time and space, swimming with strong sure strokes away from shore, away from the squeals and laughter of the other women. The hazy form of an anchored sailboat loomed ahead, and she realized she had swum out farther than usual. The voices had grown fainter. But she was unafraid. Turning on her back, she floated with arms and legs outstretched, motionless, allowing the water to cushion her, small waves lapping against her upturned breasts, washing over her abdomen and thighs, forming little rivulets around her genitals. At one with the sea, she remained for awhile in this floating position, lulled into a state of euphoric relaxation. She resolved to retain the memory of this sensation, recall it in times of tension.

But now she must start back. She discovered it was more difficult than the swim out. The tide was against her, forcing her to put all of her energy into every stroke. Struggling toward the shore, she was on the verge of panic when she caught sight of Minerva and Bernie not far ahead. They were treading water together, their hands braced on each other's shoulders, engrossed in conversation. Lee tried to push away the jealous pangs that jabbed at her. As she drew nearer, Minerva caught sight of her and pulled away from Bernie, swimming toward her. "Where were you, Lee? We were beginning to worry."

Lee stopped swimming to tread water, breathing heavily, supporting herself against Minerva's arm, strong-boned and steady. "I guess I thought I was a mermaid."

Minerva offered to tow her back, but Lee insisted she could

manage, and they slowly made their way toward shore. Soon they were among the others, still splashing and calling back and forth. Vivian was singing a sea chantey, her shrill voice piercing the air.

Suddenly they saw a car with flashing red lights coming down the road which ended at the little strip of beach. "Oh, no!" Minerva groaned. "The police!"

Vivian quit singing. "Quick everyone. Get down under the water." She motioned to the others. They all scrunched down, their knees scraping on shells and stones buried in the mucky bottom.

The car came to a stop, its spotlight swinging around toward the women in the water. Two large figures got out, silhouetted against the light, and walked toward the dinghy where Ada sat. The women remained motionless, submerged up to their necks, the bright light glaring in their eyes, Lee wishing desperately she were in bed dreaming all this. At least Elizabeth wasn't here. She was grateful for that. But what if she found out? And Arthur? Lee could not bear to think of it.

The police were talking to Ada. Then the gruff voice of one of the officers boomed out at them from an electronic bullhorn. "Attention! Everyone ashore immediately!"

"Shit!" said Vivian. Wouldn't you know? Damn cops!"

"Oh, God!" Lee said. "What should we do?" Just a short while ago she had been worried about stepping out of the water in the moonlight, and now she was expected to walk into the arms of these cops in the full glare of their spotlight. No, she couldn't possibly!

"We might try praying to the Goddess." Perry gave Lee's hand a squeeze.

"Too late for that!" Minerva said.

"What's keeping you people?" The deep voice echoed ominously across the darkness. "We want to see every one of you out here right away."

"He doesn't, like, know what he's asking for!" Melanie giggled nervously.

Lee could see Ada talking to the two men, gesturing, but with no visible effect. They remained standing, straddle-legged at the shoreline. She winced as the edge of a shell cut into her knee, but she didn't dare move.

Minerva cupped her hands to her mouth and called, "Couldn't we talk from here, officer?" Her clipped Bostonian voice sounded beautifully proper, even under these bizarre circumstances.

"Sorry, ma'am," the metallic voice replied. "We need to talk face to face. You got a problem with that?"

Minerva looked around at the others. "What now?" she asked in a low voice.

"We don't have much choice." Laura motioned the others around her. They huddled together under the protective cover of the water conferring briefly.

Then Minerva called out, "All right, officer . . . if you insist. Just a moment, please."

Forming a line and linking arms, Lee clinging to Minerva on one side and Perry on the other, the eight women emerged from the water, about waist deep, mermaids of assorted sizes and shapes, their hair dripping tiny rivulets down their necks and faces, breasts glistening in the obtrusive light. They started walking together slowly, deliberately, toward the shore, Lee squinting against the glare, feeling certain she was going to faint dead away but knowing she had to stick with the others. As they moved forward, in step, she felt a surge of strength, almost exaltation, at the bond linking them arm in arm, facing the enemy together. The water was now barely covering their thighs . . . when suddenly the voice blared over the bullhorn, "All right, hold it, ladies! That's far enough!" He sounded flustered. "Your friend here tells me you ladies reside in the Sherwood house." His shadowy figure gestured in the general direction of Elizabeth's house. "Is that correct?"

"Indeed," Minerva replied. "Correct that four of us do. The others are our guests."

"We got complaint calls from your neighbors. Don't you know there's an ordinance against excessive noise after eleven o'clock?" There was a rasp of irritation in his voice. Lee could sense the frustration of these two blustery men, their embarrassment at the prospect of encountering this group of aging women in the nude at close range, mixed with their desire to exert their dominant role.

"I'm so sorry, officer," Minerva said, ever so politely, "we were not aware of it. I suppose we might have been a trifle carried away." Her voice floated across the water beautifully modulated.

"Well . . . " the gruff voice sputtered over the bullhorn, then paused. Lee wondered how many of the neighbors were tuned in to this conversation. "Under the circumstances, Mrs. Sherwood being a respected resident of the village . . . ." The voice trailed off. He seemed to be conferring with his partner. Then the voice again. "We're going to let you ladies off with just a warning this time, but see that it don't happen again!" Lee gave a deep sigh of relief.

"Thank you, sir." Minerva did a curtsy in the water and gave Lee's arm a squeeze.

The two dark figures turned, saying something to Ada, then stalked back to the patrol car, switched off the blinking lights and spotlight, spun the car around with a screech, and disappeared down the road.

The women scrambled ashore in silence, as if afraid the slightest noise would bring back the intruders. Lee hurried over to Ada who was standing at attention by the dinghy, staring in the direction of the departing car. "Well, you folks nearly cooked your goose!" Ada said as the women gathered around her, clutching their towels and clothing.

"What did they say to you?" Lee asked.

"Well," Ada paused, relishing the drama of her role, "first they asked if I knew you folks. And my inclination was to deny I had ever set eyes on any of you, to say I just happened to take a late night stroll, but I figured they either would not believe me or think I belonged in the loony bin, so I said yes, as a matter of fact, I did." She took a deep breath.

"Then what did they say?" Vivian asked, toweling her wet curls.

"They asked where you lived, and I told them, but I said Elizabeth wasn't home, and then they said they wanted to talk to all of you, and I said I didn't think that would be such a good idea, and they got downright impudent and said they didn't need any advice from me. That's when they ordered you out of the water. I thought I'd die!"

"We thought we would too!" Margaret said with a laugh.

"It was, like, so embarrassing!" Melanie said, pulling on her jeans. "Like outrageous!"

"I think we all felt the same way, but they didn't give us any choice—so we called their bluff," Minerva said triumphantly.

"You were magnificent, Min," Lee said, "so confident and controlled." The way she imagined Katherine Hepburn might have dealt with such a situation—regal and implacable.

"You should have seen the faces of those cops when you folks started walking toward them, naked as tadpoles! You looked like a chorus line in a water burlesque show."

Suddenly Lee realized she was standing there in the glow of the emerging moon, stark naked. In the excitement, she had completely forgotten to grab her towel and wrap it around her as intended. And, even more amazing, she didn't really care. The others were still in various stages of undress, and nobody seemed to notice. She walked over to the log for her towel, dried off, and slipped into her purple coat, enjoying its comforting softness.

"I'm surprised they didn't arrest us for nude bathing," Laura said, stepping into her panties and pulling on her dress.

"I think they were too discombobulated. They wanted to clear out of here rather than confront all that nakedness." Ada laughed. "It did my heart good to watch them squirm."

"I wish you hadn't told him it was Elizabeth's house. I'd hate to get her involved in this mess," Lee said.

"Well, without an arrest, it shouldn't go on their official records. So why do we have to tell her?" Vivian said.

"Vivian has a point," Lee said. "Let's just keep it among ourselves." Minerva nodded her agreement.

"It's all right by me," said Ada. "But what if she finds out?"

"That's a chance we'll have to take." Lee was shivering now in the damp night air. She huddled into her silk coat, wishing again that she was safely in bed and none of this had ever happened.

26

Twelve days had elapsed since the eclipse and the calamitous swim in the bay. Lee had been on edge, fearing Elizabeth might find out. But she was not in the habit of chatting with her neighbors. Quince Lane, its houses spaced far apart on spacious lawns, separated by tall hedges, did not lend itself to neighborly conversations—unlike the street in the St. Louis suburb where Lee grew up, where you could gossip over the back fence or across front lawns.

Elizabeth had returned from her Manhattan overnight with John in bright spirits. She did not even inquire about the ritual—which made it easy to avoid telling her, without even so much as a white lie. Lee had tried to put the episode out of her mind. But the flashing lights, the harsh words over the bullhorn, still disturbed her sleep, tormented her dreams. She had attempted to settle back into her daily routine of writing but was easily distracted, her powers of concentration diminished.

It was a breezy Sunday morning, the air pleasantly cool, a break from the sultry heat of late August, harbinger of fall days ahead. Elizabeth was at church. The others were sitting around the breakfast table finishing their muffins, coffee and tea. Bumblebees buzzed about the blue petunias in a flowerbox on the porch railing. Through the open French doors Lee admired the patterns of sunlight on their velvety petals. A lazy morning, Lee's favorite time when she granted herself the freedom to do anything she pleased—including nothing at all. Yawning, she gave a luxurious stretch, mulling over her choices—whether to revise one of her poems or look through the *New York Times Book Review* or read a new Amanda Cross mystery *Whatever Became of Winifred?* She picked up the *Book Review* to see if any poetry was reviewed. A frown clouded her face—only fiction this week, and not much of that. The world was becoming more and more rational in its thinking. No time or space for works of the imagination.

She heard Elizabeth's car in the driveway, then the click of her heels on the porch steps and the front hallway. "How about joining us for a second cup of coffee?" Lee called to her.

Elizabeth had gone into the living room and was rattling through some papers. "Has anyone seen this week's *Village Chronicle?*" There was a worrisome edginess to her voice. Vivian suggested she try the stack by the couch. Then the sound of a page being torn out. Elizabeth entered the room, her face flushed a deep pink. "I never was so humiliated!" The words shot out of her mouth like bullets. "At least six people mentioned it after church this morning, and I didn't know what they were talking about." She glared at the four of them.

Minerva put down her crossword puzzle and looked at Elizabeth standing by the table, a page from the paper in her hand. "Liz, dear, what's the matter?"

"Why didn't you tell me?" Elizabeth said, anger coloring her words.

"Tell you what?" Vivian asked.

Lee could feel her heart pounding. She braced herself for the answer she already suspected.

"About this!" Elizabeth replied, her voice taut with rage. "This item in the *Village Tattler* column." The paper shook in her hands as she read:

> *Word has reached us that a certain group of ladies residing with Mrs. Parker Sherwood on Quince Lane, along with several guests, were reprimanded by the Village Police for creating a public disturbance in the form of excessive noise and nude bathing on Wednesday last in the wee hours of the night. No arrests were made, but the ladies were warned against future escapades. We understand*

227

Mrs. Sherwood was away from home the night the incident occurred.

She slammed the paper on the table. "What possessed you?" Her steel gray eyes were fixed on Lee who turned away to avoid her gaze. What could she say? The muscles of her throat had constricted to the point that she could not utter a word even if she knew the right ones.

She heard Minerva saying, "We didn't want to worry you, Liz. You know how these things get all blown up out of proportion. It was really nothing to speak of."

"Do you call this *nothing*?" the distraught Elizabeth demanded, her voice quavering. "You and your rowdy friends cavorting naked on the beach? Nothing? And the police coming— waking up the whole neighborhood!"

"We weren't naked on the beach," Vivian said. "Only naked in the water, properly screened from public view. Everything would have been just fine if those stupid cops hadn't ordered us to come ashore. It wasn't really our fault."

Elizabeth sighed one of her long sighs. "This sounds like another of Lee's crazy ideas." Lee could feel the blood rushing to her face.

"No, actually, it was my idea," Minerva said. "A symbolic cleansing of sorts." She got up from the table and put her arm around Elizabeth's shoulder.

"I don't see why you're so upset. They didn't get arrested," Ada said.

"You should have known better!" Elizabeth snapped. "At your age!"

Ada pushed her chair back from the table and stood up, her regal best, head high, beribboned braid hanging over one shoulder. "I'll have you know that yours truly was just sitting on the shore minding her own business when the cops showed up." She gathered the cups and put them on a tray, rattling them more than necessary in her agitation.

"Forgive me, Ada." Elizabeth looked flustered. "But the others should have known better than to behave as if this were some sort of nudist camp."

228

Suddenly Lee heard herself lashing out, pent-up words of anger. "Damn it, Elizabeth! What we did was not so terrible. We could have been smoking pot or shooting up with crack or heroin. Then you would really have something to get upset about." Elizabeth had turned white, her pursed lips and down-turned mouth deepening the creases at the corners, puckering her face as if she had eaten an unripe persimmon. Lee wished she could describe for her the pure sensuous delight of the swim, the freedom of floating unencumbered . . . But, in Elizabeth's impenetrable state, that was out of the question.

"And furthermore," Elizabeth said, ignoring Lee's comment about the drugs, "you announced to the whole world that I was away from home while you were creating a public disturbance." She gave a loud sigh of exasperation. "What will people think of that!"

"The Village of Quintauket is hardly the whole world," Lee snapped. "And besides, why is it so damned important—what people will think?" She could not hide her irritation—Elizabeth, always harping on potential opinions of some nebulous group known as people. Throughout her childhood, Lee had been plagued by this admonition from her mother. She had spent well over a half century trying to break free from it.

"The Chronicle extends far beyond our village." She pulled away from Minerva's arm and grasped the edge of the table. "The people who mentioned this at church wanted to know where I was while your little escapade was taking place."

"Well, why not tell them?" Lee said. She did not like the tone of her own voice, what her mother would have termed sassy. But Elizabeth was making her feel like a child—as if they were all naughty children who had disobeyed the rules. "I don't see anything scandalous about going to the city overnight. It's a rather common practice."

"I have my reputation to consider. The minute I turn my back, you people do something like this to embarrass me."

"Maybe she didn't want folks to know she was in the city overnight with You-Know-Who," Ada said, a gleam of mischief in her eyes.

Lee frowned. They must, indeed, have slept together.

"Say, Ada has a point." Vivian laughed. "It's John you're worried about—right, Liz? The John thing must be getting really serious. Well, well, welllll." She began humming the wedding march, "Tum tum te dum, Tum tum te dum . . . ."

"You leave John out of this!" Elizabeth's voice soared to the high decibels. Her body was rigid, hands clenched, pale skin pulled taut across the bones of her face, veins at her temples pulsing blue. "It's bad enough that you people tarnish my reputation, but at least you can leave his intact!"

"You and your precious reputation!" Lee shouted. "You're always so damned proper. I'm just getting sick of . . . ."

The front door chimes interrupted their angry exchange. And before anyone could answer it, John walked into the fracas, a bewildered expression on his face. "I heard voices so I just came on in. Is anything the matter?"

"No, nothing . . . nothing that concerns you, John dear," Elizabeth lied sweetly, her voice quickly assuming the mellow, well-modulated tones of old-monied Hamptonians.

"Merely a friendly discussion," Minerva said.

"Well, there's nothing like a lively discussion to clear the air, I always say." John gave a polite laugh, then turned toward Elizabeth. "Are you ready to go with me to the club for brunch, Lizzy?"

Lee wondered how he got away with calling her Lizzy. No one else could. Elizabeth must really care for him. He did have an appealing quality of openness, an easy-going manner, handsome in a tall, lanky way, his lean face, warm brown eyes, the shock of white hair flopping across his forehead in boyish fashion. Yes, Elizabeth showed good taste in choosing him. But then, she always did have good taste.

"Oh dear!" Elizabeth was saying. "I completely lost track of the time. I'll just go powder my nose." Elizabeth would never say I have to go to the bathroom or, heaven forbid, I have to take a pee, as Vivian might. On her way out, she cast an angry glance at Lee, as if warning her not to say a word about their argument. "I'll be right back," she said to John.

"Take your time." John pulled up a chair to the table between Lee and Vivian.

"May I take your jacket, John?" Minerva asked. He was wearing a navy blue blazer over casual khaki pants, the outfit accentuating his deep summer tan.

"No, thanks. I'll just leave it on. A bit cool today. Pleasant change." The weather was perhaps the only safe topic in this charged atmosphere.

Yes, Lee thought, with that queasy feeling signaling danger, he and Elizabeth were in love.

"Well, John," Ada said, "did you and Elizabeth enjoy the city together last week?" The question was innocent enough, but her manner and tone implied there might have been more than simple enjoyment. Her blue eyes pierced the air, staring at him across the table.

"Oh, yes indeed. It was fine, quite fine!"

Poor John, Lee thought. Clearly embarrassed but putting up a good front.

"Elizabeth told us you were going to take in a show," Ada continued. "What one did you see? I don't believe she said." Ada turned to Vivian. "Do you remember if she talked to us about it?"

Vivian shook her head. "Now that you mention it, I don't believe she did. Was it Broadway or Off-Broadway?"

"Well," John cleared his throat. His face was turning redder by the minute. "As a matter of fact, we ahhh . . . ."

Minerva meanwhile had picked up the coffeepot. "How about some coffee, John?"

"Oh, no thanks. I've already had my one cup for today. Have to watch the old ticker, you know." Lee could sense his relief at getting off the hook. "And I don't care much for decaf. As far as I'm concerned, it's got to be the real thing.

And then Elizabeth came back, neatly composed and controlled, her hair swooped back in loose waves, the harsh lines of her face, so evident a few minutes ago, now softened. Lee had to acknowledge she was lovely in her white linen suit, the pink roses of her blouse matching her pink pumps and lipstick. An ideal version of the stylish older woman, a look Lee could not rival even if she tried. "I suppose we should be on our way," Elizabeth said to John. I've kept you waiting long enough." She cocked her head prettily and smiled at him. Something about that pose reminded Lee of Nancy Reagan with Ronnie. A disturbing image. Gazing at her with open admiration, John offered his arm, and they walked together out of the room.

"Don't you think you were a bit cruel to him?" Minerva said.

"Us, cruel?" Ada said. "We were merely making conversation, weren't we, Viv?"

"Of course." Vivian could no longer suppress her laughter. "*Lizzy*, he called her. Things are getting cozy!"

"And did you notice how fast she whisked her Sir Galahad away? One might almost suspect she didn't trust us," Ada said.

"Well, one thing we know," said Vivian, arching her eyebrows, "is that they slept together."

"You're awfully quiet, Lee," Minerva said.

"I guess I'm worried." She could not put it into words— whether it was just that vague foreboding, the shadow that now and then descended to darken her mood, or if it was linked more specifically to Elizabeth and their bitter words, or to Elizabeth and John together. "I don't quite know why."

"I've never seen Liz in such a huff!" Vivian said.

"Whoever turned in that information to the newspaper ought to be . . . ." Minerva paused in search of the right word.

"Ought to be shot!" said Ada. "Of all the nerve!"

"Well, she'll get over it," Vivian said.

"Don't be too sure," Lee said. She sat, chin in hand, staring out at the petunias, now darkened by the shadow of the house. She wished she had not lashed out at Elizabeth, so ridiculously hypocritical about the whole thing. Acting scandalized by their perfectly innocent skinny-dipping, yet trying to cover up the fact that she had slept with John, pretending to be so damned moral. After all they weren't living in the Dark Ages. They were, in fact, nearing the last decade of the twentieth century, and if people wanted to swim in the nude or sleep with other people of their choosing, well, so what?

The sharp ringing of the telephone interrupted her thoughts. "I'll get it." Vivian jumped up. "It's probably Thomas. He's taking me out in his boat this afternoon." She answered the phone, then called to Ada. "It's for you."

"Who is it?" Ada asked, not getting up.

Vivian put her hand over the mouthpiece. "Sounds like Arthur."

Ada groaned. "Oh, no! Not today! Tell him I'm busy."

"He says it's urgent."

Ada got up from the table and made her way slowly to the telephone. "Hello, Son," she said in a loud voice. She never seemed quite comfortable on the phone, always talking louder than necessary. "What's new?" There was a long pause. "How did you find out about that?" She turned to the others. "A friend in Westhampton sent him the clipping." Another pause. "Now, let's not get excited. You're making a mountain out of a molehill. You tend to do that, you know, just like your Uncle Oscar." She held the receiver away from her ear, saying, "You don't have to shout at me." Lee could hear his voice across the room.

"My own mother making me the laughing stock of my friends in the Hamptons!"

"Calm down, Son. I didn't even go in the water. I just happened to be sitting there." A brief pause with some unintelligible words, then, "Yes, with all my clothes on. And nobody got arrested. So I don't see why you're so upset." Another pause. He had lowered his voice enough so that Lee could not make out the words. "You're getting yourself needlessly worked up, Son. You must remember your blood pressure. It runs in our family, you know." More garbled words from Arthur. Then Ada saying, "No, I'm not trying to change the subject. I just can't see anything in our harmless little activity on the beach worth discussing. Case closed." Ada held the phone farther from her ear. "If you persist in shouting, I'm going to hang up!" she said.

Lee could hear him clearly now. "All right," he blared, "I can see we're not getting anywhere on the telephone! Dolores and I will come out there this afternoon for a face-to-face talk with you and those other crazies."

Ada extended her arms and the telephone skyward, as if in prayer, then turned to the others. They were all shaking their heads vigorously. "No!" Lee said. "That's out of the question!"

Ada lowered the phone to her mouth. "I'm sorry, Son. That won't be possible. I just remembered I'm going out with Vivian and her boyfriend in his new boat this afternoon."

Vivian gasped, a look of horror on her face. "She can't do that!" she whispered to Lee who could not control her laughter at the thought of Ada climbing into Thomas's boat and sunning herself on the deck.

"I wouldn't want to disappoint them," Ada said. "I think his car is turning into the drive now, as a matter of fact. I'll call you later, Son. And, in the meantime, don't you worry about a thing." She hung up, smiling broadly. "Well, I guess I fixed him."

"For the time being." Lee felt a shiver down her spine. Arthur would waste no time reporting this to Kevin Maloney, just when everything was looking so favorable.

* * *

The evening had turned quite chilly, a hint of fall in the air. Lee was wearing a purple sweatshirt over her blouse. Across the front were the words of Susan B. Anthony: *Never another season of silence.* An ironic message Lee had thought when she put it on. She would be better off if she imposed a bit of silence upon herself occasionally—today in particular. She and Minerva and Ada were settled comfortably in the living room watching *Murder She Wrote.* It was a rerun, but none of them could remember who committed the murder. They liked Angela Lansbury enough to watch it again. Vivian was still out somewhere with Thomas, and Elizabeth had phoned to say she wouldn't be home for dinner.

Lee had spent a frustrating afternoon shifting restlessly from one project to another, accomplishing very little. She had tried for a couple of hours to begin a poem about her night swim in the bay but could not re-create the spell. Then she had tried writing some letters but gave up after completing one and throwing it in the wastebasket. Even the Amanda Cross mystery could not hold her interest. She had taken Daisy for a long walk, allowing her to sniff at every bush and telephone pole, enjoying the sunshine and lack of humidity in the air. But eventually she had to come home to the somber atmosphere of the house, somber from Lee's viewpoint anyway. Ada and Minerva did not seem to feel the effect of Elizabeth's outrage as intensely as she did. Minerva had spent the entire afternoon weaving, and Ada had sat contentedly on the porch sketching.

"I think the nephew did it," Ada said. "He looks guilty to me."

"Impossible. Her relatives never commit murder," Lee said.

Then Elizabeth came into the room, looking a bit wilted but still poised and proper.

"Hi, Liz," Minerva said, moving over on the couch to make room for her. "Come sit down and watch the end of this with us."

But Elizabeth remained standing near the door. She looked preoccupied. Lee wanted to say something friendly but could not think of the right words.

"Did you and John have fun?" Ada said.

"I can't talk over the noise of that TV," Elizabeth said, a note of irritation in her voice.

Minerva pressed the mute button. "Where did you go for dinner?"

"*Hobson's Choice.* After looking in on a painting exhibition at Guild Hall that John wanted to see." Elizabeth had always favored Minerva over the rest of them She couldn't be cross with her, not even tonight.

"That's nice," Minerva said, switching the TV on again.

Elizabeth gave a sigh of exasperation. "Would you mind turning off that television? There's something we need to talk about."

"But we want to find out who-done-it," Ada said. "Can't you hold off for ten minutes?"

"I'd rather not," Elizabeth said firmly. Lee noted with apprehension the set of her jaw, the stiffness of her posture.

"All right, Liz, if it's that important." Minerva turned off the TV. "Come sit here and we'll talk."

Elizabeth moved closer but stood facing them by the grand piano, her arm resting on its lid. "This isn't easy for me to say." She cleared her throat. "But I've given it serious thought and talked it over with John today, and I have finally come to a decision."

Lee glanced over at Minerva and Ada on the couch, their faces reflecting her concern.

"John has asked me to go down to Fort Lauderdale with him where he has invested in a retirement condominium." She spoke

235

very fast, almost in a monotone, as if she had rehearsed it several times.

"To live down there?" gasped Ada. The color had drained from her face.

"Let her finish," Minerva said, draping an arm around Ada's shoulder. She, too, had turned pale. They both looked somehow out of character, defenseless and old.

Lee could feel the tears welling up in her eyes—not just for Minerva and Ada, for all of them, for the end of the beautiful dream that might have been, the goal of sisterhood never quite attained. She sat clutching the arm of her chair, hardly able to believe what she had heard.

"When he asked me last week, I said I didn't think I wanted to leave Long Island, but I promised to give it some thought." She was nervously twisting her strand of pearls. "But then after what happened, well, I just decided I'd had enough of all this . . . ."

"And what about this place?" Lee asked, trying to keep her voice steady.

"I'll fly down to Florida with John next week and take a look at the condo." She was not looking directly at any of them. "And I'll put this house on the market, but stipulate that a closing cannot take place until after January 15, the date of your lease agreement. That should give all of you ample time to make other arrangements." She paused, her gaze focused on the floor. "I'll do what I can to help, of course."

"Are you quite certain this is what you want to do?" Minerva asked. "That you're not just acting on the impulse of your anger over that absurd item in the paper?"

"I'm quite certain." Elizabeth turned and walked quickly out of the room.

27

The next day Lee kept busy working in the yard to blot out the confrontation with Elizabeth, her announcement exploding like a guided missile, shattering their serenity, their very lives. Thinking about it now, and that is what her brain persisted in doing, Lee realized that she had been foolish from the start not to acknowledge, or at least be aware of, the fragility of their communal arrangement, the rashness bordering on absurdity of presuming that five mature women, no, face the truth, five old eccentrics of such diverse backgrounds and values could adapt to each other and live in harmony, particularly when one of them was Elizabeth, so conservative, so rigid, so set in her ways. She must have been out of her mind. How could she have been so totally blind to all the obstacles?

The morning had passed fairly quickly. She had turned the compost, tied up the tomato plants, clipped scraggly branches of the evergreens bordering the house, fertilized the azaleas and rhododendrons. This afternoon she was on her knees weeding the flowerbeds and loosening the soil with a trowel. The same coleus, now thriving and luxuriant in foliage, that she and Elizabeth had planted together that distant day back in June. Lee thought longingly of the rapport she had sensed during that quiet interlude. Her bones ached now from her cramped position, the pain radiating from her knees into her thighs, despite the foam rubber cushion she was kneeling on.

She had spent a restless night, waking up intermittently, too warm, then too chilly, tangled in her sheets, dreaming she was trapped in a gigantic spider web of unbreakable threads. The more she would struggle to free herself, the more they encircled her. Finally she awakened sweaty and gasping for breath. Between dreams, her mind would replay the scene with Elizabeth, and, in her blurred half wakeful state she would go over all the things she might have said, conciliatory words instead of the bitter angry ones. Then she would lie there awash in guilt. If she had not proposed the ritual, none of this would have happened. Elizabeth would not be selling the house, and everybody would be happy. But then fresh anger would do battle with the guilt, anger over Elizabeth's proprietary attitude, her unsisterly behavior. At daybreak she got up, bleary-eyed, groggy, and exhausted.

As she weeded, Lee turned over in her mind the reactions of the others to the news. Vivian had given a characteristic shrug saying, "The real estate market is in a terrible slump now. This house might take forever to sell." Then she came up with the idea that the four of them could chip in and buy the house. This had generated a temporary boost in spirits until they started thinking about where they would come up with the several hundred thousand dollars it would cost, Ada saying wryly that it would be the equivalent of flying to the moon. Vivian was at the office today. Lee realized with a jolt that she was going to miss her when they went their separate ways. Despite her frivolities, she added a certain sparkle to their group that no one else could match. Tears filled her eyes. She wiped them with a grubby hand, making muddy streaks across her face.

Minerva had been her customary tight-lipped self, the only tell-tale sign being the little nameless tune she kept humming from time to time as she sat on the terrace tying off the fringe of a woven blouse. Suddenly she stood up, announcing that she felt like having some tea, and was anybody else interested in joining her. Lee said it sounded like a good idea. Dear Min . . . how she was going to miss those comforting cups of tea! But maybe not. Maybe they could rent an apartment together, the two of them — or perhaps even a small house, not here in Quintauket but in some less pretentious area of town. Pooling their resources, they could very likely find a place large enough for Minerva's loom and Lee's word processor without infringing on each other's privacy, and yet not have to live alone. Lee smiled at the thought.

Ada, in a lawn chair reading *To the Lighthouse,* said she would like a cup too. She had been unusually quiet since last night. Probably worried—with good reason. This could conceivably give Arthur an edge in the court case.

Minerva brought out the tea tray and set it on an upturned bushel basket by a bench near the coleus bed. Grasping the handles of her kneeling stool, Lee hoisted herself up from the ground with some difficulty, slowly straightening into a vertical position. She stretched her back, then bent down to rub her legs before joining Minerva and Ada on the bench. She felt bone weary. The three of them sat quietly without the need for conversation. Lee sipped her tea, enjoying its pungent warmth, one of Minerva's herbal varieties, thinking how this might easily become an afternoon custom when they got their apartment together.

"By the way, I phoned Bernie this morning," Minerva said.

"I imagine she was surprised at the news," Ada said, reaching for a cookie.

"Yes," Minerva said. "But she came up with a rather interesting possibility."

"A possibility?" said Lee.

"Well, for lack of a better word, yes." Minerva seemed to be framing in her mind what she would say next, strangely ill-at-ease, stirring her tea, staring absent-mindedly into the cup.

Lee felt her muscles grow tense, without quite knowing why, sensing that Minerva might be about to say something she did not want to hear. "What kind of a possibility?"

Minerva continued to stir her tea without looking up.

Ada chuckled. "The possibility that we might strangle Elizabeth and bury her beneath the roses?"

"Not a bad idea!" Lee said, hoping somehow to avoid whatever it was that Bernie had suggested.

"No." Minerva put down her spoon and took a sip of tea. There was a half smile on her face and a soft glow Lee had not noticed before. "The possibility that I might move in with her. You know, she has that large apartment over the book shop, and she's alone now. She has a spare bedroom I could use, and there would be a place for my loom and plenty of storage space for my yarns." She finished her tea, putting the cup and saucer on the tray, then glanced over at Lee who sat stunned, the blood pounding in her ears, everything spinning around.

"What did you tell her?" Lee's voice sounded far away, as if coming from somebody else through a tunnel. She clutched her cup in one hand and grasped the bench with the other, holding on tight to keep from sliding off.

"I thanked her for the offer and told her I would have to think it over." Minerva was still smiling that soft, distant smile, as if already picturing herself cozily settled into Bernie's New Haven apartment. She draped her arm around Lee's shoulder. "Are you all right, Lee? You look awfully tired—and your face is quite flushed. Perhaps you overdid it today." She sounded worried.

Lee was acutely aware of the pressure of Minerva's arm on her shoulder, its comforting warmth, but steeled herself against it. Min asks if I'm all right, she thought bitterly. After demolishing my survival plans for the two of us, am I all right? How could she be so casual about all this? Why couldn't she have thought about it herself—that they might share an apartment somewhere? After all, she had been Minerva's friend much longer than Bernie. But this thing with Bernie—it was different, more intense. She could not deny it. A flood of images floated through her mind. That chance meeting in Washington, how Bernie had instantly reminded her of Min, her voice, her manner, her bearing, despite her age, a good twenty years younger, how eager Lee had been for them to meet, how they had immediately started talking and laughing together as if they had known each other for years . . . and later Bernie in her shop leaning over Min's shoulder pointing out something in a book, their heads together, nearly touching, and sitting in the ritual circle, Bernie's arm around Minerva, and together in the bay, arms linked, engrossed in each other. A physicality that suddenly formed a pattern. Subtle signs Lee had seen but chosen to disregard. Why did she have to encounter Bernie in the first place? Pure ironic chance. Or was it? Whatever the cause, it was not fair! But where was it written that life had to be fair?

She winced at the thought of Minerva occupying Bernie's

spare bedroom . . . Minerva's four-treadle loom, her shelves of multicolored yarns, her racks of handwoven dresses, tops, pants, her array of scarves and hats, and the tapestries, things that now took more than half of the attic work space. If Min were to put all that in Bernie's spare bedroom, there would hardly be space for a bed. Would she share Bernie's bed? Lee carefully set her cup on the bench and wiped her sweaty face with her napkin. "I *am* rather tired," she said, trying to keep her voice steady. "Perhaps I got a little sunburn."

"You should wear a sun hat," Ada said.

"I hate hats!" Lee could feel the tears welling up. "And I hate Elizabeth for making us split up!" She dabbed at her eyes with her napkin. She hated Bernie too but dared not say it. Of course, Min had not yet agreed to the proposal. She merely said she would think it over. But there was a sense of inevitability about it. Lee reached for a cookie then quickly put it back. She wouldn't be able to keep it down. Probably couldn't even swallow it. Glancing at her knobby fingers, she massaged her knuckles. Her hands ached from digging and pulling at the weeds. But somehow the physical pain helped ease the emotional anguish.

"Don't take it so hard, Lee dear," Minerva said gently. "Things will work out." She reached over for Lee's cup. "Let me pour you another spot of tea." Things would work out for Min, no doubt. But Lee could see no hope for herself. She accepted the tea, seeking the solace she had found earlier in its spicy warmth, but now there was a bitter taste to it.

* * *

The three women had moved to the porch where they could be in the shade and catch the late afternoon breeze off the bay. After a long, soothing shower, tense muscles relaxed, Lee felt more optimistic. Maybe Minerva was right—maybe everything would somehow turn out well. She had changed from jeans to a wrap-around cotton print skirt and sleeveless blouse. She was sitting on the swing beside Ada, comforted by its gentle motion. Minerva was in one of the Adirondack chairs crocheting the band of a woven hat, and Vivian was sprawled in the other chair, home

241

early from the office, complaining of the scarcity of clients.

A car pulled into the drive. Probably John bringing Elizabeth home. He had picked her up that morning to drive her to the hospital, and they said something about having lunch together. Then another car drove in. Who could that be? They were not expecting anyone. While Lee was speculating on this, Arthur appeared, followed by Dolores. Lee felt a sudden shortness of breath. The doubt and despair, that cloud she thought she had dispersed, quickly reappeared, nearly suffocating her.

"Hello, Mother." Arthur crossed over from the French doors to Ada, giving her his usual peck on the cheek.

Dolores quickly followed, murmuring, "Mother Abernathy, so good to see you." Ada managed to duck her kiss which landed on the back of the swing instead.

"Mrs. Sherwood tells us that . . . ."

"Never mind what Elizabeth says," Ada interrupted. "Just tell me, Son, what are you doing here?" Her blue eyes blazed at him. "I told you yesterday your presence was not necessary."

Lee sat scowling at him, but he was paying no attention to her.

"Well, when Mrs. Sherwood called this morning, I said to Dolores, 'Mother is in trouble. We must go to the Hamptons and talk things out.'" His voice sounded more nasal than usual. Lee made a mental note that he was the last person in the universe she would want coming to her rescue.

Dolores stood alongside, her face pulled into a tight little smile.

Ada looked at him, befuddled. "Trouble?" She cocked her head a little to one side. "Are you in some sort of trouble, Son? Tell me what happened." Her tone had changed from annoyance to concern. "You do have a great way of stirring up trouble, just like your father. An Abernathy trait, I suppose. His brother, you remember, Uncle Herbert? Well, he was constantly getting himself out of the frying pan into the fire. And remember that time when you were in grade school, and I had to go see the principal because you . . . ."

Lee smiled at the mix-up. Ada really should get a hearing aid but stubbornly resisted the idea. Her hearing generally seemed to deteriorate when the news was not to her liking. What was Arthur up to anyway? And what had Elizabeth said about Ada?

"*I'm* not in trouble, Mother." Arthur raised his voice to a higher pitch. "It's *you* I'm talking about." Lee could see the blood pulsing in his temples. He was clearly thrown off balance.

"Me?" Ada's voice was puzzled. "I don't understand. You said *you* were in trouble." She turned to Lee. "Isn't that what he said—that *he* was in trouble?"

Before Lee was forced to take sides between truth and illusion, Arthur responded in a louder voice, his face now quite red. "It's *you*, Mother, *you!*"

"Please lower your voice, Son. You needn't shout at me." Her posture stiffened. "Now, let's hear what sort of trouble you're talking about." Ada folded her arms and leaned against the back of the swing, gazing up at Arthur or past him to some distant year, a half smile on her face, perhaps remembering the episode involving Arthur and the principal.

Minerva pulled over two deck chairs which she placed alongside her chair. "Why don't you and Dolores sit down and tell us all about it."

They took their seats, Arthur looking uncomfortable, not prepared for this unbalanced approach.

"Now, Son," Ada said quietly, "what sort of stories has Elizabeth been telling you? And," she added with a frown, "why was she discussing my private affairs with you or anyone else behind my back?"

"I'm not just anyone. I happen to be your son."

"Well, that's true enough. And what a happening it was—the day you were born, nearly forty-six years ago." She smiled that distant smile again, remembering . . . .

"No, Mother, fifty-six years ago."

"My stars, has it been that long? Time . . . I declare, it whizzes by so fast lately, I can't keep up with it any more!" Ada studied him closely. "Well, no wonder you're beginning to look a bit frayed around the edges. In your fifties—that's a turning point, you know. But don't worry, Son, you probably have plenty of years ahead, if you mind your blood pressure, of course, and don't allow little trivialities to upset you too much. Our family, on the Merrick side that is, has a history of longevity. Your Great-Aunt Mathilde lived to ninety-six and Great Uncle Peter died just short of his one-hundredth and your . . . ."

"That's enough of our genealogy, for God's sake! You keep changing the subject."

"I'm sorry, Son. Now let's see, where were we?" She gave the swing a shove with her foot that set it in rapid motion.

"We were discussing the fact that Mrs. Sherwood invited us out here for lunch to talk over your situation."

"What do you mean, *my situation*? I'll have you to know there's nothing . . . ." As she was speaking, Elizabeth and John came out on the porch. Ada stopped the swing and turned away from Arthur to face them. She took a deep breath. "I'll thank you for an explanation!"

"Well, we ahhh . . . ." Elizabeth, startled and visibly embarrassed, cleared her throat. "That is, I thought . . . but John went along with the idea. We thought . . . ." John stood slightly behind her, shifting his weight from one foot to the other. "I mean, I got to worrying last night about you and how you would manage after I sell the house. I was distressed at the idea of you having no place to go, Ada, and I decided to talk it over with Arthur and Dolores." She was twisting her hands together as she spoke. "I thought maybe Arthur would agree to drop the court case, and the two of you could work out some sort of friendly arrangement. It just seemed like the Christian thing to do."

Lee glared at Elizabeth. Damn her good deeds! But it did point up a question they had not yet faced. Where would Ada go in January when they had to leave this house?

"And so," Elizabeth continued, oblivious to Lee's disapproving stare, "John and I invited them to meet us in Southampton for lunch at the Post House."

"You might, at the very least, have invited Ada to join you." Lee made no effort to hide her irritation.

Minerva meanwhile had pulled up two more chairs. Elizabeth sat down, crossing her legs and pulling her skirt primly over her knees. John sat awkwardly beside her, folding and unfolding his hands, staring vaguely at the floor. "You know, at Ada's age,"

Elizabeth said, "she does need to plan ahead."

"At her age? What do you mean by that?" Lee challenged. "Ada is not all that old, in today's terms—not quite four years older than you, as a mater of fact."

"Eighty-one is considerably younger than going-on-eighty-five," Elizabeth replied. "And besides, I happen to take better care of myself." She checked her neatly coiffured hair with one hand and smoothed down her well-tailored skirt with the other. "You know, Ada tends to be rather careless about her health."

There was some truth to that. Elizabeth exercised at the Omni Health Club three times a week and counted her calories and cholesterol. Ada had always scoffed at such measures. She ate with gusto whatever pleased her palate. Never one for vigorous exercise, she had used the hip injury as an excuse to be even more sedentary. But, except for slightly elevated blood pressure, she appeared to be reasonably fit.

"You're making me sound downright doddering!" Ada muttered, clearly agitated by Elizabeth's little innuendo.

Glancing at Ada to confirm her own positive evaluation of her physical well-being, Lee was disconcerted by what she could see with an objective eye. Rather than sitting with her usual erect posture, Ada was slightly humped over, her denim skirt hiked up a bit over her knees revealing the blue network of veins on her legs, her print blouse buttoned crooked with some berry stains down the front. Strands of gray hair, pulled loose from the braid, hung limply about her face, the sallow skin crinkled like old crepe paper. How strangely unkempt and frail she appeared at this moment. Lee recalled their conversation at lunch last spring—Ada saying she was not sure she wanted to live past eighty-five, considering the deterioration that accompanies the aging process.

This brought to mind Minerva's crippled friend in a nursing home, a painter like Ada, how she had given up on life, trying to starve herself to death . . . how Minerva, after the suicide of the aging Bruno Bettelheim by suffocation in a plastic bag, had considered sneaking one to her, but fortunately she was liberated by death before it became necessary. Lee shuddered. Ada would have no patience as a chronic invalid. But . . . a plastic bag . . .

would she ever seek death that desperately? Her birthday was coming up in October, and she had said nothing further about not wanting to pass that milestone. They must plan a proper celebration, perhaps their last gathering. Lee was filled with intense sadness.

"Mrs. Sherwood says your behavior has become more erratic of late, Mother." Arthur's voice grated into Lee's thoughts. "And after that bizarre episode reported in the paper, I think she has a valid point."

"Bizarre?" Ada looked bewildered. "Wait just a minute, Son." She stood up, then sank back down on the swing, as if drained of her strength.

"Don't pay any attention to them." Lee put a protective arm around Ada's shoulder. "Can't you folks see how you are upsetting her?" she said to them defiantly.

"Now, don't get excited, Mother. Remember your blood pressure." Arthur continued to ignore Lee.

"My blood pressure is my business," Ada mumbled. The fight seemed to have gone out of her. They were beating her down. She turned to Lee. "Have I been acting strange lately?" Her tone was worried.

"Of course not! Don't listen to them." She wanted to put her hands over Ada's ears or whisk her away, out of range of this attack.

"Well, you know, as one grows older, one tends to become forgetful and do eccentric little things," Elizabeth said, twisting her beads and smiling nervously. "And one needs to make arrangements before one . . . ."

"Are you implying that I'm getting senile?" Ada's face was now quite flushed. Lee, seething at their insensitivity, wished desperately for a way to change the subject.

"Well, you're certainly not getting any younger," Elizabeth said. "I've noticed how you misplace your reading glasses or your book or your sketch pad and can't always remember whether you've taken your medicine and sometimes forget phone messages and . . . ."

Lee had reached the saturation point. "Stop it, Elizabeth! We all do silly little forgetful things at any age. You have no

246

right talking to Ada as if she were coming down with Alzheimers or something dreadful of that sort. She is perfectly sane and capable of looking after herself, and you know it!"

She exchanged glances with Minerva who suddenly stood up, inquiring if anyone would like a cup of tea. Lee checked her watch. It was well past tea time. What they needed was a good stiff drink.

"No thanks, not now," Elizabeth said impatiently. And the other three politely declined with a shake of their heads.

Lee studied the four figures grouped across from the swing. Eeeny, Meeny, Miny, and Mo . . . with their rigid posture and earnest faces. She hated them with an uncontrollable fury. In truth, it was only Arthur and Elizabeth she hated. Dolores could hardly be held accountable. She just sat there stupidly nodding her little parakeet head, chirping her agreement as Arthur talked. And John was only on the fringe of it. To his credit, he had not said anything derogatory about Ada. Probably just went along with it to please Elizabeth. She had him completely charmed. Lee sadly remembered the days when she, too, had felt the quiet charm of Elizabeth. She could hear the bittersweet strains of the Chopin nocturne Elizabeth played while they all sat together on the porch waiting for word from Minerva's doctor. How close they had been just those few months ago! She gazed at the lengthening shadows on the spacious lawn, and beyond, to the water tinted pale aqua in the diminishing light. The motion of the swing took her back to that swing in Missouri where she used to sit beside her grandmother listening to her stories, certain that this wise old woman of the Ozarks had an answer for everything . . . Lee wished longingly for some of her wisdom now.

"Never mind the pleasantries," Ada was saying. "Let's get down to business and settle this once and for all." In her agitation, she was pushing the swing back and forth in a rapid, jerking motion.

"Fine!" Minerva returned to her seat and looked over at Arthur. "Why don't you tell us precisely what you have in mind?"

"Well, yes. I propose that I am willing to drop my petition for custody of Mother provided that she go to this retirement home I've found in New Jersey. It's called *Sunset House*. Mother could have

247

her own room and nourishing meals, and there's a recreation room, and perpetual nursing care, should she become ill, and . . . ."

"Perpetual care?" Ada muttered. "Sounds like a cemetery!"

"Let him finish," Minerva said calmly.

"I don't need perpetual care! When my time comes, I'm ready, and I don't want to be hooked up to any perpetual motion machines or anything of that sort. You can just forget it, Son." Reaching in her pocket for a handkerchief, Ada wiped her face which had become still more flushed and wet with perspiration.

Lee noticed that Ada's hand was shaking. That damned Arthur—and Elizabeth too! They could kill her at this rate. She tried to envision Ada limited to one room and a crowded recreation hall, trying to paint among a bunch of old people playing parcheesi or bingo or watching television. No, impossible! She stood up and placed herself between Arthur and Ada, as if to shield her. "I think we've heard enough, Arthur."

She had the eerie feeling that everything was coming around full cycle. First, Tranquil Acres, now Sunset House. For some people, perhaps such a place would be fine, but certainly not for the outspoken, flamboyant Ada. Why couldn't Arthur understand?

"Why don't you stay out of this?" Arthur's voice was becoming more high-pitched, agitation showing in every angle of his face. Lee noticed he never addressed her by name. His steel eyes targeted her. "It would cost me a mint of money to put Mother in this home, but I'm willing to do it for her sake. And she would be well rid of the likes of you with your wild schemes." He stood up and stepped to one side in order to see his mother beyond Lee who had remained standing between them.

"Don't you talk that way to Lee!" Ada raised her cane as if to whap him one, then quickly lowered it. Lee wished she had followed through. But, on second thought, that would provide first-hand evidence of *eccentric behavior*.

"And furthermore," he continued, oblivious to her threat, "it's under reliable Christian management. I'm sure I can get her in through one of the deacons in our church who's on their board of directors."

248

"How many times do I have to tell you, I don't need care!" Ada's voice quivered with rage.

"We might be better judges of that than you." Arthur was cracking his knuckles nervously.

Lee wondered how the easy-going Ada could possibly have parented such a mean-spirited specimen. There was no chance that the babies got switched at a hospital. She remembered Ada's tale of giving birth at home with a midwife. Lee imagined Ada at her easel up there in her Greenwich Village loft, painting away at one of her mammoth oils—she was into cubism at the time— large planes of red, blue, and purple intersected by heavy black lines—painting until the labor pains forced her to stop, interrupting her work only long enough to give birth . . . and the child, as he grew up, having to maneuver for her attention, standing there beside the easel, little Arthur in his Dr. Denton pajamas, his chubby little arms holding his teddy bear asking questions that Ada might have been too preoccupied to answer, being told to sit down and play with his blocks. Not an easy life for a child of Arthur's temperament. But was that reason enough to excuse all of his miserable behavior from childhood to the present day?

"Now, wait just a minute!" Vivian jumped up from her chair where she had been sitting silently, as if only half listening. "Ada told you she doesn't need that type of care. And she is the one to make the decision—not you or Dolores or Elizabeth or John, for God's sake!" Her green eyes flashed angry sparks at Arthur. Lee felt like applauding. "And, besides, it's a moot point because Ada is going to be living with me."

Ada was looking at her dumbfounded. "I am?" she said softly. "Living with you?"

Lee glanced around at the astonished faces of the others. When had Vivian dreamed this up? Or was she merely saying it to protect Ada from Arthur at the moment?

"When did you arrange that?" Elizabeth demanded.

"This morning." Vivian walked over to the swing and placed her hand on Ada's shoulder. "Well, it's not exactly arranged, but I've taken care of the preliminaries. I found it in our rental property—in East Moriches, year-round at a reasonable rate, small house, story and a half. Ada could have the upstairs to herself—a large room with good light for her studio and an alcove for sleeping. I would have a bedroom downstairs, and the two of us could share the rest of the house." Ada was staring at her open-mouthed. "It's available the first of the year for rental, with an option to buy."

"Option to buy?" said Arthur. "Where would Mother get that kind of money?"

Ada sat erect now, head high. "I'm not a pauper, you know. I do have money put aside."

"But it shouldn't be wasted on some run-down piece of property that one of these crazy ladies comes up with out of the blue," Arthur growled.

If Arthur really cared about his mother, Lee thought, why didn't he offer to put his mint of money into buying that house for Vivian and Ada, or into Elizabeth's house for all of them, rather than investing it in that stupid retirement home? She knew the answer, of course. He wanted Ada safely tucked away in an institution, well out of range of their influence. New Jersey . . . it sounded so distant, so inaccessible. If he succeeded in taking her there, they might never see each other again. Lee had the strong urge to finish him off with Ada's cane herself.

"And who would take care of Mother when she needs it, physically or mentally?"

"Would you kindly refrain from casting aspersions at my mentality!" Ada snapped. "I'm quite in control of all my faculties."

"I would take care of Ada, in the remote possibility that she would ever need special care," Vivian said.

"*You?*" He gave a sarcastic laugh. "*You?*" Are you a licensed health care worker or psychotherapist?" He scrutinized Vivian standing there in her gaudy flowered dress and red pumps, her garish red nails, heavily mascara'd eyes and lipsticked mouth, her bushy hair, overly blond. She did not have the appearance of the ideal caretaker. But, for some inexplicable reason, she and Ada always had got along well together. An odd couple, indeed, but they could quite possibly manage, one balancing the other. Vivian seemed to enjoy living on the fringe of the art world, and Ada liked Vivian's banter. True, Vivian did not fit the traditional role. But who except Arthur and Elizabeth thought Ada needed a caretaker anyway? "Mother would be out of her mind to entrust herself to the care of you or any of the rest of these . . . ."

"All right, Son, hold your tongue! We've heard quite enough of your insults." She stood up, leaning heavily on her cane. "I shall do as I choose. And I choose never to set foot in Sunset House. The very name gives me the creeps." Her face was deeply flushed, and her breathing sounded raspy. They must get Arthur out of here before Ada collapsed.

Minerva, apparently with the same thought, turned to Arthur. Her voice was firm. "We feel that Ada is quite capable of making her own decision concerning her future plans. And, at this point, you have no right to interfere."

"We'll see about that!" Arthur's face was covered with red blotches. "You can just forget about my offer to withdraw the petition. I'll see you in court on the fifteenth." He grabbed Dolores by the elbow, and they walked across the lawn to their car.

"Good riddance!" Ada muttered.

Elizabeth sat wringing her hands. "Oh dear me," she said, "I didn't think this would cause such a hullabaloo. I was merely trying to do the Christian thing to help."

John put a protective arm around her shoulders.

Lee sighed. She had heard just about all she could tolerate of Elizabeth's *Christian thing*. Of course, she should allow for Elizabeth's upbringing—the same indoctrination she herself had experienced—a world in which *Christian* was synonymous with *good*. But she was tired of making allowances for Elizabeth. Tired of Elizabeth.

Ada, her breathing more regular now, her voice more calm, turned abruptly, her braid flipping dramatically over one shoulder. She stood facing Elizabeth. "Do me a favor," she said. "Quit trying to assuage your Christian conscience, your sense of guilt, which you have assumed with good reason, I might add, for throwing us out on the street, so to speak, by trying to run our lives. We'll manage just fine, thank you very much, without you." She took a deep bow in Elizabeth's direction, then sat down, pushing aside her braid and wiping her face once more with her handkerchief.

A bit garbled, Lee observed, but she had made her point eloquently. How she would miss Ada and her theatrics! She felt strangely weighted down, as if her body were filled with lead, held in place by huge magnets. A deep sense of gloom darkened her vision. She closed her ears to the babble of voices. The realization of her aloneness slowly crept over her. Elizabeth would have John to love and cherish her; Min would have Bernie; Ada would have Vivian—provided, of course, that they won out over Arthur in court, and that was a *must* they still had to deal with. In any case, Lee would be alone, the fifth wheel, with no one. She wanted to cry out, *Wait, everybody, this is not fair!* But they probably wouldn't be listening anyway. With supreme effort, she pulled herself up from the swing and excused herself, mumbling something about going inside to start dinner.

* * *

That night Lee dreamed she was a bag lady wandering the streets of Manhattan . . . dirty, unkempt, in a stained gray sweater, pieces of it raveling away, a dingy skirt torn at the hem, shabby sneakers, her gray hair long and stringy, pulled back from her face with a rubberband, skin chapped and reddened by the cold, a plastic bag containing her sole possessions: a few books of poetry, a notebook with nothing in it, a faded photo of Minerva, some scraps of food, a raincoat, another bag tied to her grocery cart holding a collection of soda bottles and cans scrounged from the trash . . . stopping by Horn & Hardart with the cash she could get from the collection to buy a bowl of soup and a cup of coffee . . . and while checking out a trash can in the theater district seeing Elizabeth and John walk past without recognizing her, hearing Elizabeth say something about "these poor homeless people" and how they should not be allowed to clutter up the streets . . . following them far enough to hear her saying, "the Christian thing would be to put them away where they can do no harm," her monied voice trailing off into the night . . . calling after them, "you've got it all wrong, let me explain," but no response . . . finding a protected corner by a building, spreading newspapers on the sidewalk to lie on, covering herself with the raincoat but sleepless with the nagging ache of swollen joints, struggling to get up from the sidewalk, unable to move, calling out for help but ignored by the people who were stepping over her as if they were unaware of her . . . .

Lee awoke uncovered and shaking in the chill of the night. She pulled the blanket around her but continued to shiver uncontrollably for quite some time. She lay awake in her comfortable bed, with its clean sheets that smelled of lavender, watching the shadows of tree branches against the wall, wondering what her fate would be, where she would be sleeping six months from now. Not on a Manhattan sidewalk, of course. But in what cramped and lonely room?

28

They were sitting in hushed silence behind the railing of the spectator section of the courtroom—Vivian, Minerva, Bernie, and Lee, along with assorted visitors for other cases, waiting for the judge to arrive. At one of the tables in front of them were Ada and Mary Graverton, her attorney, and at the other Arthur and his attorney. Lee felt a heaviness in her chest, perhaps in reaction to the oppressive atmosphere of this room, its dark wood paneling broken only by the State seal on the center panel, the American flag, and a row of somber oil paintings—previous justices, black-robed and solemn-faced, staring down at them. All courtrooms seemed designed to dwarf the participants, with the exception of the judge, of course, royally enthroned on his bench. Lee glanced anxiously at her watch. Nearly ten o'clock. Ada's case was scheduled for nine-thirty, but their attorney had cautioned them to expect some delay. The tension of waiting . . . poor Ada would be frazzled before the hearing even got underway.

Lee tried to shift her mind to more agreeable thoughts, but it was hard to recall anything pleasant within recent weeks. Since the day of Elizabeth's bombshell, life had been far from harmonious. It had, in fact, been chaotic—Elizabeth taking off for Florida the first of September, leaving her share of the household chores for them to divide among themselves, topped by a final intensive interview of Ada by Kevin Maloney (or Mr. Baloney, as she insisted on calling him behind his back), accompanied this time by a court-appointed psychiatrist, Dr.

Penelope Greer—her questions seemingly innocuous, but just one more hurdle, Lee holding her breath for fear Ada would blurt out some of her zany remarks, Maloney and Greer leaving all of them in a wretched state of anxiety, indicating in their noncommittal manner that they would go over their notes and present their recommendations to the Judge.

Then going with Vivian to see the house she had in mind—a small white frame with sagging porch, a broken step, peeling paint, and a ragged unkempt lawn—depressing, despite Ada's cheerful insistence that it had great possibilities. Minerva had spent a day in New Haven with Bernie to check out the space and discuss financial arrangements. Lee was invited to come along but contrived an excuse to stay home. She did not want to play the role of third person in any sort of triangle. So far Minerva had not committed herself to the move. She was not the impulsive type. But Lee had little doubt about her ultimate decision.

And today here was Bernie sitting between them. Lee wished she had it in her heart to be more generous in spirit toward this whole thing. After all, she had practically thrown the two of them together. And it was good of Bernie, in this busy season for book sales, to take the day off in support of Ada.

Lee sat nervously twisting her silver and gold ring, the one Matt made for her in the early years of their marriage, the lucky ring she always wore in times of crisis. But now she was not at all sure it would help. Everything seemed to have been going awry.

She glanced at Ada, what she could see of her from behind. She looked so forlorn, so vulnerable. Rather than her usual erect posture, she sat slightly hunched over. As they prepared to leave the house, she had been in a state of nerves—her speech, though not garbled, a bit irregular, stumbling over a word or forgetting what she started to say. But who wouldn't be jittery, her future at stake? Damn Arthur for putting her through this! Lee wished she could be there at the table beside her, though in her present state of mind she might not provide much strength.

They had made certain that Ada looked her most respectable best, but that seemed to contribute to the unreal sense that the woman there at the table with her attorney was not the real

Ada. Her braid, instead of hanging down her back, brightly decorated with ribbons, was sedately wound around her head, with the intention of adding dignity. She was wearing a gray suit, purchased for the occasion, with a plain white blouse and a single strand of pearls. Ada had objected, but they convinced her this would work to her advantage. Now, Lee had her doubts. She missed the swirling skirt and embroidered top, the multiple strands of beads and jangly bracelets. Ada could as well be any ordinary old woman.

Lee, too, felt out of character in her own outfit. As a rule, she only wore dresses or skirts to weddings or funerals or some equally significant occasion. Today was one of those times. She was wearing a simple tan skirt with white ruffled blouse topped by a textured beige jacket, and dressy beige pumps that cramped her feet. Though she had been pleased with her *proper* appearance—Elizabeth could have done no better—the narrow skirt and the shoes conspired to restrict her movements and make her feel awkward, more ill-at-ease than she might otherwise have been. The only parts of her attire representing her true self were Matt's ring and the silver labris she wore on a chain around her neck, tucked among the ruffles—her *battle-axe*, as Minerva called it.

Finally the judge, a large imposing gray-haired man, entered the room, and a court officer called out in a loud voice: "All rise!" As they stood up, Ada turned and glanced over her shoulder at the four of them. Lee gave her what she hoped was a reassuring smile. How much better it would have been if the hearing had been held earlier in the summer—when they were a stronger, more cohesive unit, before the Elizabeth explosion and all those unexpected problems. But that was beyond their control. Lee had the sinking feeling that they were no longer in control of anything—their own lives or what would transpire in today's hearing.

Taking note of the judge's serious face and rigid posture, Lee came to the troubling conclusion that he was more Arthur's type than Ada's. The judge, meanwhile, was sorting through a packet of papers his clerk handed him, and after a few more agonizing minutes, their case was called. Arthur's attorney stood and presented his petition to be named Ada's conservator. Lee's mind was so scrambled, she could not take in all the words. Even if she had been more clear-headed, she would have difficulty hearing because of the poor acoustics. Despite his loud voice, the words blurred together. Something was said about Ada's *advanced age and impaired ability to make rational decisions* . . . followed by a statement concerning *impaired judgment in her choice of companions* and something else about *a lifestyle consistent with her personal well-being.* Lee could feel her rage mounting. The words were similar to those on the initial document, but more accusatory. As the attorney continued his convoluted petition, Lee noticed Ada tugging at the sleeve of Mary Graverton, whispering something and the attorney shaking her head, responding in a low voice.

Next Mary Graverton stood, speaking on behalf of Ada. Lee could hear very little. But she knew that, in essence, she would be pointing out that Ada was perfectly capable of caring for herself and did not wish to be in the custody of her son or an institution of any sort. She was a tall woman who carried herself well. With her tailored navy blue suit and heels, short black hair neatly swept back from her face, confident, businesslike manner, she certainly looked the part of a capable lawyer. But would she be a match for Arthur's swaggering loud-mouthed attorney?

There was a pause while the judge's clerk handed him some papers which he looked through. Perhaps the reports of the guardian and psychiatrist. Everything could hinge on their recommendations. Lee's hands felt clammy, and her throat was dry. She fished in her bag for a roll of Life Savers.

Then Arthur's attorney requested that he take the stand. Lee could see Ada's back stiffen. She glanced over toward Minerva who was saying something to Bernie. Vivian looked down the row at Lee with arched eyebrows. She made a comical face and rolled her eyes skyward. She seemed to be holding up well. But Vivian was always good in a crisis. Lee envied the way she could detach herself. The attorney, Mr. Bleekman, was a short, stocky fellow, strands of gray hair parted low on the side and pulled over his balding head, serving only to accentuate the roundness of his face, despite his mustache and goatee which seemed out of character. There was an arrogant aggressiveness in his manner

257

that filled Lee with apprehension. Taking a deep breath, she said a prayer, of sorts, to that vague Power out there, whatever it was, which might cast the dice in their favor. She found herself wishing Elizabeth were with them to help out with one of her Christian prayers—although, at this time, she might well be inclined to pray for the wrong outcome.

After a few preliminary questions about Arthur's background, occupation, and community activities, to establish his respectability, his attorney proceeded to the big question: "Would you kindly tell the Court, Mr. Abernathy, precisely why you feel it is in the best interests of your mother, Ada Abernathy, to be in your custody?"

Arthur cleared his throat and adjusted his tie. "First and foremost, it is evident that my mother has been wrongly influenced by these . . . " He paused, as if about the say *crazy ladies*. "these women," gesturing in their direction, "with whom she has been living for well over a year." His nasal voice carried well. "Clearly, your Honor, she needs to be free from them. Due to her physical infirmity and her unstable mental and emotional state, she is completely at their mercy and . . . ."

Before her attorney could voice an objection, Ada was standing up, red-faced. "That's a lie!" she shouted.

The judge was frowning and rapping his gavel for order. Lee could feel her heart pounding. They had warned Ada not to let Arthur get to her.

Mary Graverton had grasped her arm and pulled her down into her chair. "Objection. Conclusory statement," she said.

"Sustained," said the judge. "Strike that last sentence."

Unruffled, Arthur continued. "As a case in point, she has been involved on two occasions in strange rituals with this group, some weird sort of black magic or witchraft, totally alien to her Christian beliefs."

"Objection. Inflammatory and prejudicial."

Lee had her eye fixed on Ada. She appeared to be struggling to free herself from Mary who, with a firm grip on her arm, was saying something to her and shaking her head. "He's exaggerating!" Ada said in a loud voice.

The judge pounded his gavel again. "Miss Graverton," he said sternly, his sharp blue eyes glinting behind metal-rimmed glasses, "if you cannot control your client, I will be compelled to have her removed from this courtroom."

"Yes, your Honor."

"Objection sustained. Strike that last part."

"You may continue," the judge said to Arthur, "but limit your statements to actual facts rather than your interpretation of events."

Lee clutched the arms of her seat, feeling a strange dizziness and ringing in her ears. She must not add to the confusion by pulling anything stupid—passing out or some such, to fuel Arthur's argument.

"Thank you, your Honor," Arthur said with phony humility. "As I was about to say, these women she lives with are constantly cooking up wild schemes. It was at one of their pro-abortion rallies, in fact, that my mother fell and broke her hip." He was warming to the occasion now. "And furthermore she went traipsing off with them to Washington for another rally in a wheelchair, then denied to me that she had been there. One just cannot trust those people!"

Again Ada's attorney objected to his conclusion, and it was sustained. But the attack continued. Arthur's attorney stepped closer. "Weren't they recently in trouble with the law?"

"Yes, I regret to say." Arthur was obviously enjoying his day in court. "They were caught by the police swimming in the nude one night at a public beach."

His attorney thanked Arthur, and the judge asked Ada's attorney if she wished to question the witness. Lee was seething. Bernie, as if reading her mind, grasped her arm, whispering, "Don't get all worked up. Ada will have her turn to set things straight." But Lee knew that setting things straight was not Ada's forte.

Mary Graverton said she would not question Arthur at this time but reserved the right to recall him later.

Mr. Bleekman then called Dr. Prudence Runkles, Director of Tranquil Acres, to the stand. She was a tall, bony woman of indeterminate age, exuding nervous energy, dark hair pulled back severely from her face accentuating the narrow eyes behind horn-rimmed glasses, her tight thin lips, the hard line of her jaw. The attorney asked her to tell the Court when Ada had come to the nursing home and under what circumstances.

Dr. Runkles consulted a folder of notes. "Mrs. Abernathy entered our facility on February 10, 1989, following hospitalization for a hip operation." Her voice had an unpleasant raspy quality.

"How would you characterize Mrs. Abernathy's behavior?"

"Her behavior was erratic during the first few days. She was not at all cooperative. But with proper care and medication, we were able to bring her under control." She glanced at her folder. "She had a rather violent temper at times."

Lee was watching Ada who sat slumped in her chair staring at her hands crossed in front of her on the table. Had she given up the fight? Her attorney also sat quietly, jotting down some notes on a yellow pad.

"When and under what circumstances did she leave your institution?" His voice became louder now, preparing for the grand climax.

"The entire episode was somewhat bizarre, to say the least." She glanced in the direction of the judge. "On Friday afternoon, March 3, some women came to visit Mrs. Abernathy, and then proceeded to wheel her out of the building and drive away with her."

"Could you identify those women?"

"One of them was Lee Cranford. She left a note in the patient's room informing us they were taking her home with them. Another was Minerva Wingate who signed in at the desk and was talking to me in my office at the time the incident occurred, and another was Elizabeth Sherwood who signed in as a visitor. I believe there was a fourth person, but she must have slipped in the side entrance along with Mrs. Cranford."

Lee sat red-faced and miserable as the director recounted their actions. She made it sound so illicit.

"Do you mean to say these people violated all rules and regulations, removing Ada Abernathy from your institution without a medical release or your knowledge?

"That's correct," she smirked.

Lee could feel all the previous frustration and resentment from Ada's incarceration welling up inside of her. They had tried to talk to the director about Ada beforehand, but she was so rigid, so tangled in the institutional bureaucracy that she could not allow any elements of human kindness to enter the equation. An administrator with a heart that had atrophied to a mere cinder. A dangerous person to hold such power over people's lives.

Bleekman, having made his point, ended his questioning. Ada's attorney began her cross-examination by asking if Elizabeth Sherwood had attempted to discuss with her the possibility that Ada might have been over-medicated.

"It has not been our policy to discuss our patients' problems with outsiders," the director snapped, visibly annoyed.

"Just answer the question, please—yes or no?" Mary Graverton's voice, though soft, had a quality of firmness.

The director acknowledged that such an attempt had been made but reiterated their policy of dealing only with relatives.

"Despite the fact that Mrs. Sherwood was a close friend? And the fact that Mrs. Abernathy had been residing in her home for over a year?"

"Rules are rules," said the director coldly. "One exception could easily lead to another."

Mary Graverton moved closer to the witness. "What medications was Mrs. Abernathy receiving while under your care?"

The director, reading from her notes, responded that Ada had been on a diuretic for blood pressure, plus Dalmane for sleeping, and Haldol to relieve her anxiety and agitation, as well as her general combativeness.

The attorney then submitted for the record an affidavit signed by Dr. Gerald Stone, as Ada's personal physician, based on his examination the day they brought her home from Tranquil Acres, and subsequent visits to evaluate her medical condition. "As indicated in the affidavit," the attorney said to the judge, "Dr. Stone attributes Ada Abernathy's initial state of confusion and disorientation, slurred speech, and poor muscular coordination to adverse effects of the Haldol and Dalmane she had been receiving in the nursing home. The report points out that her

261

symptoms gradually disappeared after those medications were discontinued."

"What is your point, Counselor?" The judge's voice sounded weary or perhaps bored.

"My point, your Honor, is that Ada Abernathy has received better care and treatment *after* being removed from the nursing home than while she was *there,* placed there and forced to remain, by her son."

The director's face was splotchy red, her hands tightly clenched. Her anger was palpable. "But, the fact is . . . ."

"That will be all, Dr. Runkles," Ada's attorney said. "I have no more questions." The judge asked her to step down, and a disgruntled director had no other choice.

Mary Graverton then called Ada to the stand. Grasping the edge of the table to steady herself, Ada stood up slowly and walked with an uneven shuffling gait. She had refused to bring her cane because she did not want to appear crippled. Another error in their strategy. Ada was far more sure-footed with her cane than without. She made it, and Lee heaved a sigh of relief. Then she held her breath when Ada was sworn in, fearing one of her wisecracks. But so far, so good. The gray outfit made her skin look sallow and more wrinkled than ordinarily. Or perhaps it was just the absence of the colorful braid alongside her face.

Her attorney first asked her a few simple questions to establish that she was of sound mind—such as today's date, where she was born, her current address. Concerning her age, Ada responded with a slight tremor in her voice, "Eighty-four years, eleven months, and three days. And, in all those years, I never thought the day would come that I would have to do battle in court with my own son."

Lee felt like applauding. She looked over at Minerva who was smiling broadly.

"Please keep your answers brief, Mrs. Abernathy," said the judge.

"Would you explain your present living arrangement?" the attorney asked.

"Well, I'm living right now with those folks over there." Ada gestured in their direction. "Except for Bernie—she's the one sitting between Lee and Minerva. She lives in New Haven, but she comes over pretty often." Lee felt a flush covering her face. Next thing, Ada would be trying to explain Bernie's sexual orientation. She tried to catch Ada's eye.

The attorney quickly moved on, asking Ada to give the complete names of those she was living with, and Ada obliged. Then she asked who owned the house where they lived.

"Elizabeth Sherwood. Only she's not there right now. She and John . . . ." She stopped abruptly and covered her mouth, glancing in Lee's direction as if to apologize. "She's on vacation in Florida," she added hastily.

They had decided not to mention Elizabeth's plans during the hearing, since she had not yet made any definite arrangements and would not put the house on the market until she returned in a few weeks. Lee missed Elizabeth's calm strength. They would have a better case if she were sitting there beside them. But now she was even more upset with them than upon her initial confrontation. Her second shock came a few days later when she discovered that Melanie, her own granddaughter, was also involved in the ritual and skinny-dipping. Absolutely distraught, sighing and wringing her hands, glaring at the four of them, despite their assurances that no one else would know because the police did not list any names.

"How do you get along with these women you are living with?" the attorney asked.

"Fine," Ada said. "Just fine." Lee wished she would say more, sound a bit more enthusiastic.

"Does this arrangement present any financial problems for you?"

"Why should it?" Ada looked puzzled.

Her attorney rephrased the question. "Can you see any need for your son to assist you financially?"

"Absolutely not! He should keep his nose out of my affairs. What I do with my money is my business!" Her voice was growing louder.

"These friends you live with—do they ever try to influence you, make you do anything you don't want to?"

"Well . . . ." Ada stared at the ceiling. Lee held her breath, thinking about the times she had talked Ada into helping her with this or that project. "Well, not really. Of course, if Lee had her way I'd be involved in every good cause that comes along. But I can hold my own."

"Do you understand your son's petition—what he is asking of the Court?"

"He wants to control me, body and soul, that's what he wants. And I call it an outrage when a mother's own son turns on her!" Ada's face reddened with anger.

Arthur's attorney objected, and the judge admonished Ada to be brief and to the point.

"Has your son spoken to you about a retirement home?" the attorney asked.

"Yes. Sunset Something. One of those perpetual care places. Reminds me of a cemetery."

"How would you feel about living there?"

"I'd hate it!" she replied vehemently.

Mary Graverton thanked Ada, saying she had no more questions. Then Arthur's attorney commenced his cross-questioning. Lee said a silent prayer for Ada's protection.

"Mrs. Abernathy," he said, "is it true that you and your friends were involved in at least two moonlight rituals in recent months while residing at the home of Mrs. Sherwood?" Lee's heart sank. He was trying to make them look like witches or Satanists.

Mary Graverton objected to the term *ritual* on the basis that it was misleading, and the judge instructed Bleekman to rephrase question, which he did, substituting *gatherings*.

"Not exactly," Ada responded.

"Yes or no, were you or were you not involved in these gatherings?"

"Well, partly yes and partly no."

Lee glanced down the row and caught Vivian's eye. She winked at Lee and signaled the circular *right on target* sign with thumb and first finger.

"Try to answer the question, Mrs. Abernathy," the judge said.

"Well, the answer is—yes, there were two ahhh . . . gatherings, but no, there was not exactly a moon in either case."

"Not exactly a moon?" His voice contained a hint of sarcasm.

"Would you explain to the Court what kind of a moon is *not exactly*?"

Ada smiled and nodded her head. Lee wondered if she knew she was leading him on—or if it was all by chance. "You see," Ada said, "the first get-together was during the early evening in May, late May, while it was daylight or twilight anyway, and I don't recall seeing any moon, though I suppose it might have been there somewhere, since it can be there in broad daylight and we just can't see it until nighttime." She took a deep breath. "And the second one—well, that was after dark, but the moon was in eclipse—so most of the time it wasn't there, or hardly at all. That's what I mean by *not exactly*."

"All right." Bleekman looked a bit flustered. "Now, would you kindly tell the Court the purpose of these two gatherings and describe what took place."

"Well, the one in May was for Minerva, an energy circle is what Lee called it. In fact, they were both for Minerva, but this one was just before she went into the hospital for her cancer operation, this healing circle . . . ."

"Do you mean to say you thought you could *heal* her by some sort of witchcraft?" His voice was full of disdain.

Mary Graverton objected to the inflammatory wording, judge sustained it, and Bleekman rephrased the question.

"We are not witches!" Ada said indignantly. "I meant *healing* in the sense of boosting her morale for the operation. We all brought little gifts for Minerva. Mine was a candlestick and Bernie's was a mobile and Vivian's was . . . ."

"Never mind cataloguing the gifts," Bleekman interrupted.

"Well, we placed our gifts on a table in the center to gather positive vibes. And we all joined hands and got energy from the ground and passed it around the circle and Lee chanted, sort of, to the four directions, you know, the points of the compass, and then we invited our mothers and grandmothers to join us, only I never got along with Mama so I didn't invite her, only my grandmothers . . . ."

Lee closed her eyes in dismay and tried not to listen. Ada, true to form, was getting it hopelessly garbled, and the judge was sure to think they were all a bit balmy.

"*Ghosts,* you mean—you saw *ghosts?*" There was a triumphant note to Bleekman's voice now. Lee shuddered. He was going to make her out to be ready for a mental institution. Why didn't her attorney intervene?

"No, not ghosts. Do you believe in ghosts?" Ada looked at him quizzically.

"I'm asking the questions, if you don't mind. Please try to stay on the subject."

Ada sighed. "That's what I'm trying to do. We just *imagined* our mothers and grandmothers were there. I don't quite know why because I never did one of these before. Anyway, let's see, what next?" She stared into space . . . . "Oh, yes—next we passed around the worry rock and then we joined hands again and said good things for Minerva and then . . . well, I think that was all . . . and then Arthur arrived, uninvited, I might add, and got all upset and disrupted the harmony."

"And the second gathering?" Bleekman asked, clearly glad to be rid of the first one. "Only this time skip the details. Just tell the Court how you happened to go swimming in the nude during that event."

Ada pulled herself up to her most regal posture. "I'll have you know that I did not at any time enter the water or take off my clothes."

"What were you doing while the other ladies were performing their nude dance or whatever during the, ahhhh, energy circle?"

"That wasn't part of the circle," Ada said patiently, as if explaining it to a child who is not overly bright. "The skinny dipping occurred *after* our observance of the eclipse, when Minerva decided to jump in, to celebrate the end of her radiation treatments and wash off all that poisonous stuff . . . not really wash it off . . . nothing to contaminate the bay, you know, just kind of symbolic."

"And where were you while this nudity was in progress?"

"I was sitting on a dinghy fully clothed, minding my own business."

Bleekman was pacing nervously back and forth in front of the witness stand. "It's true, is it not, that the police came on the scene while your friends were on the beach in the nude?"

"True?" Ada said. "Well, part of it is true."

At this point, the judge intervened. "Mrs. Abernathy, please try to give straight answers to counselor's questions." Lee felt a knot forming in her stomach. It was fine for Ada to get Bleekman rattled, but antagonizing the judge was asking for trouble.

"Yes sir, your Honor. I'm simply trying to tell the whole truth, and it was not exactly true the way he worded it. *True*—the police came, but *not true* that my friends were nude on the beach. They were all in the water, quite respectably covered—that is, until the cops ordered them to come out, insisted, as a matter of fact, even though I warned them it was not a good idea, and that's when my friends started walking out, stark naked, because those cops insisted, and then the cops said never mind, stay there and . . . ." Ada chuckled. "I tell you, it was quite a sight! Those cops got more of an eyeful than they expected!"

Lee could feel the blood rushing to her face. The nude image was not one she wanted publicized in such stark detail.

"Try to keep your answers brief, Mrs. Abernathy," the judge said.

"The police came because of complaints from neighbors, did they not?" Bleekman asked.

"Yes."

"What were they complaining about?"

"Well, how should I . . . ." Ada caught herself . . . . "I mean, the cops said the neighbors said we were making too much noise."

"What sort of noise?"

Lee sent another plea to the Powers that Be: *Don't let her mention the bongo drums.*

Ada was silent for a moment, then glanced toward Lee, who was shaking her head. Ada looked away, cleared her throat and said, "Well, I suppose it was when they were splashing around in the water. All phosphorescent, you know how it gets, and they were splashing around and laughing at the sparkles and calling back and forth, and I guess the sound just carries pretty far at night, and of course, they didn't mean to disturb the neighbors.

The attorney looked directly at Ada. "Do you consider this proper behavior for mature women?"

"Objection," said Mary Graverton. "Relevancy."

"Your Honor, I am merely trying to point out that the women with whom Mrs. Abernathy is currently living, in view of their lawless actions, are not proper companions for a person of her age, indicating an impaired ability on her part, to make value judgments."

"Objection overruled. Would you answer the question, Mrs. Abernathy."

"Well, it all depends on how you define *proper*. They didn't mean any harm." Ada's face was flushed, and her braid was beginning to come unwound.

The attorney changed course. "Is it not true that Mrs. Sherwood is going to sell the house in which you and your lady friends reside?"

Ada looked at Lee and the others as if asking for help, then glanced down at her hands, saying nothing.

"Yes or no?"

"Well," she said, slowly and deliberately, "I'm in no position to predict that."

"Would you please be more specific."

"Well, she did mention the possibility, but as far as I know, she has not put the house on the market, and even if she does, that's no guarantee she can find a buyer."

"Let's assume she does find a buyer. Then where will you live?"

"That's none of your business!" Ada snapped. "I'm over twenty-one and quite capable of determining my place of abode." Her voice was quivering with rage.

Lee glanced at Mary Graverton who was shaking her head at Ada in the hope of silencing her.

The judge, meanwhile, was rapping for order. "Mrs. Abernathy, kindly try to answer the question to the best of your ability."

"I just want to say, your Honor, sir, I don't think it's right that I have to tell all these personal things about my living arrangements—and Mr. Blinker standing here casting aspersions at my friends, trying to make us seem like a bunch of common criminals."

"If you cannot see your way clear to answer the questions, Mrs. Abernathy, I shall have to declare you in contempt of court."

The judge looked at her sternly through his rimmed spectacles. "Please try to cooperate so we can resolve this matter."

"All right. If Elizabeth sells her house, I will live with Vivian over there." Ada pointed in her direction. "We'll share a place together."

Lee glanced at Vivian in her red skirt and psychedelic print blouse, flashing a lipsticked smile at the judge. She wished she had worn something a bit more conservative.

"Would you state her last name for the record?"

"I already told you when I . . . ." Ada looked at her attorney. "Her name is Vivian Gould. She's sixty-eight years old, of sound mind, and earns a living selling real estate."

"Thank you, Mrs. Abernathy." Bleekman had a self-righteous smirk on his face that made Lee want to belt him one.

The judge told Ada she could step down. Lee watched her start toward her seat when, to her horror, Ada tripped over something, perhaps the stand of the court stenographer, and toppled forward, clutching the edge of the table just in time to keep from falling headlong onto the floor. The security guard grasped her arm to steady her and assisted her to her seat—a disheveled Ada protesting that she didn't need any help. Her braid, completely unfastened, dangled crazily over her shoulder, with loose strands of hair about her face. Her blouse had come untucked from her skirt. Lee's heart was thumping double-time. The situation was getting desperate. She quickly scribbled a note to Mary Graverton and passed it down to her, asking permission to testify for Ada.

When she heard her name called to take the stand, Lee had no clear-cut idea of what she would say. But she knew she must stand up for Ada. As she was being sworn in, she began to have second thoughts. Supposing she said the wrong thing, made matters worse?

"Dr. Cranford," said Ada's attorney, "you have known Ada Abernathy for quite some time, have you not?" Lee felt a flush of pleasure at the sound of her academic title. She rarely heard it these days. Sometimes she felt it annoyed people who considered her doctorate not as authentic as that of a medical doctor. She hoped it would not antagonize the judge.

269

"Yes, she has been my friend for over forty years—ever since we both lived in the St. Louis area." Lee's voice sounded weak, strained. She could feel her hands trembling. So much was at stake.

"And would you say you understand her better perhaps than most people?"

"Objection," said Bleekman. "Leading the witness."

"Sustained. Allow the witness to draw her own conclusions, Counselor."

Mary Graverton rephrased the question. "Do you feel that you have a good understanding of your friend of forty years?"

"Ada Abernathy is a very complex individual. A woman of considerable artistic talent, with a diversity of views she does not hesitate to express. Do I understand her? I believe so—at least to the extent that it is possible to understand anyone. Throughout these forty years, she has always been unpredictable. But that adds richness and texture to our friendship. There is a quality about Ada that calls to mind Walt Whitman who said, *Do I contradict myself? Very well then I contradict myself. I am large, I contain multitudes.* And I . . . ."

Lee was interrupted by the judge's gavel. "Try to keep your responses more succinct and to the point, Mrs. Cranford." She felt the blood coloring her neck and face.

"Would you compare, for the Court, the general behavior of Mrs. Abernathy in her younger days with her present-day behavior?"

"Objection," said Bleekman. "The witness is not qualified as a behavioral psychologist."

"Overruled. She may state her nonprofessional observations, based on their long-time friendship and their current living arrangement."

Lee felt a sense of relief. "Well, I would have to say that physically, of course, she is not as agile as she used to be, but she still manages to get around quite well and can take care of her own needs. Mentally, she seems as sharp as ever, although that certainly was not the case when we . . . when she came home from Tranquil Acres where, according to Dr. Stone, she had been over-medicated." Lee looked out at Minerva who was smiling

270

and nodding her head. "In the early years of our friendship, Ada was strongly opinionated and argumentative. That certainly has not changed." Ada was leaning forward, with chin cupped in her hand, listening intently. "But I wouldn't want her to change. If so, she wouldn't be the Ada I know and love. I have never met a more versatile and challenging person—or anyone more direct and honest in her views." Lee stopped, wondering if she had said too much.

Mary Graverton gave her a reassuring smile. "Mr. Abernathy's attorney has implied that the two gatherings which took place this summer might somehow have been of a Satanic nature. Was this a correct interpretation on his part?"

"No!" Lee's voice was emphatic. "Unequivocally not! They had nothing whatsoever to do with devil worship or any other sort of evil." She felt uncomfortable with this line of questioning. Why couldn't Mary leave well enough alone? Of course, Ada's version had been totally confusing. Maybe she needed to erase any negative impressions. "They were merely energy circles," Lee said, hoping that would suffice.

"Could you give the Court a brief definition of an energy circle and explain its significance in terms of Ada Abernathy's involvement?"

"Well, yes." She hesitated. "In an energy circle, people who love nature come together to draw on it as a source of energy to provide additional strength in times of crisis." Lee sent a hasty plea to the Goddess or Whatever to forgive her for not being totally honest. "It is not, of course, a negation of anyone's Christian beliefs as was implied."

"And were these energy circles any form of witchcraft?"

"It might have seemed that way to an outside observer, but it was not our intention." Lee stared down at her hands, not daring to catch Minerva's eye. She might disapprove of her evasion. She glanced toward Arthur, who was frowning and saying something to his attorney. Clasping her silver labris, she sent a second urgent prayer that Bleekman not cross-question her and trap her into telling the whole truth. One word about feminist witchcraft or goddess worship, and that would be the end!

"Thank you for clarifying this point." Lee stole a glance at

271

Vivian who smiled and winked at her. "Now, Dr. Cranford, in conclusion, would you tell the Court whether you think it would enhance Ada Abernathy's state of health and well-being to move into a retirement home at the present time."

"Objection!" said Bleekman, standing up and striding forward. "Calls for conjecture on the part of an unqualified witness."

"Overruled. The Court, however, notes that the witness is not rendering a medical or psychological judgment—solely her own view, based on her observations as a friend. And please be brief, Mrs. Cranford."

"I sincerely believe that it would not contribute to Ada's well-being for her to live anywhere that is not of her own choosing. And I strongly feel that it is her right to make her choice freely without coercion on the part of anyone." Lee blinked back the tears welling up in her eyes. "That's all I can say."

Mary Graverton thanked her, and Bleekman, to her great relief, did not wish to cross-question. Lee wondered uneasily if the Goddess had answered her prayer or if Bleekman felt he had a strong enough case without bothering with her. She was trembling when she left the stand, making a conscious effort not to trip on the way back to her seat or to give any evidence of her frazzled nerves. As she sat down, the three women were smiling at her. Minerva whispered, "Splendid!" Bernie gave her a quick hug.

Then the judge asked the psychiatrist, Dr. Greer, if she had anything to add, beyond the psychiatric evaluation she had submitted. And she took the stand. She was a brisk, self-assured woman who gave the impression of competence. Lee tried to analyze her face, the amiable rounded contours framed by wavy gray hair. She wore a blue textured suit reflecting the soft blue of her eyes. Far less threatening in appearance than Prudence Runkles. But looks could be deceiving. "As indicated in the written report," said Dr. Greer, "my conclusion is that Ada Abernathy, despite some difficulty focusing her attention over an extended time, is reasonably stable, mentally and emotionally." Lee took a deep breath, straining to hear every word. "Her responses in Court today further bear this out. Although she exhibits a disturbingly argumentative approach to life, which might cause

272

her to be difficult company for the average person, she appears to have found a niche for herself among the women with whom she now resides. I would say she is capable of making rational decisions."

Lee glanced down the row. Vivian, Minerva, and Bernie were all sitting motionless, their eyes fixed on Dr. Greer and the judge. Ada and her attorney also sat at rigid attention.

The judge thanked Dr. Greer and asked Kevin Maloney if he had any further recommendations. He replied that his report covered all the necessary ground. Lee wondered if that was a positive or negative factor.

The room was filled with hushed anticipation for several minutes while the judge and his clerk went over some papers. Lee fidgeted in her chair. She crossed her hands tightly in her lap, feeling a twinge of pain from pressure of her ring against her finger. She was almost afraid to breathe. All eyes were on the judge when he rapped his gavel. "Inasmuch as Ada Abernathy has been adjudged mentally and emotionally stable, capable of making reasonable choices by both the court-appointed psychiatrist and the guardian, and whereas Mrs. Abernathy has made it irrefutably clear that she wishes to remain independent, the Court denies the petition of Arthur Abernathy to be named her Conservator. Case dismissed."

29

Through the casement windows in the kitchen Lee could see the old Norway maple, its dark branches forming a leafy canopy, golden in October sunlight. With every gust of wind a few leaves would swirl to the ground, carpeting the grass with bright patches of yellow. Beyond the maple a tall sassafras blazed scarlet and burnt orange. Her last season to see these trees in their autumn splendor. How she would miss them! She thought about the tea her grandmother used to make from sassafras roots, how they would sit at the kitchen table, Lee cradling the cup in her hands the same way her grandmother did, the two of them talking together, sipping the steamy aromatic liquid, savoring its tangy flavor. By closing her eyes, she could almost taste it, hear her grandmother telling tales of Ozark lore and herbal magic. She could use a cup of that tea now—and the comfort of her grandmother's voice.

The leaves were late this year, still brilliant in mid-October, their riotous colors brightening the diminishing light. As a child, Lee had always chosen summer as her favorite season, delighting in the sun and the freedom. But now, if forced to make a choice, it might be fall—a time of renewed energy, of cozy fires and candlelight—the beauty, however, tinged with melancholy, dread of what lay beyond, after the last leaves withered and fell to the ground—the dismal frosted landscape of bare branches, brown earth, the long dark nights. Those vibrant colors, after all, were only a disguise for death.

But today was Ada's birthday—no time for melancholy. Lee stood at the sink peeling carrots for beef stew—Ada's special request. The air was pungent with aroma of chopped onions browning in the large iron pot on the stove, a pot handed down to Lee through the generations. She could trace it back at least as far as her mother's grandmother. Lee had inherited the recipe along with the pot, although through the years, she had introduced a few variations. She was humming along to the melodious Second Movement of Beethoven's Pastoral Symphony floating through the speakers.

From the moment she got out of bed this morning, Lee had decided today was to be one of total harmony. To that end, she had tried to erase from her mind all negative thoughts about Elizabeth, now in Fort Lauderdale with John, or the bitter memories of Arthur's court case, or any of the problems facing their NOW chapter's plans for busing East Enders to the November rally in Washington. Ever since Elizabeth's decision to sell the house, Lee had felt such dejection, bordering on despair, she could not concentrate on her writing. To maintain her sanity, she had thrown herself with feverish intensity into chapter activities, their current focus, the National Mobilization for Women's Lives. But this morning she had turned on the answering machine to avoid any communications. Today was too special to deal with questions about buses or garbled press information. Tomorrow would be time enough.

So far, the day had progressed smoothly. She had the kitchen to herself—nobody getting in the way trying to be helpful. She loved making stew—so wholesome, so very basic. A creative act, not to be rushed, vegetables and meat all prepared in sequence until everything ended up in the pot at the proper time. As she peeled and chopped the carrots, celery, and potatoes, she felt her mother's presence . . . the two of them standing side by side, back in that Missouri kitchen, Mother explaining how to cut the carrots, how to brown the meat . . . a fleeting moment, then she was here in the Long Island kitchen again—cutting and flouring the beef, searching for the bay and marjoram leaves. She glanced at her mother's recipe box on the counter. Not that she needed it for the stew—second nature after a half century of making it.

275

But she had been using the box for a special roll recipe. After her mother's death, Lee had carried that little oak box with her from place to place without opening it for many years, hesitating to disturb that link to her past. When finally one day she pulled it out of the cupboard and touched its scarred surface, she had the eerie sensation that their fingers were touching. She had looked through the food-stained cards, clippings, yellowed scraps of paper, encountering an array of aunts, cousins, neighbors, and friends from those lost years—ghosts of her former life. Sitting there with the box that day, bitter tears streamed down her face. But now it brought a pleasant sense of kinship to times past. A community of women, nearly all of them dead, but survived by those magical little cards.

After browning the onions and chunks of beef, Lee added some water, along with the vegetables and seasonings, and a generous amount of red wine. With a feeling of satisfaction, she inhaled the rich aroma. She checked her watch. Four o'clock. Right on schedule to allow plenty of time for slow simmering. The guests would arrive around six. She carried a tray of dishes and silverware into the dining room to set the table, extended with extra leaves to accommodate twelve people. A blue damask cloth covered the table. In the center was an arrangement of lavender, red, and pink chrysanthemums that Vivian had done before leaving for work. Everything just as planned.

She returned with a tray of champagne glasses for the sparkling burgundy. She was placing them around the table when Minerva came into the room. "Have you seen Ada?"

"Not lately," Lee said. "I thought she was in the studio with you."

"Not this afternoon."

"I haven't seen her since lunch."

Minerva took a deep breath. "Ummmmm, the stew smells wonderful!" She enjoyed Lee's stew, even though she would eat only the vegetables, carefully putting aside all the meat.

"Why don't you take a look down by the bay? Ada might be there sketching." Lee was concentrating on fitting purple candles into the silver candlesticks. "When you see her, you might suggest she come in and rest up a bit before dinner. Soon it will be too dark to sketch anyway."

I doubt if she will pay much attention to that suggestion," Minerva said with a laugh. "When I come back, let me know if I can give you a hand."

You can work on the salad," Lee called after her.

After several minutes Minerva returned to the house, a worried expression on her face. She found Lee carrying in an armload of wood. "Ada's not there," Minerva said.

"Well, maybe she's in her room." Lee began sorting the wood, putting aside the pieces she would need to start the fire, stacking the rest in the rack by the fireplace.

"But her folding chair is there—and her sketch pad."

Lee caught her breath. "Are you sure? Did you look around? Maybe she just walked off to one side—you know, to try a different angle or something."

"I checked both directions along the bay, but there was no sign of her." Minerva's voice sounded husky.

"Well, maybe she went back to her room to get something. I'll check." Lee dropped the pieces of wood and rushed up the stairs, hoping to find Ada there, taking a nap or reading, having forgotten to go back for her things. "Be there, Ada," she murmured. There was no response to her knock. And even as she opened the door, she sensed she would find the room empty. It was in its usual disarray—clothes strewn about, bed unmade, nightgown and robe hanging on the bedpost, piles of books on the floor, stacks of papers, letters, and clippings on her small writing table, some clothes for laundering in a heap by the closet. Lee felt suddenly dizzy. Closing the door, she groped for the railing to steady herself as she returned downstairs. "Ada's not there." She tried to keep her voice casual. "Where could she have gone?" Lee glanced at Minerva. Their eyes met. She knew they were thinking the same thing. Had something happened to Ada—something terrible? A cold chill crept through her, cramping her stomach, constricting her lungs. "Oh, Min! Where is she?" Lee could no longer hide her fear.

Min encircled her in her arms. "Don't panic. We'll find her."

"Let's have another look down there," Lee said, hope momentarily renewed. "Maybe she's come back by now. And we

277

can have a good laugh about getting all worked up over nothing."

Lee put on a sweater, and the two women hurried across the lawn through lengthening shadows to the little beach along the bay. They found Ada's folding chair and the sketch pad beside it in the sand—but no Ada. Lee sank into the chair. "Where could she be?" she said weakly.

"I wish I knew." Minerva's face was grim.

Lee picked up the sketch pad, open to an unfinished drawing—a weatherbeaten rowboat in the foreground surrounded by scraggly marsh grass and reeds, and in the background, a shadowy figure. "It looks rather desolate. "I wonder if that's how she was feeling."

"Something might have happened to interrupt her."

Ada had been uncharacteristically quiet at lunch. Lee wondered, with a trace of guilt, if she should have paid more attention to her. But with all the preparations for the party, there hadn't been much time. And they had acknowledged Ada's birthday at breakfast, Minerva giving her a beautiful blue hand-knit sweater and Lee, Georgia O'Keeffe's *One Hundred Flowers,* Vivian saying she would have to wait till evening for hers. Ada knew about the party—so she had no reason, at least none that Lee could figure out, for feeling dejected. But Ada's voice rang in her ears, her words from last spring: *I don't even know if I want to live past eight-five.*

Minerva called to her from a clump of bushes nearby. "Look what I found!" She pulled out Ada's cane and their canoe carrier, a lightweight metal frame on wheels. During the season, they would keep the canoe strapped to the carrier in the garage. By now it would usually have been stored away, but this had been an unseasonably warm fall until the past few days. Ada could have wheeled it down without any particular difficulty. But why? "I guess that explains it," Minerva said. "She decided to go for a canoe ride."

"But why would she do that in the middle of a sketch? And why isn't she back? It will soon be dark." Lee picked up Ada's cane, rubbing her hands over its smooth wood surface, tears filling her eyes. She could not free herself from the fear constricting her throat and chest, the leaden feeling in her stomach. "I've

278

never known Ada to go out alone in the canoe. She's not that good at paddling." She cupped her hands to her mouth. "AAAAAda!" she called. "AAAAAda! Where are you? AAAAAda!"

"The wind's against you. She probably can't hear you."

"I'll get the binoculars. Maybe we can spot her out there." Back at the house, Vivian was just pulling into the drive. Quickly Lee told her about Ada's disappearance.

"We should call the police," Vivian said.

"I think it's the Bay Constable we need. He would have a boat." Lee was breathing heavily, clutching the porch railing for support.

"Why don't you sit down and catch your breath? You don't look so good."

"No, I have to find Ada." Lee was fighting back the tears. "The binoculars . . . I can't remember where . . . . Oh, Viv, what are we going to do?"

Vivian led her to a chair on the porch. "Sit here for a minute while I get the glasses. Maybe she just misjudged the time and went out a little farther than she intended." She pushed back Lee's hair that was flying wildly about her face. "You know how Ada is about time. She can't be bothered."

"I'm afraid something terrible has happened." Tears rolled down her face. "I feel it."

Vivian returned with the binoculars, offering to take them to Minerva, but Lee grabbed them and started back, telling Vivian to try to get the Bay Constable.

As Lee was running across the lawn, she saw Bernie's car turning in. Vivian could explain. She had to get back—find Ada somehow.

"Any sight of her?" she asked Minerva.

"Let me take a look through the glasses," Minerva said.

"AAAAAda!" Lee called. "AAAAAda!" But there was no response. Only the sound of the early evening breeze rustling the dry stalks of phragmites, and water lapping against the shore with the incoming tide. The golden color had drained out of the marsh grass, and the sky had dimmed from turquoise to pale gray, the landscape taking on the quality of a charcoal drawing, a replica of Ada's unfinished sketch.

279

"I see something that might be the canoe." Minerva gave the glasses to Lee.

"I think it *is* the canoe, but I can't see anybody in it." Lee dropped the binoculars. "Oh, Min, I'll never forgive myself if something has happened to Ada!" She blew her nose, struggling to control her tears.

"In this light we can't see clearly enough to know anything for sure. And, in any case, it's not your fault." Minerva gave her a comforting hug and picked up the binoculars.

"Viv is calling the Bay Constable." Lee wiped away the tears with her sweater sleeve. Min was right. She shouldn't go all to pieces.

Just then, Bernie came running down. "Vivian told me," she said, white-faced. "Can you see anything?"

"We think we've found the canoe." Minerva handed her the binoculars.

Lee thought of the times she and Ada had packed a lunch and taken the canoe over to the point of land separating their cove from the bay. Lee would paddle from the stern, steering their course, while Ada paddled from the bow, not having mastered the feather stroke. And, besides, she would never pay attention to their direction, paddling sporadically until something, a bird or fish or sailboat, diverted her attention. They would pull the canoe up on the sand and spread a blanket where they sat soaking up sun and sea breeze—Ada sketching, Lee making notes for a poem or maybe reading. Then they would cool off with a swim. Or sometimes they would just talk and watch the clouds and seagulls and passing boats. Conversing with Ada was always a delightful challenge, rather like mental gymnastics or chess. The air was growing cooler with the deepening shadows. Lee shivered and buttoned her sweater. Possibly Ada had tried to paddle over to that sandy point this afternoon. But why? It didn't make sense.

"That's definitely a canoe." Bernie was squinting into the glasses. "But it looks empty."

"Maybe she fell out," Minerva said.

"Oh, God! How could that be?" An unspoken fear cut through Lee like a knife. Suppose Ada had done it intentionally. But she hastily pushed it aside. Not Ada.

"Ada is a good swimmer," Minerva was saying, "a good strong breast stroke."

"But not necessarily in this cold water, weighed down with heavy clothing." Lee began sobbing uncontrollably.

Minerva put her arms around her. Lee felt an eerie sense of disbelief, that they could be standing helpless on shore, and Ada out there in the water somewhere, maybe drowned.

"Where is that Bay Constable?" Bernie muttered.

"I don't think there's a direct line. The police send a radio message," Minerva said.

Lee envisioned Ada, clinging to the boat, struggling to stay afloat, gasping for breath, finally succumbing, sinking to the bottom, submerged among the mucky shells and seaweed. They might never find her. She slumped down on the chair.

Bernie, scanning the water with the binoculars, suddenly cried out, "I see something! Bobbing up and down, about halfway between us and the canoe." She pointed toward the floating object, handing the glasses to Minerva.

"Is it Ada?" Lee grabbed Minerva's arm.

"It's almost too dark to see," Minerva said, giving the binoculars to Lee.

Lee held them to her eyes, but the tears blurred her vision, and her shaky hands could not hold the glasses steady. "I can't see. Take another look, Bernie."

Bernie took the binoculars. "I think it's a person."

"It's got to be Ada!" said Minerva.

Putting down the binoculars, Bernie kicked off her shoes and socks, pulled off her jacket, and stripped to her underwear. Plunging into the water, she started swimming a strong crawl stroke toward the bobbing figure.

Vivian came rushing toward them, flushed and breathless. "I couldn't get . . . he wasn't . . . so I called the Coast Guard." She paused to catch her breath. "They're sending a boat. It should be here in a few minutes."

"Good thinking!" said Minerva.

"Have you located her?" Vivian asked.

"We don't know." Minerva gestured toward the water.

"Bernie's swimming out." The women strained their eyes to watch the progress of the shadowy form, barely visible.

The next hour, or possibly longer, was a blur in Lee's mind, everything jumbled together. She remembered seeing the approach of the Coast Guard boat through the twilight haze, a motorized inflatable designed for speed, stopping near the area where Bernie had seen the unidentified form, shining its spotlight around, then after a few minutes moving toward shore . . . Bernie sitting huddled in a blanket, and a blanket-wrapped form being lifted out of the boat, carried ashore by two Coastguardsmen . . . Ada, limp and bedraggled, hair streaming wildly about her face, but alive, breathing . . . barely conscious but oh, God, yes, alive . . . Minerva talking to one of the Coastguardsmen, the other two carrying Ada to the house and up to her room, Vivian running ahead to show the way, Lee following in a daze . . . Margaret, who had just arrived for the party, taking charge of Ada, removing her wet clothes, quickly drying her off, putting on her flannel gown, getting her into bed beneath her comforter with an electric heating pad, sending Lee to her car for her medical satchel, checking her blood pressure, lungs, pulse, and finding everything satisfactory . . . Lee saying, "Ada dear, what happened?" and Ada mumbling something incoherent about the rocks . . . then sitting up in bed looking frantically about, wild-eyed, asking "Where's Bernie?" and sinking back among the pillows when assured that she was safe, murmuring, "Saved my life she . . . " then drowsing off . . . and Minerva coming in with a cup of tea . . . Bernie meanwhile showering and wrapping herself in Minerva's red plaid robe . . . Margaret saying not to worry about Ada, that she would sit with her so Lee could go down and take care of the guests . . . and Lee realizing she had completely forgotten about the party, the guests, the dinner, the time, noting that it was now seven o'clock . . . reluctant to leave Ada who was asleep, breathing rhythmically, her gray hair spread out on the pillow about her face, the color now almost back to normal.

It was not until she entered the living room that she remembered she was still in her jeans, sweatshirt, and sneakers, that her hair was uncombed, her face smudged and tear-stained. But it was too late to retreat. The guests greeted her with hugs and kisses, nobody seeming to care what a mess she was. Perry wrapped her arm about her shoulder and led her to the rocking chair by the fire which Minerva had lit. "Sit down, Lee, and let me get you a drink. You look like you need one. You're white as a ghost. Are you all right?"

Lee nodded. She had begun to shiver, not that she was cold exactly, but she could not stop shaking. "Bourbon and soda," she said, her teeth chattering.

Melanie brought the afghan over from the couch and draped it around her shoulders. "Your sneakers are, like, soaking wet. Let's take them off."

Minerva appeared with a towel and her warm slippers, and Perry handed her the bourbon. Lee huddled closer to the fire,sipping her drink, tears filling her eyes. "I'm sorry," she managed to say, looking about at the group, overwhelmed by a surge of emotions—relief, joy, sadness intermingled. How she loved them all! But how very fragile! The shivering had subsided now. "Some party!" she said, trying to smile.

Then Vivian came to the doorway inviting them to the table before the dinner got cold. Lee remembered walking into the dining room somewhat shakily and sitting down between Perry and Melanie, but from then on, her memory was hazy—as if viewing the scene through layers of opaque glass. She remembered how Bernie sat at the end of the table, still in Minerva's robe, telling about finding Ada struggling to stay afloat, about trying to tow her ashore but making very little headway, and her relief at seeing the Coast Guard boat. Then Lee remembered how they drank a number of toasts to Bernie, celebrating her courage, to Vivian for having the sense to call the Coast Guard, and to Ada, safely asleep upstairs, in celebration of her birthday and the miracle that she was alive. That she remembered. Also Arthur's raspy voice over the answering machine wishing Ada a happy birthday, asking her to call back, and Vivian saying thank God the machine was on, followed by much laughter at Arthur's expense. But she had no recollection of eating any of her stew, so lovingly prepared, nor did she remember the birthday cake Laura had baked, topped with eighty-five candles, or how she and Minerva and Vivian, serving as Ada's surrogates, had attempted to blow them all out in one breath—to the great hilarity of the others. Minerva had to fill in those details later.

30

The next morning Lee awoke with sunlight streaming into her room, casting rainbow glints across her bed from the crystal prism in her window. She stretched and yawned lazily, wondering vaguely what day it was and what she had scheduled to do. When she started to get out of bed, the room began to reel around crazily, and she quickly lay down again. Why had she gone to bed in her underwear? Suddenly the whole ghastly episode of Ada's disappearance replayed itself. Her head throbbed, and she had a queasy feeling in her stomach. She tried to remember how she got to bed and whether or not she told the guests good-bye. That part was a total blank.

She lay there wondering if she should try again to get out of bed. She ought to check on Ada. Maybe if she took it slow and easy . . . . Carefully she hoisted herself on her elbows—so far, so good—but as she sat upright, the room tilted at a dangerous angle, and she sank back. The calico cat jumped onto the bed and nuzzled her face, purring loudly, kneading its claws on the comforter. "Hi, Patches, old thing." Lee rubbed her hands through the soft fur. "Did you enjoy the party?" Patches continued to purr and knead. "You're in better shape than I." The cat curled up on the pillow beside her, still purring.

There was a knock at the door, and Minerva entered. "How do you feel?"

Lee groaned. "Don't ask! My head—everything's spinning around—and my stomach, ohhhhh . . . ." She clutched her stomach. "To put it succinctly, *lousy!*" If she closed her eyes, maybe she could get back to sleep and blank out the world a bit longer. But she would have to face it, all of it, sooner or later. "How's Ada doing?"

"She's in pretty good shape this morning. She was asking about you."

"Tell her I'll be there as soon as I can maneuver the stairs." Shielding her eyes against the sunlight, she looked at Minerva. "Did I make an utter fool of myself last night? I can't remember much of anything after Arthur's phone call."

"No, you were the life of the party."

"Exactly what do you mean by that?"

"You weren't obnoxious—just comical. You had them all doubled over with your imitation of Jeane Kirkpatrick."

"Why was I imitating her, of all people?"

"That wasn't clear to me. But you really captured her voice. Almost as good as your Nancy Reagan act." Minerva smiled broadly. "Remember—*Just say No!* in Washington?"

"Well yes, but I was sober then. Min, I'm so embarrassed! How will I face them?"

"Nonsense! It was a natural reaction after the strain."

"And all that sparkling burgundy!" Lee moaned. "Someone kept filling my glass."

"How about some apple juice?" Minerva sat on the edge of the bed.

"No, thanks. I couldn't keep it down." Lee wondered if she would ever again have a desire for food or drink.

"The pectin in apples helps settle the stomach."

"I think I'll go back to sleep," Lee said, shutting her eyes.

Minerva looked at her watch. "It's eleven o'clock. How about a cup of herbal tea?"

Lee made a face. "I'll try a small glass of Coke, if you insist."

When Minerva returned with the Coke, Lee had propped herself up in bed. She rubbed her eyes. The room had stabilized now, but her head still felt as if it were encased in a drum someone was beating on. "Is Margaret still with Ada?"

"She spent the night in Ada's room on a cot. She left early this morning. Ada was doing fine, she said, but to call her if necessary. She advised getting her to the doctor, just to play safe. But you know how Ada resists doctors."

"Let's wait and see," Lee said. "How about Bernie?" She immediately wished she had not asked, remembering Minerva sitting next to Bernie at the table, beaming at her with pride.

"Oh, she left about an hour ago," Minerva said. "She slept in Elizabeth's room," she added quickly, a little too quickly, Lee thought. Although Minerva had decided to accept Bernie's offer of sharing her apartment, she and Lee had not really discussed how she felt about Bernie—from the standpoint of a relationship, that is. In fact they had spoken only marginally about any of Minerva's plans. Lee still felt rebuffed despite any number of internal dialogues reassuring herself that it was a natural sequence of events, certainly nothing against her personally. Clearly Minerva admired Bernie tremendously. Lee admired her too. But that did not necessarily imply anything sexual. Minerva, accustomed to keeping her emotions tightly guarded, had not broached the subject, and Lee was reluctant to raise the issue. Perhaps she was afraid to find out. Minerva had never spoken much about her sex life. Lee remembered hearing about a young geologist killed in World War II. Apparently she had loved him. But now, although on friendly terms with a few men, she seemed to have no great interest in the opposite sex. She, of course, identified strongly with women and their values, as opposed to traditional male values. But that alone did not make her a lesbian, except perhaps *in spirit* if there were such a category. Lee had always resisted placing people in neat little cubbyholes. Frequently things overlapped, especially in women's lives. Sooner or later, though, she and Minerva needed to talk frankly about it. But certainly not this morning, not in her present foggy state of mind. One thing at a time.

Lee took a sip of the Coke. The dizziness would not go away. "I swear I'll never drink another drop of that stuff!"

"Do you want to put that in writing?"

Lee shook her head. "Did Ada say anything about the canoe—why she went out there in the first place?"

"She evaded the issue. Mumbled something about *a long story.*"

287

Lee looked at Minerva. "Do you suppose she fell out of that canoe on purpose?"

"It did cross my mind. But that doesn't ring true for Ada. Not at all in character."

Lee swallowed some more Coke. Maybe a shower would clear her head. She struggled out of bed and, with the help of Minerva, made her way to the bathroom.

* * *

When Minerva and Lee walked into Ada's room, she was sitting up in bed, hair neatly braided and tied with purple ribbons, intent on a *New York Times* crossword puzzle. "Well, Ada, how are you this morning?" Lee said, sinking into the nearest chair.

"Fine! Just fine!" She looked at Lee critically. "But you don't look so hot."

"Too much of the bubbly at your birthday celebration." Lee gave a weak smile. "Sorry you had to miss it."

"Me too! Minerva told me it was some party."

"You gave us quite a scare," Lee said. "What happened anyway?"

"I fell out of the canoe," Ada said hastily, looking down at the crossword puzzle. "What's a nine-letter word meaning *to continue in spite of opposition or discouragement* beginning with a P"

"Persist," Minerva said.

"No, that's only seven," Ada said, counting the letters on her fingers.

"Persevere," said Lee. As she pronounced the word, the face of Grandmother Leandra appeared for an instant. Was it another message? Or just a coincidence?

"Right!" said Ada. "How did you get so smart?"

"From Grandmother Leandra."

"You got your smarts from her?"

"No, the *word*. Never mind. We're getting off the subject." Ada had a knack for changing the subject whenever she wanted to avoid an issue.

"Now, Ada, suppose you tell us the long story about you and the canoe." Minerva's tone indicated it would be pointless to refuse.

288

"Well," Ada said, doodling along the edge of the paper with her pencil, "as you know, I was sitting there sketching, and I just got to thinking how I would like to take a canoe ride over to the point one last time for the season, and then on the way over I accidentally fell out, and, well, you know the rest."

"But why did you try it all alone?" Lee said. "Why didn't you get one of us to go with you?"

"Minerva was busy weaving, and you were making the stew."

"But why suddenly in the middle of a sketch? That doesn't make sense." Minerva's gray eyes peered at Ada. "Are you sure you're telling us everything—the whole story?"

"Do you think I would lie to you?" Ada was not looking at them. She seemed to be staring out the window or at some invisible spot on the wall behind them.

"Would you?" Minerva persisted.

Ada was silent for what seemed like several minutes. Her face had flushed to a deep pink, matching the stripes in her flannel nightgown. "Well, maybe that's not quite the *whole* story." She sighed heavily.

"Tell us, Ada." Minerva sat down on the bed beside her. "We've always been honest with one another."

"Well, yes . . . all right, the truth." She cleared her throat and fiddled nervously with her pencil. "I was sitting there sketching and thinking about being eighty-five, the big 8-5, a kind of turning point, you might say. And I got to thinking how I had entered the realm of the *old old,* and how, from now on, everything would be downhill, and the more I thought about it, the more depressed I became. And I remembered the fear I felt in court last month, knowing my fate hung in the balance. I realized just how easy it might be for me, not now but perhaps at some later date, to be at the mercy of someone else, institutionalized just because I am considered *old.*" She paused and took a deep breath. "I have always dreaded the idea of gradual deterioration, you know, when the body starts wearing out, and perhaps the mind too. I didn't want to experience that sort of decline." Her voice quavered. "And suddenly everything seemed to grow dimmer, drained of color, and sounds became fainter, as if my senses were already failing. I guess I just panicked." Ada sat quietly for a moment. Her hand was trembling as she wiped away the tears that had begun to trickle down her cheeks. It occurred to Lee that she had never before seen Ada cry. She had always seemed so fearless and tough-minded, like sturdy leather that would never wear out. Minerva handed Ada a tissue. She wiped her eyes and blew her nose before continuing. "I got to thinking all sorts of dismal thoughts about how it would be when my eyesight and my hearing failed and when I got all crippled with arthritis and had to walk with a walker or stay in a wheelchair or vegetate in a nursing home or had a stroke and couldn't talk or who knows what . . . . And so I went back to the house for the canoe and . . . "

"But none of those terrible things have happened to you yet, so why . . . " Lee interrupted.

"Let her tell us her way," Minerva said, putting a comforting arm around Ada's shoulder.

"That's the whole point," Ada said. "I wanted to leave this earth while I was still in control, you know, *I am the master of my fate, I am the captain of my soul.*" Ada sat staring past them again, perhaps envisioning herself in one of those helpless crippled states. Fresh tears rolled down her face. She wiped them away on the sleeve of her gown. "And then I got my old red sweater because I didn't want to ruin the beautiful new one Minerva gave me, figuring somebody else could make good use of it—and I wheeled the canoe down to the landing . . . ." Her voice broke, and she paused, as if it were too painful to continue. She ran her fingers through strands of hair that had pulled loose from her braid.

"Last night you said something about rocks. What did you mean?" Lee asked.

"Well yes, as a matter of fact . . . the rocks . . . ." But again, she remained silent.

"Come on, Ada, you can trust us," Minerva said gently.

"Well, I got to thinking about Virginia Woolf . . . I pictured her in my mind—you know, how she went down to the water and . . . ." She buried her face in her hands.

"Oh, no!" Lee gasped . . . the rocks and Virginia Woolf . . . . She did not want to believe it but could not deny what she was hearing. She pictured Ada walking along the desolate beach, hunting the largest, heaviest stones to fill the pockets of her sweater, then struggling with the weight of the canoe to get it into the water, shoving off from shore for a lonely rendezvous with death. "If only I had known," she said. "I . . . ."

"Shhhhh," Minerva said to Lee.

Ada adjusted the pillows behind her head, took a deep breath, and continued. "Paddling out wasn't easy. I couldn't steer the thing." She attempted a smile. Then she said something about wishing she had paid attention. Paid attention to what? Lee's brain felt foggy. Ada must have meant when Lee had tried to teach her the feather stroke. But she was having trouble now concentrating on the words, words she did not want to hear. The full horror of it had suddenly taken hold. She tried to picture Ada in the canoe, wielding the paddle to create a wild circular pattern, gradually working her way out to the center of the cove . . . paddling to where the water, where it was over her head . . . the sounds blurring together. Lee could not retain a full sentence. Words flitted around in her brain and flew away. "Worn out," she heard, then something about sitting there to catch her breath. Lee glanced at Ada who was breathing heavily, reliving the scene. "Then I . . . I somehow . . . ." Ada cleared her throat. "I managed to stand up . . . not easy . . . the rocks . . . ." Her voice was barely audible now. Lee had to strain to hear . . . "and then . . . just toppled overboard, lost my balance . . . ." Ada sat quietly weeping.

"Oh, Ada!" Lee cried. "How could you!" The anguish she had been experiencing over Ada's pain was mushrooming into a sense of betrayal. Why had she done this without confiding her feelings to them, without trying to talk it out? So unfair—unfair to herself, unfair to them. She felt enshrouded in a heavy cloud.

"And then what happened?" Minerva asked, pushing back the unruly strands of hair and wiping Ada's face with a tissue.

Through her tears, a flicker of a smile crossed Ada's face as she continued. Now that Lee had accepted the reality of what Ada had done, her brain cleared enough for her to listen and comprehend, though the horror remained. "Well, when I hit the water, would you believe it—those rocks fell right through my pockets!" She was beginning to laugh softly now. "That antiquated sweater—I forgot how worn and frazzled it was. That old yarn just couldn't take the stress of the water and rocks, I guess. So there I was, out in the middle of the cove, still afloat, and I said to myself, *Ada, you old fool, you really botched it!* Then it somehow struck me funny, and I started to laugh. I guess anybody would have thought I was completely balmy, clinging to the canoe and laughing so hard I could hardly hold on. So absurd! And then, out of the blue, an image of the four of you flashed through my mind, sharp and clear as a slide projected on a screen . . . Elizabeth sitting at the piano and Vivian leaning over her shoulder, maybe singing . . . I couldn't hear anything—all visual . . . and Lee sitting in her rocker by the fire, a beautiful blaze, holding Brother Gray, that dear old fellow, and Minerva curled up on the couch knitting. But my chair—it was empty, draped in a heavy black cloth." Ada shuddered. "It only lasted for an instant, then faded out." She sat quietly for a moment, looking down at her hands which she had been nervously folding and unfolding as she talked. There was a quaver in her voice when she resumed her story. "And suddenly I realized I wasn't ready to die yet—the whole thing had been a horrible mistake. And I thanked my lucky stars for that frazzled old sweater with the worn-out pockets."

"What a relief!" Minerva said.

"Don't you realize what a scare you gave us?" Lee said, frowning. She felt shaken and saddened by Ada's startling account but was unable to mask her exasperation at the agony she had caused.

"I'm sorry. I didn't mean to create such a commotion," Ada said, her head still bowed, as if too ashamed and embarrassed to look directly at Lee or Minerva.

"We were terribly worried! But the important thing is that you survived!" Minerva gave Ada a hug. "How did you manage to hold out until you were rescued?"

"Well, fortunately, the water wasn't too cold—not warm, mind you, but bearable. First I tried to get back into the canoe, but that was impossible without someone to hoist me in. After several tries, the canoe tipped over. So then I hung on to it for a few minutes, until I began to realize that it might be hours before anyone would spot the canoe, and it would soon be dark. So I decided to try swimming to shore. The tide was in my favor. I figured that as soon as I hit the shallow part I could walk the rest of the way. I managed to get out of my sweater and kick off my shoes. That helped. But I was just about exhausted when Bernie reached me. I doubt that I . . . ."

She was interrupted by the electronic bleep of the telephone. Minerva picked it up. "Oh, hello, Arthur. Yes, we got your message just this morning."

Ada was whispering in Minerva's other ear. "Don't tell him about the canoe."

Lee sat slumped in her chair. Arthur—all they needed right now!

"Yes, Arthur, I'm terribly sorry you couldn't get through last night. It's a shame. You see, we completely forgot we left the machine on in the afternoon." Her voice was briskly matter-of-fact. "Well, yes, Ada would have loved talking to you on her birthday, I'm sure."

Ada was shaking her head. "Tell him I'll call him back." But Minerva, intent upon her fabrication, failed to notice.

"Yes, she's right here. She slept in this morning—after the big party. It was rather late. Yes, I'll put her on." Minerva handed the phone to Ada who held it an arm's length as if summoning the necessary strength to put it to her ear.

"Hello, Arthur. Why, thank you, Son, that's very kind of you . . . . Yes, I'm sorry we missed connections last evening . . . the party? Oh, yes, it was quite a party! Never a dull moment! I can truthfully say, I've never had such a day in my entire lifetime." Ada was smiling now. "How many people? Well, now, let me see . . . ." Minerva held up ten fingers and then two. "There were twelve of us altogether. And we had champagne, lots of champagne, everybody drinking toasts. I think I had a glass too many . . . . A cake? Oh, yes, we had cake all right. My favorite— a carrot cake. It was delicious! So good, I ate two pieces. Laura, I think you met her . . . well, she baked it. Candles? Of course we had candles. Who ever heard of a birthday cake without candles? And I made a wish and then blew them out . . . . Yes, Son, I did indeed, all eighty-five of them."

Lee sat listening, with a mixture of amazement and delight, to Ada doing her act. And she felt the old warm glow of affection returning. Dear comical, unpredictable, outrageous Ada. How could she ever have survived her loss? And how could she possibly stay angry with her any longer than a few minutes?

"This afternoon?" Ada was saying. "Oh, no, Son, I'm afraid that wouldn't do at all . . . . Yes, of course, I'd like to see my present, but let's make it day after tomorrow. You see, today . . . ." She faltered. "Excuse me just a minute, Son, I have to rescue my cat. He's having a fight with Daisy. I'll be right back." Holding her hand over the mouthpiece, she said to Minerva and Lee, "What are we doing today? Quick! We can't let him come out now."

"Tell him we're going into the city this afternoon," Lee said.

"To see a play," Minerva added. "And we won't be back until late tomorrow night."

Ada relayed the information to Arthur, thanked him for his birthday wishes, and made a date for lunch the following Thursday. When she hung up, she beamed at the other two. "Well, folks, that's that! We make a pretty good team."

Lee, smiling now, got up from the chair and came over to the bed. "We do indeed." She gave Ada a hug and a kiss on her leathery cheek. "But promise me one thing, dear Ada."

"Tell me what it is before I promise."

"Promise me you'll never pull anything like this canoe business ever again."

"I promise," Ada said quickly. "I've learned my lesson. I'm a Libra, not a Pisces or an Aquarius. And a Libra is definitely not a water person."

31

Ever since she was old enough to write her name, Lee had made a list of resolutions on New Year's Eve. It just seemed the natural thing to do, a formal part of bidding farewell to the old, noting its failures and successes, and welcoming the new with fresh resolve to do better the next time around. A milestone to mark the hour of new beginnings.

On the afternoon of December 31, 1989, before jotting down the new resolutions in her journal, she was sitting at her desk looking through some old diaries she found while sorting things for the move to her studio apartment in Sag Harbor. They had all delayed their packing to keep the house presentable for prospective buyers who had been trailing through at all hours for the past three months. Lee had complained, but Minerva insisted it was the right thing to do, for Elizabeth's sake.

After Elizabeth left for Florida with John in September, it was Minerva who had made the first peace gesture by writing to her. Elizabeth had responded with a friendly letter saying she missed them and hoped there were no hard feelings. Of course, it was her life and she had a right to live where she chose, but Lee still resented the anguish she had caused the four of them. Now that there was a buyer, ironically one of Vivian's clients, who had put up earnest money, they could at least proceed with their packing. Lee had been able to rent a place in a quaint old part of town, reasonably priced. But life would not be the same.

Looking at the stacks of books, papers, and boxes surrounding her, she wondered how she had accumulated so many treasures, now to be stored or disposed of. The space would be cramped at best. The diaries she could not part with. A smile crossed her face as she opened one of them and started reading her resolutions of New Year's Eve, 1933, written in a round, girlish hand. *1) Write in diary every day. 2) Improve complexion and posture. 3) Take care of dog. 4) Keep room straight and clothes neat. 5) Work hard at school. 6) Practice 'cello and piano. 7)* **Work faster***!* Even then, at age thirteen, she had felt the relentless pressure of time and the need to excel. She sighed. Some things never changed.

This coming year would require more than good resolutions. On her own, without the ready support of Minerva and the others. Not that they would be totally out of touch. There was always the telephone. They might even write occasional letters. And they could get together for dinner once in a while. But that could not compare to living under the same roof, sharing routines, reaching out to one another at any given time.

And then there was her upcoming birthday in January, by some cruel twist of fate the fifteenth, the same day as Elizabeth's deadline for their departure. Minerva was weaving her a tapestry, something she had always wanted. No secret because she had consulted Lee on the size and color—a delicate shade of lavender interwoven with seedpods collected from the redbud, one of Lee's favorite trees. It would be quite lovely. But a tapestry, no matter how beautiful, could never take the place of Minerva herself. How she would miss her! She was trying not to think about it, but she still felt the pain of Minerva's decision. Every so often, the aching loneliness would creep over her.

Generally Lee paid little attention to her own birthdays, but this was a special one, impossible to ignore, the big 7-0 as Ada would say. She dreaded entering that ominous new decade of her life. Seventy seemed so very much older than sixty-something. During her sixties, she had felt an extraordinary surge of vitality, her creative prime. Granted, one's sixties was a bit late to start feeling in one's prime, but perhaps her age had contributed to the creative spark—the awareness of the scarcity of time, a determination to make the most of it. A productive decade for her. The one ahead was shadowy, fraught with pitfalls. The cloud of approaching deterioration and death would loom ever larger now. It was unfair—that humans were doomed to face this nagging awareness while all other animal species escaped it, simply living each moment as it came along. If only she could train herself to live that way too!

Shivering, she got up and pulled out a wool sweater to slip on over her blouse. A blustery wind rattled the shutters, whistled around the corners of the house and into every crack and crevice. It was a drafty old place at best. Elizabeth had kept the thermostat at a comfortable seventy degrees, but Minerva insisted sixty-seven was adequate and far more healthful. Lee found it easier to put on extra layers of clothing than to argue the point.

She couldn't help envying Elizabeth just a little, soaking up the Florida sunshine. Every couple of weeks they would get a card from her with pictures of shells or a beach scene with palm trees, along with breezy notes telling how she had been swimming in the pool at John's condo or bike riding or fishing in his boat. The last card had a picture of a Key Lime pie with the recipe, inviting them to come for a visit and she would bake them a pie. Lee suddenly realized that she had been missing Elizabeth a great deal—not only her cooking, of higher quality than anything the rest of them could produce, but also her quiet serenity and her music, especially that. The piano had hardly been touched since she left.

She turned on her lamp to brighten the room The late afternoon light was dwindling into the gray tones of twilight, a time when gloomy thoughts were likely to intrude. She must focus on the coming year in a positive manner. No time now for moping around, their last evening together before the chaos of serious packing. It must be a joyous New Year's celebration. Time enough tomorrow for the blues.

She placed the diaries neatly in a box which she tied and labeled. Then she glanced at the notebooks—hours of tedious notes on Shakespeare, Milton, Chaucer, Romantic Poets, Nineteenth and Twentieth Century American . . . . One by one, she tossed them into a large box marked DISCARD. Leafing through a folder of clippings marked *Tempo of the Times — 1989,* she thought back over the political turbulence and global changes of the past year, when freedom, like molten lava, spread across Eastern Europe, flowing through streets of Poland, Bulgaria, Hungary, Czechoslovakia, Rumania, climaxed by the incredible collapse of the Berlin Wall. She thought back to that magic night in November when they sat before the television transfixed, watching young East and West Berliners dance atop the wall exchanging kisses and flowers—tears and champagne flowing freely, chants of *Freiheit!* filling the air.

But, in assessing the year, those miraculous gains had to be balanced against other losses—the massacre of students at Tianenmen Square, the brutal killings in El Salvador where blood, not freedom, flowed through the streets. She had tried to express the paradox in a poem but could not capture it. Her creative power seemed to have diminished, with the upheaval in their daily lives following Elizabeth's departure—along with her sense of personal freedom. *Freedom*—such a beautiful word. Would she ever feel joyously free again? Though she had channeled her energy during recent months into the pro-choice struggle and other issues, she felt out of harmony, frustrated by the erosion of freedom for women over here, ironically at the same time some people around the globe were being liberated. Not the best of years. Countless battles yet to be waged. She gave a heavy sigh and closed her eyes, resting her head on her arms.

She must have dozed off. She was startled by the voice of Minerva who stood in the doorway reminding her it was time to start preparing the cheese fondue. They had eaten fondue last year on New Year's Eve, the five of them, celebrating the successful completion of their first year of communal life. So it seemed the appropriate meal for tonight marking the end of their time together. The four of them, plus Bernie who would arrive this evening and stay a couple of days to help Minerva pack up her weaving.

* * *

Minerva stood at the counter grating the cheese, and Lee sat at the table cutting French bread into cubes. "Bernie phoned to say she might be a bit late," Minerva said. "She was concerned about the traffic. I told her to take her time and arrive in one piece."

"Good advice. We've got till midnight to finish eating the fondue." Lee paused, wondering if this might be the time for that frank discussion she had envisioned. The opportunity never seemed right. She cleared her throat nervously, not sure how to begin. "Min, there's something I've been wanting to ask you."

"Of course. What is it?" She continued grating, her back to Lee.

"Well . . . " Lee hesitated. "It's about you and Bernie."

"What about us?" Minerva still did not turn around. "Do you mean . . . whether we have a . . . " She paused. "A *relationship?*"

From her tone, Lee decided maybe it was a rude intrusion. "If you'd rather not talk about it, that's quite all right. I probably shouldn't have raised the issue, but . . . ."

"I'm assuming, in terms of a relationship, you mean *sexual.*" Minerva paused. "And if that's your question, the answer is *No.* Now, what did you do with the Gruyère cheese? I've finished the Emmenthaler, but I know there was another chunk somewhere." She busied herself at the counter, moving the cutting board, dropping a knife in the sink, rinsing her hands, then walked briskly over to the refrigerator, still not looking directly at Lee.

"The cheese is over there at the end of the counter, next to the wine bottle." Lee could feel the blood rushing to her neck and face. This was not at all the heart-to-heart talk she had imagined. "Listen, Min, I didn't mean to offend you."

"No offense." Minerva began humming her little tune.

"I'm sorry I brought it up. But maybe we ought to talk about it."

"What is there to talk about?" Minerva had started grating the Gruyère.

"Min, for God's sake, please stop long enough for us to finish this conversation!" Lee's voice grated on her own ears. She hated the disharmony she had created, but they could not just leave the whole thing dangling, unresolved. She lowered her voice. "Come sit down for just a minute. We have plenty of time."

Minerva came over to the table, started to sit down, then turned and put the teakettle on the stove. "I'll make us a pot of tea while we talk." Then she sat at the table across from Lee. "Now," she said softly, "perhaps we should start this conversation over again."

Lee smiled and nodded. "Let's."

"I suppose . . . ." Minerva said, her gray eyes not avoiding Lee now but looking directly into hers with a level gaze, "I mean, it was a perfectly legitimate question about Bernie and me." She bit her lip and ran her hands through her hair. "It just hit a tender spot, a question I haven't truly come to terms with myself."

"You mean you don't really know?"

"I know I admire her tremendously, and we're good friends with an amazing number of things in common. And I love being with her."

"But sexually?" Lee could feel the blood coloring her face again. Why couldn't she deal with this in the same open manner she did with other issues?

"Sexually, I'm not sure." Minerva was sitting quietly now, gazing off somewhere beyond Lee, perhaps seeing Bernie with her slender athletic figure, her soft dark hair swept back from that strong lean face, so vibrantly alive. "I find her attractive."

"She's a lot like you." Lee studied Minerva's face. "Like you in so many ways—even your mannerisms . . . and she *is* attractive."

"Yes . . . but I can't say truthfully whether it is or is not a sexual attraction. Perhaps I have always kept my emotions so completely under control, on the conscious level anyway, I can't reach down deep enough to know my true feelings."

They were interrupted by the whistle of the kettle. Minerva got up to take care of the tea, returning with the tray and pouring a cup for each of them.

"Could it be that you're afraid to find out?" Lee sipped her tea, savoring its warmth and the warmth that surrounded the two of them now, a bond of affection that would always be there. How could she ever have thought otherwise?

"Perhaps." Minerva reached out and took Lee's hand. "I'm going to miss you, Lee. Sometimes I think you know me better than I know myself."

Lee smiled then looked away, not wanting Minerva to see the tears clouding her eyes.

"Certainly I've never thought seriously of . . . you know, a relationship with another woman, sexual, I mean, much as I care about women . . . I just haven't . . . I can't quite imagine . . . ." Minerva broke off, laughing. "You see, I get all flustered just trying to talk about it sensibly."

"Perhaps that's your problem. You're trying to be too sensible." Lee squeezed her hand. "Bernie seems quite fond of you. Has she brought up the subject?"

"Nothing specific." A flush crept over Minerva's face. "Beyond making it clear that her invitation for me to share her apartment came with no strings attached. I forget just how she put it. But she didn't want me to feel any sort of pressure to . . . you know."

"I know." Lee suddenly felt like singing. She went over to Minerva and gave her a quick hug. "We'd better get busy. You have to finish the cheese, and I have to cut up the apples, and we have to lay the fire and . . . oh, Min dear, let's try to stay this way always . . . the way we are, with each other, I mean. I couldn't bear it if we ever allowed a wall to form between us. It doesn't matter where we live. I mean . . . whether you're in New Haven or wherever." Minerva must not think she meant she should not follow her heart and live with Bernie. "It's just that . . . ."

"I know." Minerva smiled. "We won't allow any walls."

32

Beyond the French doors of the dining room tall pines made jagged silhouettes, casting shadows across the lawn in the moonlight. Inside, the five women sat by candlelight around the oval walnut table, Minerva at the head with Lee on one side of her and Bernie on the other, Vivian and Ada balancing the opposite end. An earthenware bowl of cheese fondue was warming on a brass chafing dish in the center of the table. Lee sat sipping her champagne and staring at the panes of the French doors, her eyes unable to penetrate the outer blackness, seeing only reflected candle flames. The dark, the unknown—the scary part of living, always on the edge of toppling into the depths. She loved the quiet, the coziness of winter evenings—as long as she could stay inside, sheltered, protected, as long as she did not have to venture forth alone into the night.

They had decided to dress up in honor of the occasion. Lee was wearing the lavender and blue silk coat with butterfly motif, the one she had worn for their eclipse ritual, only tonight, she wore it over a black silk turtleneck and black velvet pants, with a beaded turquoise belt, dangly silver earrings, and an enameled pendant Matt had made. The others had commented on how festive she looked. She was trying hard to play the part but did not feel at all festive. Her laughter sounded artificial. Not even the champagne could put her into a party mood. She thought back to that mystical August night when the coat had given her a sense of power and strength. Would she ever feel that strong again? Tonight the silk coat provided no enchantment.

Minerva looked striking in a sleeveless wheat-colored dress, textured weave of silk and linen with long fringe at the hem, over black turtleneck and tights and a necklace of irregular amber stones. She was engaged in conversation with Bernie about women artists. Lee sat watching her from the side, noting the animation of her face, the way she would laugh at something clever Bernie said, the way she would reach out and touch her hand. She could hear only part of what they were discussing . . . sculpture of Louise Nevelson . . . Judy Chicago's *Dinner Party* . . . Frida Kahlo. Lee would have liked to join in, but could not hear enough to pick up on. It wasn't as if they were deliberately excluding her—they just seemed to be in their own little realm. Her mind wandered to Diego Rivera and a bridal portrait Frida had painted, Diego fat and stolidly unimaginative, Frida wispy and mysterious. She could comment on that—or recite E.B. White's *Ballad of Artistic Integrity: I Paint What I See,* his imagined dialogue between Nelson Rockefeller and Diego Rivera about the Communist mural Rivera had painted in his building. It always made her laugh. But not tonight. Or she could talk about Judy Chicago, her bold vaginal and butterfly imagery, about seeing the *Dinner Party* in the Brooklyn Museum—the huge triangular table with embroidered runners and ceramic plates symbolizing women from early goddesses to Georgia O'Keeffe—her feeling of awe, as if in a cathedral . . . . Yes, there were ways to interject herself, expand their conversation to a threesome, but she remained silent, sipping her champagne, fighting the threat of tears.

"What's your secret, Lee?" she heard Vivian saying.

"My secret?" Lee flushed. "I don't know what you mean."

"Your secret for the fondue. It's out of this world." She rolled her eyes, dipping another chunk of bread into the fondue, twisting it to break away the strings of cheese. "Do you have some magic ingredient?"

"Perhaps it's the kirsch." Lee attempted a smile. "There was a little left in the bottle—so I just poured it in for good measure."

"Here's to Lee!" Ada raised her glass. "Queen of the Fondue!" And they all clinked glasses. Minerva and Bernie were drinking

303

a non-alcoholic sparkling wine.

"To Lee!" Bernie said, flashing her a warm smile, her dark eyes reflecting the candlelight. No wonder Minerva was attracted to her. Lee watched as she deftly placed a wedge of apple on her fork and dipped it into the fondue. She had a nice dexterity. She was eating mostly apple wedges rather than bread. Minerva also favored the apples.

Lee preferred bread drenched with the rich cheese mixture. But tonight she was only making a pretense of eating, choking down each bite. With a nostalgic pang, she remembered their hilarity of last year, the room resounding with laughter . . . stringy cheese criss-crossing from the fondue pot to their plates, one of them dropping her bread off the fork into the pot, one accusing the other of pushing hers off. Pure silliness . . . Lee laughing so hard the tears were rolling down her face. But tonight the laughter was subdued—no clowning around, no friendly arguments about whose turn it was. All of them seemed to be dipping less frequently into the fondue.

"This stuff is getting awfully thick," Ada said, swishing her bread in the bowl.

"That means we have to adjust the sterno," Minerva said. "Which way is it, Lee? Flame higher or lower?"

"I don't remember." Lee shrugged. It didn't matter anyway. Nothing mattered now. "Try higher." She picked up the pot while Minerva adjusted the flame.

"Everybody dip in!" Vivian said. "We still have half a bowlful. It's too delicious to throw out. But I suppose it would make good sandwiches." Vivian had been chattering away all evening— trying to fill the gaps of silence.

Ada was unusually quiet. She and Vivian had settled the lease for their little house and spent considerable time over there cleaning it up. A bit drab, though it would be cozier when they got their own things in. Ada insisted it would work out just fine, but Lee wondered what she truly thought. The area for her studio could not compare to Elizabeth's attic with its sunny skylights and ample space. Would the two of them get on each other's nerves, cooped up together in that little place? Tonight Ada was wearing the same outfit she had worn last year—a long Mexican skirt with embroidered white blouse and red bolero jacket. Lee smiled, remembering how, after several glasses of champagne, she had astounded them by singing *Frankie and Johnnie* from start to finish, arms waving, bracelets jangling, skirt swirling as she strode up and down and pulled the imaginary gun from her bolero. Dear Ada—such a flair for the dramatic. But tonight the fire seemed to have burnt out.

"What time is it?" Vivian asked. And just then the mantle clock struck nine, punctuating the silence. Everybody laughed, relieved to have something to laugh about. "God, I thought it was later than that!" Vivian yawned. "Why am I so tired?"

Her green eyes lacked their customary sparkle, dark circles beneath them accentuating the paleness of her skin, paler than usual. Perhaps it was the shadowy candlelight. Or maybe her dress, a garish silk, bright green, not her best color. She looked strangely old. Perhaps she had been working too hard on the house, in addition to her job and the packing. Lee felt a rush of affection for her.

Ada stifled a yawn. "Don't start that, Viv. You'll have us all doing it."

Three more hours. Lee wondered if she could hold out, keep from breaking down. She wished they could just set the clock ahead to midnight and get it over with. Everyone seemed weary. Even Minerva and Bernie had become silent.

"Remember last year how Elizabeth played *Auld Lang Syne* and we sang along?" Vivian said. Lee remembered. The four of them, arms linked, grouped around Elizabeth at the piano, Elizabeth singing a sweet, clear soprano, the rest of them harmonizing, after a fashion. When it ended, they had laughed and applauded themselves, saying they should work up a repertoire and take their show on the road.

"How about playing *Twenty Questions*?" Vivian suggested, sensing the tension as their final hours dwindled away.

Ada groaned. "Not that, please! I never could stand that game. You have to ask such stupid . . . ." She was interrupted by the doorbell. "Oh my, I hope that's not Arthur!"

"I'll get it." Vivian jumped up and headed for the door.

"You weren't expecting him were you?" Minerva asked.

305

"No, not at all. But that's usually when he shows up!"

Let it not be Arthur! Lee implored. *Not tonight!*

Vivian entered the room arm-in-arm with Elizabeth, followed by John. "Look who's here!" she said.

"Elizabeth! John! What . . . why . . . ?" Lee pushed back her chair to get up.

In the meantime Minerva had leaped up and was giving them both a hug. "Liz, what a delightful surprise! And John, how good to see you!"

Bernie got up and shook hands with both of them, asking how was their trip.

"Fine, fine!" John said. "But we're not acclimated to this weather. Roads are icing up tonight. Down there we were running around in our shirtsleeves." He looked tanned and handsome in a blue sweater, flannel pants, and gray tweed jacket.

Lee crossed the room to Elizabeth, wondering if she should kiss her or what. But Elizabeth saved her the trouble of deciding, quickly giving her a warm hug and a kiss on the cheek. "Lee, dear, I've missed you!"

"I missed you too." Lee smiled uncertainly. Missed her, yes, but had she forgiven her? It was good to see her, she had to admit that. Elizabeth was lovely in a soft red wool dress with her usual pearl necklace and earrings, her face glowing, perhaps as a result of coming in from the cold or reflecting the warmth of her dress. Or did it have to do with John? She looked about the same, yet somehow different. Perhaps her hair—cut shorter, more casual, without the stylized waves combed neatly in place. No, something beyond that, beyond the externals. This seemed to be a warmer, more relaxed Elizabeth than the one they had said good-bye to four months ago.

Elizabeth turned now toward Ada who had slowly hoisted herself from her chair and was holding onto the edge of the table, reaching for her cane. "Don't get up, Ada." She hurried over and gave her a hug and a kiss, then helped her back into the chair.

"Thanks, Liz. I'm a bit stiff in the joints these days. Not getting any younger, you know." Ada smiled. "Pull up a chair."

Lee meanwhile had welcomed John with a friendly handshake, wondering afterwards whether it might have been more appropriate to have kissed him. And Vivian escorted him to the table, drawing up a chair alongside hers. Elizabeth sat down by Ada.

"I thought I was seeing a ghost when you walked in! I truly did!" Ada said. "When the bell rang, I thought it might be Arthur. Never dreamed it would be you and John."

"Oh, were you expecting Arthur tonight?"

"Lord, no!" Ada said with a laugh. "But as I was telling Minerva, that's usually his cue to come on stage, when he's least expected. What a relief to see it was you!"

"It's just a shame you two don't get along," Elizabeth said. "Why don't you bury the hatchet and start the New Year on friendly terms? That would be the Christian thing to do."

Lee frowned. Elizabeth pushing Ada about Arthur, as if he hadn't disrupted their lives enough. And still harping on the *Christian thing*. Maybe some people never really change.

"Enough about Arthur," Ada said abruptly. "You folks look like Florida agrees with you. But what brings you up here at this time of year?"

Elizabeth looked over at John with a strange smile, and he smiled back, but neither of them spoke. Minerva, meanwhile, offered them some fondue, saying there was at least twice too much and couldn't they help clean it up. Elizabeth thanked her, saying they couldn't eat another bite, having just finished dinner at the Quintauket Inn where they were staying. John said he wouldn't mind a glass of champagne. Vivian brought out two glasses and opened another bottle, and everyone raised their glasses to welcome the guests.

Overwhelmed by sadness, Lee glanced at all of them grouped around the table, thinking how harmonious it appeared to be, how a stranger peering in the window would describe the scene as a cozy New Year's Eve celebration, this happy gathering of people joyously toasting the future together. Who could tell, from a window view, that this was a farewell dinner? She looked at her watch. Ten-fifteen. Another couple of hours and the waiting would be over. The atmosphere had lightened up since the arrival of Elizabeth and John, but only because their presence provided a temporary distraction. It did not alleviate the pain and

307

loneliness that lay ahead.

Vivian turned to John, then looked at Elizabeth across the table. "You haven't told us why you happen to be up here in the dead of winter instead of basking in the sun. Has something gone wrong with the house sale?" Vivian would lose a sizable commission if the deal fell through.

"Well, yes and no," Elizabeth said, with that same vague smile. "John and I have something important to tell you."

Lee looked over at John whose face had reddened beneath his tan. He was staring into his champagne glass, toying with the stem.

"An announcement?" said Ada. "Well, what do you know!"

"Don't tell us you're expecting!" Vivian arched her eyebrows in mock surprise.

"Vivian, don't be ridiculous!" Lee hated it when Vivian carried on that way.

"Well, if Sarah and Abraham could do it, why couldn't they?" Vivian said with a laugh.

"No, the only thing we're expecting is another great-grandchild, well, I mean John is. His granddaughter, the one living in Fort Lauderdale."

"No offense, Liz. I was only kidding," Vivian said. "I'll bet I know . . . . You're getting married and you want us to come to the wedding, be your bridesmaids." Her voice had climbed to a high pitch now, the words coming out in little squeals. "How exciting! Have you set the date?"

"No, that's not it." Elizabeth blushed. "Not that we haven't considered the possibility. But it seemed entirely too complicated, what with social security and pensions and taxes and our assortment of heirs and so on."

"What is this—*Twenty Questions*?" Ada demanded. "I thought I said a while ago I didn't want to play that game. Why don't you simmer down, Viv, and let Elizabeth tell us whatever it is she's trying to tell."

"A splendid idea," said Minerva. "Do tell us, Liz."

"Well . . ." Elizabeth gave a nervous little cough. "It does have to do with the house deal in a way, but that's only part of it." With the same erect posture Lee remembered, she sat gazing into the darkness as if trying to formulate the words. The shadowy light accentuated the network of wrinkles fanning out from her eyes, pulling at the corners of her mouth.

Lee wondered what news she could have that would possibly be of any real importance to them. She braced herself for the worst, but after all, what else could Elizabeth do to hurt them? They were prepared to get out on the fifteenth. If there was a delay in the closing or something of that sort, it was irrelevant. They still had to leave.

"I guess I'll start with the real estate part first." Elizabeth took a deep breath. Lee noticed she was twisting her pearls. Invariably a danger sign. "You see, our respective attorneys have been giving us trouble, quibbling over every little provision in the contract, raising new issues every time we solved one, and . . . ."

"Those damned lawyers can really botch things up!" Vivian said. "I wish they'd just keep out of it and let us handle the closings. It would be much smoother—and speedier too."

"And so," Elizabeth said, taking a sip of champagne, "John and I decided on the spur of the moment to come on up here to straighten things out."

"Strange I didn't hear about it at the office," said Vivian.

"They didn't know it because we just arrived this afternoon," John said. "We haven't been in touch with anyone. Just packed our bags and took off. You know how Lizzy is when she makes up her mind. There's no stopping her." *Yes, we know,* Lee thought grimly, *only too well.* "Had to get on stand-by for a flight, but luck was with us. And here we are." He lifted his glass, glancing around the table at each of them. "Here in time to share New Year's Eve with all of you wonderful gals . . . uh, I mean women." He looked over at Lee with a shy grin. "Skaal!"

Lee raised her glass and smiled back at him, wondering if Elizabeth realized her good fortune. John was such a genuine, good-hearted fellow.

"When we got ourselves settled over at the Inn," Elizabeth continued, "I took out the contract and started going over it before calling the attorney. And then suddenly the strangest thing happened." She paused, smiling vaguely. "This is going to be difficult to believe, I'm sure, but it's true. As I was looking at

309

that contract agreeing to sell this place . . . ." She glanced around the dining room as if trying to absorb every little detail. "As I was studying that contract line by line, I suddenly got to thinking how much I was going to miss this beautiful old house where Parker and I were so happy and where we raised our chihldren . . . and my garden . . . and how very much I would miss all of you . . . and how I hated the prospect of living my life out in Fort Lauderdale, so flat and uninteresting, with its maze of look-alike streets and its steamy humidity, even the palm trees, the monotony of them, and all those decrepit old people everywhere you turn . . . ."

"We're a bit on the antique side ourselves, you know!" Ada interrupted with a laugh.

"You know what I mean." Elizabeth took another sip of champagne. "And so I said to John, 'I can't go through with it. I just can't sell the house!' And, of course, he looked at me as if he thought I had lost my mind, but then . . . ."

That's true!" John said, laughing. "I couldn't believe I'd heard right—until I saw that determined expression on her face, and when Lizzy gets that look, she means what she says." He drained his glass and reached for the champagne bottle. "So I told her it was, of course, her house and her decision."

Lee sat motionless, dazed. Did that mean Elizabeth was coming back? What about John? He seemed to be taking it in stride. But would he live here with Elizabeth or down in Florida? She snuffed out any glimmer of hope that was beginning to flicker inside of her. She must not allow herself to hope . . . .

"Let me get this straight. You're not selling the house?" Vivian's face had turned pale. Lee supposed she might be thinking about her commission going down the drain.

"Is that what you said, Liz? Or was I hearing things?" Ada asked in a tone of disbelief. "My hearing is not so great these days."

"That is indeed what I said." Elizabeth smiled at Ada and held out her glass toward John who poured her a small amount.

"Better take it easy, Lizzy. You know how this goes to your head."

"Tonight who cares?" she said with a laugh, taking another drink of champagne. She looked around the table as if expecting

310

some sort of response, but the only sound was the ticking of the clock. "Well, what do you think?" she asked. The silence continued, palpable in its intensity. Lee sat immobilized, numbly wondering what Elizabeth was expecting in the way of a reply. Taking the house off the market did not necessarily mean she wanted them back. Why did she have to be so vague?

Finally Minerva broke the silence, her voice slow, deliberate, showing no outward sign of emotion. "And so what are your plans now?"

"Well . . . ." Elizabeth held her glass to the light, squinting through it toward the candle flames, twirling it with her fingers. "Well," she repeated . . . and then, to Lee's amazement, her eyes filled with tears as she looked around the table at the group. "John and I have talked it over for the past several hours." She paused to wipe her eyes with a lace-trimmed hanky. "And we were wondering . . . ."

"What Lizzy is trying to say is . . . ahhh," John hesitated. "You see, I want to spend some time in Fort Lauderdale . . . my son and his family . . . and the grandchildren . . . and the second great-grandchild on the way . . . don't want to lose touch . . . but want to be here with Lizzy most of the time." He smiled and reached across the table to take her hand, gazing at her with admiration.

Lee had trouble following what he was trying to say, uncertain whether it was her brain, clouded by champagne, or incoherence on John's part.

"So we were wondering . . . ." He cleared his throat. "Wondering if you folks thought there might be room here for me to . . . ."

"John sold his house in Southampton last fall," Elizabeth interjected, "and . . . ."

"So we wondered," John said, rubbing his finger under his collar, fiddling with his tie, "if there might be . . . if we could all six perhaps . . . ."

Lee looked over at Ada who was sitting in open-mouthed amazement and Vivian, leaning forward on her elbows staring at Elizabeth in obvious disbelief.

"You mean you're saying you actually want us . . . you're

inviting us to stay on?" Lee said to Elizabeth, her voice sounding strangely weak and quavery. "The way we were before?" Hearing those words, she realized the absurdity of such a desire. Even if they miraculously came together again, it could never be the same as before—when they first started out, imbued with a kind of innocence, blithely unaware of the jagged edges of co-existing within one household.

"I realize that you have all made other arrangements, but if it's not too late . . . ." Elizabeth paused, her face quite flushed now, her gray eyes gleaming with tears behind the gold-rimmed glasses. "I had no idea how much I would miss all of you—dear flamboyant Ada, Vivian with her vivacity and wit, Minerva's artistry," she smiled over at her, "artistry with fabrics and life itself, and Lee's earnest endeavors, her crusades . . . . Whatever would I do without you, *all* of you?" She took off her glasses and wiped her eyes. "It just suddenly struck me this afternoon when I was going over that contract what a foolish mistake I had made—and how I wanted everything back the way it used to be." The tears were trickling down her face now. Lee had never known her to break down this way, allowing her emotions to crack that mask of perfect composure. It was indeed a new revised edition of Elizabeth.

"So we figured maybe I could move in with Lizzy," John said. "That is," he added with a shy grin, "if you women can put up with me."

"The question is, can you put up with us?" Ada asked.

"And can you cook?" Vivian asked.

John nodded. "Nothing exactly gourmet, but edible."

"He's far too modest," Elizabeth said. "Last fall he took a course in Chinese cooking. You should see what he can prepare with a wok."

"Well, then, it's a deal, as far as I'm concerned," said Ada, "provided we can get out of our lease."

"Not to worry. I can work it out," Vivian said brightly, "though we might forfeit some money." She glanced at Lee. "Why so solemn? I'll help you with your lease too."

Lee attempted a smile and thanked her for her offer.

Vivian turned abruptly to Elizabeth. "Are you sure you mean

this, Liz? Or is it just New Year's Eve sentimentality and perhaps a bit too much champagne?"

"Oh no, I do mean it." Her tone was serious. "I'm quite sober— well, reasonably sober anyway, and when I made the decision this afternoon, I had nothing at all to drink. I've never been more sure of anything!" She glanced around the table. "Where is Minerva, by the way?"

"She's in the living room talking to Bernie." Lee tried to keep her voice casual. She had noticed the two of them slip out of the room, and from her place at the table, she could see them sitting by the fireplace talking softly together.

"Minerva was planning to move in with Bernie, in her apartment over the book shop, you know," Ada said.

"Oh, I didn't realize . . . ." Elizabeth said, flustered, her face turning a bright pink. "That is, I don't remember that she mentioned it in any of her letters. I suppose I just took it for granted that Minerva and Lee would find a place together."

"Well, Bernie offered her the space at very little cost," Lee said quickly. "She could hardly afford to turn it down." She sat fighting back the tears. Throughout the time Elizabeth had been telling how much she had missed them and wanted them together again, Lee had the uncanny sense that she must be dreaming it, that any minute she would wake up and return to the old reality. Seeing Minerva and Bernie in the living room, she felt the familiar fear knotting her stomach, choking the air from her lungs. Everything rested upon Minerva's decision. This beautiful dream might indeed come to an end. She must prepare herself for that very real probability. Of course, being together with the others would be better than living alone. But how she would miss Minerva!

The wind had increased in velocity, rattling the shutters, howling around the house and down the chimney. Sleet bombarded the windowpanes. Lee shivered and drew her silk coat about her. Not that she was cold. It was the sound of it. The mantle clock struck eleven, and John got up to peer out the French doors at the storm. "I think, my dear, it might be wise for us to start back to the Inn," he said, "before this weather gets any worse."

313

"But you can't leave now!" Vivian said. "We have to drink a toast to our reunion and our new beginning for the New Year."

John had walked back to the table and was standing behind Elizabeth, his hand resting on her shoulder. How handsome they looked together, Lee thought, and how very happy!

"I'd love to stay a while longer," Elizabeth said, "but I think John's right. It could be rather slippery, and you never know what sort of drivers will be on the road. We can stop by again in the morning."

Lee thought about Bernie's clothes and personal belongings strewn around in Elizabeth's room and said a silent prayer that no one suggest they stay overnight. With Elizabeth's penchant for neatness and privacy, not to mention a touch of homophobia, it could be an awkward situation if they were to go up there. And just then she heard Ada saying, "Why not spend over?" Lee was shaking her head, but Ada was oblivious to the signal. "Then we could celebrate in proper fashion," she said, her cheeks a rosy red, her eyes shining.

Elizabeth's face brightened. She looked up at John. "What do you say, dear? We could drive over to the Inn in the morning. It would be far safer."

John said he guessed that would not be a bad idea. Lee panicked. Somebody had to say something.

"I'm not so sure," Lee said after momentary hesitation. "You see, ahhh, Bernie . . . well, that is, ahhh . . . ."

"What she's trying to say is that Bernie is using your room," Vivian said. "But we can work that out. No problem, really."

"She was planning to stay here for a few days to help Minerva pack up," Lee said, unable to hide her embarrassment.

"Oh, I see." She sounded disturbingly like the Elizabeth of former times. Her hand went up to her pearls which she began twisting around her finger. "Well," she sighed, "I guess we'd better get back to the Inn."

"No, wait!" said Vivian. "This is ridiculous. You can't go out in that storm. We'll set up a cot for Bernie in one of our rooms. She won't mind, I'm sure." She came over to Elizabeth and John and gave them each a hug. "We won't have it any other way."

"Yes, that settles it," said Ada. "Now, let's get on with the celebration."

314

"I think they have a point," John said. "If Bernie doesn't mind, we're better off here."

Elizabeth smiled a half smile, saying she supposed so. And Lee hoped for the best.

Vivian started pouring the champagne and called to Minerva and Bernie to come in for an all-round toast, and Lee filled their glasses with the nonalcoholic wine. The two women entered the room arm-in-arm, Minerva saying, "We have something to discuss with you, a proposal." She glanced around the table at each of them. "And we'd like your *honest* reaction." Her voice was serious, but there was a glow of happiness on her face. Bernie, lovely in a loose-knit red vest over winter-white wool turtleneck and pants, looked apprehensive. What were they up to, Lee wondered. She could feel her heart pounding, and a constricting dryness in her throat. She took a sip of champagne, steeling herself for whatever lay ahead.

"Well, make it quick," Vivian said, "before this champagne loses all its bubbles."

"As you know, I was planning to move in with Bernie over the book shop, but with Elizabeth coming back, that left me free to stay here, but of course Bernie was disappointed. She had been looking forward to it." Minerva took a deep breath. "And so this idea evolved that maybe Bernie could sell her book shop and move in with us."

"I think I could sell the shop for a pretty good price. Someone was inquiring about it just last week, but at the time, of course, I wasn't interested." Bernie looked over at Minerva with a smile. "In recent months I've been getting into the business of selling out-of-print books by mail which is proving to be quite profitable. I could probably expand that—enough anyway to make a comfortable living."

"She could move into my room with me," Minerva said. "There's plenty of space for another bed. And we could partition off part of the attic studio into an area where she could store her books and operate her mail-order business, if it's all right with Ada to share that space—and, of course, if it's all right with Elizabeth and the rest of you to add another person to our group."

Lee was listening with a strange mixture of emotions—joy and relief that Minerva wanted to stay, but pierced by the pain of having to share her with Bernie. She tried to push aside the jealous pangs, reasoning sternly with herself that this would be considerably better than giving up Minerva altogether. She wanted to say something—something positive, but could not find the words.

"It's fine with me," said Ada, beaming. In her present state, Lee thought, anything would be fine with Ada.

"What a great idea!" said Vivian. "That will make seven of us. A lucky number! But, wait a minute." She looked at Bernie. "Are you a good cook?" Vivian and her cooking questions. Not too appropriate for one who specialized in TV dinners.

Minerva and Bernie were looking anxiously toward Elizabeth who had been sitting staring at her napkin, folding and unfolding it as she listened. "Would it be all right with you, Liz?" Minerva asked. "It would cut down on the expenses for the rest of us, of course."

Here was the true test—Elizabeth. Had she really changed— or was she the same old up-tight, conservative person she had always been? Lee glanced at Bernie standing there so beautifully strong-looking, yet so vulnerable at this point, vulnerable to possible rejection, Bernie who had suffered more than her share of rejection in her lifetime.

"Well, Liz, how about it?" said Ada. "Can you put up with another one of us?"

Elizabeth looked over at Bernie and Minerva, still standing together at the end of the table. She remained silent for what seemed like an age as they waited, scarcely breathing. Could she open her heart to Bernie, welcome her as one of them? "Well," she said, a smile slowly softening the lines of her face, "why not?" She turned to John. "How do you feel about it, dear?"

"Fine, fine!" he said briskly. "Doesn't matter to me. I'm outnumbered any way you want to count."

A wave of guilt washed over Lee for being so judgmental of Elizabeth. And now she was forced to confront her own reservations about Bernie, her deep sense of rivalry. Would she, too, be willing to accept her with an open heart and mind?

She could feel Minerva's gaze. They were expecting her to say *something*. Getting up from her chair, Lee went over to the two of them and put her arms around them both, hugging them close. "Welcome, Bernie!" she said, tears brimming her eyes. "You're going to be a splendid addition to our group." She felt a flood of joy and knew she was speaking the truth.

"Thanks, Lee," Bernie said softly. Her dark eyes were also filled with tears. Minerva was smiling, her eyes a silvery sheen in the candlelight.

"Here's to the seven of us in the new decade of the nineties!" Vivian held her glass high.

"Cheers!" said John, gallantly extending his glass toward each of them in turn before taking a sip.

"Skaal!" Lee lifted her glass and smiled at Minerva. She wanted to say something about living together in sisterhood, but then remembered John and how she shouldn't exclude him. But she couldn't say sisterhood and brotherhood. Too overblown. She would have to figure out a way around that, but not now.

"Blessed be!" said Bernie, her voice husky with emotion.

Ada was sitting at the telephone dialing a number. "Hello, Arthur?" she said. "Yes, Son, it's me . . . No, nothing's wrong. What makes you always jump to the conclusion I might be in trouble?" Ada was shaking her head in annoyance. "I'm fine. Just wanted to wish you a Happy New Year!" Lee had trouble believing her ears. Maybe it was the champagne. "How about you and Dolores coming out tomorrow?"

Lee looked at Vivian who was making a comical face, her hands raised skyward as if seeking an explanation. Elizabeth was smiling. "What a fine idea! Tell them to come for brunch," she called to Ada.

"No, Son, I'm serious. We have all sorts of good news to share with you . . . . No, it's too involved to explain over the phone. Come out around eleven for brunch, and we'll tell you all about it. Bye, Son." Ada turned from the phone with an embarrassed smile. "Well, what's everyone staring at?" She took a sip of champagne. "I decided Elizabeth has a point. Maybe it's time we call off our feud, Arthur and I . . . at least start the year with a clean slate. But no guarantees, mind you."

The old clock made itself part of the celebration, resonantly striking the hour of twelve.

317

"I forgot to bring out the bells!" Lee said. "We were going to ring them at midnight the way we did last year."

"Never mind the bells." Elizabeth got up from the table and walked over to the piano, carrying her glass which she set on the bench beside her. Then, to Lee's amazement, she began to play *Pineapple Rag*, her foot tapping in time to the music. The others gathered around, John leaning over Elizabeth's shoulder, humming along, Vivian doing a little shuffling ragtime step, Ada tapping her cane, her braid swaying back and forth as she moved to the rhythm of the song, Minerva between Lee and Bernie, her arms draped over their shoulders, the three of them harmonizing and improvising the words as they went along.

"I didn't know you could play ragtime," Lee said when Elizabeth paused to take a drink of champagne.

"There are probably a great many things you don't know about me," she replied with a laugh, her face aglow.

* * *

Alone after the others had gone upstairs, Lee moved over to the fireplace where she tossed on another log and a handful of kindling, poking it into a blaze. She sat quietly in her walnut rocker, listening to the slow ticking of the clock, thinking over the incredible events of the evening, still a bit dazed, wondering if she would wake up in the morning to a different reality. Watching the flames encircle the log, sparking sizzling, then dying back into red-gold embers, she must have dozed off. When she opened her eyes, she saw Minerva entering the room with a tea tray. "I thought we might celebrate the beginning of the new decade with a cup of tea together," she said, smiling at Lee.